A SOUVENIR FROM ELANTHIA

Dominic Miles

A SOUVENIR FROM ELANTHIA

DOUBLE DRAGON

Chapter 1
Asha's Lament

The library on Hanis was a warren of a place, dug half into the mountain to keep the occupants from the planet's desert sun, built around a series of light wells and glass-roofed courtyards that looked like green houses and broke up the monotony of tiled floors and white walls with a welcome touch of colour. There were roses, she noticed, as she crossed the plaza in front of the anthropological section, big as dinner plates. They must be genetically modified, she thought, and really too much of a good thing. They had taken an object of beauty, super-sized it and spoilt it in the process. The colours were insipid, not vivid, the reds were not that blood colour of real roses, they were more like a scarlet wash and the white had a slight greenish tinge to them, which reminded her of caterpillars.

Her friend Esmee would have laughed at her description, she knew, would have been amused at the way she picked apart all these strands of modernity that surrounded her. But Esmee was a long way away and a long time ago, or so it seemed. She had become a librarian because she liked old things, books in particular; the smell of them, the feel, and that was even before you got to the content. But, in truth, she had little to do with books. There were, of course, still collections of them at the central and in the local hubs, but in reality what she dealt with were discs and hard drives of one sort or another. Though it still all came down to words in the end.

She looked up through the glass dome, before she went through the doors to the anthropology section. The sky on Hanis always had a red tint to it no matter what time of day, something to do with dust particles in the atmosphere, she thought, though she hadn't paid much attention to the orientation talk on the shuttle ride over. She could also just glimpse the top of a jagged, red spire of rock, part of the ring of serrated, broken mountains that framed the campus. But the glass was covered with a film of the same red dust and instead of giving her a sense of infinite space, the dome made her feel as if she was in a bubble, separate and alien from the desert world around her.

Karin was at the desk in the anteroom, working on a monitor. She glanced up as Robyn scanned herself through the door using her identity badge. Security here wasn't exactly state of the art - the place was, after all, a library - so it was something of a low priority. The woman smiled at her. Like all the co-workers she had met here, she seemed friendly, but also rather unengaged. Not the sort of person you could get drunk with and have a good laugh, she thought.

Karin was so blonde and Germanic-looking, her ethnicity was written on her face like a label. She had thought there had been a frisson of interest there, the other night at the welcoming reception, but perhaps she had been mistaken. The vile, ersatz stuff they called vodka here, could do that to you.

"Does anyone ever go out there?" She asked, just to make conversation.

"On the surface, you mean?" Karin answered. "Some people work out there, miners, engineers and so on."

"No. I mean out there to walk, have a look around. Is it even possible?"

Karin shook her head and smiled in an ever-so-slightly condescending way.

"It's possible, but not really practical; temperatures are too high in the day and there's the risk of sandstorms. It's a really hostile environment."

As she walked on down the corridor, Robyn regretted making the effort. What sort of stupid question was that? She asked herself. And why do I seem to be as awkward as an adolescent here? She had felt her face reddening as she left Karin and couldn't really understand this reaction. She thought it was because she felt so much out of her own environment here; she had got used to her life on Thera, her water-side house next to Lake Kara, her daily work routine at the Institute. She had taken this assignment to break out of that cycle, to challenge herself. She was starting to think that she had made the wrong decision.

She suited up and scanned herself through the air-lock. The vault she was working in was programmed to maintain an optimum level of humidity and temperature to protect all the records. It was also a dust-free environment, of crucial importance on this planet where the abrasive red dirt seemed to get everywhere.

Shelby was already at his station and nodded to her. Though drinking and eating were technically forbidden in the vault, he had a travel cup in front of

him and pointed to a flask on a side table as he
nodded to her. Not much of a greeting, she thought,
but he seemed the strong silent type. He was over
six feet and absolutely gorgeous; slim, graceful and
the colour of dark honey. Not her cup of coffee of
course, but quite personable. With looks like his, he
didn't need to make an effort with women. Yet,
truth be told, the short time she had worked beside
him, she had found him easy-going and relaxed. She
also appreciated the fact that he didn't chatter; she
liked to get her head down and absorb herself in her
work.

She poured some coffee from the flask into one
of the recycled cups, wondering how her society
had gone from pottery to pewter, reached some apex
of functionality and design and then plummeted
back to nasty, plastic cups that burnt your fingers
and sloshed your drink everywhere. Then it was
back to archiving.

At one time, it was said, all the knowledge of
the world, of old Earth, could have been stored in
one room. So a scholar in Renaissance Italy, for the
sake of argument, could amass a library in his house
and be confident that he held the world's knowledge
in his hand. Just an illusion of course, even at the
time, but a tenable one at that. And if you went
further back, that great, lost library of Alexandria,
which in some ways the library on Hanis resembled,
could have well made a case in its time for being the
vessel of its own world's knowledge.

In Robyn's time, the guardians of knowledge
had abandoned these illusions; their job was no
longer just to amass and conserve knowledge.
Instead, because of the snowstorm of information

8

that was a constant blizzard, overwhelming everyone everywhere, their task had been subtly altered. In fact, now they had to harvest information, gleaning the important relevant facts and winnowing out the chaff, the misinformation, the bizarre and weird mis-directions and the just plain lies. As she thought about it, she was happy with this harvest metaphor, though aware that many of her contemporaries wouldn't quite get it; they weren't very informed about old, traditional agricultural practises.

The job was not to suppress information, but to filter it and send it to the central Hub. The theory was that this body of knowledge, this narrative, would stand on its own and remain, long after the babble of other voices had died out. That was the theory at least.

If it hadn't been for the way she felt about this place, Hanis and the people she worked with, she would have had to admit that she had pulled a plum assignment out of the mix. In truth, if she hadn't felt so lonely and so detached from the others - not necessarily through anybody's fault but her own - she would have felt that, at last, she was truly fulfilling her role as a librarian and historian.

She had been given the task of assessing the archives of some of the commercial expeditions, carried out by a number of corporations that had won the contracts to explore and develop trade with the Copernican sector of the far galaxies. It was recent history, as only the advent of sub-light travel had made such exploratory voyages feasible.

What fascinated her were the anthropological records that the corporation ships had kept as one of the stipulations of their contract. As part of their commercial agreements, they were bound to a policy of respecting the indigenous peoples that they came across and a commitment to minimal interference in their societies. To demonstrate that they had obeyed these regulations, they had been entasked with describing and recording everything that they encountered. There was a plethora of recordings, film and statistical data. Her job was to combine it into some sort of narrative, a historical overview of the inhabited planets in the sector that would be uploaded to the Hub.

In practise, some of the information was patchy and of dubious value. Some of the expeditions had employed anthropologists, but most of the records had been compiled by miners or security details and were often more focused on the exotic rather than the mundane.

As she logged into her work-station, she cross-referenced her work schedule with the diary on her hand Pad. One word came up – 'Elanthia'. It meant nothing to her for a few seconds, and then she recalled what it was. A small, dusty planet on the edge of the Copernican sector. Nothing much of note there, it seemed from the quick scan she had given it; a classic pattern of contact, contract and consolidation. In company speak this meant that the expedition had made first contact, which must have been friendly or positive enough to lead to a trading agreement or contract, which in turn led to a process of development in the consolidation phase. This was a subtle, delicate process of helping the planet's people to help themselves, without due interference, but with enough technological and scientific input

10

to better their lives and set them on the path of self-help. Or so the theory went.

So Elanthia was on her to-do list, but didn't look particularly promising. She was sorely tempted to shelve it for now and get on to some of the meatier, more appealing planets, but her librarian's analytical sense wouldn't let her. She should do this in order. She could give Elanthia a morning, perhaps a day, and console herself with the prospect of getting stuck into Shabaz, or Consignia 1, tomorrow.

She started to look at the material more methodically. As she thought, there was nothing much of interest. The planet was classified as a B2 planet with a breathable atmosphere. It had a longer year and correspondingly longer seasons. Most of the population was concentrated in the equatorial belt of the planet that was drier than old earth, which was always the benchmark they measured planets by, but reasonably habitable.

The exploitation contract had been won by the Sung Yang Corporation and first contact had come through one of their survey ships the 'Sir John Franklin'. The survey team had reported an indigenous population at Point 5 of the Intergalactic Anthropological scale, which would put it at or around the level of pre-Conquest Meso-America, ancient Mesopotamia or late Dark Age Europe. The scale was a nonsense anyway and had long been discredited, though as no one had come up with an acceptable alternative, it was still in use.

So the description told her very little and the images she viewed, while intrinsically of interest, just gave her a patchwork picture of the place. She looked to see if there were any records of indigenous archives of any sort, whether written documents or pictographs on stone or pottery, but the expedition reported that there was only an oral culture, reliant on memory and the passing down of these memories across the generations. That in itself wasn't strange; there were many examples of similar cultural models, in old earth cultures, and across the galaxies.

The first expedition had landed near the equator on the central continent, which was itself like a vast archipelago of sizeable land masses around an inland sea. It had landed in the kingdom, or empire - the translation of the vocabulary was apparently problematic - of Melanthera, which seemed to be the dominant state at the time. But there had been some problem at the contact stage and things had stalled. It was only some years later, when Melanthera had been partially overrun by a nomadic people called the Hvassara, that viable treaties had been negotiated. Because what the planet did have, was the richest range of minerals that you could wish for, all just waiting for extraction. From what she read, the consolidation phase was a model of practise, with the Hvassara and the local Melantherans coming on in leaps and bounds, from pastoral nomadism to the brink of the industrial revolution in a span of a decade.

It all seemed straightforward enough, though the part of her that was a historian regretted the lack of primary sources. So much had been compiled after the fact, some years later, and many of the original records had been re-edited over time and with hindsight. That was the problem with these virtual records, they were too easy to tinker with, to fine polish.

She could hear Shelby moving, getting up out of his chair and stretching and, checking her Pad, she saw that it was lunchtime.

"Canteen?" He asked walking over to her station, then looking at her screen.

"What are you doing?"

She told him and explained her frustration.

"Well, you could try and access the 'Sir John Franklin's' mainframe; they must have archived it at some point.

She moved over so he could use her keyboard. She didn't know what cologne he was using, but it smelt good, or perhaps it was just his shower gel. For a moment, as he leant over her, she felt just a twinge of regret that she played, as it were, for another team. Though she suspected that, even if she hadn't, she wasn't even in the same league as he was.

"Oh, that's slightly strange," he said, and she let her reverie fade away.

"It's classified and not accessible."

It was his turn to be intrigued now. He told her that it was unusual for these expedition records to remain secret.

"Perhaps it's a mistake," he said, "I'll try something else."

He fiddled at the keyboard for a while and then said:

"There you are. I've got it. Some of these records were backed-up by expedition members directly onto the Hub, by-passing the mother ship; it was against protocol, but often happened."

He stood up and let her at her screen again. The files were listed in date order, most headed as daily logs, but a few records stood out as they had other titles. She scrolled through, until one title seemed to catch her eye. 'Asha's Lament' it said. She touched it and it opened.

"Asha's Lament is an epic poem or saga that was written almost contemporaneously with the fall of Melanthera. It describes the life of the hero Asha, and how she came to prominence. It also describes the siege and final battle for Melanthera and is valuable both in terms of historical and cultural significance as one of the last completed works of the canon of Melantheran literature."

She was conscious of the fact that Shelby was hovering impatiently behind her, reluctantly waiting for her to finish so they could get to the canteen. She knew he was partial to the soya burgers and they were likely to run out, unless they got there in good time. But she was glued to the screen. There was a link to a translation of the Lament of Asha and she touched it, but an error message came up.

"That means it's classified," said Shelby behind her. From his tone she could tell that he thought that was an end to it. But to her it was only the beginning. The records had said that there was no written literature, yet that was contradicted by this report. She was supposed to write a true and fair assessment of Elanthia's history, but how could she do that if she had to omit an important part of its culture, its own historiography.

Yet she could not believe that the Hub was suppressing or omitting information. All the librarians had an ethical responsibility to be objective; they were expected to be critical also, but they weren't supposed to create partial histories or skew the narrative. It must be a mistake, she thought. She could refer it up to her supervisor here, Dr. Simeon.

She turned her screen off and went to lunch. Luckily, there were three soya-burgers left, but as she sat with Shelby and some others at the long, studiedly archaic table, looking out through the tinted picture window at the desert beyond, she couldn't stop thinking of 'Asha's Lament' and knew that she would dream of it in the night to come.

Chapter 2
Asha

"So it was that the maiden Asha looked out from the mountain, while watching her flock of Hvass and saw the star falling from the sky. She had a vision then, of the city Melanthera, and knew that she should take up the sword of her father and, with the blessing of her people, travel there to fulfill the destiny that the star foretold."

Gamelon, the priest stopped reading from the hvass skin scroll and looked up satisfied with himself. Berendal poured him more of the fiery liquor they called kassa in Melanthera, and which like nearly everything in this land, seemed to originate from hvass, this being their fermented milk. He, himself, was drinking what the Star People would call "wine" as it was fermented from a sort of fruit. It amused him how they had to find an equivalent for everything the Melantherans ate or drank. And of course, according to them, their version was always better.

"Is that how it happened?"

He turned to the tall, dark woman opposite him. As always she was nursing that long, two-handed sword in her lap and her arms were not far from her bundle of throwing spears and her hvass hide target. It was as if, Berendal thought, she expected a mountain lion to walk into the place.

She nodded silently, but her eyes fixed on him and made him uneasy. He knew her interest in him wasn't in any way amorous; she was one of the Sisterhood and had taken a vow of chastity and continence, that was why she was drinking water, which was a perilous enough act in itself in this flea-pit of a place.

They had come in with their caravan; this was the first oasis east of Melanthera. Circumstance had thrown the three together and who was he to question whether it was fortune or some god's will. There were, after all so many gods, in Melanthera. The Star People were different. They had one god, or so they said, but he was fast coming to believe that their one god was really money.

"Is that how it happened?"

Gamelon had an irritating habit of repeating things. Asha nodded again and fixed her eyes on the priest. She seemed continuously ready to pounce, like one of those lions she had fought up on the high plains and whose skin she wore now, over her spare frame. Berendal soon tired of looking at the two of them and instead scanned the room.

There were a few Hvassara there, in their short hvass leather breeches and conical riding hats, but there was a truce of sorts in force so that wasn't strange in itself and, anyway, within the walls of the caravanserai it was neutral ground. They were, however, renowned for their treachery and double-dealing so he decided that he must be careful. He was more interested in the serving girls though; they were local Harradim, graceful and shy, with their head-veils, their arms heavy with bangles and each bearing the delicate, little ring they wore in their left nostrils, signifying they were unwed. Out-of-bounds, he knew, but he could dream.

Asha, meanwhile, had not taken her eyes off the little priest, who had again filled his earthenware cup with kassa. He will be drunk soon, she thought, and it reminded her of her uncle and how he used to drink the kassa and would often beat her for some supposed transgression. Then she thought back to what the priest had said. Though she'd nodded, it hadn't really been like that. When she'd seen the star fall, she'd been pissing in a hollow on the mountainside; it hadn't been a mystical experience, with the smell of hvass dung in her nostrils and the wind blowing the edges of her robe into her stream of water, even though she had crouched there to be out of that eternal, maddening gale. She had stood up cursing and only then had her eyes noticed the streak in the sky.

She hadn't really had a vision of Melanthera, rather it had occurred to her that it was there the star would fall and, as she crouched in her piss-stained robe, she had looked around her at the hvass and decided she was mightily sick of them. So next day she had stolen away, said a few words of farewell to her uncle who was drunk and semi-conscious again on kassa and taken up her father's sword, her only legacy. Though her uncle, of course, thought otherwise; that the sword was his.

So she'd started her walk that day, her cloak and her weapons on her back, the parcel of dried food perched on her head and her water–skin around her belly. And this, apparently, was how legends were born and grew and were changed in that growing. She would let the priest have his own story, but it wasn't hers.

Chapter 3
Dr. Simeon

Robyn felt a degree of trepidation as she made her way up the stairs to Dr Simeon's offices. She had met the man very briefly when her rotation had arrived at the library. There had been a drinks reception in the canteen in the evening, to which they had been so cordially invited that it was obvious that they their attendance wasn't optional.

Simeon had stood on a chair and given a very formal welcoming speech while the sparkling wine was handed out. He had expressed the hope that they would all enjoy their time there and find it profitable, not monetarily of course, he joked, though the salary was handsome enough, but in terms of knowledge gained.

He'd then shaken their hands, working down their assembled line like a monarch, but had slipped away as the reception got going and the terrible, noisome vodka started flowing. She'd been glad of that, as she'd drunk a little too much and it was bad enough letting your co-workers see you in that state - though quite a few of them were as worse for wear as she was - without making such a formative impression on your boss.

She had got the impression, though, that there was so little to do here, stuck in such a harsh environment, that all their relationships and interactions were a little too intense and over-cooked and you either found solace in drinking or the gym. Of course, there was sex too, but, as of yet, she couldn't figure out where, in her case, this fitted in.

Arriving up at the top floor, she noticed that a real effort had been made here to give the place a collegiate feel, all early twentieth century Oxbridge, with artificial wooden panelling and replicas of old furniture. Quite frankly, it didn't work, but she decided to keep her opinion to herself. The receptionist on the mock-mahogany desk waved her through. Robyn knocked on the already open door and a non-committal voice said:

"Come in."

Simeon was sitting at his desk, totally engrossed in work, staring over lowered glasses at the terminal screen. That explained his lack of interest, she thought, as she stood there in the doorway. The glasses were one of his affectations; most people these days had their eyes lasered to correct any sight defects, but he clung to his spectacles, as he also hung onto his mock-tweed jackets and bow ties.

"I wanted to see you," she said, feeling nervous and hearing how it affected the tone of her voice. "I have a question about some of the records I'm reviewing. There seems to be an anomaly."

She could see that she had his interest now. He'd raised his eyes from the screen, pushed his glasses up his face and fixed her with a look, which partly suggested outrage and partly surprise. The records were sacrosanct she knew, there could be no anomalies. In the secular religion of Librarianship, the integrity of the records was the article of faith they all espoused.

"What exactly do you mean?"

20

It was only after she had explained the situation, what she had found, that he asked her to sit down. He scratched his head and looked around, then offered her coffee. His people skills weren't up to much and the act of working out how he was going to make, or otherwise procure, the coffee seemed to stymie him. In the end, it never materialised.

But he did give her a hearing of sorts. He sat back on his chair, his fingers steepled, and was silent as she said her piece. Afterwards, he grunted a few times, but still said nothing. Just as she had given up hope of getting any response, he said:

"It does seem to be an interesting case. What I think you have to bear in mind is that on many of those early expeditions, the personnel were... how can I put it... less than adept at interpreting some of the material that they encountered. After all, many of them were technicians or engineers, with just the minimum of training, a couple of days of an anthropology course at best, so the records aren't always that great."

She thought that he was going to leave it at that, but she pressed on.

"I appreciate that Doctor, but it's quite a major mistake to make, omitting the fact that a society had a whole canon of literature that has, to all intents and purposes, disappeared from the record."

Simeon sighed, whether through tiredness or frustration it was hard to say:

"I can see why this would concern you Ms. Harper, but you'd be surprised if I told you of some of the completely bizarre errors in the records that I've come across in all my years of doing this. On

21

Tantalus 6, a mining survey team identified what were basically prairie dogs as a sentient species and even started to negotiate with them. They'd seen the intricacy of their burrows, their underground towns, and confused a natural instinct to build as architecture. It's one of many classic, well-documented cases."

She got the hint of accusation in what he said. You haven't done your homework, was what he meant to imply.

"So you think this is misinterpretation," she carried on. She was getting a little angry now. She felt patronised.

"I seem to recall that on some of the Copernican sector planets, the societies there had developed a rudimentary way of recording trade transactions, very much like some of the early cuneiform tablets on old Earth. It's not really a literature as such, more like an accounting system. You'll need to check this out, but I would surmise that the early expeditionary parties that came across this system were too inexperienced to interpret it for what it actually was and misinterpreted it as a written literary tradition. In other words, they got over-excited and carried away."

She also understood the implication of this; he was saying that she was the one who was getting carried away now.

"But what about the Sir John Franklin logs?" She asked him, more direct now, less amenable. "Why are they effectively sealed?"

"Oh, that's easy to explain. These corporations are quite paranoid about commercial security and see spies everywhere. It's standard practise, that's all. Everything of interest was uploaded to the Hub, any sensitive commercial details were classified."

His slightly smug smile said it all. The interview was obviously over, so she nodded a farewell, which he returned, and made her way back to her section. Nothing he'd said had set her mind to rest. His use of the example of cuneiform was particularly inept; languages like Akkadian may have initially developed writing as a means of recording trade, but this script was soon in use for other purposes like codifying laws and transcribing mythological tales. Had he never read the "Epic of Gilgamesh" or the "Laws of Hammurabi"?

She wondered if she had made a mistake coming to him, but the system was strictly hierarchical and she had worked long enough in libraries to know that. Shelby had told her to let it drop, that it wasn't worth it for some piss-ant little planet at the arse-end of the universe, as he so succinctly put it, but she'd always been stubborn. She told herself that she should leave it there, but she'd found Simeon markedly irritating. She'd expected to be patronised, but had felt dismissed like an errant child.

So she was in something of an inner turmoil when she got back to her station and turned her monitor back on. I should just finish this section of the report and get on with one of the more interesting planets, she told herself. I'll go down the canteen tonight and blow off steam about Simeon with my co-workers, have a few drinks, starting getting to know them better, flirt with Shelby or Karin or both of them. A picture of Esmee came suddenly and unbidden into her head, but she tried to banish it. What was it they said, if you fall off the horse, the best thing to do is get back on it, though it would be a different horse in this case.

She thought she should get back to work and was just about to open the next batch of files on Shabaz, when her fingers, as if they had a life of their own, typed Elanthia into the Hub's search engine.

Chapter 4
Berendal And The Star People

Kevorkian, or Kev as he was known to the rest of the team, scanned the base with tired eyes as he came out of the pod. He pulled on his sun-glasses against the glare and was tempted to pull up his bandana over his nose to filter out the dust, but policy dictated that your face should not be covered or obscured from the indigenes in these first contact situations.

Melanthera was supposed to be a major city, the jewel in the crown of the central continent and the archipelago of inhabited islands that the territory was made up of, but all he could see around him was many-storied houses made of mud-brick that were so shapeless and eroded they looked as if they were melting. And everything was jumbled together; there were no clear patterns of streets, just a maze of alleys and every so often open spaces, where invariably, animal skin tents were pitched, as half the city seemed to be nomadic or semi-nomadic. They always seemed to be coming or going and, always also, driving before them herds of animals.

So apart from the heat, dust and the oppressive glare, the unfathomable, eternal comings and goings grated on your nerves. If you walked the streets, you were likely to get trampled or crushed; in a good-natured sort of way, because, he had to admit, the people seemed relatively affable.

They'd demonstrated this affability in the way they had let them set up this forward base just inside the city walls in the bazaar-like market space before the Hwrathka gate. His bosses at Sung Yang had been suitably impressed by this positive attitude at first, until they'd realised that the Melantherans were just treating the "Star People" as they called the expeditionary team, like any other traders. And the expeditionary team, in turn, were becoming more and more frustrated at the way the Melantherans were so singularly unimpressed by the obviously superior technology that they'd brought with them. They seemed to regard the base, with its prefabricated and self-sustaining habitation pods, its perimeter fence, floodlights and other apparatus, not with awe as they should, but with a sort of mirthful tolerance, as if the circus had come to town.

They were a little more impressed by the shuttles that set down and took off, but the crowds who gathered to witness these events were like the audience at a football match, chattering and jostling, cheering at the moment of take-off or landing, but, to be frank, not over-awed, not intimidated, not even overly impressed.

In fact, the Melantherans were probably the most unimpressible people he had ever met. Their attitude could only be described as blasé, not a term he readily used but which had been explained to him by Berthaud, one of his colleagues, and which he found particularly apt. But while they were unimpressed by material goods or technology light years ahead of their own, they could become ridiculously over-excited over the smallest of things. A pauper in the most disreputable rags would carry himself like a prince because of the blood that flowed through his veins. A face tattoo of a certain kind could silence a crowd and set traders to packing up their stalls. A man reciting, what Kev took to be poetry, could bring the marketplace to a halt and render silence everywhere.

He couldn't fathom these people, and that word was also apt, there were depths to them that he had no way of reaching. He saw a prime example of what he was talking about down by the galley pod in conversation with Berthaud. Once they'd analysed the linguistic patterns and fed them into the ship's main-frame, they hadn't been long in coming up with a translation programme. It was by no means perfect, but it would serve. Berthaud was trying to fine tune it, so she was using every opportunity to talk to the locals and was in conversation with one now.

It was the one who called himself Berendal and who seemed to fancy himself as some sort of poet. He was ragged, dusty - but to be fair everyone was dusty to some degree - and looked to be impoverished; but he obviously held himself in high esteem, the way he strutted around like a denuded peacock. He wore the hooded poncho-like cloak that they all wore, over the similarly ubiquitous loose tunic and voluminous trousers. He had on the short boots that were generally worn, either those or sandals. All the leather here stank, because it was cured in animal piss and retained a tang that was strong, though not particularly unpleasant. He was completely unadorned, except for an ornately worked belt that he wore around his waist that bore a curved scimitar-like sword. He had the dark-olive skin of the city people and their dark eyes and he

27

was obviously trying to charm Berthaud, as he had brought her a rather wilted handful of flowers, some non-descript blue things.

They were deep in conversation, though Berendal was obviously rather impatient with the intermediary of the translation programme on Berthaud's hand Pad, and the woman was getting more and more frustrated with him. As Kev came up, she said:

"He's spent half an hour reciting poetry to me, but the vocabulary is too exotic for the machine to pick up. I think he also asked me out to dinner, either that or he wants to marry me."

Kev wondered what going out to dinner consisted of in Melanthera, he doubted that it would have been described as a gourmet experience and whether Berthaud's stomach could have taken it.

"Berendal," he interrupted the man in mid flow, but he could see that Berthaud was glad of the break, "tell me again about the Hvass and the Hwrathka."

Berendal looked at him as if he was the slowest pupil in the class, but did as he was asked:

"The goddess Elanta gave us two great gifts, the Hvass and the Hwrathka. The Hvass feed us and clothe us, they give us life."

Kev knew that the Hvass were those goat-like creatures that were everywhere on this planet. They were the main form of domestic animal, kept for their milk, their wool and their meat. Even their hides were tanned for leather.

"Without the Hvass we couldn't live. They also give us Kassa, which makes men happy and women happier."

Kev looked at Berthaud, he didn't know what Kassa was.

"Cheese?" The woman guessed.

So cheese made men happy and women happier? It was possible, Kev thought, after all there seemed very little else to amuse people here.

"But Elanta also gave us the Hwrathka, into which she put her strength, so that they could carry for us and help us build palaces and temples to the goddess."

The virtual gap between words and translation made things difficult, but he tried to get more details.

"Berendal, let me get this right. Hwrathka are those big creatures."

He had seen one when they were invited to an audience at the palace, they were the size of elephants, but shaggy and horned like highland cattle. They were beasts of burden and beasts of war. The Empress, or so they had translated the title of the ruler of Melanthera, had invited the whole team to the reception. Initially they had been loath to go, but they all carried their side-arms for personal protection and, in a society where the apex of military technology was the composite bow, they felt that the risk was acceptable. Anyway, a shuttle would be standing by with support if they were compromised.

They were not allowed to use vehicles in these first contact situations, so the walk to the palace had been a long dusty one, though as they had done it in early evening it hadn't been too hot. It had, though, turned into a bit of a procession as many of the market traders and a horde of children had followed them up the steep track to the palace, which was part residence and part citadel.

There were eight of them, precious few against the milling crowd, but the Empress had sent an escort of guards with turquoise cloaks and veiled helmets, sinister enough to keep curious onlookers away, and a detachment of the same soldiers had been left to guard their camp. The Empress had stood with the other members of her court before them as they came in through the palace gate and greeted them. He did like that about Melanthera, nobody stood on ceremony, and they had then reclined in the pavilions that bordered the palace gardens, as a parade of dancers, conjurers and fire eaters performed for them.

Berendal had somehow sashayed his way in with them. He seemed to be representing himself as the interpreter, though, truth be told, it was Berthaud's Pad that was doing all the work. He had been a useful intermediary though, helping to explain the origin of the various foods and drinks on offer. First contact situations were always difficult, breaking bread and taking wine with your hosts had an almost sacred significance in most cultures, but, because of the differences in microbiology, teams had to be careful about what they ate. Some things an alien stomach could just not tolerate. When things became established, you could set up systems to monitor the local food, though teams usually just stuck to their rations.

The feast was marked by the fact that food and beverages weren't pressed on them. The Empress, a benign elderly woman, seemed to look on them with a degree of sympathy and sadness as courses were shown to them and quickly taken away.

Berthaud whispered to him, halfway through the second course:

"Berendal seems to have given them the impression that we all have rampant diarrhoea."

That seemed to explain things and also the rank of concerned looking servants who seemed to have been tasked to take them to the latrines and attend them. Later, these looked slightly disappointed that their services hadn't been needed.

Towards the end of the meal came the ceremonial toast that ended all Melantheran feasts, according to Berendal. This did involve drinking the local spirit, but Kev reckoned that this was reasonably safe as long as it wasn't too strong. One of the techs had done a quick, surreptitious analysis with a testing kit and that didn't pick up any noxious substances. Berendal said something about Kassa to him, but he told him he thought that they would skip the cheese.

The ceremonial toast went on and on and though Kev's team tried to be moderate in their consumption of the fiery liquor, the dictates of politeness, as their hosts kept pressing it on them and re-filling their golden cups, meant that most of them were a little drunk by the end of the meal.

Berendal, in particular, was all smiles and seemed exceedingly pleased with himself. He kept nodding towards the Empress, who smiled benignly back, and the other members of the court seemed pleased too, as they lifted their hands in the universal gesture of contentment that seemed ubiquitous in Melanthera; two open palms held out and upwards, or "jazz hands" , as Davies, one of the Techs, had dubbed it.

Berthaud, sitting beside him, was busy on her Pad with the translator programme and eventually leant over and whispered to him:

"From what I can gather and it's not exactly straightforward, this stuff is regarded as a cure-all for stomach ailments, so they're convinced that the more we drink the better we will be."

Well, at least they weren't trying to get them drunk deliberately.

The worst, though, was yet to come. Just as all the Melantherans seemed to have drunk their fill and were looking markedly merrier than before, a flock - which was an appropriate description considering their exotic plumage - of dancers bounded and leaped onto the floor from the sidelines and started up a strange formal, dance. They formed lines and circles and moved according to stately, studied patterns, as a pipe of some sort and a drum drew out a hypnotic, repetitive rhythm.

"It's like some of those old European folk dances, circle dances that sort of thing," Berthaud said, but Kev was no wiser in spite of her comment.

The dancers were both women and men and all marked by the vividly dyed clothes they wore, made of a silk-like material that clung to their lithe bodies. The pavilion's floor was a blurring pattern of watery blues, vivid scarlets, greens and yellows. The Melantherans were obviously enjoying the spectacle and were making their "jazz hands" gesture again.

Berendal was back at Berthaud's side trying to explain something.

"From what I understand of what he's saying," she told Kev, "this is a courtly dance from a place called Piroush, which is one of the islands at the edge of the central continent. I think it's where the Melantherans are supposed to have originated from, but I'm having some difficulty understanding the detail."

Kev nodded and thought to himself that that phrase could sum up all of these encounters. They were always having difficulty "understanding the details"; it was frustrating the things that escaped them, the subtleties they couldn't understand.

The dancers all seemed to be young and attractive; they had the olive skin of the Melantherans and the dark, raven hair. From what they had seen so far, the Melantherans were boringly uniform in their ethnicities and physical characteristics. Because their people seemed to have inhabited this central belt of the planet and had never settled in any of the northern or polar regions, which were mainly ocean anyway, they did not mirror the diversity that you saw in old Earth's peoples. They'd never had to evolve to deal with different climates and so were strikingly homogenous.

Suddenly there was a pause in the music, but then it started again and the Melantherans all raised themselves up from their couches and cushions, some not exactly steady on their feet, and joined in the dance. And out of the melee that was the dance floor, a group of the brightly garbed dancers swooped on Kev and his team and, despite their protests, manhandled them onto the dance floor, where the once stately dance had now become something wilder and frenetic.

The members of his team were looking to him for guidance, as the laughing dancers tried to demonstrate to them the steps of the dance. Berthaud looked terrified and only Davies, who had probably drunk too many toasts, was looking as if he was enjoying himself.

"It's one of their customs... so dance!" He said, as a beautiful young woman with flashing eyes and a ready smile grabbed him around the waist. He was close enough to smell the musky scent she wore and, over it, a sharp odour of sweat and the all-pervading smell of dust. They did smell different these Melantherans; they smelled more alive somehow than the sterile, showered ship's personnel he was so used to.

There was something about Melantheran women, he had noticed, a frankness, an openness. And there was a liveliness, an energy to Melantheran life. They were always laughing or squabbling or crying. Some might say they were highly-strung or over-emotional, somehow primitive in their response to the stimuli of life, though you might also say, he thought - but perhaps it was the alcohol talking - that they were more alive somehow.

He was even starting to enjoy himself, when he suddenly noticed that most of the Melantherans had stopped dancing and were watching the Star People. They were obviously enjoying the spectacle immensely; though some of them, particularly the dancers, tried to make an effort to hide their amusement, many of the revellers, the more drunk ones mostly, were almost hysterical with laughter. A couple of them were even rolling on the floor. Only the Empress, who had never left her couch, seemed unmoved by the spectacle, but just smiled benignly down at all of them.

The dance broke up and everyone resumed their seats. One of the Empress's retinue, a tall rather gaunt young man with a pronounced hook nose - Kev presumed he was a court official or some sort of nobleman - made some comment out loud and many of the audience laughed, until they noticed the stony expression on the Empress's face.

Berthaud asked Berendal what he had said and at first the man was reluctant to answer. Then he said something and Berthaud used her Pad to translate to it to Kev.

"Apparently that was one of the Empress's generals, Kal Quintal, and he said that although the Star People were rich in goods and knew many things, they couldn't dance and had no sense of rhythm."

Kev grunted. He thought it was actually a pretty fair assessment of things.

That wasn't the worse though, the worse came next. One of the Empresses' servants made an announcement that Berthaud didn't catch in time and then Berendal sprang forward and launched into what Kev presumed was some kind of poem, which went on and on and was seemingly endless. Some sorts of fruit juices and sweetmeats were served to them, though they didn't partake of them, but the performance did go on for an unseeingly long time. From what Berthaud gathered, Berendal's poem was some sort of tribute to them called something like "A Hymn to the Star Men". It was too full of strange vocabulary and syntax for Berthaud to translate on the spot, but she recorded it for later.

Finally, the feast ended with a visit to the Hwrathka quarter of the palace where the big beasts were stabled and trained. They followed the Empress out from the pavilion and through a series of courtyards and gardens until they came to an ornate gate, guarded by more of the masked spearmen. They passed through and before them was a vast parade ground that took up most of the walled plateau that lay beyond the hill-top palace. Arrayed in front of them were ranks of the big beasts, bigger than elephants and covered with the same sort of coarse hair that Kev imagined mammoths would have been covered with. They were impressive, with their curled horns, their broad shoulders and square heads, snorting and pawing the ground.

Kal Qintal stepped up onto a small, man-made hillock and gave a command, motioning with a red-painted staff as he did so, and the animals started to execute a series of manoeuvres - impressive enough considering the size of the beasts - which reminded Kev of synchronised swimming on old Earth. They wheeled in circular formations, crossed and crossed again, advanced, executed turns and ended the display with a thundering charge that ended some few metres from where they stood. Some of his people looked on the brink of turning and running for cover, but Kev stiffened them with a backwards glance and held his ground, figuring that if the Empress could do so, calm and stately in her blue silken robes besides him, so could he.

36

He was most sorry for the Hwrathka drivers, perched between their shoulders and the two archers, in a sort of mini howdah atop the beast, who looked positively sea-sick as the big creatures broke into their lumbering run.

As they walked back down the hill later, flanked by their mysterious masked guards, Berthaud asked him what he thought of the Hwrathka.

"Big ugly brutes for the most part," he said as the violet Melantheran dusk settled on the land in the same way as the dust was settling on them, "and they reeked of dung and urine."

Berthaud looked thoughtful as she considered his remarks:

"I don't know," she said. "I think there was something terribly noble about them."

Now, in the dust and glare of Hwrathka square the memory of that night had already taken on a strangely unearthly quality, as if it had all been a dream. Berendal was saying something, Berthaud translating. Then he walked away.

"What did he say?" Kev asked her.

Berthaud shook her head and said:

"If I understood him correctly he said that there was no point answering your question as the very fact you asked it made him think you would never really understand what the Hwrathka meant to the Melantherans."

Kev took off his cap and ran his hand through his hair. The poet probably had it just about right, he thought, there was no way Kev or the rest of his people would ever really understand the Hwrathka, the Melantherans or the whole damn planet.

Chapter 5
Hymn To The Star Men

Robyn's head was thumping when she woke up and her mouth was so dry she thought her tongue was stuck to the roof of her mouth. Hanis was a good posting in that they all had their own quarters and she was glad that she wasn't sharing with some young air-head, especially when she woke up like today with such a colossal hangover.

As usual, she blamed it on the terrible ersatz vodka, but she suspected, in truth, that it was really down to the amount of the foul stuff she had actually imbibed and her consumption was, as usual, relative to her own sense of burgeoning unhappiness. This after all had been the plum posting; the job that would get her career back on track, but equally importantly would get her life back on the rails.

The shower and toilet cubicle were just a metre or so away from the bed; these were indeed private quarters, but, having been built by the Colonial Engineer Corps, were more like the cramped cabins you got on a starship than terrestrial rooms.

In the bathroom a strange woman's face looked out of the mirror at her. It was standard practise to use your Pad to read your temperature and your various mineral levels when you got up in the morning, but today she daren't. Instead, she started trying to remember what had happened last night in the canteen and later, when she and a few of her colleagues had retired up to the euphoniously named star lounge, a glorified viewing platform at the top of the library.

She knew that she had been flirting, some might say outrageously, with a number of her colleagues, one of whom she thought had been Karin. She didn't think she had made a pass at Karin; in fact she was pretty sure she wouldn't have known how to do so after all these years. Karin was very Germanic in the way she drank; it didn't seem to outwardly affect her - no flushing, no slurring, no unsteady feet - until suddenly she did something, spilt her drink or dropped her glass, and you realised she was totally and gloriously drunk.

Staring in the mirror she saw the truth written all over her face. She was lonely and even though she had convinced herself she could be brave and independent, she missed Esmee; missed her warmth, the scent of her, the cosy evenings spent in their apartment together looking over the lake. She had thought she could go out there and find new love, or at least diversionary sex, but she didn't know where to start.

And there was also this business of Elanthia; it had intrigued her at first, seemed to be a challenge, but now it was starting to make her uncomfortable, as if there was a sinister edge to it. That might have been why she got so drunk last night, she thought, as she looked in the mirror, savouring the excuse. Especially since she had found the 'Hymn to the Star Men'.

The Hub's search engines had proved to be virtually useless to her research. It was as if they had been programmed with some software that could weave an illusory, electronic web over the planet's history. It was almost as if the Hub would only sanction the orthodox, received view of Elanthian history, that it was piss-poor planet with a primitive, limited culture. She had been looking for the 'Asha's Lament', but could find no reference to any such work or anyone named Asha.

The closest she got to learning anything new, was the list of Elanthian names that she eventually winkled out of the system. She presumed it was the work of some anthropologist or ethnologist with one of the first surveying teams or the One God One Church missionaries that had a contract with Sung Yang and eventually turned upon most of their planets. It was a partial list, a work in progress containing twenty-six names and an attempt to translate and analyse the meaning of them.

She found the name Asha, which according to the author of the list, originated in the western central continent of Elanthia and was associated with the semi-nomadic pastoral peoples of that area, dubbed the Mountains of the Moon by the Sung Yang teams for no obvious reason. Asha was apparently a common girl's name amongst these mountaineer tribes and probably meant 'beloved'. All this was guesswork, however, because the author was basing the translation on Melantheran, the language of the central continent associated with the city states of the area. It wasn't clear if the Moon People, as they had come to be known for want of a better name, spoke Melantheran, a dialect of it, or a completely different language.

Frustratingly that what all she found, but, on impulse, she copied the list of names and did a multiple cross-referenced search on them. She came up with some leads, but they all turned out to be dead-ends; similar sounding names in other languages or obscure references to records of the first contact groups, giving no more than allusions to the name itself and no other details.

She had just decided to give up and get back to the work on Shabaz, when something tangible came up. One of the names that she had inputted was Berendal; it had figured on the list, but had no other reference beside it, no translation or explanation. She was somewhat surprised to find that the link led her back to Shabaz or, to be exact, a list of literature from the Shabaz federation.

She clicked on the link to the title and found that it took her to a translation of what was presumably some sort of poem called 'Hymn to the Star Men' by the afore-mentioned Berendal. She had only a basic grasp of the linguistic landscape of Shabaz, but she knew straight away that this was no co-incidence of name or confusion of text. The poem was written in Melantheran, or rather rendered in the transliterated alphabet that the Sung Yang anthropologists had used to capture the language and its flowing script.

She could think of no other explanation except that it had been misfiled, purely and simply, and, in this way, had escaped whatever catastrophe had happened to the rest of Melantheran literature. Perhaps there were other texts scattered around in the shadowy, electrical corners of the Hub, like old books misplaced on cob-webbed shelves in some abandoned part of a vast library, all that remained of their lost voices.

The text was a learned article by some linguistic researcher, which attempted to translate and analyse the poem. The author, a previously unknown academic called Anthony Lao, had a rather spiky, over-blown style and seemed to take a very critical position on the poem.

In fact, he spent a substantial part of the article discussing whether the form the text was written in could be called a poem, as the metrical and rhythmic structure was so obscure. He came to the conclusion that it was some sort of performance piece, not an enormously original finding as the text clearly stated that it had been performed at an imperial reception for one of the first contact teams in the Melantheran citadel.

According to Lao, the original text, which had later been transliterated, was taken down, presumably verbatim, by a scribe as it was performed. He'd used the word 'hymn' in the translation as he had surmised, on very little evidence, that the reception was some sort of religious occasion and he theorised that the Melantherans had thought that the 'Star Men' were gods of some kind, or, at least, god's servants.

She knew the type, she thought, as she read the article; always finding some sort of religious significance in the things they examined, every piece of writing was a sacred, every big building a temple, every government a theocracy. It had been an academic fad, a few years back, to interpret these newly contacted cultures in this way.

She remembered how one of her lecturers at Hub College had said that, if they considered their own culture where every room had a screen in it connected to the Hub, how easy it would be to see these focal points of the room as sacred shrines to some distant god. But in a sense they were, she thought. Perhaps the Hub was what many of them had instead of a god.

Whatever the title really was, the piece was obviously written as a eulogy for the visitors, these Star Men from a distant place.

"When the Star fell from the sky, we did not think to see such wonders.

They stood before us in all their finery, no leather for them, no wool or linen."

The leather, wool and linen referred to were translations of some similar Melantheran materials.

"They came in all their glory, with all their clever things, that sung and flashed and twittered like birds.

They carried no swords or spears, but came in peace to trade and make alliances."

She doubted that the Star Men had come to trade and make alliances, but, according to Lao, it was a Melantheran phrase that signified that the contact team had come in peace.

"Their faces were fair and they were fertile, their ships that sailed the sky had many herds and many fields of ripe corn."

Again, according to Lao, this was a stock Melantheran way of flattering the contact team, implying they were handsome, healthy and wealthy.

"Why did they come to our city? Why are we so blessed? Let us wish them health with cheese."

Lao thought that "wish them health with cheese" was equivalent to blessing them, though to her it sounded more like a toast.

The poem went on for many verses in this style, but then its tone started to change.

"See how abstemious they are, sniffing their drinks! How their attendants hover, ready to honour them! They eat in such a dainty way, shaming our appetites. Look at them dance, they have the grace of antelopes!"

Something occurred to her as she read the verse, and then re-read it and referred to Lao's notes. The word he had translated as antelope was originally written as hwrathka and, from her research into Elanthia, she knew that hwrathka were big lumbering beasts, one of a very limited range of domestic animals, who were, according to all the records she had read, as graceful as elephants.

Suddenly she understood what Lao had completely failed to grasp. The poet, Berendal, was poking fun at his guests; he was being playful, even sarcastic. She re-read the text with new eyes; it was hardly a poem written by a man who was over-awed by the Star men. He flattered them, said nice things about them, but he wasn't above making fun of them in a subtle, rather affectionate way. The Melantherans weren't overwhelmed or daunted by the strangers, as the histories would have her believe; they had a much more complicated attitude.

She managed to find a record, more of a blog really, written by one of the officers of the first contact group, Dr Marie Berthaud, who also described the reception and how the contact team hadn't eaten anything for obvious reasons, having had no opportunity to do a definitive test on the food. She mentioned the obscure little fact that the Melantherans had thought, because of this, that the crew all had diarrhoea, which made the reference in the poem to "attendants ready to honour them" quite funny. It had all been there for Lao to see, but instead he chose an interpretation that fitted in with his own pre-conceptions.

She spent some time reading the poem, starting to appreciate the nuances of meaning, the sub-text that ran through it, giving her a new insight into how the Melantherans looked at things and how this Berendal thought. She turned to Lao's notes again to find out if he had written anything about the poet, but the academic's knowledge was sparse. He wrote tersely that Berendal was some sort of minor poet or bard, who had acted as some sort of guide or liaison for the first contact team.

She realised it was later than she thought, when the night maintenance engineer came through the doorway and gave her a quizzical, surprised look. She glanced down at her Pad, it was long past dinner, that mutually-agreed communal time that the team spent eating, but she would still be able to get something to eat in the canteen, though the soya burgers would all be gone. She copied the documents, the poem and the list of names, onto her desktop, making sure they were in her Shabaz file rather than the Elanthian one. As always, she synchronised her desktop folders with those on her Pad. Taking work home with you, in fact carrying it around everywhere, was just a fact of life these days.

That strange, almost intangible feeling that she had started to have about Elanthia was becoming more real, more pressing now. The sinister edge she'd felt, like those involuntary shivers you get, someone passing over your grave as they used to say, was taking a clearer form. She was starting to be convinced that there was something amiss here, shoddy record keeping or misapprehensions couldn't account for this. Someone, somewhere had tried to suppress the truth about Elanthia, but the shadows and echoes of it were still there, ghosts in the Hub's machines.

Chapter 6
Asha's Journey

It was another time, another place. Asha had sought out the shade of a borriba tree, beside a pool in the terraced gardens below the Palace mound. There were, of course, hvass here, grazing around her. In fact, in Melanthera, it was very difficult to get any distance away from hvass, they were always present. The result was that there was precious little grass left in the gardens and only the few plants that were too bitter for the hvass's undiscerning palate.

It was close to the mid part of the day and the sun, Elanta's torch, was hot and the wind that blew, as always, was gritty, dry and tasted of metal. Thought the ground where she sat was dusty, scoured of any plant life by hvass, and there was hvass dung all over the place, the shade of the borriba glade was pleasant and the pools that flowed from the springs in the rocks above gave, at least, an illusion of coolness.

Though, when she was younger, she had got heartily sick of hvass, living with them and shepherding them every day of her young life, she now gained a sort of comfort from their presence, their simplicity. For what else did they do all day, but eat, dealing with their ever-present hunger, sleep and occasionally rut. She wondered if, when Elanta had given the hvass to them, the people, whether in fact it had been an elaborate joke. But she quickly checked herself, that was after all blasphemy, and she must maintain her purity of thought, as truly befits one who is of the Sisterhood. At this thought, she felt a gripe in her guts and let out a fart. Abstractedly, she wondered if there was a link between flatulence and blasphemy, or whether it was the diet of pulses she had to rely on now she had eschewed meat, as part of her religious dogma.

Though she felt somewhat rested in the shade of the tree, she felt particularly on edge that day. She felt her nerves tensed, her muscles coiled, as if she was a mountain lion waiting to spring out on its prey. She hated this inaction; she needed something to distract her. But the something, when it came, was more of an added irritation, rather than a distraction.

The red-robed, beggar priest Gamelon had found her again and she knew that he would, as usual, pester her with his questions. He would always ask her what had happened, trying to sort the happenings and places into some sort of order. He would also ask her how she felt about this and that, which was in many ways worse. How was she to know what she felt? Her feelings changed like the wind, like the sun when a cloud passes over. But at this moment her feelings were clear, she was irritated by the shambling presence that approached her and wouldn't leave her in peace. As usual, he had a flask of kassa with him and was half-drunk, his habitual state.

"Oh, brave and magnificent Asha," he said, as he drew near and then sat, uninvited, a short distance from her. She noted that he wasn't coming too close; he had had experience of her temperament before, how suddenly it changed.

"I have come again to seek you out and hear tales of your exploits and to feast my ears on your legendary courage and prowess in arms."

To Asha, there was little difference between Gamelon's mouth and a hvass's arse, both produced dung.

"You were going to tell me," he said, "about the early days of your journey, how you made your way, after many adventures, out of the mountains and defeated a horde of Hvassara. How the people of the lowlands kissed your feet and raised you up as one of the chosen ones, one of the Sisterhood, who keep their faith with Elanta and keep the people safe."

She could not remember promising him anything of the sort and it was unlikely that she had, in fact, spoken more than a few terse words to him. She knew, however, that even if she loosened her tongue to him, which was doubtful, he would write what he wished anyway and it would bear a poor relation to the truth, whatever the truth was. There would be a horde of Hvassara and she would defeat them, it would be written so in his history.

She closed her eyes and tried to block out the murmur of his voice, concentrating instead on the rustling sound that the hvass made when they moved and the rhythmic grumbling sound they emitted, as they chewed and digested what little grazing they could find. She had been a different Asha in those days.

The journey out of the hills had been a time of both wonder and fear for her. Every day seemed to bring new sights, new taste and new smells. She had not realised how big the land was, how long it would take her to follow the hvass trails through the bare hills and down, ever downward, to the flatlands below. She had walked into villages, expecting the hospitality that all Moon People would give, as long as your clan wasn't warring with theirs, but had found suspicion and a grudging sort of charity.

These people, she noticed at once, were shorter than her people and their skin was a shade or two lighter. To her they looked uncomely and wan. Though they fed and watered her, she realised that they did it out of fear. Her people, she found out later, had often raided these settled villages and, such was their reputation, that the villagers were loath to offend even a single warrior. They kept her on the edge of their villages and, at first, this lack of human contact had made her somewhat lonely. Though she had spent much of her life alone with hvass, she had always felt part of a family, a clan; now she was solitary like an old, mountain lion.

Every day, there was something new to see; when she first saw a windmill being used to pump up water from a well, she was in awe of it. When she first tasted the fruit that the villagers cultivated, so different from the berries that grew in her homeland, she thought she'd had a taste of heaven. All these things, these sights, smells and tastes, made her feel that she was stranger journeying in another world and that she would never be able to find home again.

Then one day she met the Hvassara, but not a horde of them, only four riders. She had seen their fire a long way off across the plain, getting closer as she topped each rise of the gently undulating land. That they did not seek to hide their camp, or seemed in any way perturbed by her approach, seemed to mark them down as lacking fear, a trait she found attractive. As was her people's custom, she crouched down on her haunches a little way from the camp, waiting for the gesture that would beckon her in, offer hospitality. It was not long in coming.

Though her face remained impassive, she was intrigued by the little men, in their short leather breeches, with those strange, little hats, that had a conical peak and then descended into flaps that covered their necks and, dividing over the ears, fell down in two flaps on either cheek. They were all bow-legged from a life in the saddle and had a curious rolling walk. Though the villagers had spoken a similar dialect to hers, these men's language was unfamiliar. She couldn't understand any of their words.

Their shaggy mounts, hobbled and grazing in a depression nearby, were a surprise to her. Later she would learn that they were haras, a bigger cousin of hvass, bred by the Hvassara for riding and carrying, and capable of a swiftness she had not seen before.

Though she caught them giving her sidelong glances when she sat down, their eyes suspicious and appraising, they fed her a bowl of some stew they had cooked in a large, iron pot over the fire. It was some sort of meat, not hvass. She thought it was maybe a rodent of some sort, but she was hungry. She did, however, almost choke, because the meal had a fieriness about it. Something she had never tasted before. For a brief second she thought that she had been poisoned, but when she saw them laughing at her choking and spluttering, she guessed that they meant her no harm. They just had

52

different, novel tastes. In later years she would get a taste for that fiery, Hvassaran spice that they had borrowed from the Harradim of the desert oases.

After the meal, they produced a skin of kassa. She had always been wary of the drink, had seen how it had robbed her uncle of sense, practically of life. But here she felt it would be impolite, a breach of the code of hospitality to refuse. After a few sips, she looked on these men differently. They felt like comrades, like friends. One of the men, older than the others, loosened his belt and made a show of laying aside the long knife that he wore in a sheath on it. He motioned to her to put aside her sword, but she pretended not to understand. She did notice, however, that the three younger men made no move to take off their belts and knives, and also noticed, her warrior's instinct still sharp even after the kassa, that they kept their small, curved bows close at hand, even if they were not strung.

The kassa started to act on her senses. Later the old man had crept closer to her, had taken to lifting the skin to her lips and started patting her arms. He even at one stage put a hand on her sword hilt, motioning her to put it aside, away from her lap where she cradled it. She'd taken his hand from the sword hilt, but then he had put it on her shoulder. As she looked at the young men across the fire, she recognised a hunger in the looks that they were giving her and not for more food or more kassa. She had never been with a man, but, after all, they were not that much different from hvass in the rutting season.

Abruptly, she stood up, almost knocking the old man over; the three young men across the fire were reaching for their knives. Asha pretended to be drunker than she was, stumbled a bit and mimicked pissing, crouching down in front of them, to their amusement, and lifting her shift. As they were laughing, she stumbled from the fire into the darkness, the sword cradled in her arms like a child.

She had really needed a piss, so, going just far away enough not to arouse suspicion, she crouched down in the grass. She could hear muted voices from the men around the fire and the muffled sounds of movement. She had no doubt that they would try and make her captive when she returned to the fire. She also knew what would come next. If she was fortunate, they would not kill her afterwards, but would trade her as a slave. She knew this, it was just as if they had actually told her so, but part of her was still shocked that these men, creatures more like, would act this way and breach the sacred, universal rules of hospitality. If you had invited someone into your house, your camp, fed and watered them, it was a sin to then abuse them in some way.

Though there were four of them, Asha knew that she had one advantage, that they thought she was drunk and incapable of resistance. She had had to leave her throwing spears and shield by the fire, so as not to arouse suspicion, though no-one would go out into the darkness totally unarmed in case there were lions about. Someone shouted something from the camp and the others laughed. She started walking back and then let out a cry, pretending she had fallen, calling for help. She could see two figures, silhouetted by the campfire behind them as they approached her location; they hadn't even drawn their knives so sure were they of their prey.

She took off her shift and let it fall on the ground, then moved a few paces away, her two hands on the sword hilt ready to swing the weapon. As one man bent over the shift, puzzled, she struck at the one who had remained standing and cut him down. She kicked the other in the head and then pounced on him. She used the rope that he had brought with him to bind her, to choke the life out of him.

Hearing someone else approaching, she rolled off him and lay still in the grass. She could hear her breath panting, hear her heart racing, thought the sounds might betray her, but just as the figure neared, as she could her the soft fall of his feet on the grass by her, she rose like a mountain lion, the creature she had fought and killed so many times before, and knocked him senseless with the butt of the sword.

Then she walked slowly toward the fire. The old man was there standing by the flame, busy stringing his bow, but he looked up with a gasp as she came into the light. She was stark naked, her ebony skin reflecting the low, burning flames. She gave him just a glimpse of what he had wanted, what he had paid his life for, before she removed his head with one stroke of the long sword. After she had made sure the other men were really dead, she washed off their blood with water from their skins and donned her shift again. She did, after all, prize her modesty.

Sleep, she knew would be impossible here, the blood would attract lions and other predators and she could not be sure that these men were not part of a bigger party of Hvassara. She collected up her few possessions and walked over to the haras. She did not want to leave the creatures hobbled like this, prey to any predator, but she knew nothing about the animals and was, quite frankly, frightened to approach them. Were they savage? Would they sense that she had sent their masters on their way to the shadow world? As she crouched, contemplating the creatures, she suddenly became aware of a sound, coming from - or so it seemed - the ground near where they were grazing.

Walking over, keeping a wary eye on the haras, she saw that what she had first thought to be a uniform swathe of grass, was, in fact, not so. There was a patch of this grass that, even in the soft pre-dawn light, looked discoloured, yellower than the green around. She realised that this uprooted grass was covering something. A pit-trap, she thought, as sometimes they used to trap lions, but, when she tentatively cleared off some of the grass with her sword, she saw, beneath a covering of branches cut from the low shrubs that grew in clumps hereabouts, a more exotic creature in the hole below.

The creature was a woman dressed in some sort of red robes. A red shift, covered by a hooded cape of the same colour. The woman had the same olive skin as the villagers, darker than the three Hvassara, but not as dark as her own and a long flowing head of hair, black with a hint of copper amongst the tresses. The Hvassara had made an effective prison, but, using a rope she found in the camp, she managed to get the woman out of the pit.

"Sister, I'm grateful." The woman said, when she had loosened the gag.

Though the woman was filthy and weak from hunger and thirst, she looked with concern up into Asha's face; upwards, because like all of these people she was much shorter than Asha.

"Are you well? They didn't ill use you?"

When she took the woman back to the fire, stirred up the ashes and got a blaze going to warm her up, the priestess - for that was what the red robes signified, Asha later found out -looked out over the bodies around the place and then at the headless corpse, which Asha had dragged just a little way off from the hearth. She seemed to be weighing up the scene, looking from one corpse to another, then looked hard at Asha.

"You did this yourself?"

Asha nodded.

"Then what are you? Angel or demon?"

She gave the priestess a little time to recover, but then hurried them on their way. She was still unsure whether more Hvassara would turn up. The woman was familiar with the Haras and took one to ride, but she couldn't persuade Asha to do the same. The Moon Girl felt safer and more secure on her own two legs. Asha had no idea of where exactly they were going, she was still vaguely heading for Melanthera, but the priestess, whose name she said was Amala, thought she knew the direction of the nearest town and a convent that would give them shelter.

Though Asha had never had much truck with words, Amala proved to be a garrulous companion. From her she found out the story of her abduction;

how the caravan she had been travelling in had been attacked by Hvassara and she had ended up in the custody of the four warriors, part of the booty divided up between the members of the raiding party, which had then split up, fearing pursuit.

Asha had asked her if they meant to sell the woman as a slave, but Amala tutted and threw her head back, the universal gesture for 'no' amongst the people of Melanthera.

"No. They knew they could get more money, if they ransomed me back to the Sisterhood. That's probably also why they didn't rape me, if that's what you were wondering."

It had crossed Asha's mind. Though the woman possessed a sort of strength and seemed kind and warm-hearted, she appeared to have none of the physical power and martial prowess needed to stay alive on these plains. To Asha, anyway, the fact of rape was an alien, somewhat surprising thing. Amongst the Moon People there was raiding, fighting, even death on occasion, but they didn't generally rape. Women were abducted, but were then quickly married, often by mutual arrangement with the prospective spouse.

From Amala she found out that amongst the Hvassara it was something of a standard practise and even the red robe didn't always save a priestess from this fate. Sometimes the very chastity they practised was the attraction, an added touch of spice.

Asha found out about the chastity in another way. It was cold on the plain and when they made camp that night, keeping the fire low so that they wouldn't be spotted, but afraid to sleep without it

58

because of predators, it was natural that the two women would share their sleeping blankets, keeping close to share their warmth. But when Asha had started to touch and caress the woman, to do the sort of things that the girls that herd the hvass did at night for a little bit of mutual comfort and release, Amala stopped her.

"You are a very beautiful woman, Asha, and I'm tempted and a bit flattered. But I'm one of Elanta's Sisterhood and we really are chaste, not like some other orders."

Asha had felt rebuffed at first, but as the woman talked as they travelled and she found out more about the Sisterhood, it started to sound attractive. They didn't drink alcohol either and after her last night on kassa, she felt she could do without that as well.

The city that they eventually got to, after three days, was on the very edge of the territory of Melanthera, just a dusty, ramshackle frontier town, but to Asha it was a fabled place of tall towers and palatial buildings. She didn't see - or if she did, didn't notice - the cracks in the walls, the shifting courses of brick-work and the gates hanging off their hinges. At the convent behind the temple of Elanta, which every sizeable place in Melanthera boasted of, the Sisters made them both welcome. No-one questioned Asha, no one sought anything from her.

She found out that she could be a Sister and still go about her normal life, carry on her journey. Thus it was that she took her vow one afternoon in the temple, the sun slanting in from outside making

golden panels on the floor, all the Sisters assembled
and Amala holding her hand and smiling at her.

Chapter 7
Weekends On Hanis

For Robyn the weekends on Hanis were deserts of time, which stretched out to the mirage of a horizon she could never quite reach. As on most of the outer planets, where bases and colonies had been carved out of, or set down on, a hostile landscape, the inhabitants of the facilities on Hanis had tried to adhere to the pattern of work and leisure that had become a custom and tradition of Earth's industrial ages. Day length on Hanis almost matched that of Earth, so they could follow a pattern of five slightly longer days of work and two of rest.

This pattern mainly applied to the civilian establishments on the planet. The mines and the other extractive industries followed a shift pattern that ensured continuous working, though the work was so mechanised it only necessitated a small teams of technicians and engineers. The military, as always, followed their own patterns of activity.

Hanis itself was sparsely populated; the mines were the reason that humans had first ventured here. First had come the surveying ships and the prospecting teams, then the drills and digging rigs, followed by the Defence Force bases to protect them. The library had been set down in this alien landscape like some leviathan of an ocean liner run aground on a distant strand. As the new cities were built and the new-found planets coalesced into commercial and industrial networks, which in turn fed and were nurtured by the existing web of the older planetary economies, the library on Hanis would be the Hub's outpost in the outer planets. A reminder that knowledge was the heart of this power, that wealth and economic growth were underwritten by the Hub and its almost mystical power to harness and channel the wide ocean of information that flowed around the planets and everyone on them.

The denizens of the library didn't mix much with the other groups of humans on the planet; there was no collective communal space. It was if they were effectively sealed in their own society, in the same way that the library was hermetically sealed from the desert landscape. So the team of senior librarians that managed the place, had done what they could to ameliorate their situation and soften the sense of isolation. The staff were encouraged to arrange sports tournaments and social events; there were book groups and singing clubs, film societies and arts circles. But mostly there was a pronounced tendency towards drinking too much and an almost morbid fascination with the rather, bland limited fare that the canteen produced.

Robyn found that Sundays were her worst day. Friday and Saturday nights tended to be party nights, which meant that they tended to gather in small, department-based groups in the canteen or one of the bars, to talk, drink and flirt. Occasionally there was music and some dancing, but mainly there was Friday night karaoke, which would never involve Robyn.

So Saturday was taken up with recovering from Friday night and the menial tasks of housekeeping, though in truth these were kept to a minimum, as her quarters were well-equipped and laundry and cleaning were taken care of by the domestic staff. But Sunday was a vacuum that her own nature abhorred, filling the aimless hours with memories of Sundays by Lake Kara, the coffee houses and restaurants, the pleasure gardens and boat trips, all those days spent with Esmee, when they were together and Robyn felt like half of one entity.

On the worst parts of Sunday, the late afternoon hours that were particularly forlorn, she would gaze out of her sealed window at the desert mountains and sky, which topped the compound walls and gave a lie to the false, green oasis that surrounded her under its protective doom, and feel like she had irrevocably lost that other half, that twin, and would never be able to become whole again. The loneliness at those times was so acute that it was like a physical pain.

When she had lived on Lake Kara, she had liked to run. Nearly every day, if she could part herself from her warm bed and the sleek, comfortable shape of Esmee beside her, she would run on the paths that wound in and out of the groves of cedar trees that fringed the Lake. She had tried running on Hanis, but here it wasn't the same in anyway. There was a circular corridor which ran the length of the upper storey of the library, designed for walking and, running and cycling, with a panoramic view through an enclosing tunnel of glass. She did take some pleasure from just running this circuit, nodding a greeting to others she met on the way, but it was not the same as those early morning runs by Lake Kara, when she felt her soul being borne up on the wings of the birds that lifted from the lake as she passed, knee deep in the warm mist. But there was some consolation; it was while pounding the sterile metallic corridors of the library that she met Abi.

Robyn had avoided the running clubs that other librarians seemed to favour; running, she thought, like masturbation, was something best done alone and not in random company. Besides, it gave her space to think and she'd rather do that than engage in mundane conversations with people she hardly knew. But if you kept going jogging at the same times, you tended to bump into the same people, runners being creatures of routine. Abi was one of these, someone she saw most days but didn't really note. Until one day, when the end of their runs had coincided and they were walking back to the accommodation levels, they fell into conversation.

It remained something of an enigma to Robyn, how she had become so close with the woman. They had started to run together, quietly, but companionably. One day Abi had told her about the sauna and the hot-tub and they fell into the routine of going there after running. It was on the first occasion that they went, after they had dressed together in the changing room, that Robyn noted with surprise that Abi had put on the fatigues of a Defence Force soldier.

Though Robyn didn't like to admit it to herself, her social circle on Thera had been limited; almost exclusively she'd mixed with artists and intellectuals, so the military was an alien territory she'd always thought of as masculine and remote. Abi was part of small unit of Defence Force soldiers which was in charge of security at the library. She was an intelligence officer and had some responsibility for vetting and monitoring the staff, though she was vague about what she actually did.

Abi was different to anyone that Robyn had become close to before. She was tall and slightly mannish; she was almost intimidatingly fit and well-muscled, though compact. She had been named Abigail, but would only answer to Abi. She'd told Robyn that her parents, a diplomat and a development expert posted to one of the Tantalus planets, had adopted her when she was a baby from one of the local temples. Though her voice had the modulated tones of the inner planets and she often sounded like the career soldier she was, the dark skin and yellow-green eyes of her Tantalan ancestry gave her another dimension, an exotic allure.

As to their relationship and its nature, this was as equally unclear to Robyn as to any casual onlooker. She had to admit to herself that there was something about the woman that she found attractive; it was hard to think you could look deep into those eyes without getting bewitched by them. But she was unsure whether it was anything other than friendship or, indeed, should be. Abi was, also, not exactly forthcoming with her own feelings, presumably it was all part of the military thing.

Whether it was a courtship or a friendship, she soon stopped trying to fathom it. Though on the face of it they were very different people and were drawn together by circumstance, as it was, they seemed to get on reasonably well. The weekends seemed gradually less forlorn as they grew closer and Sundays became a day to look forward to rather than one to endure.

During the time that she was getting to know Abi, Melanthera and other Elanthian matters had been replaced by more pressing issues and had receded into the background of her mind. She's had a request from the Hub for a finalised version of the Shabaz files - a core history with hyper-linked sub-sections - which had taken up most of her time over the few weeks that had elapsed.

On one of the Saturday evenings that she was increasingly spending with Abi, a chance remark brought it all back to her. They had spent the night in her quarters, not that there was much else to do in the library, and had opened a couple of bottles of the Theran wine that Robyn had brought with her. The dark, almost black, colour of the wine brought Lake Kara back to her. And with Lake Kara, came Esmee. But as she told Abi about the wine, and how Thera had an optimum climate for grapes and a perfect soil for making a Malbec-like wine, she found she could visualise Esmee and think of her without that habitual grief and sadness.

"It's good wine," Abi had said. "It reminds me of the stuff we used to get when I was stationed in Melanthera. That stuff was almost black. I don't know what they made it out of, some fruit like grape, but not exactly the same."

She talked a bit more, but Robyn missed some of what she was saying. She felt a sudden frisson of shock pass through her, a physical shudder. Elanthia, until this moment, had been something that she had encountered, but at a theoretical distance. The thought that it was a real place - that the things she read about had actually happened -

had always been there in her mind, but she'd been somewhat removed from it until now.

"So when were you stationed in Melanthera?" She asked.

Abi was garrulous that evening, the wine had loosened her tongue. She said that she'd been stationed in Melanthera at the end of the war; a war that was news to Robyn.

"It's not really a place many people have heard of." Abi said. "I'm surprised you know it. Melanthera's a pretty shitty place anyway. Hot, dusty and crowded and there was all the war damage. We were there as part of the peace-keeping force, which meant protecting the Sung Yang personnel and making sure the locals didn't kill each other. They were always fighting, the Elanthians."

Abi wouldn't say much more, talking had sobered her a bit and she quickly regained her usual reticence about her work. Robyn tried to draw her out more, but she didn't say anything else. Finally Robyn gave up.

"After having to look over the files of the place, it's interesting," she said, "to meet someone who's actually been to Elanthia and met the people."

Abi laughed.

"Robyn, they're all around you. Half the cleaning staff are Elanthians."

She had of course seen the self-effacing, olive-skinned men and women who drifted around the library like ghosts. They came and went from her quarters like benign invisible beings. Seldom encountered, they would, if spoken to, return your greeting with a nod and withdraw as soon as possible.

So these were really the men and women she had read about? The dark, vivacious Melantheran beauties, the poets and the priests. Could they be the same people and, if so, what had happened to change them so much?

But she thought this was just the drink talking. Of course people were never really like they were in their own songs and poems. We all put a gloss on things, we all exaggerate. Perhaps her Elanthia was just a poet's fantasy after all.

That night they slipped into her bed together. They'd had a lot of wine to drink and it seemed the natural thing to do. Nothing else happened, but she took pleasure in the fact that there was someone else beside her and, when she woke in the early hours, she pushed herself up in the bed and watched Abi sleeping. The woman was dead to the world and could probably sleep through a minor earthquake, she thought.

As she lay there, she made a resolution. Now that the Shabaz work was over, she'd go back once more to the files on Elanthia. What Abi said had made her curious and she needed to find the answers to the many questions she had.

Chapter 8
Asha At The City Gates

For Berendal the night and the morning after hadn't lived up to his expectations. He had spent most of the evening in the pleasure house by the Hwrathka Gate. There had been a crowd there, filling out the tables, celebrating the first vintage of last year's borriba berries. Earlier in the evening, before the light went and the Star People locked their gates and set their sentries, he managed to persuade Berthaud to accompany him to a table outside the place to taste the newly- made drink. To his great surprise she didn't spit it out but tasted it and said:

"This really tastes like French wine, a Cahors or a Madiran."

And when he looked puzzled, she explained further:

"In my old country on Earth, where my parents came from, they used to make a fermented drink from a fruit called grapes. It was almost like a religion to the people, they'd been making it for a thousand years or more."

She poured herself some more.

"This is really good," she said. "You could export it."

Then she bade him goodnight and made her way back to the compound.

Berendal was pleased at Berthaud's reaction, but a little offended that she thought a man of his literary talents should give up poetry for the trade of wine merchant. The Star People, he thought, just didn't understand the way Melanthera worked; they were predictably gauche and awkward in any social situations, despite all his attempts to tutor them.

He shrugged off any offence; he had, after all, a certain sentimental attraction to Berthaud, though whenever he saw her she was always in those shapeless, drab clothes that the Star People wore. He did wonder what she would look like in Piroushi silk, but he suppressed the thought, thinking that he was entering dangerous ground. The Empress had made it clear that the Star People were honoured guests and not to be interfered with in any way and that probably included him plighting his troth, though in truth this hadn't stopped him reciting the occasional love poem to her when the fancy took him.

The breaching of the borriba wine barrels was always something of a festival in Melanthera and the pleasure house would always provide a cartful of free wine on the evening of the vintage's launch. So Berendal set himself to the onerous task of drinking the wine and at the same time composing a poem in praise of this year's crop. This involved quaffing large quantities of the drink, with the result that, when he was ready to deliver the poem, he was not at all steady on his feet or clear in his speech. It didn't matter though, because nobody was.

As he staggered out of the house in the early hours of the morning, he had glanced over at the Star People's compound, where the dour-faced sentries paced back and forth behind the wire. He wondered that they would all close themselves off in their metal huts, rather than join the celebration.

He doubted they would have slept with all the singing and dancing going on.

He spent the next hour or so serenading a Piroushi girl who lived in one of the allies of the market quarter. He had difficulty finding the right place at first - even to him the city's narrow streets, overhung by leaning buildings, were a maze - but eventually he found her house, the closed door topped by vivid blue Piroushi lamp.

He spent a good deal of the next hour reciting poetry to the girl and thought he saw a glimpse of her face behind the closed shutters or at least an indefinable shape flitting across the shadow cast by her bedroom's lamp. But his charms did not win him entry to her boudoir that night, instead an irate neighbour threw a bucket of piss over him and he was forced to retreat to the square before the gates again to wash himself as best he could at the fountain.

He must have sat down on one of the outside tables of the pleasure house and fallen asleep, because it was there he woke up to the light of dawn, with the already hot sun pouring down like honey on him. Feeling tired and not in the best of health, he walked over to the Star People's compound to see if he could persuade them to give him a draught of the health tonic that they took every morning. It was a powerful, pleasurable thing that cleared the head and helped you put thoughts back in your brain after a night such as he had had. He asked for Berthaud and when the guards motioned that she was sleeping, he asked for the elixir, for 'coffee', but they were not accommodating. He wondered if he had pronounced the word right, but it was hardly a difficult sound to get around his tongue.

He took himself off into the shade and it was thus, sitting in the dust beneath a wall of the pleasure house, he saw the guards open the Hwrathka Gate for day and the figure that strode through it before everyone else. She was followed by a caravan of Harradim, leading a train of over-burdened harras, and at first it seemed to him that this magnificent creature, a head taller than the Harradim men behind her, was leading an army. She was dressed in the red robes of the Sisterhood, but wore a cape of some sort of animal hide over her shoulders; probably, he thought, the skin of some lion she'd killed. Slung on her back was one of the big, two-handed swords that the western mountain tribes used and she carried a bundle of throwing spears and had a hvass hide target she'd slung over one shoulder. Her skin was dark, almost black, and she had the long angular body of her people, a long neck and a thin face with high cheek-bones and, as he saw when she came nearer, the darkest, fiercest eyes.

Though, in truth he was slightly wary of her and found her intimidating, he had already started composing a love poem to her in his head, because he was so struck by that savage beauty, that barbaric grace, that he was finding it hard to catch his breath. She stopped just in front of him, and looked around her. The view from the Hwrathka Gate and the square before it was quite impressive, he thought, if you hadn't had to stare at it for most of your life; the narrow streets and tall buildings of the town, a veritable warren, climbed the hill towards the

Empress's palace, winding through the gardens of the Temple quarter and up onto the plateau that the citadel enclosed.

For a moment, an almost indiscernible change came over the woman's face as her eyes flickered up towards the plateau, taking in all that lay before her, and her mouth opened in astonishment, but very quickly that look of child-like wonder was gone and her face set again in that implacable warrior gaze. And as he rose from the shadows they flickered downwards to look at him. Though he smiled at her and gestured welcome - hands open, palms up - she did not react, but just stared at him. As was as if, he thought, she was deciding whether to kill him, eat him, or copulate with him, the last being the least likely.

"Welcome, Sister," he said, "to the city of Melanthera." He couldn't help puffing up his chest and standing on his toes, trying to make himself look a bit more impressive. But the woman carried on staring at him, meeting his eyes in a very un-Melantheran way.

He smiled at her, feeling a little uncomfortable under that unforgiving gaze and said:

"Sister, I would be happy to render you assistance. To guide you where you need to go or to show you the sights of the town." Still no response. He looked around, the food stalls at the edge of the square, where the market would be setting up soon, were open and so he tried another tack.

"Come, you must be hungry. Take some food with me."

A barely perceptible bow of her head signified agreement and he led her over to one of the stalls

73

that he often frequented, where they sold the hot soup the nomads liked to drink in the mornings with a dollop of hvass-milk yoghurt. Just as she was lifting the wooden bowl to her mouth, as they were sitting on a table in the shade of a borriba tree near the stall, he had a horrible feeling that he might have made a mistake; she might not have tasted the hot spice that flavoured the food before. She might think he was trying to poison her. But when she had tasted, she looked at him again and gave another almost imperceptible bow of her head. She liked it; he was relieved. He was in no mood to be chased around the square by an irate Moon Maiden wielding a broad sword.

He had chosen the stall - as usual after a late, drunken night - because he found that the hot, spicy soup and the sharpness of the yoghurt helped to clear his head and chase away the fumes of the borriba wine. As the woman ate, she looked around and he stole a few surreptitious glances at her. She was young, he saw; her height and the way she carried herself had made her seem older than she was.

He was intrigued that she wore the robes of a priestess. He knew that the Sisters didn't all live in convents and often walked among the people following other occupations, but he could not recall seeing one with such a martial air before. Perhaps this was how it was with the western tribes. He, himself, had no wish to find out; those far barren hills had little attraction to him, he was city-dweller after all. But, he suddenly thought, what if all the women there were like this? Then again, he considered the matter, beautiful they may be, but also well-armed and deadly; a combination that he'd best stay away from.

When she had finished her bowl of soup, she just sat there. In truth he had little money left, but he called the tea-seller over and gave the boy some of the last of his coins for a pot of the brew. To his surprise the woman started talking:

"This is good," she said, in that heavy, cloying western accent.

"It's durgan root tea," he said, in reply.

"I know," she said, just a hint of irritation in her voice. "I know what durgan root tea is, but this is different."

Oh," he said, a bit taken aback, "we add spice to it. It's a Melantheran thing."

"It's good," she said. "I like it. Thank you."

He acknowledged her thanks and then she was silent a while. She had that calm and self-composure that he'd seen before in people who made their living by herding animals and raising crops. She had none of the impatience of the city dweller, none of that restlessness; she seemed remote from and unconcerned by the bustle that was already starting up as the market stalls opened up around them.

"So what brings you to Melanthera?" He asked, trying to make conversation, filling in the spaces of her silence.

"I want to see where the star fell." She answered.

He said he could take her there and asked her name.

"I am Asha." She said.

So it was that he took her the short distance across the square and towards the compound of the Star People. He was surprised that she hadn't notice the metal fences before, the shining cabins and the strange, insect-like machines that seemed to clutter the enclosed space. They stopped some distance from the gate and Asha crouched down in the dust gazing at the place, for all the world like the hunter she was, contemplating the spoor of a lion she was tracking.

Berthaud and Kevorkian had been up in the town meeting what passed for the local Chamber of Commerce, a sort of merchants' guild. It had been a frustrating event; the merchants and traders of Melanthera didn't seem to have much of a work ethic when it came to maximising their profit. Like all the other city people they had met, they seemed hedonistic and shallow, never deferring their everyday gratifications. Capital and investment meant nothing to them; they liked money, but only so they could spend it on enjoying themselves.

They saw Berendal and the woman, Asha, before Berendal saw them. Kev groaned and said:

"What does that scarecrow want now?"

For the Star People, Berendal had become, as Kev was wont to describe him, the "ace scrounger". He seemed to have a fascination with them, their food and their equipment, that few Melantherans shared. Kev considered that one of their biggest mistakes had been introducing him to coffee; since he'd sampled the beverage, he was forever hanging around the gates asking for 'kuffee' as he pronounced it.

Berthaud had thought that Kev and the others were being a bit unfair when it came to Berendal. She had noticed that the Melantherans were a generous lot. If you made the mistake of admiring something, they would just as likely give it you; so you could end up with a lot of unwanted stuff. Berendal was just expecting the same sort of behaviour from them and they had more to give than he had, so the exchange was rather one-sided.

Berendal saw them and greeted them. All Melantheran gestures of greeting - apart from the hug that they enthusiastically employed all the time - seemed to involved lifting your hands and showing your palms and there seemed to be some subtle language in these signals. Berthaud was just about starting to grasp the meanings. Berendal also shook hands with them; a habit, like coffee, that he had embraced with enthusiasm. As he got close to them, Berthaud was aware of some sort of unpleasant smell that hovered around him; a combination of the piss-smell of leather, a sharp tang of spilt wine and an overlay of more piss. She thought he had probably had a heavy night, after their wine tasting rendezvous.

The figure with Berendal stood up. Berthaud was amazed how tall she was in comparison to the poet. Berendal was telling them that she was from one of the western mountain peoples. From what she had gleaned, she knew that these were clans that lived a semi-nomadic life, herding their animals and growing what crops they could on those bare hills. She was quite taken aback by the way the woman carried herself and the relaxed way she hefted her weapons, but she was even more intrigued by the red robes the woman wore. She knew that these marked her down as one of the Sisterhood, an order of holy women who seemed to play an important role in Melantheran life, but were still a mystery to her. They were priestesses and lived like nuns, but were also healers and arbitrated disputes. And she didn't know how they related to the male priests she had also seen around the place, similarly red-robed. As usual with affairs Melantheran, there was a chaotic nature to the order of things.

Berendal said the woman's name was Asha and that she had "come to see where the star had fallen". It wouldn't be the first Melantheran they had taken around the compound, nor the last. It was Sung Yang practise to have an open door policy when it came to indigenous people, though this had its limits. You couldn't just have them wandering around, but escorted tours were encouraged.

The usual areas of interest were the canteen, where the Melantherans took much pleasure and indulged in a degree of hilarity, tasting the Star People's food. The other areas of interest were the living quarters, where the showers - "the house fountain" as the Melantherans called it - caused great admiration and the bunks caused more mirth. The Melantherans thought it hilarious that people would choose to sleep one on top of each other. These people loved their cushions and their silks, if they could afford them, and they marvelled that the Star People, so materially rich, could sleep on such Spartan mattresses and in such rudimentary beds.

Berthaud could see that Kev was reluctant, but she, as the ethnologist, was in charge of relations with the local people, so she took responsibility.

There were some problems at the gate, as the security detail insisted that Asha should leave her weapons with them. The woman was reluctant, but once she was ensured that they would be returned she concurred, though she kept alert and wary all the time she was parted from her armaments. Looking at her lithe body and the way she carried herself, Berthaud had no doubt that the woman could give a good account of herself in unarmed combat as well as armed.

It so happened that some of the guards were putting the robot dogs through their paces and the two Melantherans were intrigued by the creatures. It was hard to explain what they were as, by some evolutionary quirk, Elanthia had never had a canine equivalent to domesticate and use for hunting and herding. It was also difficult to explain the purpose of the things, as they were primarily a weapon of war, used for scouting and to support patrols. The guards, who were like all security details from a Sung Yang defence and protection unit, quickly put the creatures away, not wanting to expose their military secrets. There were always tensions between ethnologists like Berthaud and the D and P units. Even Kev, though he was more of an engineer than an ethnologist, was ill-disposed to the guards who kept themselves apart from the other, who they referred to scathingly as 'civilians'.

Asha, unlike the other Melantherans, didn't get much amusement out of the canteen or the living quarters. No smile or even the ghost of amusement passed over that solemn face; she didn't let anything rattle that self-composure. While Berendal enthused to her about the coffee they gave them and the chocolates, the woman just gravely sipped at her drink and hardly tasted the sweets. There was a nobility, a presence to her, that Berthaud really admired. It was like meeting somebody from a child's story book, a knight or some other hero, in the flesh.

To Berthaud, even though she did not understand all the exchanges between Asha and Berendal, it was evident that the poet was treating the woman in a very patronising way. This in itself didn't surprise her. She knew enough about the citizens of Melanthera to recognise this quality of theirs. The city dwellers had an amazing self-confidence; a conviction that they were cleverer and more cultured than the rest of the people who inhabited the Empire. They really thought of themselves as at the centre of the world, but, interestingly, they didn't exclude others from this; as soon as you gravitated to the hub of hectic life that the city was, you were part of it. You, in turn, could look back at your old home, whether in mountain or desert or on one of the islands, and wonder how you ever lived in any other place but the city.

The only time that the woman asked a question, was when they took her back to the gates. As she was taking up her weapons - with a relief that she tried to suppress, but which was all too evident - she looked directly at Berthaud, her dark, brown eyes piercing and acute, and asked:

"Why did you come here?"

And for a moment, before she grasped for the standard textbook reply, Berthaud was lost for words.

Chapter 9
Elanthia: The Unauthorised Guide

In the days that followed, Robyn started to feel a change come over her. She realised that for the preceding month or so she had just been drifting, following her daily routine, but not really engaging with the tasks. She effectively worked on her own, receiving any instructions through her Pad or her workstation and it was easy to grow listless and lethargic. She could not fathom why she had changed in the last week or so, perhaps it had been her friendship with Abi; though she did not want to read too much into their time together, fearing that she could easily get swept away if she took a swim in those waters. Because there was something fierce, something intense in Abi, which occasionally, just once or twice, she had seen emerging from beneath that calm, ordered veneer of good manners and conviviality.

She was honest enough with herself to realise that, at the core of her restlessness and despondency over the last few weeks, had been the fact of her missing and mourning for her time with Esmee. After they'd split up, amidst the vibrant, bustling and beautiful streets of Thera, she had felt that she could do anything she wanted, that she could find other lovers and live her own life away from the woman she had once thought that she would never part from. She had told herself that she almost welcomed the split, that she could now concentrate on her own career, no longer feeling like an adjunct to Esmee's glamorous life of artists, theatres and endless receptions.

She had taken the Hanis assignment to get away from Esmee, but in the claustrophobic corridors of the library, stuck behind the sealed windows that separated them from the heat and dust of the red clay planet, she had learnt that she had taken her lover with her, in mind not body. On Hanis, in the boredom of the evenings and the long weekend afternoons, she had spent too much time alone, too much time brooding over what she had had and what she had lost. The sterile diversions of the canteen, the bar and the karaoke lounge just managed to underline the fact that she was stranded on this rock in the endless sea of the universe, while Esmee's life went on, and so did the endless round of social events and dinner parties, and, she was sure, other lovers.

So she did not know where her newfound energy, her newfound interest in her work, had come from. But partly, she thought, it was somehow tangled up with Elanthia. Ever since she had first come across the reference to the 'Lament of Asha' and had found the misfiled 'Hymn to the Star Men', the little planet had been at the back of her mind, but she'd been too apathetic to do much about it. But now, with her new zeal for her work and the fact that Abi had brought home to her that she was dealing with the Elanthian present as well as the recent past, she felt that she needed to find out more.

After she had uploaded the Shabaz documents to the Hub and had received a guarded, but positive response, Robyn started to consider her dilemma.

She still had Elanthia on her 'to-do list'. It was obvious to her that what the Hub expected was the expurgated version of Elanthian history; she was worldly enough to realise that the records were sealed for more than commercial purposes and that someone had gone to a lot of trouble to suppress huge chunks of information about the planet's history.

As a librarian Robyn knew that she was supposed to have an ethical responsibility to find and preserve the objective truth of things. But, of course, the truth was always going to be a difficult thing to grasp and perhaps she was being too subjective about Elanthia, perhaps she was guilty of seeing only a partial picture.

So she decided that for the present she would compile two documents; one the bland, orthodox history that the Hub would expect, the other her own private, unauthorised history of the planet. It filled her with some degree of trepidation to embark on this course of action. She'd never done anything like this before and it was strictly against all regulations. She thought it was probably a disciplinary offence, but she resolved that she would keep her alternative record until she had time to consider what to do with it. Besides, if it was discovered, she could make out that it was just a set of notes and aide memoires.

Robyn knew she was a good researcher; she took a professional pride in it. She seemed to have almost forgotten that fact over the last few weeks and had acted more like she was cutting and pasting other people's words rather than sifting out the facts and creating her own narrative.

She had undertaken numerous searches of the Hub, entering 'Asha' or 'Berendal' as key words with no result, so she decided to take a different approach. Most of the records she had accessed so far were from the corporations which had made the first contact with planets like Elanthia and Shabaz and developed commercial relationships with the indigenous peoples thereafter, but there were also other categories of records. Those of the military were effectively sealed to her, so, for instance, there was no way she could find out any details about the Defence Force's involvement in Melanthera - Abi's 'peace keeping' days - apart from a series of terse press releases giving bare facts and figures. But she had more fortune with the diplomatic records kept by the confederation of the inner planets.

Though it was, in practise, the commercial companies that had carried out most of the negotiations with governments and rulers on the outer planets, the confederation, keen to remind corporations like Sung Yang that they were officially representing the inner planet's government as well as their own interests, had made sure that any meetings or contacts with the indigenous peoples of the outer planets had been minuted.

Just before lunch, Robyn had found what, to her, was a golden nugget of information amongst the catalogues of dross. It was a record of a meeting between the Empress of Melanthera, the same Empress who had figured in Berendal's 'Hymn to the Star Men', and a senior executive of the Sung Yang Corporation. The meeting had been documented by the same Marie Berthaud whose records she had accessed before. It wasn't a formal set of minutes, more a distillation of what had happened.

Berthaud wrote that she had accompanied a Director Carstairs to the Empress's palace. Carstairs had apparently been impressed by the veiled guards who had escorted them and the musicians that preceded them, as they progressed through the town and up the dusty road to the palace gates. Berthaud noted that, although the cymbals and pipes that heralded them drew a crowd at first, as usual the Melantherans were hard to impress. Though Carstairs had undergone the genetic modification and cosmetic remodelling that was a fad of the super-rich and was, as a result, nearly seven foot tall, athletically muscled, golden haired with eyes of an almost supernatural blue, the Melantherans hardly shot him a glance.

There was a slight, but marked, undercurrent of sarcasm in Berthaud's tone as she described Carstairs and Robyn wondered how the woman had got away with actually writing and submitting it in the document. She reported that Carstairs had been very careful about where he put his hand-crafted, synthi-leather shoes and how he had constantly worn gloves, even in the heat of the Melantheran noon. When the Empress had taken hold of his shoulders, in what the contact team referred to as 'the Melantheran hug', the man had almost shied away, which would have been disastrous in terms of protocol.

Berthaud added a note about the Melantheran hug. It was, apparently, more an attempt to lift you off your feet than a real hug. You were kept at arm's length, but firmly grasped about the shoulders and ever-so-slightly lifted. The first time Berthaud had been 'hugged' in this way, she wrote, she had almost lost her balance, to the great amusement of the Melantherans.

The Empress had met them in one of her garden pavilions, where the fountains and the shade trees helped to ameliorate the effects of the Elanthian sun. Carstairs had apparently spread a handkerchief before he sat down on the couch that had been offered him. Robyn got the feeling that Berthaud clearly didn't have much respect for Carstairs.

It was when Berthaud listed the personnel at the meeting that Robyn gave an audible start that drew a quizzical look from Shelby.

"Interesting reading?" He asked. "You are really getting into it these days."

She made some innocuous remark in return.

"Not a criticism, Robyn. It's good to see you enjoying your work. Now what about those Soya burgers."

She couldn't not go to lunch with Shelby, so she had to wait and pass an interminable lunch hour before she could get back to Berthaud's record of the meeting. Powering up her terminal afterwards - suffering from indigestion, having bolted her food - she started reading again. Though the "Star People" had only taken Berthaud and a security detail with them, the Empress had had her usual retinue of guards and servants to attend her.

"As usual," Berthaud had written, "the poet Berendal had offered to serve as interpreter, though, in practise, we used the translation App on my Pad."

But this wasn't what had made Robyn cry out; it was more the fact that she had found a digital photograph from the meeting. Berthaud had said that the Melantherans didn't like being filmed. When it was explained to them, they had thought of it as an odd thing to do unless you had such a bad memory that you couldn't remember things. Thus, they couldn't see any point to it and were loath to be captured on video. However, they would begrudgingly, let the "Star People" take still photographs, though they thought these far inferior to the portraits their artists produced that, in their words, "could capture the soul as well as the face."

So Robyn could actually look on the face of Berendal and the others gathered in that pavilion. Oddly, they were formally posed, like a Victorian photograph; the Empress seated in the middle, on first glance a grave-faced elderly, woman, thin and almost bird-like, but, on further study, Robyn could see a glimmer of amusement in her eyes. She had a high fan-shaped headdress and a simple long robe in that purplish-shade of blue which seemed to be the Melantheran colour.

Then there was Carstairs, blonde and tall and serious; a sort of Byronic figure, in his long coat with its high collar, or so he probably saw himself. Berthaud was a small, compact dark-haired woman, standing next to him in drab fatigues, a cap pulled over a head of black curls. She looked serious and concerned, as if something troubled her.

And then there was Berendal. He was standing there with a wide grin on his face. The poncho-like cloak looked a little threadbare and had faded to a washed out blue, his baggy trousers were a garish purple, a contrast to the drab, sober colours that the Sung Yang people wore. He stood there with that smile on his face, his arms akimbo, as if he was utterly and absolutely pleased with himself. He had a thin face framed by a dark, sparse beard and a head of black curls; ironically he looked a little like Berthaud. He was younger than Robyn had thought; she had supposed that the composer of the "Hymn to the Star Men" was some venerable old court poet.

When she got over her initial surprise at discovering the photograph, she read on. Berthaud described how the Melantherans, as always, were very difficult to pin down. The meeting had been called to discuss the question of mineral rights. The Sung Yang surveyors had found nearly every mineral known to man on the planet, in abundance, and wanted the Empress to cede them mining rights. The conversation meandered over hwrathka and hvass and all the standard Melantheran obsessions until, eventually, Carstairs broached the central subject, asking straight out, contrary to all protocol, for the Empress's agreement to Sung Yang starting mining.

Berthaud said that the Empress had been quiet for a while and it looked for a moment as if she might ignore the request, but then she had looked directly at Carstairs and said:

"If I understand what you are saying, you want to dig holes all over my country to get the metal that you need."

Carstairs reluctantly agreed that this was the case and the Empress went on.

"Unfortunately, I can't allow that. The Melantherans spend too much of their time looking ahead of them and not down at the ground. They'd fall in the holes and so would the hwrathka and hvass. I can't have that happening."

Carstairs had looked in astonishment at Berthaud and then said:

"But we will give you wealth and riches and we'll mine the minerals ourselves. We'll dig underground, there won't be holes that the people will fall into."

The Empress threw her head back and clicked her tongue in what Berthaud explained was the 'Melantheran no', not the expression of displeasure that Carstairs took it to be, just a standard negative response.

"If you tunnel beneath my land, it will all collapse when we get the next earthquake, then where will we be."

There was a bit more conversation, Carstairs pressing the matter, the Empress talking about everything but the matter at hand; about the palace hwrathka, the harvest, the summer retreat she was looking forward to in Piroush. In the end a very subdued Carstairs had followed Berthaud and the rest of the detail down the hill to the Sung Yang base.

Robyn sat at her workstation and thought about what she had read. Sung Yang and the other corporations only had one reason for exploring and exploiting the outer planets and that was mining. Trade could be lucrative, but what was really at stake was the inner planets' hunger for minerals and the corporations' need to extract and ship as much as they could. To Sung Yang, and Carstairs, the

Empress's refusal would have been a major set-back.

Robyn saved a copy of Berthaud's report in her Elanthia folder and then, on impulse, did a search for 'Dr. Marie Berthaud' in the Hub. She got very few hits, one or two on personnel lists. A couple of articles in academic journals, but, just as she had resigned herself to the fact that she was following another blind alley, she found a reference to an article in one of the Hub's archived news feeds. The article was called 'the Berthaud affair'.

Chapter 10
The Empress And The Moon Maiden

The Empress sat on her divan in her pleasure pavilion and tried to listen to the priest sitting before her, but she had so many other things on her mind. And the afternoon was hot; even up here on the plateau, there was hardly any breeze and, what there was, was like the hot breath of the desert that was ever present, ever in her mind.

She knew that it was past time to go to Piroush, to her summer palace, where the island winds would keep the days cool, or at least bearable, and she would be able to sleep at nights, not waking from bad, cursed dreams in a fever-sweat. She couldn't bring herself to go, she had too many cares. She was too old for this, she told herself, too weary, but she was also too inured, too used to looking after her people, these strange and amusing creatures who she loved like as if they were her own children.

The priest - what was his name; was it Gamelon - was some sort of chronicler and the authorities at the Temple of Elanta had asked that she grant him an audience, a number of audiences as it turned out, so that he could continue with his compilation of the history of her reign. He had told her that it was to be entitled: 'the shining path of our Empress Sun'. She had suggested a more prosaic title: 'the history of the reign of Empress Mila the Third'. He had of course agreed. You couldn't, after all, argue the outcome of the game with an Empress, though she was sure that he would eventually try and foist on his account a grander title.

Gamelon had been asking her about her girlhood, though she couldn't really see how relevant that was. She did remember those dances and receptions in Piroush, where she and her mother had spent most of their time while her father was away fighting some campaign or other. She had made it an unwritten rule of hers, when she as a slim, young girl had ascended the throne, that she would avoid the path of war whenever possible. Too many of the young men that had courted her had not come back from battle.

She thought she had been quite successful in doing so, she had fixed their borders with the western tribes through treaties and trade. A man would, after all, rather sell something to his neighbour than kill him. You could only loot a village once, but you could sell grain to it every year. She prided herself on being an Empress of peace, but, of course, there were always the Hvassara out there in the desert on her eastern borders, eternal and uncompromising.

In her bleakest moments, she'd thought you couldn't deal with them with anything else but force, but she had strived to make some sort of pact with them. The trouble had always been that there was no-one really that you could make a deal with; there were so many tribes all with a different leader, some with many leaders, so by the time you had made an alliance with one people, another was raiding your outlying settlements. The Hvassara, she knew, would always be with them; the nomad always hungry for the food of the farms and the riches of the towns.

Now there were these Star People. Her meeting with the man they called Director Sinclair had been followed by others. The small woman always brought them, the Star People leaders. They would be dressed in their crude, uncouth finery and the small woman would use her speaking device to interpret, though she had quite a few of their words ready on her tongue. It was always the same story; bribery and veiled threats, more of the latter and less of the former lately. She had been tempted to have one or two of the envoys thrown into the cells beneath the Hwrathka stables, but that would, though amusing, have been against the laws of hospitality and diplomatic protocol.

The small woman she liked, though. She thought that she should invite her to a private dinner, though the Star People were loath to go anywhere on their own. She felt that she could find out a lot from this woman, who looked a little Melantheran and seemed to be imbued with natural good manners. She would, of course, have to put up with the presence of that scape-grace Berendal, who seemed to have attached himself to the Star People and the small woman. What was her name? She was sure she had known it once, but she had known so much over the years that it was no surprise that things slipped from her mind.

Poets, she thought, were a bit like kobo flies; the creatures were irritating and annoying, but ultimately they had a use, as they morphed into the larvae that spun Melantheran silk. Her people liked their poets and their poetry, though in her opinion

Berendal's verses were an acquired taste; too many poems about unrequited love. He did serve another use, though, he provided a valuable set of eyes and ears to keep her informed of everything that the Star men did; his curiosity and down-right nosiness had its advantages.

She had to admit to herself that the meeting with Director Sinclair, which had set the tone for the others, could have gone better. She shouldn't really have used the opportunity to make fun of him. She had, of course, known that their mines would not cause the ground to collapse and she knew that the Melantherans, whilst sometimes shockingly inept and often downright stupid, would not really fall into the mine-shafts.

It had really been a way of buying herself time. She knew what sort of power these people had, they had after all flown between the stars and it had probably taken them hardly more time than it would take her to get to Piroush. She did not doubt that they had weapons that could outmatch the bows of her soldiers and that could stop the legendary charge of her hwrathka that no enemy had ever been able to stand against.

She sighed and brought her attention back to the present:

"Where were we Gamelon? Surely you have enough for that chapter."

In his flowery language the priest informed her that perhaps he needed a little more detail. He wants to know all the ins and outs of a hvass's arsehole, she thought to herself and then, remembering she was the Empress, tried to suppress the thought and the laughter that threatened to come with it. She had, after all, to maintain her imperial gravity.

The time seemed to drag on as the priest asked his questions and her mind drifted off to that other time, before she became this imperial being and had to put all her other life, her only real life, behind her. It had been such a long while now and she wondered how much longer this existence would last. Ever since the Star people had come she'd had a feeling which she had tried to suppress; more a premonition really, that would come on her suddenly as she turned a corridor in the warren of the palace, or when she woke suddenly in the half-light of dawn and before the rest of the citadel was awake. Or even in the full light of day, when she followed the mundane tasks of court and ceremony that made up the work of ruling.

And the premonition told her, as sure as the aches she felt in her bones at the end of the day and when she rose, that a bad time was coming for Melanthera; that the Star People's coming had been a portent of this new age, the end of the days that were and had been. This she knew, this she was convinced of, but what to do about it was a question she could not answer.

On a number of occasions she had called her council together to discuss 'the matter of the Star People' as they all called it. They were a mixed and motley bunch and, or so she sometimes thought in her darkest hours, as much use as a three-legged hwrathka. There were the three generals, generally led by Kal Quintal, the other two being too fat and complacent to form their own opinions. That was one of the problems in pursuing a policy of peace, she thought, your soldiers lost that leanness of mind and energy of the spirit that war bred in them.

Then there were the three priests, the high priest of Elanta, Dorak, with his two aides, one a bookkeeper, the other a philosopher. Dorak's stock phrase, when asked to make any decisions was: "As Elanta wills it." In practise, this meant that, unless the choice was directly relevant to the Temple, and most importantly to its revenues, the High Priest would abdicate all responsibility.

The Sisterhood were supposed to have three representatives on the council, but only ever sent one; a practical bustling woman, who was the mother superior of the biggest convent in Melanthera, which was situated opposite the temple complex of Elanta, just outside the palace walls. She had to admit that the Sisterhood, or at least Sister Alethea, were more practical and prosaic than the priests. And such was the rivalry between the sisterhood and the priesthood, that Sister Alethea would always tend to disagree with anything that the High Priest agreed with. The only thing that united the Sisters and the Priests was a mutual suspicion of the military.

The Empress thought that this tension and squabbling between the three main parties of state was what had kept Melantheran politics healthy and had helped to bolster her position as the monarch. She could never get consensus, so she usually had to make the decisions; and had always been sure to give a sop of comfort or consolation to each party. It had seemed to work well enough up to now. And the days when the Emperors had been over-extravagant, or mad, or both, were long gone. She had to maintain a certain pomp and ceremony, as her position demanded, but she had no intrinsic interest in wealth.

She had, after all, everything she needed and if there was a surplus of grain in the granary or of wine in the cellar, it could be shared out to the people on the feast days, of which the Melantherans had many, or given to the temples and convents to be distributed to the poor. Though she did not court popularity, which would have been beneath her imperial dignity, she had some awareness that she was generally liked, if not loved, by her people. If things went wrong, of course, they might blame the Empress, but often, too, they would blame the generals or the priests, so blame was shared out equally and never coalesced into the sort of resentment that brought down thrones.

The 'matter of the Star People' had originally only figured as an item added at the end of the list of things the council met to discuss. Increasingly though, it had climbed the agenda and took more and more time at meetings. The traditional council of nine had been supplemented by a representative from the merchant's guild, who represented the views of the traders and craftsmen of the city. Once a year the Empress would convene a Grand Council, where representatives from the villages and provinces of the whole Empire would attend and air their grievances, but they were not represented on the smaller advisory council. The country people were mainly farmers and herders and were obsessed with weather, crop yields and all things pertaining to hvass, so she doubted that they could have contributed to the discussions in any meaningful way.

At the council meetings, the Star People had their partisans, or at least one. The representative of the merchants tended to be a supporter. The merchants had been flattered by the Star People's willingness to meet them and treat them as some sort of commercial partners. From what the Empress had found out - through Berendal and others - nothing very tangible had come from these meetings, as there was precious little to trade yet. Some of the merchants dealt in the minerals the Star People were interested in, but in negligible quantities. And the Star people shipped in all of their own foodstuffs, so there was no possibility of trade in these commodities, which somewhat intrigued the Melantherans, who couldn't figure out how people could survive without the bounty of the hvass; its hide, milk and meat.

So though the merchants were getting no immediate and present benefit from the Star People, they had been courted by promises of a golden and prosperous future, which to them would involve lots of money and little effort. Though the merchants were avid supporters of the aliens, they were not effective in pressing their case. The merchants' representative - often a different person each time as people came and went with caravans - was usually cowed by the presence of the clergy and intimidated by the generals, particularly Kal Quintal, who had a markedly arrogant and superior manner.

As to the other representatives, the priests tended to be non-committal and fatalistic; what would be would be. The generals had, at first, wanted to eject the Star People. Kal Quintal, in one of the first meetings after their arrival, had asked leave to assault the base with the hwrathka and to seize the aliens as hostages. She, of course, had not allowed this. But in later meetings, the generals, mainly Kal Quintal again, had changed their attitude. They seemed eager to learn about the Star People's weapons, so obviously superior to theirs, and to spend their time scheming about how they could get their hands on these armaments.

The only person who gave her even a crumb of comfort at these meetings was Sister Alethea. The woman seemed to appreciate their predicament, though she had no real answers. When the matter of the mining concessions had been discussed, after the Empress's meeting with Director Sinclair, the merchant's representative had been an avid supporter of the Star People's proposition and, to her surprise; the generals had given their guarded approval. It had only been Alethea who had shared her concerns.

"This could change our world," she had said, "it could be the end of the Melanthera we know. They will bring more of their people, more of their machines. They will bring their own gods, and cast ours into the shadows."

This had caused a stir and the meeting had ended in some consternation. Afterwards, as the councillors left, the Empress had motioned to Alethea to hang back. She had asked the woman what she thought they should do; something as Empress she seldom did.

"I'm sorry, your Highness," the Sister had replied. "I really don't know what we can do. I have a feeling that, whatever action we take, the Star People will have their mines, their metals. That's why they came here and they won't leave till they have gutted our land."

The Sister, usually so composed, became visibly upset; her eyes filled with tears and her hands twisted the fabric of her robe.

"All we can do is wait and see what happens and act as best we can."

That was the problem the Empress thought; we, none of us, know what the best course of action is.

She forced herself to come back to Gamelon and the present. She did realise that his history, however verbose and self-satisfied the man was, could be of great importance. It just might be the record of Melanthera's last days.

Just as the priest was asking more questions about the early days of her reign, there was a welcome interruption to the drab routine of the day. A guard came in - one of her veiled Barossi - and said that the poet Berendal was craving an audience and had a companion with him, a Sister. Though she did deign to give Berendal these private audiences - he was her spy after all - the man could be tiresome and demanding. And she was somewhat irritated that he had brought someone with him. It smacked of the sort of thing the poet would do to impress a woman. But, this time, the interruption was welcome, so she asked the guard to bring them in, much to Gamelon's chagrin.

A few moments after, Berendal came in, seeming to fill the room as he usually did. He gave a quick obeisance, bobbing down to his knees, then rising up as she gave a dismissive gesture of her hand. Following behind came a tall woman, with the dark skin and angular features of the western tribes, the Moon People as some called them. She was dressed as a warrior, but also wore the robes of a sister. The Empress was old enough to remember the old orders of warrior priests and priestesses, but they were now only a thing of memory and myth.

The woman was young, a maid really, and the older woman wondered what it would be like to be so young again. She had almost forgotten those days of youth, the vigour of your body and the passions of your heart; she remembered some of it, but those memories were like distant echoes that came to you unsought.

She beckoned for the woman to approach and saw that she had tears in her eyes. The Moon Maiden almost threw herself on the floor in front of the Empress, so eager was she to prostrate herself. The Melantherans didn't stand much on ceremony and the Empress, underneath the mantle of ceremony and spectacle, still thought of herself as Mila, that young girl who had come too early to the throne. It was easy to forget that to some of her people she was this distant, dread figure; almost a demi-god. She noticed that Berendal and Gamelon were slightly embarrassed by this display; they exchanged quizzical glances.

"Rise up, child," the Empress said to the Maiden. "And tell me your name!"

The woman rose up to her knees, a look of something nearing rapture on her face.

"If it please, your Highness, I am Asha."

"It does please me, Asha. Now come and sit by me and tell me your story."

Later Berendal and Asha left the Empress's presence. The woman was still somewhat stunned by what had taken place. Not only had she met the Empress, the great monarch who held the whole of Melanthera, town and hinterland, in her palm; she had actually conversed with her, seen her smile and laugh as she told her story. It was all such a wonderful, but awful thing.

Berendal watched Asha as they walked out of the pavilion and into the palace gardens, the Barossi guard keeping a wary eye on them as he led them. In all the days he'd known her, all in all a few weeks now, he'd never seen her so affected by anything, never seen any emotion on her face until now. He was also glad that the Empress, as he'd hoped, had given Asha a position in the palace. She'd been sleeping on his floor and eating his food for all this time as, while she could shift for herself in the wilderness, the town was a different place. She had been up to the convent of the sisterhood, but for some unfathomable reason couldn't find a place there. She was now, so the Empress had bade her, to present herself at the palace gates in two days' time to take up her new job as the Empress's bodyguard.

It was not that he wanted to be rid of Asha; he had, in fact, grown fond of her. She had a simplicity and innocence that he found charming and strangely touching. On that first day he'd spent with her, when a young man had plucked the sleeve of her robe - a typical gesture of one of the street hawkers in Melanthera - she had put the boy on his back with a knife at his throat in scarcely a moment. He'd had

102

to explain how things worked in the city; try and give her a street-sense that she lacked.

He also found her extremely beautiful. That first night when she had undressed in that small attic room of his, he could clearly see the shape of her body outlined against her shift by the light of his lamp. He'd only tried to touch her that once; he could not help but put his hand on her thigh as she sat down beside him on the bed. After she'd twisted his arm almost out of its socket, she'd informed him in no uncertain terms that she was of the Sisterhood and took her vow of chastity seriously. His arm had felt numb for almost a day afterwards, but it was almost a relief, truth be told, as thoughts of and plans to seduce her did seem to have taken up a lot of his energy up to that point.

As it was, she did not seem to bear him a grudge for trying - after all some of the Sisters weren't as chaste as they made out - and they settled into an easy comradeship after that. Even though she wouldn't share it with him, he'd offered her his bed, but she'd tried it and pronounced it too soft to sleep on; she preferred his floor.

The Barossi guard left them at the citadel gates and they made their way slowly down the road to the city below. It was the hottest time of the day and Berendal pulled his hood up to shade him from the furnace heat of the sun. A carriage, the fast kind drawn by a team of three haras, passed them at speed and enveloped them in a cloud of white dust. He coughed and pulled his neck scarf up to cover his mouth and nose. He glanced at Asha. The woman strode on oblivious, seemingly immune to the sun. The heat didn't slow her at all; in fact he had to hurry to catch up with her.

As they got almost to the foot of the hill, a number of pleasure houses beckoned, with their cool, dappled gardens and the soft sounds of fountains, like a special kind of music, underlying the silence of that afternoon, when even the hvass were sleeping. He tried to tempt Asha with the prospect of shade and a cool drink, but she would not be drawn from the path and the purpose she had set for herself. So he left her there, to carry on whatever journey she was making, to whatever destination she had in mind. Awkward and infuriating as she was, he thought he would miss her when she was gone.

Chapter 11
Above The Canyon

As they breasted the ridge above the canyon, Robyn felt the furnace heat of the wind, that rose up from the chasms below, hit her in the face like a blow. Though her head was covered by the hood of her service jacket and her mouth and nose were covered by a scarf, she still felt as if she had just been slapped by a myriad of small hands. The goggles protected her eyes, but even their rubberised seal could not completely keep out the gritty, red dust that flew about the atmosphere, making everything hazy and unreal.

The path to the viewing platform was precipitous; it descended from the crest of the ridge in a series of steep, switch-backed trails and, apart from the wind, she had trouble getting her breath. It wasn't as if she hadn't been warned; the young geologist from the South Star Corporation had told them about the strength of the wind and also the thinness of the atmosphere at this height. There was less oxygen and it was affecting her brain. She felt like an old woman as she staggered down the path gripping tight to the handrail, as if one more gust would pluck her from the face of the mountain and whirl her off into the depths below.

She glanced at the three people ahead of her; the geologist and the two data analysts from the library that she only vaguely knew. They seemed singularly unaffected; the young SSC scientist was shamelessly flirting with the two women, who were giggling and whispering conspiratorially like two schoolgirls. Robyn thought that, ultimately, it didn't matter how much effort and resources you spent on educating people, they all surrendered to their hormones in the end.

She looked around at Abi, who was following her. The woman gave a thumbs-up in return, the stock military gesture. Surprisingly, she saw that Abi looked like she was suffering too, under that veneer of confidence and capability she wore. The woman's breath was laboured and she also seemed unsteady. Robyn thought that it didn't make any difference how fit or strong you were, the lack of oxygen affected people in diverse ways, despite their muscle tone, fitness or constitution. She turned away, knowing that Abi hated showing any sign of weakness or demonstrating any fallibility; ironically, that in itself was one of the woman's flaws.

It was Abi who had told her about the trip. They said that Hanis's Great Canyon was much grander than its equivalent on Earth; twice as deep and much more splendid. SSC was one of the major mining conglomerates on Hanis and, as one of its 'Corporate Social Responsibility' sidelines, it was developing an embryonic tourist infrastructure to open 'Hanis's wonder' up to the other planets.

Robyn and Abi had joked that while Earth had, or once had anyway, seven wonders, Hanis just had one, or two if you counted the red dust that got everywhere even in the hermetically sealed atmosphere of the Library, causing much crotch-scratching and a resulting run on skin creams and other oils. They'd laughed about this for quite a while, in the midst of another night drinking Theran

106

wine. It was becoming a habit, Robyn thought, but they never seemed to progress further.

When SSC had advertised the excursion, there'd been a massive take-up from the library staff. In reality, though Hanis was a good posting in terms of salary as work on the outer planets always carried a special service bonus, most of the library staff were terminally bored. In terms of demography, they were mainly young, mostly active and had a lot of surplus energy to burn up. There was a specific kind of cabin fever that they mostly suffered from; though the base seemed vast on first acquaintance, it quickly became stifling and claustrophobic. The corridors were long, but boringly similar, the quarters mirrored each other. The public spaces soon became drab and dreary. The landscape outside, that spectacle of red desert, constant wind and blinding sun, soon became hostile and oppressing.

Abi had told Robyn that SSC, though they purported to be offering the trip as a friendly gesture, were really using them as guinea pigs to see if there were any glitches, before they offered it on the open market.

"They'd rather kill one of us than a tourist," Abi had told her, "as they might sue, whereas we'll all have to sign waivers."

Robyn had said that she was amazed that anybody would want to visit such a benighted planet, but Abi had shrugged the comment off.

"You'd be surprised, Robyn. The more adventurous sorts get quite a kick from these outer planets. A bit of exotic, rugged landscape, so they can convince themselves they've risked their necks, then a few days and nights on somewhere like Shabash, watching the natives and wandering around the alleyways and bazaars of the towns. They go home then with their photographs and films, having written their travel blogs, and get most of their loom-woven carpets and hand-made silks taken off them at the space port by customs, in case they are spreading germs. That's what SSC wants to buy into."

"Sounds like your type of thing, Abi," Robyn said; only realising afterwards how bitchy she had been.

Abi's face was composed as usual, but a flicker and a filming of those deep, green eyes betrayed the hurt. That and the way her shoulders seemed to stiffen, her whole stance became less relaxed.

"I've had enough of that in the Defence Force to last a lifetime." She replied.

Robyn had made some excuse, said that she was joking and Abi had relaxed again. But Robyn had surprised herself; why was she starting to make catty, hurtful remarks to the woman. It was as if she was trying to break through that blank facade, to get any emotional reaction, even if it was anger or pain. So Robyn had gone on the trip partly as a penance for her behaviour to Abi. It was all internal of course, in Robyn's head, but she was making a particular attempt that day to be nice.

The company had picked them up from the Library's landing pad in one of their cruisers for the short hop to the salt lake on which they were building the hotel complex. As they approached from the air, Robyn wondered again about the advisability of the trip, as beneath them the rolling desert, which gave way to the glistening salt pans of the dead lake, looked like the most god-forsaken place you could imagine. They landed in a swirl of dust that took ages to settle and then transferred to crawlers, the tracked land vehicles that were the staple form of transport on the surface.

Thought the dust had all but settled when they made the short walk from the cruiser to the land vehicle, it felt like they were walking into an oven. Though nearly every inch of Robyn's skin was covered, she could almost feel it drying out, been robbed of moisture in the dry heat. She tried to figure out in her head what the opposite of humidity was and whether there actually was such a thing as nought per cent humidity, but soon gave up. Climbing up into the inside of the crawler was a welcome relief; though functional and basic, it had a sealed cabin and was air-conditioned.

The vehicles set out at their slow, ponderous pace towards the hotel complex. This was a strange, fairy tale like place of towers and spires, built to resemble a mountain-side with windows threading its surface. The place was still being built and had not been sealed yet, but they were taken to the main hall and lobby which had been finished, driving straight into the garage underneath the building and then taking the lift up to the main floor.

This was all built like a classical temple with polished mock-marble floors and columns. Lunch had been laid out in a sumptuous banquet on long tables. The food looked good, but as she took a plate and started to tuck in, she saw Shelby just in front of her, shaking his head:

"It looks better than it tastes, Robyn," he said. "Just like the stuff in the Library canteen, really, only all dolled up."

"No soya burgers?" She asked. And he sadly shook his head, as if this private joke of hers was much more serious than she thought.

He wandered off and suddenly Abi was there.

"Is that a friend of yours?" She asked. She was trying not to frown, but her forehead was creasing.

"A work colleague. He sits at the next station to me." She continued to pile her plate up. "Surely you've seen him around?"

"Not that I can recall," the woman answered.

Robyn realised that Abi was jealous, when the woman proceeded to sulk for the next half hour; being terse and non-communicative, but throwing longing little glances at Robyn, when she wasn't supposed to be looking. It was all getting a bit complicated, Robyn thought, when she was fetching what passed for coffee for them both. But when she returned to where Abi was sitting and saw the evident discomfort on her face as she watched Shelby from a distance, making the rounds of all the attractive women in the room, Robyn took pity on her.

"He's very handsome," she said and Abi nodded in reply.

"But he's really not my type."

As they climbed back on the crawlers, Robyn had seen that Abi seemed happier, almost elated. Mood-swings to deal with too, she'd thought, then tried to vanquish the thought.

The crawlers had followed a track up the side of a dry valley, climbing ever upwards to the ridge.

There'd been a running commentary coming through the intercom from the geologist in the lead vehicle. The driver of Robyn's crawler, fourth in the line of five, had seemed bored and distracted. He's probably, she'd thought, more use to hauling cargo than people, especially people like us; information whores as the miners reputedly called them behind their backs. He'd perked up a lot though, when he had to help the two pretty data analysts down from the doorway of the vehicle.

Now, as the viewing platform loomed up out of the dust clouds and mini-tornados that scoured the ridge, she felt glad that they hadn't served any alcohol at lunch-time; she was light-headed enough. The place was a glassed-in dome that partially cantilevered over the steep slope and was in part buried in the hill-side. The automatic doors - enormous iris valves that blinked open and then blinked closed behind them - led into a corridor that acted as an airlock and once through this they were in that large, cavernous internal space. There were gasps from the party, as they realised that the cantilevered part of the dome had a partially glassed floor, allowing them to look down on the canyon walls and the dark, deep valley it enclosed.

The view was truly spectacular; she gazed down on the coloured and layered bands of rock, the earth slips that had caused landslides that were a mile or more long. The canyon was at least twice as deep as its counterpart on earth, over two and a half miles in places. The instability of the geology, and the tremors that occasionally shook this part of the planet, had made a landscape of towers and pillars that were all strangely carved by the wind and softened by the movement of the earth. It was, to Robyn's eyes, like an old-fashioned wedding cake, a thing of many strata, all misshapen and melted, as if it had been left out in the non-existent rain.

But what really fascinated her was that, looking down into the depths of the chasm, she could see movement; flying creatures, the strange, lace-winged fire-lizards that were the only species so far identified on Hanis. She had never seen them before, they were confined to these high places, but now she watched fascinated as they glided on the hot thermal winds which rose up from the valley floor.

She had not noticed that Abi had come to stand beside her. Suddenly, the woman took her hand:

"It's marvellous, isn't it?" She said. But then they were both silent, lost for words and not wanting to ruin the moment with banalities, holding on to each other as if there were no glass floor beneath their feet and they were about to plunge into that abyss and make their attempt to fly like the fire-lizards.

On the way back they spoke little. In fact the whole party seemed to be dogged by a feeling of listlessness, a forlorn mood; now that they had seen what they intended to, had had a day out, but inevitably had to go back to their quarters in the library. Back to the same four walls, the same view, the same dull grating routine, the harsh light of morning and the empty darkness; staring out from those picture windows at night over the moonless desert, the sky just punctuated by the odd point of light, a star or a shuttle landing, you could imagine anything whether wonder or horror.

Back at the Library, Abi followed her to her quarters and, with no invitation, followed her in turn to bed. It was the first time Robyn had slept with anyone, had sex with anyone, since that last time with Esmee, not counting masturbation of course. Abi was fierce and passionate, an energy that Robyn could not quite match. She let her body drift, let the waves of passion lap over her. Out of politeness, she eventually turned the tables on Abi, pushing her down on her back and making her come. It took ages, or so it seemed, but when she did, she was surprisingly emotional. Even crying in Robyn's arms.

Abi slept well, spent and content, as if she had been striving for this, working hard up to this moment. Robyn, in contrast, dozed a bit and then woke. Once this would have been everything, the warm, sensuous shape of a lover in her bed; that wonderful feeling of satiety, that counterfeit warmth that you could call love. But now it wasn't enough; her mind was elsewhere. She was in a city called Melanthera, on a planet called Elanthia, and she could hear strange voices calling out to her.

Chapter 12
Evening On Piroush

To Asha the islands of Piroush were like another realm, a paradise that should not be of this world, but of the next. When she, a part of the Empress's entourage, had had to climb the walkway onto the ship that would take them like a swift bird across the inland sea, she had been as perplexed by the strange craft as she had, the night before when they arrived at the port, been astounded by the body of water that lay before her, a silver mirrored surface that reflected the face of Elanthia's moon and her two smaller consorts.

She had steeled herself for all this newness. In truth, she had known of the existence of the sea and had known that there were craft that crossed it, but the reality had been different from what she had imagined. When she had got over her fear, made all the worse by the fact that she couldn't show it to her companions - especially the sinister, veiled Barossi, who hardly acknowledged her - she started to enjoy herself. She liked the way the craft glided over the water; she liked to watch the sails fill out with the light, cool breezes that played upon the waves. It was cool on the sea and somehow invigorating after all the dust of their journey, the slow procession from Melanthera in a caravan of carriages and wagons.

Her days at the palace had been few. The Empress had decided, a week or so after Asha took up her duties, vague as they were, that it was time for the annual pilgrimage to Piroush. Melanthera got too hot for the Empress and her court at the height of the summer, though to Asha it was cooler than her own western mountains. When the cavalcade had set out, Asha had taken up her weapons, wrapped her blanket and her food bundle around her and prepared herself for a long walk, but she had been told by the officer in charge of the Barossi, in none too gentle terms, that she would be riding in one of the wagons. The Barossi were the only ones who would be marching; it was a point of honour with them and they did not want her trailing after them.

She thus had another new experience; she'd never ridden in a wagon before. Apart from the driver, who sat up a little apart on a high seat where he could control the team of haras, she shared the vehicle with the priest that they called Gamelon and two Piroushi girls, hand-maidens of the Empress. After the first hour she had started to feel cooped up and uncomfortable in the back of the vehicle. They travelled with the awning down as the dust thrown up by the carriages and wagons ahead rose in clouds which blew back on them.

There wasn't a lot of room in the wagon box, as various bits of furniture and bundles of supplies took up most of the space. The Piroushi girls - thin, soft-limbed creatures made for a life of indolence - lounged at the back of the wagon on bundles of bedding and curtains. Asha had heard it said of Piroushi girls that they were only good for two things, dancing and love-making, and wondered what sort of servants they made. She thought that they probably came from aristocratic families and had been sent to court to find favour for their kindred.

She had noticed that the Empress surrounded herself, as a result of diplomacy and her policy of building alliances where she could, with the scions of tribes and vassal nations. Most of these people had some function or other in the royal household, like the Piroushi girls, but were, in truth, mostly redundant. It did occur to Asha that she perhaps came into this category; perhaps she was just a convenient token representative of her people. In the end though this didn't matter, she had a sacred duty to serve the Empress and it was up to the Empress to decide how.

The Piroushi girls were a little scared of her and left her alone. On the first night, after the vehicles had stopped and the camp had been set up, to escape Gamelon and his endless chatter, she had found her way back to the wagon early and settled down to sleep beside the two girls. Amongst her people, in the villages, the unmarried girls always slept together, so it was natural to lie down beside them and would have seemed impolite of her not to do so. The pile of bedding was a little too soft for comfort, but she laid the broadsword beside her, the hunting spears close by and curled up in her blanket, one hand on the sword's hilt as was her custom.

She woke up in the night hearing whispering and, by the faint light of the lanterns that were hung around the edges of the camp and dimly lit the wagon's interior, she saw the two girls both wide awake, holding each other and watching her as if she were a sleeping lion. As she lifted herself up, hand still on the sword hilt, one of them gave a gasp and the other buried her head in her companion's shoulder. Asha gave them a look of disgust and went back to sleep. Scared of their shadows, she thought, but after that, she was careful to sleep outside the wagon on the ground.

The priest was more of an irritation than the Piroushi girls, as they mainly dozed, giggled or complained in those soft, vacuous voices. Gamelon was different in that he was garrulous and sought to engage her in conversation. He had an endless fascination for her and her people; he wanted to glean every useless piece of information about the western mountains and the western tribes he could from her. A few times she had felt her fingers itching and moving towards her knife, as the man droned on interminably, but she remembered what Berendal had taught her, that you had to act a certain way amongst these people, however irritating they were.

Berendal had taught her many things in the brief time they had together; though he had been often equally irritating. He also had that effect on her that an orphaned baby hvass had when she was a herdswoman. Its bleating was annoying, but you made allowances because it was helpless and also endearing in the way that baby animals are. She had thought it amusing when the poet had tried to sleep with her, turning those baby-hvass eyes on her, so she had only hurt him enough to make him quickly reconsider his position.

Even Gamelon eventually seemed to run out of questions that she could answer, but then he took it upon himself to tell her things about Melanthera and other parts of the Empire, as if he had decided to, in some way, become her unwanted teacher. Her silence and lack of response eventually started to quieten him.

It was only when Gamelon started asking her about herself and her journey to the city, almost as an after-thought on one interminably hot afternoon when they were crossing the desert, that his interest was awakened again. She could see how his eyes fixed on her, but became gradually unfocused, dreamy, as she described how she had followed the fallen star. Much later, she would realise, that it was at this point, somewhere in a place with no name in the midst of the desert, that the legend of her life was born; the wilderness its reluctant mother with Gamelon as midwife.

When their ship anchored in a wide calm bay after two days sailing, she saw a landscape like no other seen before. The green hills fell down to the water, interlaced with rivulets that plummeted in falls of crystal water off cliffs into the sea. Blue waters lapped gently at white sands and, between the shore and the emerald forest that climbed up to the mountain heights, was the Empress's summer palace; a vast, sprawling, low complex of pavilions and airy apartments, where silk hangings and wooden partitions enclosed a space that was neither indoors or outdoors, but a strange mixture of the two. The climate of the islands was sultry and hot, fierce showers would fall on some days, but there were also light, cool breezes coming off the sea and the constant sound of water - waves lapping or streams running - a cooling counterpart to the afternoon heat.

Evenings were the best time. The heat of the day seemed to evaporate, any rain clouds cleared, and the sunset made a golden path that stretched over the horizon as it were an open road to other worlds. The Empress had the tendency to rise early and take a walk in the forest or along the shore-line, then to rest in the afternoons. Evenings were spent eating and drinking in one big company, with musicians and Piroushi dancers and all sorts of entertainers. After a week or so of this routine, it was hard, even for Asha, to keep the languor of the days at bay. She could sometimes find an off-duty Barossi to practise her swordsmanship with, though generally they didn't like sparring with her as she was a woman and the Barossi were notoriously patriarchal.

Intriguingly she found herself often in the company of the Piroushi hand maidens, who had become less wary of her. In the late afternoons, the girls were often sent off to collect the madra berries the Empress particularly liked, that grew in the foot-hills above them and she would be given the task of guarding them. She was not sure against what threat, as the place seemed isolated enough and there seemed no predatory wildlife on the island. The girls' names were Kusha, who had the darkest jade eyes, and the glossiest hair, as well as lips that permanently pouted, and Annesh, a wisp of a girl with hair that was almost bronze in colour and light green eyes that always seemed to bear a burden of sadness. She had asked Kusha about this one day and the girl had said:

"She misses her family. Even more so here than in the city, as they are not far away."

Kusha, the more talkative one, told her that the island they were on was called Khetmis, and, apart from the palace and a small fishing village on the other side of the mountains, it was uninhabited. The main island, Piroush, the city state from which the whole archipelago took its name, was a day's sail away. She thought that the Empress would probably visit the city on her way back to Melanthera and she said that Annesh and her were counting the days.

Asha had guessed correctly that the girls were the daughters of two of the lords of Piroush and she looked on them with a certain, new-found sympathy; understanding that they too had taken a path not of their choosing, but to which they had been called by duty. She still thought them soft and weak, too ready to cry if they twisted an ankle or pierced their hand on a thorn bush, but she had grown to like their soft, graceful manners and the way they took care of each other. She did, however, make sure that she fitted in an extra sword practise after spending an afternoon with them; she didn't want their softness to rub off on her.

She thought herself lucky during this time that Gamelon didn't bother her. He spent his time following the Empress around or closeted up with her. His new duties had sobered him; he was no longer wed to the flask of kassa he used to carry with him. A courtier told her that the priest was writing a history of the Empress's reign, which in itself was strange to her as her people had no need to put down on scrolls the memories that they kept and passed on from old to young.

The languid unchanging routine of the days stretched into weeks and Asha found it increasingly hard to stop herself succumbing to the lethargy that the island encouraged. Even the Barossi became indolent, not helped by the fact that the scale-like breastplates they wore, the long spears and shields they carried, were not suited to this climate. Plus the fact that the face-veils they affected had been created for dry and dusty deserts, not this humid, tropical climate.

The result was that none of them were ready for the raid when it came. Asha had been lying on her divan in her apartment, when she heard the noise; soft footfalls and whispering from across the courtyard. She first thought that it was perhaps Kusha and Annesh come to play a trick on her and smiled, though, if it was them, she would pretend to be cross.

Then she heard that unmistakeable sound, that strange rattle that emanates from the throat of a hvass as you slit it from ear to ear. But there were no hvass in the palace. In a moment she had slid back the wooden panel that made up her door and crossed the courtyard outside. She knew that a guard was always posted at the head of the corridor that led to the Empress's quarters and she quickly found the Barossi; he was lying on his side with his throat cut. She could visualise how it had happened; he was probably sitting there, dozing in the sun, unaware of the death that was creeping up on him.

She did not have time to think on what the threat might me or from whom it might come. She knew the Empress would be in her sleeping quarters and feared there was little between her and the invisible assassins but a few flimsy wooden panels. She ran quietly on her bare feet to the corner where the corridor snaked around on itself - the place was a veritable maze - and looked around the edge of the wall. She quickly counted five figures that she could see, bunched up as if waiting for instructions; two had bows, three swords or short, bill-like weapons. Fools, she thought, not to guard their rear, as she quickly loosed two of her throwing spears at their backs.

The dull grunts and exclamations of pain told her that she had found at least one mark and then she heard feet running back up the corridor towards her. She saw an open doorway in front of her and dodged into the room sliding the panel shut. She heard feet come running around the corner and stop, then heard what she thought were two voices, whispering. She focused on the voices, intuited from their sound their relative positions and swung her sword in a two handed stroke, cutting through the panel and into flesh. The flimsy wall fell outwards, covering the body of the man she had felled with that first stroke.

The other man seemed more surprised by her appearance than afraid and took a split second to recover and bring up his sword. But he was too late, her second stroke had already slashed his stomach open. He collapsed at her feet and, at the same moment, she heard screams from down the corridor. She stepped over the body quickly and ran around the corner, ignoring the wounded man who was huddled against the wall of the corridor and the corpse that lay near him, both victims of her spears.

She saw an archer further down the corridor taking aim at her and ran as fast as she could towards him. He loosed off his shaft and then fled and, as she tried to dodge the missile, she felt a sharp pain on her left arm. Glancing down, stopping only momentarily, she saw that the arrow had grazed her upper left arm, but the fold of the red robe she wore had afforded some protection, making the wound a trifling thing; she'd got worse from her practise bouts. The archer had been too unnerved to take aim properly and to draw the bow back its full length.

She ran on then, pursuing the archer out of the doorway at the end of the corridor and into a scene of chaos. At first she couldn't quite make out what was happening, who was screaming and who was fighting who. The archer had run out of the corridor in such a hurry that he'd tripped over a body lying on the ground in the doorway and stunned himself. Asha put her foot on his back and would have driven the sword into his neck, but saw that one of the other assassins was advancing towards her, sword in one hand and a small round target in the other.

She left the archer for later and concentrated on her attacker; looking past him she quickly took in the scene in front of her. The body of a dead Barossi lay in front of the doorway opposite and she surmised that the Empress must be in the apartment behind the door. Another Barossi was holding off two of the assassins, she could also hear noises coming from other parts of the palace; the tell-tale sound of men shouting, the cries of the wounded and the chinking of clashing weapons. She saw out of the corner of her eye that her archer was starting to raise himself up, unsteady but still a threat.

The man who faced her was smiling; like all the assassins he had a gaily-coloured scarf wound around his head, wore some sort of padded jerkin or brigandine, and short voluminous trousers. His curly hair and kohl-lined eyes reminded her of the Piroushi girls. He slashed at her with his curved blade and she parried. He said something obscene to her, something he'd like to do to her. His smile told her that he had underestimated her, so she kept backing up as he came towards her.

"Put the sword down, girl," he said, "you might cut yourself."

His smile got wider.

"Put it down and I won't be too rough with you."

She knelt down and bowed her head. He didn't know what she was doing, but thought the fight had gone out of her. He hesitated for just a moment, deciding what to do with her; should he kill her or take her captive? Then suddenly she sprung up and dealt him a back-handed stroke of her sword. He tried to parry, but he just managed to deflect the sword slightly; instead of striking him on the head it sunk into his shoulder and hit an artery. He died with the smile still on his face.

Quickly, she pushed him aside seeing the archer was up and advancing on her drawing a long, wicked-looking knife. She looked over and saw that the Barossi guardsman was sorely pressed. Just then, she saw Gamelon emerge from the mouth of the corridor, brandishing a staff. The archer, seeing himself sorely pressed on both sides, lost his nerve and ran away across the courtyard.

She let him go and advanced across the yard, just in time to see the Barossi fall, over the body of his dead comrade. Too late, she thought, as one of the assassins kicked his way into the Empress's room, but the man immediately staggered out again an arrow buried in one of his eye shafts. Before the other assassin could enter the room she was on him; he was already winded and out-of-breath from the fight with the Barossi and looked as if he had a wound in the leg.

He was aggressive though and rushed at her, as if he knew his strength was nearly spent and he needed to kill her quickly. One feint, one parry and then a cutting stroke that nearly took the man's head off, finished it. She looked up from the body to see Gamelon watching her, an astonished look on his face.

Quickly, she made her way to the doorway, but, wary of the archer, she called out before entering:

"Highness, are you alive? It's Asha."

She pushed into the room to be faced by Kusha, bow drawn, arrow nocked. When she saw Asha, she lowered the bow and started weeping.

"Kusha," Asha said, "you have done well. You kept the Empress safe, but you must still keep up your guard, there could be more of these people out there."

The girl nodded, raised her bow and resumed her position watching the doorway. Gamelon and Asha went through another doorway, under a silk awning, and saw the Empress sitting on a divan.

"Well," she said. "I suppose you have come to save me."

A detachment of Barossi turned up soon after and a gaggle of courtiers and serving women fussed about the Empress, who remained cool and aloof. Women were rending their robes and men were shouting in angry voices, but the Empress remained composed. Barossi officers shouted commands and there was a lot of clanging of spears and running to and fro in the corridors as the soldiers and the servants scoured the palace looking for intruders.

"Where were all these people," the Empress asked Asha, "when they would have been of some use?"

Annesh had found Kusha and both girls, though unwilling to leave the Empress, clung to each other and took turns to weep or made comforting noises. Asha now looked on Kusha in a new way. She might be soft on the outside, and the killing might have taken a toll on her, but she had proved brave enough when she had to be.

When the palace was secure they sent parties out to pick up the trails of the raiders. They had come over the mountain, so that they could surprise the palace. The sheer size of the place and the labyrinth-like nature of its corridors had been their downfall. The Barossi reckoned there'd been about thirty of them, but they'd split up into small parties to find the Empress and got lost or confused by the lay-out of the place.

The party that had struck lucky – or unlucky on reflection - the ones that Asha had fought, had killed the lone Barossi and then followed the corridor to the Empress's courtyard. A young Melantheran maid had raised the alarm as they emerged from the doorway, she had thrown a tray of drinks at them and screamed. It was her corpse that lay in the doorway of the corridor, her body that tripped the archer. But the alarm she gave, and paid for with her life, had probably saved the Empress, alerting the remaining Barosssi. Nobody doubted that the assassins, who it was thought were Piroushi pirates, had come to slay the Empress, but nobody could think of a reason.

Asha had been with the party that cut the trail. Even in this terrain that was so strange to her, she was a good tracker; the skill was the same, you just needed to adapt it. She was faster than her companions and got well ahead of them. Cresting the ridge of the mountain pass that the raiders had taken, she could see below her a party of some seven or eight men, some wounded, limping down the trail.

She saw them enter a belt of forest and, though she knew she should really wait for her companions to come up, she descended the slope and made a wide circle, entering the forest off to the flank of the path they were following. She thought she heard sounds, someone crying out, a scuffling of running feet, so she lowered herself into a low line of bushes, worming her way forward.

She got to the edge of a clearing and was taken aback by the sight she saw. The men she had been following all lay about the open ground; at first she thought they were exhausted, but then she saw the bloodied throats, the severed limbs and the discarded weapons. These men had fought something and lost. She heard a strange noise in the distance, something like bird noise, but harsher and less musical. Then she saw them. Two shapes at the other end of the clearing, retreating through the trees; she only got a glimpse, but she was sure. She had seen these things before. They were what the Star People called robot dogs.

The way it would be written down, the way Gamelon would record it, the assassination attempt that was made on the Empress in the forty-eighth year of her reign, was carried out by a band of Piroushi pirates, whether on their own volition or on the behest of another was not known. All that could be said was that the attempt was defeated.

There were many brave people that day; there was the lowly Melantheran maid, Azuri, who gave the alarm and her life with it; there was the Piroushi lady, Kusha, who held the Empire's last line of defence on that threshold in Khetmis. Then there was Asha, the Maiden who followed the Star. She had killed five of the attackers and fatally wounded another. She had pursued the survivors up into the hills. That day a hero was born, a legend that the Melantherans would weave and cling to in the dark hours that were ahead for them.

Asha had told the Empress what she had seen. How the Star People's creatures had played some part in the raid, how they had killed the last of the pirates, sealing their lips and stilling their voices. Only one other person had been told and that was Gamelon. That verbose, pompous, bladder of a man had been transformed by the news and the anger that he felt.

"Highness, we must let everyone know that the Star People have had a hand in this. We must shout if from the temple towers, carry the news across the desert and to the frontiers of the Empire."

128

The old woman had calmed him, sat him down and talked to him softly and sadly.

"And what would that achieve, my faithful Gamelon? In their anger the people would want to wipe the Star People off the planet. They'd attack the compounds that have been spreading all over the place. And to what end?"

Gamelon sat, head bowed, unable to answer.

"I'll tell you. It would give them the excuse to make war on us, to subdue us. So we will act publicly as if they had nothing to do with this. But in private we must take care and be prepared for the days that are ahead of us. Days that will try and test us as never before."

Chapter 13
Berthaud

In the morning Robyn had slipped out of bed first and made tea. Abi was on an early duty shift, so Robyn could hurry her out of her quarters without needing to make excuses. They'd kissed each other good morning and been tender together, so Abi went off with a smile on her face. But as soon as Robyn had touched the console to seal the door, she immediately started to wonder what she was doing. With hindsight, she thought that she should have known it was always going to lead up to this. And hadn't this been what she wanted all along? Part of her acknowledged this and welcomed it, but another part of her was less easily convinced. Had she just sleep-walked into this, like she usually did in her life?

She tried to put it all out of her mind as she showered and dressed, but the words Esmee had said to her on that last terrible morning, when she packed her bags, the tears streaming down her face, played in her head;

"You are never satisfied, Robyn. You don't know when you've got a good thing and you never will."

By the time she set off to work, she felt hot and flushed. Knowing that they kept the temperature at a steady nineteen degrees Celsius, she wondered what was happening to her. Perhaps it was her hormones, she thought; a reaction to the night before. She must have been out of condition or out of practise.

She felt terribly self-conscious as she stalked down the corridors, as if everyone she passed, each vague acquaintance she met, knew about her and Abi. The claustrophobic society of the Library was a hive of rumour and gossip. It was inevitable that word would get around that she was 'seeing' Abi. She hated all that, all the baggage that went with these things. Up to now, she'd successfully kept herself and her business under the radar. Now she'd be part of the great emotional epic of the place, the rollercoaster of relationships. But so what, she thought, by the time she got to the changing room and was suiting up.

When she emerged from the airlock, Shelby was waiting for her with a mug of coffee in his hand. She didn't know how he did it; this was the real stuff he got, not the genetically modified, hydroponic version that you usually got on bases like this with most the caffeine stripped out. She smiled at him and that seemed to be thanks enough.

She liked that about Shelby; he didn't make a fuss about things, didn't seek any reciprocity from those little kindnesses he did for you. Not like Abi, she thought, and then suppressed it. She knew she'd been unfair, but couldn't help thinking that things might have been easier, if Shelby had been her cup of tea. She knew that the jury was still out on Shelby, the gossips had not quite got a handle on his sexuality yet. It was rumoured that he batted for both sides, but she, after all, was in an entirely different game.

The kick she got from the coffee was just what she needed to get started on her work. She'd been tasked with checking the transliteration of a collection of scrolls from one of the Shabaz temple archives. Just when she'd thought that she'd finished her work on that planet, they'd found more material that they wanted collated. This was one of the occupational hazards of her job; nothing was ever really finished or finite, there was always some other source or document being uncovered, something that would lead you to revisit or re-examine what you thought you knew. Except when, she thought, they didn't want you to revise the history of the place. When it was tied up in a neat, sealed parcel like Elanthia.

It should have been exciting, dealing with actual artefacts rather than electronic documents. She'd been down the corridor to where the conservation technicians were cataloguing the scrolls and scanning the text. She'd stood there trying to pretend excitement, but all the time her thoughts had been elsewhere, thinking of Berthaud and what she had written. Now, as she peered at her screen and looked at the scanned text, using the translation programme and checking it for syntax and sense, she kept losing concentration, kept drifting off in her thoughts to what she had found out about Berthaud.

The news feed article that she'd found about the 'Berthaud affair' on the Hub hadn't exactly been informative. It had been one of those general magazine-type pieces that tried to handle important issues or controversies in science in a popular way. The fact that it treated 'science' as one homogenous whole, rather than intricate inter-locking patterns of disciplines, said something of the superficial way in which it addressed it subjects. It had been written by a reporter more to entertain and inform, than to advance knowledge.

It purported to be a discussion of the Berthaud affair, but it managed to be hardly informative at all, as to what the affair actually was. It was more a discussion of the ethics involved in ethnography and anthropology, and the need for scientists to be objective in their dealings with the societies they encountered on other planets.

The author, frustratingly, took for granted that the reader had some prior knowledge of the 'affair'. She scanned the text, a few of the passages staying with her:

".....The facts of the matter are recent and are doubtless familiar to our readers. Dr. Berthaud's actions, the choices and decisions that she made during the siege of Melanthera, supporting one faction in what was basically an inter-tribal war, has become a case-study of how easy it is for the ethnologist or anthropologist to lose their objectivity.....

.... It has always been clear to scientists in this field that the cultural and historical baggage that we each bring to our work, can be as much to do with our conscious as our sub-conscious. We should therefore ask ourselves what there was in Berthaud's history, her cultural memory, that allowed her to indentify so much with one faction of the Melantherans. In other words, what made her decide that one tribe was the 'good guys' and the other was the 'bad guys'.....

.... We can see from the Berthaud affair that concepts such as social justice, equity and the rights of the individual are, though in many ways the underpinning of our society, subjective judgements and values that have no place in objective, scientific study..."

It was clear that the Berthaud affair did involve the same Dr. Marie Berthaud who had been the ethnologist on the Sung Yang surveying mission on Elanthia and that she had somehow got mixed up in some sort of war on the planet. Robyn wondered how this was connected with Abi's time on Elanthia, whether the peacekeeping mission she had mentioned was linked; looking at the date of the article she thought that there must be a connection. She wondered if she could raise the subject with Abi, but somehow she doubted it. The irony was that though they had slept together, they weren't that intimate yet.

Again, after reading the article, she'd searched for more references to Berthaud, but couldn't find anything more. Then she'd looked for information about the peace-keeping operations on Elanthia. The DF records were either classified or sealed, which wasn't much of a surprise, but she did find a terse reference to an 'Operation Accord' on the force's own Hub. Like all organisations and corporations, the Defence Force spent some of its time and money in telling the public how efficient they were at their job and why they needed financial support, recruits and contracts. One of the pages on the Hub had a chronological record of DF present and past operations, just a terse commentary with little detail:

"Operation Accord: Defence Force units were invited by the political authorities of Melanthera to provide a peace-keeping force between warring

134

factions and to suppress terrorist activities by subversive elements. Part of the DF's mission was to protect Sung Yang personnel on the planet, who had become a target for extremists. The mission was accomplished after two planetary years and all units, with the exception of support and training elements working with local forces, were withdrawn."

Just when Robyn had thought that she was destined to wander through a series of blind alleyways, never finding her way to Berthaud and the key that she held to what really happened in Melanthera, a chance remark of Shelby's changed everything.

They had been at dinner and she'd been venting her frustration - indirectly, not being specific - about the difficulty in accessing the ethnological records of the survey expeditions to the outer planets. It was a habit of theirs to blow off steam with each other, but that day he surprised her.

"It is difficult," he said, "if you go through the Hub."

She knew, vaguely, that Shelby was some sort of economist, that he was part of a team recording and analysing the commercial and economic activities of the corporations on the outer planets.

"You know, Robyn," he said, "most of the work that I'm doing and some of the other guys are doing, is sponsored by corporations like Sung Yang and SSC. They wanted to get the record straight, so they uploaded an enormous amount of information to the Hanis main-frame. It's mainly raw data, and there's no search facility, but it is catalogued and it just takes some old-fashioned research to find what you want."

He'd told her that she could access it; anyone working in the Hanis library could, just by entering her own login details and password. When she'd expressed surprise that the records weren't better protected he'd said:

"They've got other ways of making sure that nothing leaks out of Hanis."

It was a throw-away remark, or so she had supposed at the time.

Robyn thought it was supremely ironic that the information that she had sought was hidden from her in plain sight, on another part of the network that she used every day to do her research. Each section of the library on Hanis had its own research portal, so that the economist, microbiologist - or whatever scientist you were - could access the most relevant parts of the Hub. But in addition to this, there was a less sophisticated information portal which took the user to the records and other information actually contained on the library's mainframe. As Shelby had told her, though this was not accessible to casual users, any member of the library staff could access it.

She spent some time wading thought the contracts and spreadsheets that made up most of the records. They were organised according to commercial categories and not yet cross-referenced, so it wasn't an easy task to find what she really wanted, but she eventually found references to Elanthia in a section on mining concessions. The Sir John Franklin's ethnology records had been deposited in a sub-folder almost as an after-thought; as if they had only had some marginal relevance.

She quickly scanned the information that afternoon and then settled down in the days that followed to more thoroughly reading the records in any spare time she had. This was usually at the end of the afternoon, so Shelby got used to the sight of her working on as he left his station for the day.

Many of the reports were routine and not all were by Berthaud; other ethnologists had been deployed as the Sung Yang Corporation increased its presence on Elanthia. It was not a complete record either; there were significant gaps, anything not relevant to business or economic transaction had been left out. Just before the trip to the Great Canyon, she had come upon an intriguing report from Berthaud, though she hadn't had a chance to read it until now.

It was a log entry that gave a detailed report on what Berthaud called 'the Melantheran way of business' and detailed the customs and practises of merchants in the city, but, just at the end of the entry, Berthaud had added something, as if she had felt the need to record it quickly.

"Received a message from Director Carstairs, in orbit on the Sir John Franklin, he told me to make myself ready to attend a meeting of the Grand Council with him in the next few days. I replied that the Empress was away at her summer palace in Piroush. He, in turn, replied that the order stood. He was expecting some political changes in Melanthera imminently.

Later, Berendal appeared at the gates of the compound. Very quiet at first, but then told me that there had been an attempt on the Empress's life in Piroush. I'm not sure why he sought me out with this news. I did ask him who was responsible for the attempt. He told me that it was rumoured to be pirates. I walked out later in the city with him at his invitation. There seemed to be an extremely tense atmosphere and, according to Berendal, various rumours were circulating about the Empress and the assassination attempt. Berendal told me the Empress was returning from Piroush, whether this is official news or another rumour is uncertain, but Berendal is usually a good source of intelligence about the place.

I had distinct feeling that Berendal was leaving something unsaid; that there was a hidden agenda. I could see a lot of movement of troops of various sorts in the town, including mercenary units like Hvassara horse-archers, who were usually billeted outside the walls. As we passed through the main streets, I could see that many of the side –streets were being sealed off by gates I'd never seen used before, that I thought were purely ornamental. Some of them were so rusted up, it was taking whole gangs of men to shift them. Militia units of citizens were manning the gates.

I tried to draw Berendal out about what was happening in the Palace, as he had told me that the gates of the citadel were closed. I knew that the Grand Council were nominally in charge when the Empress was away. But when I questioned him about this, he gave one of those aggravating, childish smiles of his and laughed, telling me that Kal Quintal wanted to be the new Emperor. He then abruptly shut up, as if he'd said too much.

Back at the base, I reported the matter to Kevorkian, the civilian manager, and Johnson, the commander of the Defence and Protection Unit. Johnson reported that a unit of Barossi guardsmen had taken up position in front of the base. Their commander had informed him that they were there to protect the base from "ruffians and market scum." I emphasised to the two senior members of staff that I felt that we were witnessing a coup taking place in Melanthera and that this was a very unusual state of affairs. The Empress was more than just the political authority, but also a religious leader, seen as Elanta's representative on the planet.

Johnson wanted to contact the Sir John Franklin for reinforcements, which he said, "were on stand-by," but Kevorkian over-ruled him, saying that the base wasn't in immediate danger and we had a policy of non-interference. Later, I contacted Director Carstairs. He asked me to confirm that the Empress was alive. I replied that I could only report what I had been told. He told me to stand down and await further instructions.

A full report of these events, including my analysis, has been submitted to Kevorkian"

As Robyn sat at her desk now, thinking about this last entry of Berthaud's - the last one she had accessed - she decided that she would have to stay late again to see if she could find the woman's next log entry or the report that she had mentioned But Robyn was hot again and her head had started swimming. She turned to Shelby:

"Is it me," she asked, "or is there something wrong with the air conditioning in here?"

He quickly crossed the space between them and put his palm up to her forehead.

"It's you," he said. "You're burning up."

So Robyn, who was never sick, became an integral part of 'the Great Canyon epidemic', which, by its end, had affected almost a quarter of the party that had embarked on the SSG excursion. It baffled the Library medics, but eventually the SSG company doctors linked it to the fire lizards. It was supposedly some virus that lurked in their droppings, just waiting for a passing host. Though she could not remember seeing any fire-lizard shit, it was apparently dried out and blown all about the place by that infernal, never-ending wind. SSG sent over an antigen, which made Robyn suspect they knew of the virus's existence from previous experience, and, as a result, the victims suffered little more than flu-like symptoms for a week or so.

Robyn had spent the first couple of days in sick bay, but had then, dosed up with the antidote, been allowed to go back to her quarters; where Abi would take care of her, if and when her rota allowed, which in reality wasn't that often. Thus it was that Robyn got to know her first real Melantheran. Her name was Khamis. She was one of the ghosts; the cleaners who came and went via the network of service tunnels which ran alongside, over and under, the wide corridors of the Hanis library.

Their first meeting had been strange, like a scene from a dream. It had happened as Robyn dozed on her bed, her forehead still seeming to bear the cold traces of Abi's lips, that farewell kiss that she had bestowed on Robyn in the manner of a nurse rather than a lover. Robyn had been sleeping lightly, her fever giving her strange, waking dreams and, at first, the soft kiss of the service door opening, the rustle of overalls and the soft padding of feet, seemed a part of some sleepy imagining. Then she saw the small willowy figure. The dark, glossy hair in two braids, the dark, opalescent eyes looking down at her with initial fear, then concern. Then she felt a pair of gentle, deft hands lifting her up, propping a pillow behind her.

"Drink this," the voice said, strangely accented, but soft as silk, "it will make you better. It's durgan root tea."

In this way Khamis arrived in her world, a fugitive from another.

Chapter 14
How Berendal Held The Gate.

The whisper had gone around the crowds in the marketplace. From the shy Harradim girls, getting water at the well for the food and teas shops, it had passed to the pleasure girls, doing their laundry at the trough, from there a Piroushi dancer had turned it into a song and, as she pirouetted in one of their strange, bird-like dances, she'd spread it from stall to stall.

Then two musicians, dressed in that shabby finery that marked them out as Melantherans, took it up as a refrain, adorning it with music from lute and tambour. Even the Barossi guardsmen, still and stoic, like statues in the morning sun - which was so hot that everyone else haunted every sliver or space of shade - were heard to be murmuring it, until, with one harsh command, their officer put a stop to it. Finally, the whisper, which was also a song, turned into a shout, as a ragged urchin-like boy hopped and skipped in front of the implacable Barossi, bawling and yelling:

"The Empress is coming! The Empress is coming!"

A ragged cheer when up from the crowd; a Melantheran cheer, which was more like an ululation. It was ragged, because everyone there was confused as to whose side they were on, and, more importantly, whose side your neighbour was on. You didn't want to shout for the Empress, if the person next to you was a Kal Quintal partisan.

Berendal was standing with crowd of morning drunks and sleepy serving girls in his favourite place, outside the Hwrathka Gate pleasure house. He'd just taken Berthaud back to gates of the base which now, he could see, had been sealed. The watch –towers along the base perimeter were manned and the sun glinted on the metal of weapons and the body-armour of the soldiers who stood guard there.

He'd wanted her to see, to understand what was happening. Quintal had been spreading the rumour that the Empress was dead and that the army now marching on Melanthera was a hostile force. Then there had been that fast haras rider, one of the Empress's messengers, who'd somehow got entry through the Hwrathka Gate. Almost collapsing from exhaustion, seated under a borriba tree in the market square, unable to go further, he had told anyone who would listen that the Empress lived and was on the way back to the city.

Berendal didn't know what had happened to him. He'd soon disappeared, led away by a squad of Hvassaran mercenaries. But news in Melanthera was like a brush fire on the hills in summer; one spark and everything was alight. So it was that in the space of an afternoon, neighbourhoods were closing their gates, weapons were being handed out from basement arsenals; some so rusty and in need of repair that they were practically useless.

At about the same time the citadel gates were closed, as if the people themselves were the enemy, and Hvassara and Barossi started expelling Melantheran soldiers from gate-houses and towers, under the supposed orders of the Grand Council.

143

Kal Quintal had let it be known that there were suspected traitors amongst the Melantheran soldiers and he had taken precautionary measures. In fact, no-one doubted that he had more faith in the mercenaries' loyalty to him, bought with money, than the local, city garrison.

As Berendal stood there, he wondered at his fellow citizens. The Melantherans, at any hint of trouble, were out of their houses and on the streets, desperate to find out what was happening. It would have been more sensible, he thought, if they had been hiding in their cellars, but they were basically too curious. Even if arrows rained, and spears arced, still they'd be there, poking their heads around corners to see what was happening, not wanting to miss it for the world.

The Barossi had arrived just after he'd escorted Berthaud back to the base. Though he hadn't shown it, he had started to get worried for her safety on the streets. There was an underlying resentment to the Star People that had gradually been building up over the last few months. There were more and more of them, all over the place, setting up bases like this one and their craft - those ships that sailed in the sky - could be seen hovering overhead even in the most remote places.

One of the western tribes had even captured the crew of one of them that had unwisely landed in their territory and the Empress had ended up paying a ransom for their safe return, feeling that the duty of hospitality she'd extended to the Star People obliged her to do so.

The veiled guardsmen had taken up position on the square in a solid phalanx facing the Hwrathka gate, the base to the left of them, the market to their right, so it was unclear why they were there; to protect the base or to threaten the gate.

At the Hwrathka gate, nervous faces peered out of the narrow windows and from the towers above. The gate was like a self-contained fortress, as it had been designed to be. Beneath its great arch, wide enough to take two Hwrathka abreast as the name suggested, were two gates, one outer and one inner; above this were living quarters for the garrison and the winch rooms which controlled the opening and closing of the great wooden doors below. Above this floor were storerooms and defensive loop-holes in the walls, culminating in battlements flanked by two towers.

In theory, the gate and gate-house were impregnable. Even if the walls around it fell, a determined garrison could hold out for a long time until relieved. In practise, the garrison wasn't, at this moment, very determined. It consisted of some twenty one Melantheran soldiers, commanded by an elderly and rather portly junior officer. Because Melanthera hadn't been under the threat of any hostile action for decades, garrison duty tended to be the preserve of the old, the weak and the stupid.

Thus it was that the force which held the Hwrathka gate, on that morning the most strategic military position in the whole Empire of Melanthera, was a motley and mostly unenthusiastic crew. Even some of the veteran warriors, who stiffened the spine of the force, though once fierce and intimidating, were too arthritic to climb the ladders or too myopic to shoot straight.

When the Barossi arrived, the officer in charge of the Gate, named Kalen, had scratched his head and wondered if they had come to relieve his force. He had a grog shop, a side-line that he was very concerned about. He'd seen the crowds assembling and was worried that his wife wouldn't be able to cope with their thirst. He was even more confused when a force of Hvassara archers arrived and formed up near the Barossi, the two respective commanders engaging in what seemed to be a heated conversation.

He was leaning out of the window, trying to listen, when a rotten fruit of some sort hit the shutter close to his head. He reeled back, but then looked out as he heard a hissing sound, someone trying to attract his attention. He vaguely recognised the man below; he was a well-known denizen of the pleasure houses and had been known to drink at Kalen's grog shop, trying to swap a poem for a cup of wine.

"Psst! Kalen! I've got some wine for your lads. Let me up!"

There seemed no harm in it, thought Kalen, as he signalled for one of his men to lower the rope ladder to Berendal and to use the small winch to pull him up. He had told the truth and was bearing a skin on his back.

"From the grateful citizens of Melanthera to our brave soldiers!"

It was silver-tongued flattery, but it did the trick. The garrison stood up straight, pushed out their chests and held their cups out while Berendal poured. But while the poet was toasting them, even more preposterously, a shout came from one of the look-outs above and Kalen looked out of the

146

window again to see the office in charge of the Hvassara approaching with a small detachment of the archers. The man was waving a hvass skin scroll closed by seal.

"Who is the officer in charge?" The man asked. He was small, like all Hvassara, with that bandy-legged walk. The helmets the Hvassara wore were metal copies of their conical hats and marked them out as foreign mercenaries.

Kalen looked around and then quickly realised the man was talking about him, so he stuck his head further out of the window and hailed him.

"I have orders here," the Hvassaran captain went on, "from Kal Quintal, the supreme protector of the Empire. You are to surrender the Hwrathka gate to me immediately. Now, open up! Tell your men to get their things and go!"

Kalen scratched his head. He didn't know what to do, but then, orders were orders. His men had already started to collect their sleeping rolls and their few possessions. Most had houses or rooms in the town, so kept little in the gate house. One of the older men, a veteran of many wars, had come down from the tower and was standing looking out over the square.

"Who are those barbarians to give us orders?" He asked.

Kalen sighed; the old man Draga, was always being difficult.

"Orders are orders." Kalen said, but Draga shook his head.

"Orders should come from the Empress, not that hvass's arse Quintal."

There was some uproar at this and an argument started, but suddenly a voice cut throw the muttering:

"You can't give up the gate," said Berendal.

Two more cups of wine had fortified Kalen enough to politely decline the Hvassara officer's request and he had only just got the window shutter closed, before the first arrows hit the wood just where his head had been a moment before.

Later, in the afternoon, Berendal looked out over the square from one of the loop-holes above the gate arch. He did this very carefully, conscious of the fact that the Hvassara were highly accurate archers, as they had already proved, killing the old man Draga and wounding two young lads. Draga had breathed his last propped up against the pillows of the divan in the officer's quarters.

"All I've done all my life is soldier," he said, "and what I wanted to be was a ..."

But he had died before completing the sentence.

Looking out, Berendal could see that most of the crowd had scattered or taken cover, Some of them, it was true, were treating it all more like a spectator sport than the bloody, little skirmish it was. A number of crumpled bodies, inert and strangely doll-like, lay strewn on the ground in front of the inner gates, proof that the garrison also had teeth and could bare them. The Hvassara, after an initial rush intended to frighten the defenders into surrender, and which got them nowhere causing instead a number of casualties in their ranks, had formed their own make-shift siege works, making a barricade across the square from market stalls and over-turned wagons. Every so often an archer would bob his head up and let fly a shaft, trying to discomfort the garrison as much as possible.

The Barossi had withdrawn, but only a little further back from their original positions on the square. They were now crouched down behind their shields in what passed for an "at ease" position in their military philosophy. It was still unclear what they would do, though the Hvassara didn't seem to see them as a threat. It was while surveying the ranks of the veiled guardsmen that he saw the dust cloud from the road that descended from the citadel and, calling out an alarm to the others who were dozing or on guard, he followed the progress of the strange procession that came into view at the far side of the square. There were more Hvassara and a number of wagons pulled by three Hwrathka. These weren't war beasts, but draught animals, pulling two catapults from the imperial arsenal and wagons full of ammunition and scaling ladders.

Berendal had a horrible, giddy feeling of helplessness as he saw the Hvassara unhitch the catapults and the wagons. Two parties then detached themselves to serve the artillery pieces and the rest, pushing the wagons before them, started to cross the square. The Hvassara already in front of them started firing to cover their comrades.

Then everything happened quickly and at once. The catapults were shooting bundles of cloth soaked in pitch at the gate-house, intending to set it alight. Quintal must be desperate, Berendal thought, if he plans to burn us out. The small force was badly stretched between returning fire and trying to extinguish or kick away the burning bundles that were landing on the tinder-dry, wooden floors. When shrill cries came from the battlements above the main gate-house, Berendal rushed up there to see what he could do. They used the last of their water supply to quench the flames, hauling up the barrels and hacking them open, so that a wave of liquid met and fought the fire that was taken hold.

Just when this danger was past, the first scaling ladders hit the walls and up came the Hvassara, swarming up the makeshift wooden structures like spiders. Berendal grabbed a pike and fended off one of the ladders, sending its occupants down onto their comrades below; he didn't see them fly, but heard their cries. But then more Hvassara erupted over the wall of the battlements and he drew his sword, saying a quick prayer to Elanta, regretting all the drinking he had done, all the pleasure he had taken with girls, and bemoaning the time he had wasted when he could have been practising his swordsmanship.

He didn't have time to be scared. A pinched, little Hvassara face, contorted with rage, and then another, loomed out of the smoke towards him slashing with the wicked short blades they carried. The first one fell over - the floor was extremely slippery - and he managed to parry the next one's sword and land a blow on him with his sword hilt. This one disappeared into the smoke to be replaced with another and the same frantic and fatal dance of slashing, cutting and parrying carried on.

He felt no pain, thought he knew he was wounded in several places. The smoke, which still hung around them, the heat of the sun, the arrows and missiles which were still coming over - even though they were hitting the Hvassara as well as the defenders - all conspired to turn the afternoon into a nightmare, a vision of the underworld. Is this what heroes crave? Thought Berendal. Is this what they want? I'd rather a cup of wine and a warm, soft Piroushi girl.

Then, suddenly, they came no more. Instead of the noise of battle that had been in his ears on the rooftop, the grunting sounds of exertion, the gasps and screams of pain and pleasure taken in killing, there came another sound. There was music on the air. A stately, slow, but unstoppable song of pipes, counterpointed by cymbals and bolstered by the rhythm of drums. But there was a deeper rhythm also. He looked around him, all the Hvassara were dead or dying. So were many of the garrison. Three of them were left standing and while the two lads who were with him pushed off the last of the scaling ladders and dealt with the remnants of the fire he looked out, away from Melanthera down the Imperial road and saw coming towards him a great dust cloud, rolling across the land like a sea wave.

It was the Empress and the army she had collected on her way home. He listened to the music again and understood what that deep underlying rhythm was. It was the tramp of thousands of feet and, even deeper still, the thud of hundreds of Hwrathka hooves, like an earthquake coming towards them.

Out in front he could see the vanguard. A force of spear men and archers led by a familiar figure. He could not mistake her, even at this distance; the tall erect stance, the flaring of her orange robes in

151

the dying sun, as surprisingly the day was used up already. It was Asha.

Seeing her, it was only then that he cried. Only then that he stated shaking uncontrollably.

"Open the gates, Kalen," he shouted. But Kalen was dead, throat opened by a Hvassara knife.

"Open the gates!" He cried again." The Empress is here!"

This time he heard the great winches creak. Then he raised himself up from the wall and went looking to see if there was any wine left.

On the square below the Hvassara, in some confusion after being thrown back by the ramshackle band of defenders, mistook the meaning of the opening of the gates. Battle deafened and tired, they thought they had won, surging forward through the arch, only to stop suddenly, appalled at the spectacle that faced them, a full-blooded, full-throated army.

They hesitated, waiting for orders, but most of their officers were dead. And then that demon in priestess's robes was amongst them, hacking and hewing as if she were cutting timber. The vanguard crashed into them and they turned to run, only to find that the Barossi had finally decided which side they were on, or had always been on.

It was all too much for the spectators. Melantherans weren't that keen on Hvassara at the best of times, especially foreign ones, so they joined in, throwing anything they could lay their hands on. Some of the more disreputable elements of the market denizens took advantage of the prodigious piles of Hwrathka dung and flung them at the fleeing men.

The mercenaries broke and ran, trying to run the gauntlet of the crowd and avoid the spears of the Barossi. As most of the alleyways and side –roads were barred and the gates manned by armed citizens, they had no choice but to stream backwards towards the citadel, pursued by Asha's vanguard and a considerable number of Melantherans citizens who were either too foolish, too drunk or too aggressive to know better.

When the Empress arrived at the citadel gates they were wide open. The council came out to meet her, newly liberated from their cells by the loyal Barossi. Kal Quintal had fled; it was rumoured that he had escaped in a dung cart, hiding under a particularly fragrant load. When Berendal was told this, he made a quip:

"All glory ends in shit!"

Then started to compose a poem on that theme in his head.

Later the Empress asked to meet the defenders of the Hwrathka gate, those who weren't dead. She was amazed, though of course didn't show it, when she saw Berendal standing in front of her with the few others who had survived. She was even more surprised when she found out that it was the poet who had stopped them surrendering the gate-house to Quintal's forces. She asked him to approach to accept her deepest gratitude. He did so, that aggravating, but now strangely endearing, smile still on his face.

Later again, after he had washed himself and been given fine clothes by the Empress's steward to change into, he wandered the Palace gardens, an honoured guest now, until he found her. She was unmissable; the tall, dark-skinned figure outlined in silhouette against the setting sun, the moon and her consorts rising in the opposite orb of the sky.

"I thought I was dead," he said as he approached her and she turned to face him, stern and implacable as always.

"Then I saw you, Asha. I saw you coming at the head of an army and I knew I would live."

She looked into his eyes and, to his surprise, hugged him. A little too enthusiastically, almost lifting him off his feet.

Then he saw she was with someone. A Piroushi girl by the look of her; she had the darkest jade eyes, and the glossiest hair, as well as lips that permanently pouted. He started to compose a love poem in his head, leaving aside for now the epic he had been intending to write, and would write later, about how he and his comrades held the Hwrathka Gate.

Chapter 15
Khamis

All that time she spent in her bed, all those days which seemed interminable, but were few enough really, Robyn became fascinated by Khamis. The cleaners came and did their work when most of the Library's personnel were at their own jobs. They tidied, took the dirty clothes to the central laundry, stocked the fridges and cupboards like a ghostly army of elves or fairies, benign and benevolent to their human masters. Seeing Khamis work, Robyn was amazed at how low-tech all her cleaning equipment was; vacuum cleaner, dusters, various sprays. Then she realised the reason for this. When labour was so inexpensive and readily available, there was no need to develop a more efficient technology; why have self-cleaning rooms when cleaners came so cheap?

What surprised Robyn even more was the care that Khamis took of her, coming back after her work was done to brew durgan root tea for her.

"I shouldn't really be here," she would say. "But I think you need this." And she would produce the tea and perhaps a few sweet cakes or biscuits. Robyn noticed, though, that if Abi arrived Khamis would quickly go, slipping away like an afternoon shadow slides into the evening.

Abi saw her once or twice and made a few grumbling comments:

"What's she doing here at this time?"

Or: "Doesn't she ever get her work done?"

Robyn noticed that Abi, who did seem to be prone to possessiveness, never seemed jealous of Khamis. The woman just wasn't on her radar in that way.

Though Khamis was loath to talk about herself, in the long stretches of time in those afternoons when they were together, Robyn asked her questions and she eventually relented.

"You're Melantheran?" Robyn asked.

The woman nodded: "I was born in Melanthera, but my family was from Piroush."

Robyn remembered some reference to Piroushi dancers in the information she had compiled on Elanthia.

"Piroushi are dancers? You are famous for it?" Robyn asked.

The woman laughed as if she'd made a joke:

"Among other things," she answered.

The woman was so gentle, so full of a sort of grace, that though Robyn had hundreds of things she wanted to ask her, she didn't want to intrude on that core of her being that Khamis seemed to want to keep secret. So the questions and answers came in fits and starts, gradually and softly.

"How did you come to work here?" Robyn asked one day.

"Oh," Khamis replied. "I thought you would know that. They take a work quota from the camps. For us the money is very good and we can send it back to our families, those that are left."

"The camps?" Robyn asked. "There are camps."

Khamis looked at her as a parent looks at a child, indulgently, but with a slight edge of annoyance.

"The refugee camps. All the Melantherans here are from the refugee camps. After the war there were many refugees."

She wanted to ask more, but, as usual when the questions became uncomfortable, Khamis slipped away saying she had work to do.

Another day Khamis asked her a question, asking what she did.

"I'm a sort of historian," she said, not sure if the woman would understand. "I compile histories of the outer planets, so that everyone can read them. I did some work on Elanthia."

Khamis for the first time grew upset, even angry:

"Make sure then that you tell the truth. They tell so many lies about Melanthera, about us."

The anger flared briefly, but disappeared as quickly; as swift and soft as Khamis slipping out of Robyn's room through the service door.

Though Robyn had found her time with Khamis surprisingly pleasant, it had also been somewhat frustrating. There were areas, things that she couldn't delve into. Khamis would either clam up, and then leave on some excuse, or reply with some throw-away remark like:

"They would say that."

Or: "If you only knew."

Then she asked the woman to tell her, let her know. But Khamis would just say:

"Perhaps one day."

But then one day Robyn got better and that seemed to be the end of her relationship with Khamis. She would make an excuse to come back in the day or leave late for work, but their time never seemed to coincide.

She started back into the routine of work; nights with or without Abi, but mostly with. They fell into the habitual cycles that couples have. The evenings in, searching the Hub for old films to watch together. Their early morning runs, somehow more intense now, followed by the intimate ritual of showering and changing together and then breakfast, as Abi watched the news updates on the Hub. Or the nights when Abi would come in late from a duty rota and Robyn would wake up and share a glass of wine with her, before dozing off together on the divan.

However, every so often, just when Robyn was becoming inured to these changing patterns of her life, just when she was beginning to enjoy them, she would occasionally catch a glimpse of one of the ghost army of cleaners; or in the canteen, at lunchtime or in the evenings, she would look into the eyes of one of the serving staff for just a moment too long, looking for some trace of Khamis in each Melantheran face. Once, just the one time, she found one of those synthetic red roses left in a glass of water by her bed. She knew who had left it, but had to get rid of it quickly when she heard Abi coming in.

Back at work, she tried to make some sort of synthesis of all the information she had found on Melanthera. It was, in truth, a patchwork quilt of sources; she had the text of one poem - the 'prayer to the Star Men' - various logs attributed to Berthaud and a variety of other references from the library's records to flora and fauna, culture and trade. There were still pictures and some film; though surprisingly few of these, probably due to the Melantherans' disdain for these captured moments. She had made copies of the documents and kept them in a password protected folder on the desktop of her workstation, uploading them to her Pad as well.

She tried to figure out a chronology of events. She had documents that covered various aspects of the first contacts that the Sung Yang teams had on Elanthia, particularly with the Melantherans. She then had those logs of Berthaud's which referred to a palace coup, but seemed to imply that there was more to events than initially seemed. The report Berthaud had submitted was untraceable. She also knew, from the brief reference to the "Lament of Asha", that after these events, and not long after considering the dates, Melanthera had been besieged and there had been a final battle. During the siege, Berthaud had become notorious for taking sides.

Then there was the reference to the D.F.'s peacekeeping mission on Elanthia, which must have immediately followed the siege and battle. From Khamis she knew that probably a sizeable number of Melantherans had ended up in refugee camps. It seemed to her that the documents and sources that she had were like the fruit on a tree, perhaps a borriba tree she thought wryly, though she'd never seen one. And each fruit grew on a branch. They in turn grew on a bough, which led on the solid, monolithic trunk and down to the roots below. At the centre of the tree were these various shadowy figures; Berthaud, Berendal and Asha, whoever she was. Somewhere there too, though her analogy became slightly vague here, were the enigmas that were Khamis and her lover, Abi, all connected to this web of deed and circumstance. And, of course, there was that anonymous author of the 'Lament', another spectre at the feast.

Later, after events had toppled on her like a tower of books, she would realise how naive she had been, thinking that she could go on with her side-line, her alternative history of Elanthia. But she had, up to this point, led a privileged life; one of that interplanetary class of people whose professions and skills served the centre so well and were handsomely rewarded for doing so. She had taken her freedom, academic and personal, for granted through all these years she had served the Hub.

Her first inclination of anything amiss was when, one day, Shelby suggested an early lunch, something he wasn't usually in the habit of doing, being a creature of routine and pattern. They made the usual play of words and small-talk as they walked to the canteen, but as they sat in a quiet corner of the dining hall, Shelby's face suddenly turned serious.

"I need to warn you Robyn," he said.

Robyn smiled and suppressed a laugh at first. She thought it was the start of some elaborate joke.

"Robyn, this is serious! I don't know what you are doing, but someone has been in and accessed all the material on your machine."

He told her how one of the maintenance men had visited their work-room on one of her rest days and spent a lot of time on her work-station.

"He said he was installing some sort of update, but you and I know that the maintenance guys always do their stuff after hours. They're rostered to operate in the evenings, when no-one is working; it's easier for them that way," Shelby went on.

"Also," he said, "haven't you figured out yet that there are an awful lot of maintenance men for this facility? Most of them really are technicians, but there are also a number of them who are there to maintain the security protocols rather than the hardware."

Robyn frowned. She couldn't, at first, understand why anyone would be interested in what she was doing. It might have been against some work regulation, some disciplinary code, but it wasn't exactly subversive. She said as much to Shelby.

"Robyn," he replied, "much as I love you – platonically, of course - you are colossally naive. Why do you think there's so much security here? Why is so much encrypted or fire-walled? Officially, the Hub's a filtering mechanism, excluding the irrelevant details, getting to the central core of information, constructing a narrative. That's true, in a way, but it actually constructs a partial narrative, leaving out the uncomfortable, inconvenient facts and pieces of data that detract from that narrative."

He sighed and went on.

"I don't know what you've been doing and, to be honest, I don't want to know, but you've obviously found a stream of information that was never supposed to enter the river. Someone wants it dammed up."

She'd never seen him so serious and suddenly she started to feel scared.

She spent all the rest of the day in a stew of confusion and indecision. She didn't know what to do. That evening she felt too tense to deal with Abi; the woman noticed and commented on how quiet she was. Luckily, Abi was on a night shift, so she didn't have to explain herself, spending all the hours of darkness in an agony of insomnia. In the middle of the night she woke up and retrieved her Pad from her jacket pocket. Though it was against every security protocol that she could think of, she copied the Melantheran files onto a memory card and spent an hour or so thinking where she could hide it. She knew that if they searched her quarters, their electronic surveillance devices could easily detect any Pad or electronic storage device. Then she thought of a place.

It was a forlorn hope, because she was not at all sure if Khamis still came and went or whether another ghost had taken over. She also wasn't even sure if Khamis could read, or at least not Robyn's language. In the end, she decided to leave a small box of chocolates, real chocolates from Theran cocoa beans that she had been keeping for a special occasion that had never happened. She left a note stuck to the box saying:

"A gift for Khamis from Robyn."

Inside she put the memory card under the chocolates with another note:

"Please keep this safe for me. Sorry to ask you to do this, but it's important."

Stupidly - probably because it was in the middle of the night and at that worst time when you doubt that you will ever get to sleep, as the day you don't think you will be able to cope with draws near - she spent ages wondering how to sign off, eventually deciding to add:

"With much affection, Robyn."

After she had written it, she felt that it sounded rather feeble, but was too tired to do anything about it. Then she lapsed into welcome sleep; so deep that Abi, coming in after her shift, didn't disturb her.

Then next day she dragged herself out of bed, allowing herself a minute or two of resentment at the way Abi slept, so peaceful and content, like the proverbial babe-in-arms. On the way to the work-room, just as she was passing Karin's desk, the woman called out to her.

"Did you check your mail this morning?"

In truth, she hardly ever did, as few people wrote to her.

"Well, if you had," Karin went on, "you would have seen a message from Dr. Simeon ordering you to his office first thing."

Robyn tried to make light of it, to shrug it off as unimportant.

"What have I done now?" She asked, not expecting an answer, forcing a smile onto her face.

Karin's blue eyes, glacial and indifferent, looked back at her. She didn't return the smile.

"Yes. I wonder what you've done.

Then she turned away.

All things considered, Dr. Simeon was extremely understanding and even, to some extent, sympathetic. After giving her a stern lecture about the disciplinary offence she had committed in accessing classified information, for which he said there was no excuse, he adopted a more conciliatory tone.

"Of course, I understand the temptation. It is in our nature as Librarians, part of our work, our skill set, to find out information about things and it is so easy to get side-tracked by the lurid and dramatic. To find yourself down some back alley looking into the shadows. I blame myself, in many ways. When you came to me, I should have been more understanding. I should have seen the signs."

He smiled at her in what she supposed he thought was a paternal way.

"I'm sure you've got a ...." he paused, as if searching for an apt word, "good career ahead of you."

He'd obviously discarded 'brilliant', Robyn thought, but at least 'good' was better than 'reasonable'.

"But you have got to understand one important factor of our work."

He stopped again, as if for effect, and smiled at her once more. A wolf looking at a lamb, the wayward notion came into her head.

"We do not only spend our lives ascertaining the truth, we are also guardians of it. We keep the ordinary people away from the darkness, keep them in the light. We must not confuse them, we must not lose our focus on truth, unadorned truth."

164

He poured himself water, not offering her a glass, she noted.

"I think you lost your way, my dear," she winced at that, but didn't correct him. "To paraphrase an ancient expression, you could not distinguish the wood from all the individual trees. But that's what we do, focus on the wood, the whole entity rather than the detail."

She nodded and said nothing, the anxiety of the last day and the sleepless night making her passive.

"There will be a disciplinary procedure. I do not want to pre-empt its findings, but in all likelihood you will transferred off Hanis. I would not think that you will face dismissal. I hope not."

She nodded again, as if that was all she was capable of.

"However, there will also be a parallel enquiry carried out by the security people, as you did access classified material. So you will be suspended immediately until further notice."

With that he dismissed her, sadness rather than anger on his face.

Then it was the walk of shame, back to her quarters, past all her, now former, colleagues. The rumour mill had been grinding away and the blank, noncommittal looks they gave her showed Robyn that they knew she had been guilty of some transgression.

Back in her quarters, she lay on her bed and felt a bit like crying. She was, it was true, rather damp-eyed and felt like a child that had been banished to its bedroom, unloved and unwanted. Then she saw it, another flower in a vase. Another rose. And a note under the glass:

"Thank you for the gift. You are my friend and
I am yours, now and always. K."

Chapter 16
Gamelon And The Churchmen

The saying came into Berthaud's head as she crossed the square outside of the citadel gates:

"First comes the trader. Then the missionary. Then the red soldier."

The square outside the citadel's main gatehouse was really a parade ground, kept clear of people, animals and the market stalls that tended to grow like mushrooms in the rain in every clear space of Melanthera. From the square, the road descended in steep, partially-stepped dusty bends down to the city below, flanked by neighbourhoods of houses that clung precariously to the slopes of the hill.

The view from the square was almost breathtaking. Before her as she walked she could see Melanthera spread out like an illustration in a book of fairy tales, a bird's eye view of the sprawling metropolis, the houses built so closely together that they gave the impression of trying to burst out from the city walls that encircled them, like a belt that was one notch too tight for its wearer.

On either side of the square, gardens built into the hillside made a cool resting and waiting place for those who had business inside the palace and might have to wait or linger to see it done. It was what was going on the garden nearest to her that had brought the quotation to mind. The One God One Church people were holding an open air service amongst the fountains and in the shade of the trees, sermons and singing blasting out over the hot, still square and drifting down to break the silence of a Melantheran afternoon into fragments.

Who had said it? She thought and then, stopping at the edge of the gardens taking refuge from the sun under a tree, she put a search into her Pad. She was in range of the base's network so it was straightforward. She soon found out that the words had been spoken in 1879 by King Cetswayo of the Zulus and referred to his experience of the British Empire. To her it sounded poignant, a lament, even maybe a premonition. Because, from what Berthaud knew of that piece of history, the Zulus had done all they could to avoid war. After it became inevitable, they had even wiped out a whole column of Queen Victoria's red-coated soldiers, but had ultimately been defeated by the sheer industrial and economic power of their enemy.

In this case, in Melanthera, they had been the traders; Sung Yang had won the contract to develop the planet and she was one of the team. It was the same really; there was a parallel. Once the Empress had let the traders in, the One God One Church people - who were sub-contracted to Sung Yang, having tendered for the missionary concession - had followed, as it were, through the back door as part of the whole Sung Yang package. She wondered when the soldiers would come, but then thought that in reality they were there already. She was about to submit her report that afternoon about the events surrounding the attempted coup. She had discussed it with Kev and he had advised her against submitting it.

"Delete it, Marie," he'd said. "You'll just make trouble for yourself. The Empress's days are numbered, unless she does an about-face and agrees to the mining concessions."

She knew he was right, knew that Sung Yang would get what they wanted in whatever way they could, but still she felt she needed to act. Even one voice raised, to alert those higher up the management chain than Carstairs and his team, might find a sympathetic listener, someone willing to act, though the chance was slim.

She pondered things as she sat there, watching the two Barossi guards that trailed her, who had both retreated into a patch of shade. She thought this was very unlike Barossi, who seemed usually to stand to attention most of the day. Perhaps they were getting soft, or lax out of view of their officers. The Empress had sent them as an escort when she summoned her that morning. There was still some unrest in the town, some turmoil, but the presence of even just two royal guardsmen provided a safe passage for her. They were silent and dutiful, walking a pace or two behind her, only speaking when it was necessary and never hurrying her on.

It was not the first time she had been up to the palace and, at first, she had been flattered by the Empress's invitations. But although the Empress was always cordial and the meetings were informal, almost social occasions, Berthaud had quickly got the impression that Her Highness Mila the Third was a wily old bird. While the meetings were ostensibly about Melanthera and were staged to give Berthaud as much information about the place's history, culture and religion that she could digest in one go, they had also turned into a two-way exchange; the Empress finding out as much about the Star People as Berthaud was finding out about Elanthia.

The subject of the coup never came up directly; conversations with Melantherans were anything but direct, they took coyness and understatement to extremes that even the British, in their imperial heyday, had never reached. But they seemed to be doing a lot of hinting.

As usual, it was Berendal who had been most forthcoming. He seemed, somehow, to have attained a favoured position with the Empress; as also had the young woman, the statuesque huntress or priestess, whatever she was, from the western mountains, who was also usually in attendance, seemingly as some sort of bodyguard. It had been one hot, dusty afternoon that Berendal had let the biggest of his hints slip out. They had been drinking the ubiquitous durgan root tea - it was like a tisane of some sort, it, vaguely tasted of liquorice and was not really to her liking - when suddenly he had said:

"Those metal creatures I saw, when I brought Asha to you." He nodded towards the woman, Asha, who as always, remained impassive and silent.

"You call them dogs, do you?"

She had to explain, again, that they were actually copies of dogs; it was difficult to find the vocabulary. Berendal nodded and asked:

"Have any escaped?"

She said she doubted it, too tired and sleepy in the heat of the afternoon to explain that they were incapable of acting on their own initiative. In turn, she enquired why he was asking.

"Oh," he replied, "it's nothing. It's just that Asha thought she saw one down in Piroush."

170

Asha's implacable expression broke open for just a flicker of a second and Berthaud thought that the look she fixed on Berendal was some sort of warning. Whatever it signified Berendal changed the subject, pointing to an extremely attractive, olive-skinned girl who was serving the Empress.

"Have you met Kusha?" He asked." She's Piroushi and you know what they say about Piroushi girls..."

Kusha's beautiful eyes fixed themselves on Berendal and for a moment Berthaud thought she was about to strike him. He quickly finished the sentence:

"They are very beautiful and they are fantastic dancers."

Berendal and the other attendants, including Kusha, started to laugh at this, but Berthaud didn't get the joke. She noticed that both the Empress and Asha retained their dignity, though while Asha's face was as immovable as stone, the Empress had what you would probably call a twinkle in her eye; the slight, discreet suggestion of a smile around her eyes.

On her way back to the base she had thought more about what Berendal had said and had become convinced that he was sending her a message. Even she had heard the story of the attempted assassination of the Empress; Asha's martial deeds were the talk of the market-place, and every time you heard the story the number of attackers grew. Berendal 's remark was odd and frankly absurd, unless he was informing her surreptitiously that Asha had seen one of the robot dogs in or after the attack.

She knew that a special section of the Defence and Protection Unit had picked up two of the dogs a week or so before the coup. The rumour had been that they were headed for the polar regions of the planet, virtually unknown even to the Elanthians, but when the soldiers had equipped themselves from the compound's stores for the supposed mission, they hadn't taken the sort of gear that you would need for an arctic climate and there was no sign of cold-weather clothes or any other polar gear on the cruiser's manifest, as Davies, the very talkative Tech, had pointed out. In fact, there'd been a lot of talk on the base, mostly from the men, speculating on what the real mission of the 'specials' was. In her experience men often had a boyish enthusiasm for these clandestine military operations and the soldiers who carried them out.

The base banter that she remembered took on a sinister undertone now. She did not doubt that Sung Yang were capable of mounting an assassination attempt on the Empress, using some sort of proxy force. And she remembered how Johnson had said there were DPU troops on standby on the day of the coup and the mysterious mission that Carstairs had wanted her for.

So, sitting there in the shade now, it seemed to her that the red-coated soldier was already well on the way to Melanthera and the advance guard had already arrived. She turned what Kev had said to her over in her mind, the inevitability of the thing; that Sung Yang would have their mining concession and Melanthera under its thumb, whatever she did.

Talking of ethics, of her responsibilities as an ethnologist, as she had to Kev, had sounded somewhat hollow; she had after all, with many others of her profession, taken Sung Yang's money. It was the first pay cheque that had compromised her ethics, she thought, so to talk of them now seemed somewhat futile. So she sat there, not wanting to venture out in the sun, thinking of whether she should make her stand or just let it wash over her.

She turned to distract herself and looked at the gathering around the One God One Church people. The audience members were few and those that listened had spread themselves out under the shade of the trees. The height of the afternoon was a bad time to draw Melantherans out of their houses and away from their siestas.

The crowd seemed to be comprised of what was generally referred to as 'ruffians and market scum'. The indigent and the iniquitous, she thought. A hard house to play for, as they used to say, before entertainment became virtual and remote, flesh replaced by shapes evoked from electronic static. She did, however, notice one familiar figure in the red robes of a priest. Gamelon, she thought his name was. He was often in attendance when she visited the Empress and would, if not cut short by a wave of the imperial hand, bombard her with questions about the Star People.

She didn't really understand their priesthood; it seemed a fluid profession, encompassing someone like Gamelon, who seemed to have no particular religious duties, or at least none that were clear to her, as well as more orthodox clergy. He was, it seemed, some sort of historian, so she should have felt a certain academic kinship with him.

It was the same with the Sisterhood. She could not really comprehend the subtle relationship they had with the people; they had a spiritual role it seemed, but were also healers and sages. They were even warriors, unless Asha was an exception to the normal rule. She wondered if Gamelon was here to add another chapter to his history or whether he'd come to get some professional tips. Who knew? When she stood up to go, he saw her and raised a hand in acknowledgement. She waved back.

Gamelon saw the small Star Woman leaving and waved to her. She had been a bit of a disappointment to him, as she didn't seem to be as enthusiastic in exchanging knowledge as he was. From what he understood of the Star People's strange society, she was some sort of historian too, though everything she was told seemed to go into the small box she carried, whereas a Melantheran historian had to keep it in his head and then write it all down laboriously on Hvass skin. He had to say, though, that she was one of the most approachable of the Star People, not like those guards who had, more than a couple of times, treated him with suspicion at the gates of the compound.

On balance, he liked the woman, but it was difficult forming a friendship with her, professional or otherwise, as Berendal had a tendency to keep her to himself. He seemed to dance attendance on all of them, all the Star People, always sniffing around the compound, but he particularly seemed to like this Berthaud. Gamelon did think it was quite humorous the way Berendal's currency had suddenly soared in value; it was all about being in

174

the right place at the right time. Though it was generally held that he had acquitted himself bravely at the Hwrathka gate.

Gamelon shifted his attention back to the man who was giving the sermon, a tall white haired-man in the matching jackets and trousers that the Star People wore, with a white sleeveless robe thrown over it. He was asking the crowd, beseeching them almost, to let God into their hearts. This was one of the problems that he had with their religion, one of the contradictions. If God, as they seemed to be saying, had created them and was omnipotent, why did they have to 'let' their God into their hearts? Surely he could come and go as he wanted. He also understood that their God had allowed his son to be sacrificed for the sins of the people. This sounded rather unfair to Gamelon and, again, if he was so omnipotent why had he let it happen?

What was also confusing was the idea of one indivisible god, that also was divided into three persons. He was especially confused about the Holy Ghost. He could never find out what that aspect of their God really was. He'd talked to the OGOC people at length, but they were surprisingly vague about this spirit. Earlier in the day he'd tried to explain the Melantheran approach to the gods to one of the missionaries, a callow, yellow-haired youth with bad skin and protruding teeth.

"We like having many gods," he'd said, "that means they don't get lonely and feel the need to intervene in human affairs." Like your god does, he nearly added.

"Besides, there's a lot of work for them to do and this way, with so many of them, they don't have to be busy all the time and can specialise."

The youth had nodded inanely in response. He knew these missionaries didn't understand, however impressive their efforts to learn the Elanthian languages were. Unfortunately, knowing words didn't always bring understanding of their meaning.

They'd been open to his advances, had spent some of their time talking to him it was true. He'd even had one or two meetings with the white-haired man giving the sermon, Archdeacon Andrews. But Gamelon had soon learned that though the missionaries would talk, they wouldn't listen. They feigned an interest in Melanthera and its culture, but only so they could more easily sell this new religion to them. And to Gamelon it was like the pitch you'd get from a market trader selling borriba grapes; slick, subtle, but not altogether truthful.

The Elanthian religions weren't keen on proselytising. In Melanthera, the priests and sisters tended to think that it was up to people to embrace their own religious affinities; it was a matter of personal choice. The Piroush were renowned for their godlessness, making the occasional offering or dedicating the odd festival to their sleepy, indolent deities. Among the Hvassara, the cult of the sky god was the only allowed religion, and they and the Barossi were famously intolerant of other faiths, but in general, throughout Elanthia, missionaries, and their inherent need to convert the unfaithful, were rare and exotic beasts.

The white-haired man ended his sermon in their customary way, with a holy song:

"All people that on earth do dwell sing to the lord with cheerful voice."

Gamelon could see that it was the white-haired man and his acolytes around him, all similarly attired with a white robes worn over their ordinary clothes, who were doing the singing. Even though the words had been translated into Melantheran, the crowd just seemed to be humming or making whatever noise they saw fit, so that the surprisingly sweet and really quite melodious singing got mingled in with a cacophonous discord emanating from the more over-enthusiastic members of the audience.

He also noticed that the guards standing behind the OGOC people did not join in the singing. They mostly looked bored and hot, standing there in their black-visored helmets, their body armour catching the sun, their hands always close to those short, blunt-barrelled weapons they carried. He'd heard from one of the palace servants how, during the time the Empress was away, Kal Quintal had asked for a demonstration of the Star People's weapons and, it was said, had been very impressed and probably a little intimidated by their power. He'd never seen one fired, but knew that in some way they threw little pellets at great speeds from their barrels and these could go through a man. He'd told Asha about them, but all she'd said was;

"There's little honour in fighting with such things."

But she was a throwback from a past age and he knew that many of the generals had understood the uses that such fearful implements could be put to.

177

When the singing was over, Archdeacon Andrews had invited the audience to eat with them:

"Friends, break bread with us. Drink deep with us, as you would drink deep of His spirit, His charity, and His glory."

It was the signal the crowd had been waiting for; they fell on the tables that the OGOC acolytes were setting out like ravening beasts. Soon people were fighting over loaves of bread and Andrews, looking uncomfortable, shouted out:

"There's plenty for all brothers and sisters, be patient."

The harvest had been bad that year and there were plenty of hungry people in Melanthera. No-one was starving, the Temples and the Sisterhood saw to that, but nobody really had their fill of food either. Gamelon could see that the guards were looking nervous and were glancing at each other. One or two had lifted their weapons, so he stepped forward.

"Behave yourselves!" He shouted. "These people are strangers, guests. Let's not leave them thinking that we Melantherans have no manners!"

His speech did have some effect, some of the crowd did grow a little shamefaced, but what he said next had even more effect.

"I can have some of the Empress's Barossi here in seconds and they are so hot and bored that they'd love to break a few heads, so behave and take your turn."

Though the concept of the queue was totally alien to Melantherans, the crowd did stop jostling and formed a vague sort of line, grudgingly giving way to their neighbours. The Barossi had a fiercesome reputation, so they didn't need a second warning. It turned out that Andrews had spoken the truth; there was plenty of food, so that fact also calmed the people down.

As Gamelon approached the tables, determined to see that his instructions were carried out, Andrews detached himself from his companions and approached him.

"Thank you, friend," he said, "for your assistance. You are most welcome here. Though we wear different robes, we are both fellow men of God."

The difference was, thought Gamelon, that he didn't have to bribe a congregation with food or have armed guards standing by to back-up his message. He did, however, out of politeness, allow Andrews to take him aside to a low bench by a fountain and took the fruit juice that the man proffered, rather disappointed that it wasn't wine. Perhaps, he thought as he sat there, we can have an intelligent conversation about religion, an exchange of mutual respect. Andrews sat by him and started talking:

"Now, friend, let me tell you about our God. The one True God"

Gamelon made his excuses and left.

Chapter 17
The Prisoner Of Hanis

The news of her suspension didn't go down well with Abi:

"For goodness sake, Robyn, what did you think you were doing?"

Robyn was temporarily abashed; it was a new side of Abi she hadn't really seen before, an angry side.

"I didn't know that it was classified," she replied, though she knew she was not being completely honest with her lover. "I admit, I got carried away and should have realised I was getting mixed up in security issues, but I just thought it was commercial stuff. I thought it was restricted access because it was economically sensitive, honestly."

"You don't get it Robyn do you?" Abi almost spat the words out. "It's all the same. If something's classified, if it's secret, if you access it, you've breached security. Full stop! Get that into your stupid head!"

Abi was really furious now and was shouting, ranting at her. Robyn wondered for a moment if the woman was going to hit her. She would hit her back, even though Abi was stronger than her and, after all, a soldier. Robyn had done martial arts classes, for fitness it was true and she'd couldn't quite remember when she had last hit somebody, but she'd put up some sort of fight.

But abruptly Abi calmed down and sat down on the couch sighing:

"I'm just so disappointed, Robyn."

Robyn tried to make it up with her, tried to be sorrowful and penitent, but, in truth, she thought Abi was over-reacting. Soon though, it was all academic. Abi had collected the few things she had left in Robyn's quarters and was standing by the door.

"We need to take a break, Robyn, until this is all over."

The anger had gone now, Abi's face was a mask of misery. As the door slid open, she turned briefly:

"For god's sake, I've got my career to think of. I could be the one who ends up interrogating you."

That was it. The end of Abi. Robyn didn't really think they were taking a break. Rather she saw Abi as the crew taking to the lifeboats as the good ship Robyn sank beneath the waves. She told herself she wasn't going to cry, but she did, of course. She lay on her bed and tried to stop her head spinning, to somehow still that incipient throbbing just behind her forehead that she knew was the precursor of a headache. It was when she had laid her head on the pillows and smelled the perfume of Abi's hair and skin on the pillow-case that the tears came. She suddenly felt so lonely, so isolated here. Her job, her career, was fast disappearing down the toilet bowl and that tentative, hesitant relationship she was building with Abi had suddenly been blown away, like a handful of the planet's red dust, blown to the four corners of the place.

But after a while, after she had cried herself out, she remembered Khamis's note and knew that she had at least one friend here. She so wanted Khamis to come, to slip into the room in the way that she previously had, but, of course, she didn't. No-one came that morning and in the afternoon the only visitor was another of the cleaners; an older, moon-faced woman, who didn't seem to understand. when Robyn asked about Khamis, tried to ascertain why this new woman had taken her place.

That wasn't the only visitor that she had. In the middle of the afternoon, just as she was planning to go and have a run, to brave the gauntlet of accusing or sympathetic faces, the door buzzer sounded and she opened it to two security guards, dressed in their black uniforms. One of them was familiar; she was sure that she had seen him dressed as a maintenance man before, but she wondered if her mind was playing tricks.

The taller one of the two, a young, fit-looking man with cropped hair and a thin angular face, gave her a command as soon as he entered.

"Sit down, Ms. Harper!"

Though these were her quarters and they were the intruders, she meekly obeyed.

The tall man sat down opposite her on the second divan, but the other man - the erstwhile maintenance man, a middle-aged fellow, with a freckled complexion and red-hair that was now nearly gone - stood as if on guard by the door.

"Ms. Harper," the tall man started, "we have a serious, a very serious, matter to discuss with you. I am conscious that you have been suspended from your job for accessing classified material. That is an ongoing issue and will be dealt with in due course."

He sat back, seeming to relax, but his eyes, keen and cold, never left hers.

"But there is another issue. It appears that the material you accessed was copied and taken out of a secure environment."

Without speaking, Robyn got her Pad and handed it to him. She thought that would be it, but he looked slightly surprised by her action.

"Ms. Harper," that title again, she wasn't used to being called that, "you'll find that all the files on your work-station and on this machine have been erased. They were, in fact, erased yesterday, remotely and at the same time. I'm referring to the fact that you copied the files onto another device, probably a portable memory of some sort."

Robyn felt a sick, cold feeling of panic hit her stomach like a punch in the gut. How could they know? She thought. Had they taken Khamis? She could only imagine how much trouble the girl would be in if they had.

"I'd advise you not to say anything, Ms. Harper. I would suggest that, instead, you think deeply about your situation. We know that you copied the files. We also know that they are not in your quarters. That suggests you passed them to somebody, which in turn makes your crime - and yes I did say crime - more serious. It's one thing accessing classified information, but attempting to disseminate it can be classed as subversion. Rather than a rap on the knuckles, you could be looking at a custodial sentence."

He stood up:

"We'll leave you now. To think about what you've done. You are confined to quarters. Your door will be locked remotely. You can expect to be interrogated in the near future and then transferred to a holding facility. Your only option is complete honesty and co-operation."

He left then, the door swishing open. The older man, before he too departed, looked her up and down.

"You silly bitch!" He said as he walked through the door.

Robyn was shaken, suddenly the enormity of what she had done struck her. But at the same time it all seemed unreal, a gross over-reaction to her actions. She'd compiled a collection of files on Elanthia, not passed on military secrets to some enemy. She picked up her Pad, to check if the files had truly been deleted and saw that she had message. It was from Shelby:

"Keep your chin up, kid!" It said.

She typed out a reply and tried to send it, but realised that her access to the wireless network had been somehow jammed. They'd cut her off from the outside word. She tried her door control, just to check if they had sealed her in. The door wouldn't open, so it was true. They don't need prisons, Robyn thought, they just alter your door code. They don't even have to leave their desks to do it.

Because they'd cut off her access to the network, she couldn't even access the Hub to watch the news or find an old film, so she lay on her bed and thought. What should she do? Part of her wanted to come clean, to tell them everything, as if wiping the slate like this would somehow erase what she had done. It might work she thought. She was probably going to end up in jail, but everyone knew that there were prisons and there were prisons. A top security jail on Hephaeston was a lot different from a minimum security establishment on Thera. She let her mind embark on a day-dream; perhaps Esmee would visit her, the hard-bitten con, and, when she was released, there would be a reconciliation. She might even increase her sexual attraction, with the added allure of notoriety.

There was, however, one problem with this. To throw herself on their mercy she'd have to sell out Khamis. Khamis, who was only doing her a favour, but had inadvertently engaged in what they would invariably describe as a subversive act. She also knew, at a visceral level, or, at least guessed, that what they would do to a Melantheran would be worse than what they would do to her. So, she decided, there was nothing else for her to do; she would have to be brave, to tough it out. But she had no idea of what she might face.

Someone brought food for her that evening, a female security guard, brusque but not unkind. To Robyn it seemed that the woman looked at her with a degree of sympathy, like you would look at someone who'd done something stupid. She had a bad night, then just after she had eaten breakfast they came for her, the same two.

They took her with them to the lift and then down to a level that she'd never been to before. The walls here were unfinished, and, unlike the interior of the library, there had been no attempt to adorn the place or pretend it was anything more than utilitarian. They did not use handcuffs or restraints of any sort. There was, after all, nowhere to run. They took her to a featureless room, all white with nothing on the walls. A table and three chairs the only furniture. Then they left her there for what seemed an age.

After an interminable time - during which she was careful to try and keep calm and not show any signs of fear or panic knowing they would be filming her - the door opened and, to her surprise, Abi came in. She didn't say anything, but took the chair opposite her. They were both silent for a long while and then Abi spoke, her voice cold and calm, the consummate professional.

"They've given me a few minutes with you, Robyn, to see if I can get you to be sensible. You really have no option now, but to totally co-operate with them. You will definitely be charged with an offence, all you can do now is to mitigate the seriousness of that charge. Just tell them everything, tell them what happened to the files and you've got a chance, a good chance I think, of emerging at the other end of this mess."

With that she stood up and, just as she passed Robyn, briefly touched her cheek. It was just a slight, brush of the fingertips, but to Robyn it felt like an embrace.

Later, in her quarters Robyn would go over the interrogation in her head. The tall, fit one had done the talking. He'd kept asking the same questions, trying to catch her out, but she'd stuck to the story she'd thought up. She told them, admitted, that she had copied the files onto a memory card, but she said that, in a panic, she had thrown it away down the rubbish chute in her kitchen. The rubbish went straight into the heating plant, so there was no way for them to check. Inwardly, she'd thought that her story was plausible, but it hadn't convinced the tall man. After what seemed like hours, he finally finished his interrogation.

"Well, Ms. Harper, it's out of my hands now," he said. "I find it hard to believe your story. Very hard."

He sighed, ran his hands over his face and his voice, when he again spoke, sounded sorry.

"You will be taken to a facility where they have the means of finding out the truth. I hope for your sake what you have told us today is the truth, or it will go badly with you."

With that he stood up and left the room, leaving her with the red-haired man, who also stood up, crossed to Robyn and slapped her hard across the face. Then he left, not saying a word.

The tears came to her eyes. They would of course, she told herself, anyone's eyes would fill up if they were slapped. She worked hard to stop herself crying more, knowing that they would be watching her. The slap sobered her. She wondered how she would hold out against that sort of physical brutality. She just wasn't inured to it. She'd had an easy life really, well-fed and nurtured, not having to scrabble for a living or live on the mean streets of a slum or a refugee camp like Khamis. She remembered reading something about Earth's Second World War. How the German secret police, the Gestapo, had tortured Allied agents. How it had been accepted that they would always break under torture, that they were told to hang on long enough so that their comrades could get away or relocate before they inevitably told all. She must do the same, she thought, hang on for Khamis. Though, truthfully, she doubted how long she would be able to hold out.

Later, after they had given her time to stew in her own thoughts, or so it seemed, the woman security guard came in to take her back to her quarters. Robyn's lip hadn't been cut though it felt sore and bruised. He'd also caught her nose, which had bled slightly. She felt as though she had a black eye, but wondered if it would show so soon. The woman was surprisingly gentle and solicitous as she led her by the arm, as tenderly as a parent.

Before she left her she hovered in the doorway for a moment:

"I'll bring you some more food later," she said. "I'll also bring you something to put on your face. It probably feels worse than it looks."

She hesitated, turning to go, then added:

"There's been a run on cruisers, some trouble up at the SSC mine, so you'll probably have a bit of a wait before they transfer you."

Then she was gone and Robyn went straight to the bathroom cubicle to look at her bruised, battered face in the mirror. The woman had been right, it didn't look that bad; there was a smear of blood beneath her right nostril that she wiped off and her nose was looking slightly puffy on one side. Her right eye, or at least the skin around it, looked a little bruised and was discolouring slightly. She turned and went back into the main room and through into the bedroom, taking her clothes off, trying to throw off the cold, clinical smell of the interrogation room which clung to them. As she was taking her robe from the wardrobe, she glanced at the table by her bed and saw the note:

"You are not alone. We have sent our prayers to Elanta, to protect you. Your friend Khamis."

Chapter 18
Harradim Hearts

As the ranked masses of the Hvassara horse archers galloped around Asha's small command, riding in ever decreasing circles, coming closer and closer to the front rank where the Melantheran pike men stood, dusty and unmoving phantoms in the shimmering heat of the morning sun, Berendal said, under his breath so that no-one else would hear:

"This wasn't one of the Empress's better ideas."

But Asha's hearing was keener than he'd thought and she turned to glare at him. He knew that the questioning of Mila's orders was a sacrilegious act to her; those western mountain tribes treated the Empress as if she was a demi-goddess, but the Melantherans were more sanguine and sophisticated. He was dusty, though, and thirsty. The kobo-flies were biting, like malevolent little demons, and he was in no mood to apologise. Besides, at that moment he was in mortal fear of his life. Asha's hand had gone to the hilt of her sword, so he followed suit, even though his short, curved blade looked rather pathetic besides that great weapon of hers.

But, suddenly, the Hvassara stopped as if on one unspoken command and a choking cloud of dust rolled over them. Asha's hand relaxed and she turned to Gamelon, who stood the other side of her, the red hood of his robes up and over his face to keep off the sun, the dust and the flies.

"It's as I told you," he said, "that's the manoeuvre they call 'the wheel of battle', next comes the final flourish!"

His muffled voice seemed almost enthusiastic and then Berendal heard it, the sound of a thousand insects in flight, a buzzing and hissing, as hundreds of arrows were launched into the air and fell like a deadly rain. Now's the test, Berendal thought, of whether this is just the way they welcome allies or how they greet unwelcome visitors. Whether the arrows fall on us or around us.

But when the dust cleared, blown away by the eternal wind, he could see around the perimeter of their small force that the arrows had fallen just short of the front ranks of their men, for all the world like a bizarre, low fence that marked their position and separated it out from the desert around them.

"It's just as you said," he turned and spoke to Gamelon, who had let the hood slip from his face, "and it was quite a dramatic greeting."

"You sound surprised," the priest laughed, "and I must say that you looked a bit perturbed and uncomfortable a little while back."

Asha stood between them, silent as usual, but looking singularly unimpressed. Then, after a few moments, she remarked:

"It will take them an age to pick up all those arrows."

Then she abruptly walked away.

It was still something of a surprise to Berendal that he had ended up on this mission. A few short weeks before he had been back in Hwrathka Square, hanging about his old haunts in the market quarter. His sojourn at the palace had been ultimately short-lived and it was all, or mostly all, to do with Kusha. He felt that she was, in many ways, mostly to blame, because of the fact that she was such a vision of beauty. In truth, though, he had found her fey and fickle and somewhat impervious to his charms and, more disastrously, to his poetry.

There had been, after all, a problem of rank and social position. The Empress's old chamberlain had taken him aside one day and tried to give him a subtle, vague warning, talking of the purity and quality of the ancient blood-line of Piroush, how untainted it was. He realised some time after the meeting that the old man had been, by implication, denigrating his own standing in Melantheran society. In point of fact, by such standards, he was not worthy enough, in a number of ways, to pay court so obviously to a Piroushi princess. Class and social status could be surprisingly fluid in Melanthera, but even so, there were limits.

The affair had come to a head when he wrote what he thought was one of his best love poems, entitled 'the jungle rose of Piroush'. The poem told the story of the quest for the rare, fabled jungle rose of Piroush and how a young man had travelled far and faced many ordeals to find the rose, which, when he plucked it, turned into the fairest maiden, who surprisingly seemed to have the same hair, eyes and fair face that Kusha had. He might have got away with the close similarity had he not then gone on to describe the maiden as a having a 'vulva like a honey pot'.

He'd been very proud of the simile, others had been less impressed. Asha, who seemed to be overly protective of the two Piroushi princesses, Kusha and

192

her friend Annesh, had been livid. He had not even officially launched the poem yet, he was keeping it for one of the afternoon audiences that the Empress held in the palace gardens, where dancers, singers and poets would vie to win her favour and approval. He'd only read the poem to some of the serving girls, when they'd been about the laundry in the kitchen yard, and, though they had giggled, they'd seemed quite taken by its romantic sentiments. Servant girls, in his experience, always went moist-eyed at any mention of love or hearts aflame with passion.

The servant girls must have told the other servants and, through the usual palace rumour mill, the fact and content of the poem must have got back to Asha. When she'd eventually found him, off guard as it were, sitting sleepily in the mid- morning by one of the fountains after too much wine the night before, she'd lifted him up bodily with her two hands, slapped him and dunked his head in the fountain. It had all been extremely undignified, but luckily not witnessed by anyone else.

It had fallen to the chamberlain to send him packing. The old man had said that, while the Empress still had affection for him, she had thought it best that he no longer lived in the palace. Neither of them had to actually state the reason. He had been granted a small pension in acknowledgment of his bravery at the Hwrathka Gate and he had been told to keep up his contact with the Star People, particularly Berthaud, and to report back to the Empress at regular intervals. He was also told that, if he valued his freedom and his health, he would abstain from reciting the 'jungle rose of Piroush' in public, as Princess Kusha had a rather irascible father and a number of potentially dangerous cousins.

When he'd left the palace, it was true that he'd felt a bit down-hearted. But as he descended the winding road in the hot morning sun, wearing fine clothes and with money in his pockets, he realised that life, after all, hadn't served him that badly. On reflection, Kusha, he thought, had a tendency to behave like a spoilt child, often the problem with princesses he had found, and he had no doubt that tales of his bravery would be circulating in the market quarter, making the women long to be seen on his arm.

He could also do with some time away from the stuffy confines of that place, where he had been expected to adhere to their arcane and arbitrary codes of behaviour. Things always had to be done in a certain way and there were so many taboos and restrictions. And there was Asha, always watching him it seemed, always there at his shoulder if he was sneaking another skin of wine from the kitchen, or always turning the corner when he was trying to coax a kiss from one of the servant girls in some dark corner of the palace corridors.

So the world had seemed as new, when he walked down to the town from the palace that day. And, it was true, he had spent what seemed an immeasurable, almost endless time of drinking, dancing and paying court to as many women as he could, steering clear of Piroushi girls this time, his heart still too tender. It had not all been pleasure, though, as a number of times he had been up to the palace with Berthaud, who seemed more and more keen to gain a hearing from the Empress. To Berendal's chagrin, he wasn't always privy to these conversations. The two women would often closet themselves up alone to discuss things. Such was the trust that was placed in Berthaud that the Empress would not even have her Barossi guards in attendance.

It was after one of these meetings that Gamelon caught up with him as he crossed the square alone in front of the palace, Berthaud having departed some time earlier. He had come to know the priest in his time in the palace; the man was ubiquitous and talkative so you could hardly avoid him.

As they walked in step down the road that led back to the town, the priest told him of the latest task the Empress had entrusted him with.

"The Lady Asha has been commanded to lead a diplomatic mission to the Hvassara and I've been ordered to accompany her."

This surprised Berendal. He'd noticed that Asha was always referred to now as the Lady Asha - rather than just plain Asha - after her meteoric rise at court. He'd often felt that she should, really, have been just a little bit more grateful to him for introducing her to the Empress in the first place, but Asha wasn't one to express gratitude, even if she felt it, or any other feeling if it came to that. But he was somewhat taken aback that Asha had been picked for a diplomatic mission, as she was neither subtle nor tactful.

"I was brought up on the eastern plains, just on the frontier, so I speak Hvassara and know their ways. I was honoured to be chosen."

"I'm very glad for you, brother priest," Berendal answered, wondering why the man was telling him this and whether one of the pleasure houses that were strung along the road was open and served wine that was drinkable.

"And I'm glad for you, brother poet, as you're coming too."

It transpired that the affair of the 'jungle rose of Piroush' had become more entangled; somehow a copy of the poem had reached Piroush. This was not surprising in itself, as the merchants and traders that travelled the length and breadth of the Empire, would always carry more than just trade goods; letters, poems and works of literature were often bundled up and borne along with the merchandise. The hvass skin scrolls didn't weigh much and people were avid to read anything they could lay their hands on.

There was a delegation from Piroush due in Melanthera in the next few days and the Empress had thought it advisable to get Berendal out of the way, rather than have him skewered by some Piroushi noble-man. Though he was as irritating as a kobo fly, she still had some affection for him and, besides, he was a useful source of information on the Star People. Also, though she'd told no-one this, she regarded the 'jungle rose of Piroush' as one of his better poems, more subdued and less high-flown in its rhetoric than some of his other ones, though it was true that the ending verged on the pornographic.

So it was that Berendal turned up the next day at the eastern gate, having wrested himself from the arms of the girls at the Hwrathka Gate pleasure house, who had sobbed and entreated him not to go. Like all Melantherans, they were mortally afraid of the Hvassara, and thought that he was going to his death.

The square before the eastern gate was a dismal place of trampled earth and treeless, patchy lawns where armies and caravans had always, from time immemorial, been marshalled in readiness for the dangerous, often deadly, road to the east. Outside the walls were the tanneries and the shambles; all the dirty, undesirable industries that the city needed but sought to keep at arm's length. As a result of this, a strong stench of dung, rotting offal and piss hung over the square like a malevolent spirit. This was one of the poorest neighbourhoods of Melanthera; only those who could not afford to live higher up, or by one of the other gates, would live here.

A number of ragged and feral-looking urchins watched the soldiers as the caravan formed up. Most of the troops were Melantheran pike men, there were no Barossi in the force as, though the Hvassara and Barossi were neighbours, they were also, as sometimes happens, implacable enemies. There was also some light cavalry, mounted on haras and a force of archers from Piroush. Berendal decided to give these latter a wide berth, just in case. There were no hwrathka, as the great creatures, while formidable in war, were slow moving and not well-equipped for the arid plains and desert of the Hvassara; they needed gallons of water and tons of hay to function properly.

Berendal was surprised by the sheer size of the train of pack animals, but Gamelon, who had greeted him as he strode up, said:

"An embassy to the Hvassara basically involves giving the relevant chiefs as many presents as you can carry. If you want to make a treaty with them, you've got to buy it."

As he mounted his haras, he saw Asha, also mounted, and waved to her. She acknowledged him, but not with any enthusiasm. He wondered if she was still angry with him.

They'd left the city soon after and spent days crossing the plains, the landscape getting drier, the vegetation more sparse, until they were crossing an arid steppe of rolling undulating hills, which seemed to go on forever, nothing else on the horizon in all directions. They spent the nights, when they could, at Harradim oases. Though they were too big a force to be welcome within the caravanserai walls, Berendal could usually persuade Gamelon to share a flask of wine or a cup of kassa on the tables the Harradim set out beneath the stars in the evenings. And once or twice, to his surprise, Asha accompanied them.

On the tenth day they'd encountered the first Hvassara. These scouts had followed them and not made contact, but a day later a larger force had turned up and there'd been a brief parley. When the Hvassara were sure of their peaceful intent, they'd let them pass, following up the parley next morning with their traditional greeting.

"It's a demonstration of their martial prowess," Gamelon told him, as they brushed the dust off themselves and prepared to move out, "it says that you may come in peace, but this is how we fight, how we can roll over you if we want."

Berendal nodded, listening intently, he'd previously had little to do with Hvassara, except, of course, for the mercenaries that he'd encountered at the battle of the Hwrathka Gate.

"There's always been this hostile, but dependent relationship between us and the Hvassara," Gamelon went on. "They are unbeatable on their plains; seldom, if ever, has a Melantheran army bested them out here in their world. But bring them into our world and, if they have to besiege a city or attack a well-defended position, they are at a loss."

The caravan was moving on, their column screened by the Hvassara horsemen, riding in two columns of their own, parallel to the Melantherans.

"The thing is though, they've always needed us. They want the things we have, the things we make; our wine, our food, even our women. They despise us, but they can't really live without us."

The Empress had timed the embassy to coincide with the Hvassara annual assembly of the tribes. This was a coming-together of all the varied and various Hvassara people from all over the vast steppe lands that were their home. Some of the Hvassara groups were antagonistic to each other or even involved in open warfare, but this meeting was the main religious festival of the nomadic peoples, the annual festival of their god. The Hvassara were not a particularly imaginative people and something about living out there on the barren plains made them pragmatic and economical with words; the rendezvous was simply called 'the gathering' and their god was 'the Sky God'.

A day later, the small force of Melantherans came upon the edges of 'the gathering', a vast encampment amidst the plains, on the banks of the main river that flowed through the country from the unseen mountains to the north, the Amatis. It was only the flow of the Amatis, from the snow-capped and desolate heights leagues away, that enabled the Hvassara to come together like this. The arid nature of their land, the lack of water and animal feed, made it necessary for them to live in small, fast moving groups, but the Amatis and the lush grasslands of its fertile banks gave them this one time and place where they could come together.

As the Melantherans passed they got a curious, but mixed reception. Some of the tribes from the furthest east or south had little knowledge of them and they were thus just a curiosity. But some of the groups were more hostile; the women, in particular, throwing hvass dung at them or bearing their arses as a show of disdain. Berendal had never seen Hvassara women before. Unlike the men they mostly went bare-headed, sometimes affecting a grass-woven hat at the hottest times of the summer. They wore skirts rather than breeches, but the skirts were slit at each thigh, so that they could mount their haras more easily. They wore a short sort of tunic of hvass skin, not properly cured, and wore their hair in plaits that they often wound around their heads like a cap. Berendal noticed that both the men and the women tended to piss where they stood, the women crouching down in front of the strangers with no shame or attempt at concealment.

Like their men folk, the women were small and had that strange rolling gait and bandy legs that a life-time of riding had given them. These people, Berendal thought, seemed positively uncomfortable off the back of their haras; the earth to them was best seen from a saddle. As they passed through the various tribal camps, Berendal noticed that many of the women and the children were bathing in the wide pools that the Amatis flooded through as it flowed along the valley.

"They don't usually bathe," Gamelon told him, "there's not enough water for that, so this is a luxury to them. Usually they cover themselves with hvass fat to keep the sun off and to keep warm at night, so, what with the smell of the rancid fat and the uncured hide, you can smell a Hvassara encampment before you even see it."

The women who stood as they passed to peer at them, unabashed by their nakedness, all seemed to be ageless. The sun had burnt them brown and wrinkled the skin of their faces and necks, while the white-yellowish skin below was usually covered up, thus making a strange and striking contrast. Berendal, as a poet, had always been appreciative of all the forms and shapes that female beauty took. From the stark, simple grace of the Moon Maidens of the Western mountains to the full and luxuriant beauty of the Piroushi, he'd always convinced himself that there wasn't a woman from all of the tribes or peoples of Melanthera that wouldn't have an attraction for him. But the Hvassara women were different; there was something quite formidable about them. He wouldn't admit it to himself, but they intimidated him.

He noticed that, though nearly all of his other companions were overwhelmed by awe, curiosity or just plain fear, Asha as usual sat unmoved and implacable on her haras. He knew that she usually avoided riding, that she was uncomfortable on an animal's back, so he wondered if, in part, her stony-faced self-absorption was due to trying to keep her seat on the creature. Gamelon had told him that she'd wanted to walk, as usual, but the Empress wouldn't allow it; the Hvassara would have scant respect for a leader who wasn't mounted.

As they passed through the various camps, they saw the portable sky-altars; strange shrines of banners, flags and animal skeletons which were the only vehicles the Hvassara had. They'd carried or dragged them before they borrowed the idea of wheels and wagons from the Melantherans. The other sight they saw as they passed the camps was prisoners; either slaves going about their work or chained prisoners of war, usually Barossi, looking strange without their customary face veils; having been stripped of all their clothes, their big, muscular bodies seemed pale and vulnerable without their long shifts.

In Berendal's long talks with Berthaud - usually as they walked around the city on the way to, or back from, some new thing he had thought to show her, Harradim wrestling, a Barossi religious festival or the like - one thing that had always fascinated her was the Melantheran's attitude to slavery. While Melantheran society wasn't a model of equality, even though they were markedly more relaxed and informal than many people when it came to their monarchs and nobles, one thing that marked them out, in anthropological terms, was the lack of the institution of slavery, or anything relating to it like serfdom.

Berendal had tried to explain it to her. It all came down to, or at least so he interpreted it, the personal relationship between the people and their god Elanta. Though she was one of a number of gods and goddesses, she was in some ways unique, as she was, at least in part, the very earth they stood on personified. So, as they came from the earth and returned to it, it could be said that they were owned by the earth, or Elanta. Thus, it followed that one person couldn't own another, as they all belonged to Elanta.

In truth, it probably wasn't as simple as Berendal had put it to Berthaud and the situation with regard to slaves probably wasn't as clear cut on the eastern fringes of the Empire, where Melantherans lived close by and, in some cases, intermingled with Hvassara and Barossi. Even in Piroush, it was not unknown for people, if in debt or fallen into poverty, to indenture themselves for a number of years as servants, but, generally, it was true that Melanthera was not a slave-owning society and the imperial and religious authorities had no truck with slavery.

It was one thing that Gamelon had warned Berendal, Asha and the officers of their military escort about.

"The Hvassara do take and trade slaves. You may even see some Melantherans amongst them. However outraged you, or equally importantly your men, feel about this, you are not to act rashly. We do have a supply of money to ransom Melantherans and others of our allies we find as slaves. But we can't make the Hvassara release them unless they want to."

There had been a general, but reluctant, acceptance of this.

"Before you go, my lords and Lady Asha, there is one more thing," Gamelon continued. "Something you all probably know already, but I need to remind you of it. This is the festival of the Hvassara's Sky God and as part of this they make sacrifices. Including human sacrifices. Usually, but not always, warriors captured in battle. As we are at peace with the Hvassara, they should not have any Melantheran prisoners, but it is important that none of us or any of our men are seen to be interfering with this practise, however abhorrent we find it."

Berendal looked carefully at the Barossi prisoners they passed, wondering if they were destined for this fate, knowing that there was nothing he could do if they were.

They spent an uneasy week or so with the Hvassara, a round of talks and meetings with the various chieftains and uncertain, anxious nights. Some of the young warriors would take delight in riding around their camp in the dark hours and trying to stampede their haras. Complaints about this behaviour fell on deaf ears or were met with shrugs; whichever chief they complained to, always maintained that the young warriors belonged to another tribe.

There was one area of the encampment where they felt relatively safe. A central market area had been set up and traders had come from the Empire and beyond for this one annual opportunity to sell their goods to the Hvassara. The market area was policed and patrolled by warriors who would tolerate no violence or insult to the traders or any other person attending the trade; the Hvassara relished this one opportunity to buy these exotic goods and would not tolerate any interference with the commerce.

A few days into the week, when Asha and Gamelon were meeting one of the chieftains nearby, Berendal feeling bored and listless, decided to take a walk through the stalls. There were few things to divert him in the encampment, he'd soon tired of watching Hvassara women bathing, and a turn around the gaily decorated stalls tended to liven up the days and help him forget the anxieties and disturbances of the nights.

It was there that he saw her for the first time. She was dressed like a Hvassara woman, so he probably would not have remarked her, until his attention was drawn by the beating that her mistress was giving her. He had noticed the elderly woman before, as she wandered around the market with her retinue of bodyguards. He had thought that she seemed fat for a Hvassara woman, as the combination of hard living and scant food supplies kept them thin. She was also loaded up with necklaces and armlets. Instead of hvass skin, she wore a Melantheran silk tunic and trousers of the same stuff. This could well have come from the horde of goods they had brought with them and which Gamelon had already started distributing. Berendal had marked her out as a chieftain's wife or mother and given her a wide berth, consciously trying to keep out of trouble and not looking at the pretty girl slave who trailed her.

The noise drew him; the cheers and the whistles of the audience. He turned a corner and before him saw the spectacle. The onlookers had formed a circle and he had to push his way forward before he could see what was going on. He saw the old woman's arm before he saw her. It was rising and falling, the riding quirt that she wore on her wrist, like most Hvassara, was being used to beat something or someone. As he drew nearer he could see the pretty slave girl on her knees, bent over, her head touching the floor as the old woman whipped her unmercifully on the back and buttocks. In her free hand the old woman was grasping the slave girl's long black hair, pulling it and keeping her on her knees.

Berendal looked around him; there were a number of Hvassara warriors amongst the onlookers and a few of the market guards, who did little but laugh at what was taking place. Almost unconsciously his hand went to his sword hilt, but a hand grabbed his arm and a voice at his shoulder said:

"Friend, I don't mean to interfere, but, if you as much as show your blade, you'll die and they'll probably kill the girl too. Hard as it is, you'll just have to watch and hope the old crone tires."

It finished soon enough; the old woman probably realising that she didn't want to ruin or kill such a valuable piece of property. She stalked off, leaving one of her guards to get the girl to her feet and pull her along behind him. As she passed, she looked straight into Berendal's face, a look of entreaty in her eyes. He could see now that she was Harradim, one of the oasis people, probably taken in a raid. She wore the nose ring and had that quiet grace that Harradim women had. He knew he must help her, despite what Gamelon had told him.

The market trader who'd intervened was from one of the coastal towns to the south and had learnt Melantheran from Piroushi traders. He told Berendal what had happened over a bowl of kassa taken, as he said, to steady their nerves. The girl had gone to fetch a necklace made of bright, opalescent shells from one of the stalls and had been unlucky enough to have the string break as she carried it. The shells had flown everywhere and the old woman had grown apoplectic with anger.

"She is the first wife of one of the premier chieftains, Karas," the trader said, "so no-one will interfere with what she does. She could have cut the girl's throat and the guards wouldn't have done anything, whereas, if you'd as much as looked the wrong way at her, they'd have killed you."

As he bid farewell to the trader, the man said:

"The old woman comes to the market every day. She won't pass up the opportunity to spend some of Karas's money, so take care if you're here tomorrow."

That day, though, marked the end of Berendal's aimless wanderings in the marketplace. Asha, never having appreciated the use of patience, had grown restless and frustrated by the constant delays and excuses that she received from the Hvassara chiefs when she asked for an audience, and had taken drastic action. The chieftains, while avoiding meeting the Melantherans, were avid for the goods they had brought to seal any compact. Every day numbers of Hvassara warriors, aides or officers of the chiefs, would show up at Asha's camp, knowing that they would be given gifts to take away. It seemed to Asha, and Gamelon didn't contradict her, that the Hvassara were playing a deliberate game of taking as much as they could without giving anything in return. So Asha made a drastic move; she let it be known to her visitors that the Melantherans intended to strike camp and depart if a meeting with the chieftains could not be arranged.

This was a risky manoeuvre, Gamelon told her, as the Hvassara were notoriously volatile and might have taken it as an insult or an act of war, which could well have resulted in the massacre of the whole party. But, in the end, the ploy worked. After some angry exchanges with envoys, it was agreed that a gathering of the main chieftains, whose lands bordered the Empire, would be called and Asha could present her case. And Berendal would be one of the delegation. The poet hadn't really considered himself as having any official status; he'd thought that his place on the mission was more a question of removing him from sight for a short space of time. But as the Empress had appointed him, for whatever reason, he was an Imperial officer and had to act as such.

The gathering of chiefs had been set up on a plateau-like expanse of land someway down river, where the steppe dropped to the river valley in a series of stepped, sandy bluffs. The Hvassara chieftains had set up their hvass hide pavilions all around the site, leaving space in the circle at one end for one of the portable sky altars, positioned above the river bluffs, and opposite the sacred wagon, facing towards the endless plain, a wide entrance corridor. When Berendal rode up with Gamelon, Asha and a small escort, they found the chieftains gathered in a semicircle in the middle of the place, flanked by servants and body-guards. They were bidden to sit down a little way off and wait.

"I'm not quite sure what we are waiting for," Gamelon had just spoken, when he was answered by a sound that was somewhat akin to a thousand thunder-claps and also to a thousand hvass stampeding. Hard to describe, but familiar. One of the Star People's sky ships was heading towards them out of the horizon, skimming the steppe like a stone on water.

All was chaos for a few moments, haras reared, hvass ran all over the place, joined by screaming children; women wailed and warriors rode around aggressively, but aimlessly, in circles. The craft set down outside the camp, raising a vast cloud of dust, out of which emerged a number of the Star People all in the same drab green uniforms, except for the escort of soldiers they had with them, dressed in black, armed and armoured.

The Star People, in their turn were conducted into the circle and seated opposite the Melantherans. To Berendal's surprise, one of them waved a brief curt greeting and he recognised Kevorkian. He waved back, earning a disapproving glare from Asha. Melantheran diplomats, he knew, had their dignity to preserve and were above such petty niceties.

Of all the chiefs, Karas was the most imposing, bejewelled and dressed in silk like his wife, but taller and bulkier than most of the other Hvassara. His face bore the scars of battle, his eyes seemed almost hooded and his thin, sharp features seemed to hold no humour or pity. There was a sizeable group of Hvassara women flanking each chief, their wives and concubines, brought with them as another crude flaunting of their wealth, and Berendal could see the woman from the market amongst them. But thought they were attended by numbers of slaves, he could not see the Harradim girl in their company.

Berendal, of course, had no experience of such meetings, diplomacy being an obscure and arcane art to him, but the proceedings seemed enormously tedious. The sun was hot and though awnings had been set up, it was markedly noticeable that the chieftains and the Star People were well-shaded, while the Melantherans had only a few skimpy strips of cloth to serve them. And the wind blew constantly off the steppes beyond, bearing dust and sand that made you itch and cough, making Berendal think that it was no wonder that all the Hvassara he met seemed to always be irritable.

The chieftains, one after another, talked at length, Karas being first and longest. They all had their translators; the Hvassara had men amongst their ranks who spoke Melantheran and the Melantherans had Gamelon; the Star people had someone, but not Berthaud, with one of their translation devices. Each Hvassara chieftain gave a long rambling history of his tribe and then an account of his own deeds and martial prowess. It was all very repetitive, enumerating hvass taken, haras caught and, least importantly it seemed, slaves taken.

When Berendal was almost asleep, it was the turn of the Star People to speak, pointedly asked to go before the Melantherans. Berendal was impressed that one of their number stood up and spoke in Hvassara, rather than using their little machines. Ultimately, the man said very little, professing friendship to the Hvassara and, right at the end and almost as a throw away remark, to the Empire. The Hvassara seemed inordinately pleased by this and deeply touched, which seemed something of an overreaction to Berendal. They stood and stamped their feet in the traditional Hvassara way of applauding, while the Star People did that clapping their hands together gesture that they used, which was strange to the Melantherans as herders used a similar gesture to call hvass.

Then Gamelon spoke. He talked of the long friendship between the Hvassara and the Empire, omitting all the wars and border raids. He said that the Empress had personally sent them, her emissaries, with gifts for her dear friends the Hvassara and she gave them in the hope that their friendship would continue and the peace between their peoples would endure. Gamelon gave, to Berendal's thinking, a good, if rather overblown, address about peace. How men would be able to tend their herds without scanning the horizon all the time for raiders and mothers would put their babies to bed safe in the knowledge that no-one would come in the night with fire and sword to carry them off. However, it didn't seem to impress the Hvassara, there was some foot stamping, but

211

noticeably less than for the Star People, but the latter did, Berendal noticed, politely put their hands together.

Then the talking was over and there were various demonstrations of the Hvassara's martial prowess, all involving riding, archery and swordsmanship in various combinations.

"Is it all settled then?" Berendal asked Gamelon,

"Who knows?" The priest answered. "Hvassara don't sign treaties, and so we just wait and see."

Asha, who had been sitting beside Berendal silently, suddenly turned to him with a smile on her face:

"If we get back to our borders without having our throats cut, Berendal, we can call it a success. And you can write a poem about it. A different and better choice of subject than your last one."

As Gamelon stilled his laughter, trying to maintain some ghost of dignity, Berendal wondered how Asha had suddenly got so talkative and why she had chosen to remind him of his last poem; it wasn't as if she ever read anything. He was wondering whether Asha could actually read, when he saw the girl.

He'd been idly looking around the circle, bored by another display of haras-archers hitting targets while leaning half-way off their mounts, when he looked towards the sky altar just as a crowd of prisoners were being ushered from behind the tents towards the open ground in front of it. They were mostly Barossi, but amongst them he could see that one slim, figure, her black hair and dark skin contrasting with the pale skin of the other prisoners.

212

"Gamelon," he asked, "those prisoners, are they for sacrifice?"

The priest nodded: "The sacrifice will seal what has been said at this gathering. It will make it like an oath to their god. That's partly why they've kept everything vague. They can't break their oath, if it's unclear what's been agreed."

Berendal tried to keep the fear he felt for the girl out of his voice as he asked:

"Most of them are Barossi, but there are some others as well. They're not prisoners-of-war, or are they?"

"Prisoners-of-war, somebody who has transgressed in some way, slaves that have tried to escape," the priest said, "you don't have to do much to end up there. Spill some wine on your master's clothes and you could end up as a sacrifice to the Sky God."

Berendal didn't say anymore, but Gamelon looked at him quizzically:

"I hope you are not thinking of trying to free any of them," he nodded his head in the direction of the prisoners, "that would be foolish. And before you ask, no, they won't sell them to us. They are the Sky God's property now."

Their conversation was suddenly interrupted by a commotion at the entrance to the circle. A team of haras was dragging something heavy into the open ground at the centre. The Melantherans hadn't seen its like. It was a long metal tube, mounted on a sort of small cart. It was being towed by a wagon. A group of Hvassara detached the small cart from the wagon and started, or so it seemed, feeding its mouth. They pushed in some sort of powder, then a round stone-like object. They then stood back as one of their numbers took a lighted taper and touched the back end of the tube.

There was an almighty roar, like the throats of many hwrathka charging into battle, a sound to freeze the blood, and the stone was thrown out of the tube's mouth and off into the steppe, eventually bouncing a few times as it came to ground. That might have been all the more impressive to the Melantherans, if the cart the tube was on hadn't shot backwards as the stone was discharged, causing the little team of Hvassara to run in all directions to get away from it, falling over each other. The cart careered towards the seated conclave of chieftains, who in turn beat a hasty retreat, pushing wives and servants out of the way. The cart stopped well in front of their ranks, but the damage had been done. The Melantherans, instead of being shocked and in awe, were doing all they could to stifle their laughter.

When the chieftains had come back, brushed themselves down and tried to maintain their dignity, it was time for the giving of presents followed by the feast. The Melantheran wagons were brought in and were duly plundered with only grudging thanks. In contrast, the Star People's gifts seemed sparse and ungenerous, but the Hvassara thanked them all the more.

As the food and drink was brought, mostly rough Hvassaran fare - lots of barbecued hvass meat, hvass cheese and yoghurt - Asha said:

"I think the Star People already gave their gifts. That infernal device that we saw, it smells of them.

The Hvassara wouldn't have come up with a weapon like that without help."

Gamelon sniffed at her words: "It will never catch on, Lady Asha, it's too noisy and cumbersome."

The feast also involved endless quantities of kassa. Gamelon had warned them that this was the dangerous part of the proceedings, the Hvassara got drunk and obstreperous early on in the afternoon, and it was important to keep sober and act calmly, ignoring any provocation. Whole embassies had been murdered over arguments involving who took what choice cut of meat.

The feast also involved the mingling of the three parties. This was intended to instil a sense of friendship and peace, but, as the Hvassara got more and more drunk, it became an uncomfortable process. Berendal had just avoided two warriors, who were fighting over a bolt of silk, one of the Melantheran gifts, when he encountered Kevorkian. They managed a halting conversation. Kevorkian had a cup of kassa, which he was staring balefully at. Berendal knew how suspicious the Star People were of any food and drink on the planet, but in this case it would have been rude, if not disastrous, for them to refuse the drink. In truth, they had little to say to each other. The question that Berendal wanted to ask, what the Star People were doing here, was the one that he knew Kevorkian wouldn't answer. Kevorkian made some comment about cheese, and then wandered off.

The feast went on until the end of the day and when darkness fell most of the Hvassara were either staggering or dead drunk, supine in a variety of positions like the remnants of a massacre. Berendal didn't make a conscious decision, he just found himself walking towards the captives, picking a Hvassara knife up on the way, from where its owner had dropped it during some brawl, having left his own sword back in camp.

A fire had been built near the altar, so he had a beacon to guide him by. He slipped around the back of the tents, avoiding amorous couples, and kept to the shadows, pausing when he got closer. He could see two guards huddled by the fire. He could also see that they were passing around a skin of kassa, so he told himself that he only had to wait. It wasn't long until he saw one's head nodding and then the other slipping off into the darkness. He'd thought the man had gone off to piss, but when he started towards the prisoners, he realised that the guard had done the same thing. They were both heading for the same prize, the Harradim girl.

The guard hauled the girl up onto her feet; none of the other prisoners protested and the girl just gave a groan as she tried to balance on her stiff legs, as he dragged her off behind the tents. Berendal waited until the Hvassara had laid the girl on the ground, cut the hobbles on her legs and was loosening his trousers, until he made his move. One simple and fluid motion and the guard was dead, his throat cut. It took Berendal longer to calm the girl, but suddenly she recognised him by what light there was and grew peaceful. He had just turned and was leading her off, when the other guard loomed out of the darkness, coming at Berendal with his short spear.

"I am dead," Berendal thought, "and all over a pretty face."

But a shadow detached itself from the ground and pounced on the guard, just like a mountain cat would; there was a tumble of bodies, a crack of bone and then quiet. Afterwards a familiar voice said:

"Quick, we have to move the bodies, make it look as if they quarrelled over their loot."

It was Asha. She stood there naked, a vestige of light from the guards' fire playing on the planes of her face, the sharp angle of her hip bones and the elastic muscles of her back. They dragged the guards nearer their fire, leaving the Harradim girl in the shadows. They put weapons in their hands, spilled kassa around and scattered the Melantheran gifts that the men had helped themselves to. Berendal was worried about the prisoners, whether they would clamour to be freed, or give the alarm to gain a reprieve. But the few Barossi who saw what they were doing kept silent, stoic as always, knowing that they couldn't save all of them. As a final act, Asha dropped one of the guard's knives near them, to give them a fighting chance.

Behind the tents Asha washed the blood off her body and quickly donned her clothes.

"You'd better get the girl back to our camp." She said. "And be warned, if you're discovered there's nothing we can do for either of you."

Berendal nodded and asked:

"But how did you know?"

"You are easier to read than any of your turgid poems. I could see what you were looking at and I

217

thought I'd better make sure you didn't make a mess of it."

He thanked her, but she answered:

"Don't thank me. It was a stupid thing to do."

Next day they rode out, their mission over. There was disarray in the Hvassara camp; they were told by a Hvassara interpreter that apparently the guards' who had been assigned the sacred task of guarding the sacrifices' had forgotten themselves while in their cups and killed each other over a bolt of silk. It was an ill omen, he said, as most of the prisoners had escaped. They would be recaptured, he told them, afoot as they were on the steppe.

If the Hvassara had counted, they would have noticed that the Melantherans had one extra pike man in their ranks; a small, slightly built fellow, who kept his head down, his face hidden by his helmet.

Chapter 19
Robyn Through The Looking Glass

Robyn did not know if it was the noise that had woken her from her sleep or the nightmare she was having. In the dream the red-haired security guard kept slapping her, over and over again, and she could feel the blood flowing out of her mouth onto her shirt. She put her hand to her mouth and came away with small, tiny teeth. Then, she didn't have a top on and he was leering at her, leaning towards her with a syringe.

She woke, her heart beating so fast it was threatening to burst, her body soaked in sweat, the covers stuck to her skin. Then she heard the noise. Someone was coming through the door; there was no mistaking the soft, hydraulic hiss of the mechanism. It figured that they would come at night, she thought. They wouldn't want any disturbance in the corridors as they dragged her away, kicking, biting and screaming. But, she thought, I'm too scared of them to do any of that. I'll go with them quietly, telling myself the lie that I'm saving my energy.

She really wanted to pull the sheet over her head to pretend it wasn't happening, as if by not seeing them, she could banish them. But then she thought she should dress, rather than be dragged down the corridor naked or in her underwear, which might not be too clean. So she got up, unsteady on her feet and started pulling clothes out of the locker, wondering what you wore for interrogation and imprisonment. Loose clothes, she thought, and then told herself how ludicrous she was to be even considering her options. At least it's over, she thought, all the waiting is past.

But something was wrong. Whoever had entered her quarters was moving around tentatively, more like a burglar than a security guard. For a terrifying moment she wondered if they had sent someone to kill her. It would, after all, clear up all their loose ends. The suicide of a mentally unbalanced Librarian would save them a lot of effort, but then she remembered they wanted information from her. A voice calling in the darkness put an end to these thoughts.

"Friend Robyn. Are you there?" It was Khamis.

The girl came into the bedroom. She was wearing a head torch, which made it look like she had a halo, an angel rather than a burglar.

"I was checking to see if the other one was here," the girl said. "I don't think she likes me and I think she might stop me from helping you."

"Abi's long gone," Robyn said, surprised at how her voice caught on the words and a sob welled up in her throat.

Khamis switched her torch off and put the light on.

"Put these on please, Robyn." She said her name tentatively, as if testing it on her tongue.

Khamis gave her a loose tunic and trousers, the garb of the cleaners and other domestic staff in the Library. There was also a head torch and a swipe card on a lanyard.

"You must be quick," she said. "And you can take nothing with you."

Robyn dressed quickly, smelling her own sweat, wishing she'd had time for a shower. When she was finished, Khamis took her hand and pulled her through the living room and kitchen and out through the servant's entrance into a service corridor.

"But how..?" Robyn started to ask. But the girl silenced her, putting a finger to her lips.

"Later!" Khamis said.

Robyn had never been in the service corridor; she doubted that any of the Library staff had. It was wide enough and high enough for one cleaner and a trolley, with occasional bays that were, she thought, effectively passing places. There were panels set at floor level, which gave some light, coming on as they went by, and she could see the service doors of the various quarters as she passed, with once or twice a lift shaft giving access to other floors.

After ten minutes or so, Khamis opened a hatch in the wall of one of the bays, it was an old-fashioned manual door with a lever for a handle, and signalled for her to put her head-torch on.

"We have a long climb," she said, "two floors down this ladder and then another corridor."

The girl climbed onto the ladder and Robyn followed, closing the hatch as instructed by Khamis before she started descending. At first Robyn was frightened, it was very dark and the beam of the torch only partially lit the way, but as she got into the rhythm of the climb she started feeling that it was all somehow unreal. Was she still dreaming? She asked herself, but then her foot slipped on a rung and the resulting jerk brought her back to reality.

"Take care!" A voice instructed from below her in the darkness.

After what seemed like an interminable time, Khamis opened another hatch and then they were out in another corridor. This one seemed more like a maintenance tunnel; there were cables and pipes all along the walls and they had to stoop to walk. After ten minutes or so, Khamis called a halt, pulling her gently into a low space under a battery of pipes. From somewhere she produced a flask of water and Robyn, suddenly realising how thirsty she was, drank deeply. The Piroushi girl also produced a packet of biscuits and they sat side by side, eating and drinking in silence for some minutes.

"Can we talk now?" Robyn asked and the girl nodded.

"How did you do it? I thought they had locked down all the doors." Having said it, Robyn suddenly thought how it sounded. What she really meant was how did a Melantheran cleaning woman beat a sophisticated security system.

"You still have some friends here," Khamis said, "and my people learn quickly."

She smiled: "They see us pushing the laundry trolleys, serving dinner and cleaning up their mess and they think we're like some sort of dumb animals."

"But what friends do I have.... apart from you, of course." Robyn was strangely touched by the idea that there were others in the Library thinking of her, looking out for her.

"There are others, but I can't tell you who. You know why." Khamis answered.

Robyn thought back to the white interrogation room and nodded. She did know why.

They didn't stop for long. Khamis took her through a maze of maintenance tunnels and then down another ladder. Eventually, she turned a corner in a dark corridor, entered a room and climbed another ladder to some sort of storage loft. In the loft was bedding and some more supplies of food, in packets like army rations.

"We need to sleep now," Khamis said. "It's cold down here, it's not heated like the living quarters, so we'll need each other's warmth. I hope you don't mind."

Robyn, though she was hardly thinking about sex at that moment, did not think that she would take much persuading to cuddle up to this beautiful, young Piroushi woman. But something in Khamis's tone struck her. It was the note of apology. What have we done to these people that they feel they have to apologise for being close to us, being intimate with us? We've turned them into slaves, she thought, we don't name it as such, but it's basically the same thing. We've bred in them in the camps a sense of worthlessness. It made her so angry and sad that she took some time getting off to sleep, though Khamis seemed to have no such difficulty. Once in the night, she woke with a start. Khamis was saying something, calling out in her sleep:

"They're killing the hwrathka." She kept saying it over and over again in distress. So Robyn held her and tried to calm her. The girl's eyes opened once and she smiled faintly. Then she went back to sleep and spent the rest of the night peacefully.

They spent three days in the loft. Khamis explained to her that there was no surveillance on these levels, so they were relatively safe. They'd laid a false trail, hacking into the passenger manifest of a cruiser leaving the library on a shuttle trip to the Hanis transport hub and entering her details, as if she'd used here Library I.D. to board the craft. It was done more to confuse security than to convince them that she was gone.

They'd changed the cleaning crew on Robyn's floor some time ago, after someone had complained about Khamis. Robyn thought that it was probably Abi, and down to jealousy rather than any other suspicion. It had been fortuitous, though, as Security was now less likely to suspect Khamis of being involved in Robyn's escape.

They - whoever they were - had decided that it was not safe for Khamis to go back to work in any section of the Library that was under security surveillance, just in case she was picked up for questioning. The supervisors and under-managers were mostly Melantherans, it was the sort of work that many of Robyn's people regarded as too menial for them to do, so it wasn't difficult to re-assign Khamis.

"We have to be careful, though," the girl said, "there are informers even among my people."

On the second day Robyn got up the courage to ask Khamis about her nightmare and what she had said in her sleep. There was something guarded about the girl and Robyn often felt like she was intruding when she asked personal questions. She'd thought Khamis wasn't going to answer, at first; the girl looked upset and uncomfortable. But then she sighed and said:

"It was something from my childhood. Something that happened in Melanthera during the war. I will tell you one day."

After the third day Khamis felt that it was safe enough to take Robyn to the servants' quarters. These took up nearly a whole floor of the basement and someone, no-one was sure who, had dubbed it the 'Underworld'. It would have been unsafe to try and pass Robyn off as a Melantheran, so she had been given the identity of a Theran migrant worker and assigned to a four-berth dormitory with other women migrant workers.

As Thera was an affluent planet, there were few migrant workers from there. Those that were there would often have some sort of shady past; a criminal record or some past political transgression. A Theran identity was plausible for Robyn; she had, after all, lived on the planet for years.

Khamis had told her that it was only for a week or so, but she still felt bereft being parted from the girl. They'd spent only a few days together, but she'd probably been closer and more intimate with Khamis in those few days than with all her years with Esmee. The fear they lived with had stripped away the barriers. They lived close together, flesh by flesh, the smell of each other's bodies in their nostrils, like animals. And when Khamis said goodbye to her, if only temporarily, she felt her loss keenly, as if the girl was her only link to the real world, her only link to herself, to Robyn.

They'd assigned her a job in the laundry; she needed to do something, or the women she shared with would have got suspicious. Though the washing and drying was all done by machine, she was amazed at how much manual work was still involved, sorting and cataloguing the dirty clothes. Ironically, it wasn't that different from library work, if you substituted clothes for books. It was a lonely time, she would eat in the workers' canteen on her own and spend most of her free time, what little there was, watching films on the public Hub terminal. Initially she'd been a little wary of the women who shared her dormitory. One, an ex-con from Hephaeston with tattoos up both arms, seemed particularly predatory, but the woman turned out to be all bark and no bite. She would, anyway, come back from work exhausted and just want to sleep.

One night, as she walked down the corridor back to the sleeping quarters, in a particularly gloomy mood, thinking that she had, effectively, just swapped one prison for another, someone touched her arm. It was Khamis, standing in the shadows as she turned a corner.

"Come with me," the girl said. And when Robyn started to speak, she put her finger on her lips gesturing for silence. Robyn was so glad to see her she almost kissed that finger.

She led her off down a corridor deep into the Melantheran part of the 'Underworld'. Robyn hadn't been here before and was amazed at her surroundings. They've almost created their own town, she thought. The walls had been painted in the earth colours and sky blue that Melantherans used to paint their houses with, or so Khamis told her.

"It's all against regulations," the girl said, "but nobody bothers us down here."

Khamis took Robyn to a large room that had been painted all around with trompe l'oeil pillars and prospects of fountains.

"This is our temple," Khamis said. And drew her aside to wait as the service, or such Robyn thought it was, came to an end.

It was simple gathering of people in a semi-circle being addressed by an older woman in red robes. Robyn couldn't understand the words, but felt a thrill to finally hear Melantheran, the fluid and fluting tones of the language, the rhythms and cadences. After ten minutes or so, the woman in the red robes finished speaking and, as the congregation filed out, she turned towards Khamis and Robyn, beckoning them over.

"This is Alethea," Khamis said, by way of introduction, "she supervises the bakery by day and in the evenings and on weekends she is a Sister. Do you know what that is, Robyn?"

Robyn nodded.

"I think so," she said.

"Khamis," Sister Alethea said, "it is better if you do not use our friend's name, or use her Theran name instead."

She smiled and looked at Robyn.

"We know that you are a friend and we know how it is you have come to this place, which must really seem like an Underworld to you. As if you have truly fallen from grace."

She stepped forward and took Robyn's shoulders. I'm actually getting a Melantheran hug, Robyn thought, childishly thrilled.

"You should know that, for your safety, we have kept those documents and records that you gave to our daughter, Khamis, and have got them to safety. They will form part of that canon, that history of our world that we are trying to piece together, like one of your jig-saws."

She laughed at this, showing small white teeth.

"All of us are grateful to you, and we know you have suffered. But soon, very soon, we will get you to a place of safety."

A place of safety, Robyn thought, was there such a thing? She felt that she would never be safe again.

Chapter 20
At The Hwrathka Gate

From one of the towers on top of the Hwrathka Gate, Asha looked out at the massed armies of the Hvassara below them. The high midday sun was glinting off the metallic barrels of dozens of the infernal machines that Berthaud had told the Empress were called 'cannon'. Hvassara were digging ditches and raising palisades to protect these weapons; other Hvassara were drilling, out of bowshot, with the smaller versions of the cannon that Berthaud had told them were called 'muskets', which could also throw a ball over a great distance, or so Berthaud said. It was all so unlike the Hvassara, who had always been raiders, known to hit and run, but never to invest a place. Asha pointed the batteries of cannon out to Gamelon, who was standing next to her, a helmet sitting incongruously on his head.

"I thought you said that they'd never catch on," she said. But Gamelon stayed silent.

Berendal, standing by them, was silent, deep in thought. He'd been given command of the Hwrathka Gate again, because of his successful defence of it the last time it was threatened. He somehow doubted that this situation would be in any way similar to the last one and he had little confidence in his abilities to command. He knew, though, that every Melantheran would be called to arms and he was better-placed up here in this gate-house than on one of the long stretches of wall.

It was always the Hwrathka Gate, he thought, this place had figured so much in his days of late and, in truth, he couldn't quite make out if it had a benevolent or a malign influence on the events that were overtaking him. When they'd returned from the mission to the Hvassara, he'd returned to the market square just below them, heading back to his rooms, the Harradim girl following him. He was trying to work out what to do with her. But then Berthaud had stopped him before he had even got home, just as he was introducing the girl to the pleasures of borriba wine on a table outside the pleasure house. She had asked for an audience with the Empress, stressing how important it was that she be seen as soon as possible. Berendal had led her to the palace straight away.

Berthaud had been slightly bemused by the slim, graceful figure of the young woman who followed them, keeping a pace or two behind Berendal. She knew enough about the ethnic make-up of Melanthera to recognise the girl as one of the Harradim, but she was confused to find her there with Berendal. What she knew of the Harradim told her that the women were kept close within their communities and avoided mixing with outsiders if possible. Yet this young woman seemed inseparable from Berendal.

She tried to ask him about it, jokingly:

"Did you get married, Berendal, since I last saw you?" But uncharacteristically he seemed irritated and somewhat worried by the question.

"It's a very big, long story," was all he would say about it, though she was very impressed that he managed to say it in her own language. Say what you would about the Melantherans, she thought - and some of the others like Kev did say a lot about them, not much of it good - but they were bright and quick learners.

She realised that she had grown fond of these people, their zest for life, their humanity and the way that Mila, though practically all-powerful, managed to run a state that was fairer and more equitable than many of the so-called democracies on the inner planets. That was why she had decided to do this, to see the Empress and tell her what was going on. She knew that it meant that she was abandoning the objectivity that her profession demanded, that what she was doing was unethical, but she was driven by circumstance.

There was little formality these days, when she visited the palace. They were admitted by the Barossi guards and taken straight to the gardens, where, as usual, the Empress was spending the afternoon amongst the cool fountains and airy pavilions of the place. Berthaud noticed that she was alone, apart from Asha, who was like the woman's shadow, and the loquacious priest Gamelon. The guards also admitted the Harradim girl, who seemed unwilling to let Berendal out of her sight, making the poet even more uncomfortable. As they stood there waiting for the Empress to finish putting her seal on a number of scrolls, Berthaud was surprised to catch an amused look on Gamelon's face. Gamelon was highly amused by something and it seemed the joke was on Berendal. Asha as usual was stone-faced; does nothing move that woman, thought Berthaud

231

When the Empress had finished, she asked Berthaud to be seated on one of the divans. Asha and Gamelon also sat down followed, more tentatively, by Berendal; the Harradim girl taking up a position on the floor by his divan.

"Your lady, or whatever she is, can sit on one of the divans," Mila said to Berendal, "she doesn't need to crouch on the floor."

"Thank you your Highness," the poet answered her, looking uncomfortable, "but I think she prefers the floor. Long years of habit, you know."

Gamelon was smiling again and Berthaud got the definite impression he was trying hard to suppress his laughter. How surreal, she thought, with what I have to say.

"Friend Berthaud," the Empress said, "you catch my advisor at a difficult time. As you can see from his face, he is worried and concerned about friend Berendal's domestic arrangements. But I think he can put that aside, as I see from the look on your face that you have something serious to say."

Gamelon looked chastened and, suddenly, his attention was on her.

"Can I speak freely, your Highness?" Berthaud said, conscious of the Harradim girl nearby.

Mila turned to the Harradim girl:

"What is your name, child?" She asked.

The girl took a while, stuttering out her name, almost struck dumb by the fact she was in the Imperial presence. She was called Noor.

"Noor." Mila said. "Can I ask of you a favour? Would you go the kitchens and fetch us some cool borriba wine? This guard will show you."

The girl went off with a Barossi.

"I doubt she bears any goodwill for the Hvassara, but just in case," the Empress said and bade her to carry on.

So Berthaud told the story. How the decision had been taken at a senior level to bypass the Empress in their quest for mineral rights. How her people had sent a mission to the Hvassara and opened up negotiations. It had not been a success at first and there'd been a few bad incidents. But eventually the nomads, and one chieftain called Karas in particular, had recognised that, as the Hvassara chieftain had put it: "in a haras race between the Empire and the Star People, you wouldn't bet on the Empire."

Commercial rules meant that Sung Yang couldn't directly intervene in internal conflicts on Elanthia, so they had decided, as an alternative, to persuade the Hvassara to invade the Empire.

"They wouldn't have taken much persuading," Gamelon had responded when she said this. "And we've seen those new weapons they have. I didn't think the Hvassara had thought them up on their own."

Berthaud told them that her people had recognised that the relationship between the Empire and the nomads was balanced. While the Hvassara could dominate the steppe, they were unequipped, practically and in psychological terms, to take on standing armies and fortified positions. So her people had decided to tip the balance.

They had introduced a technology that, though simple in their terms, would usher in a revolution in Elanthian warfare. They had given the Hvassara gunpowder and the means to make cannons and muskets. It was a technological leap, but not too high a jump for Sung Yang to lose the option of deniability. Putting out the story that the Hvassara had invented gunpowder off their own backs was just about plausible; it could be passed off as a natural evolution. It was much easier to explain this away, rather than giving them modern weapons and training. They'd probably even get ethnologist like Berthaud to write learned papers about how the Hvassara had leapfrogged a few stages in their development.

Berthaud stopped and looked at the faces of those assembled there. They hardly looked surprised, it seemed to her that she was confirming what they mostly guessed.

"I probably don't need to tell you that there is a Hvassara army marching on Melanthera, with covert help from my people, the Star People as you call them."

The Empress nodded and, seeing that Noor had returned with a tray, said:

"Take some cool wine to slake your thirst."

She sipped her drink, the cool, sweet liquid was welcome. There seemed to her to be a sad look in Mila's eyes as she smiled at her. As if the Empress knew and well understood the ordeal that they were facing.

Berthaud went on: "I should also tell you that the Star People are going to abandon the base here and evacuate all their personnel."

"So we must thank you for telling us this," the Empress replied, "and bid you farewell."

"With your leave, Highness," Berthaud answered, "and if you can find me quarters in the palace, I intend to stay."

The older woman smiled and said: "You are welcome to stay with us."

Berendal looked out from the tower at the Hvassara army and then turned to look down at the market square. Where the Star People's base had been was just an open stretch of ground littered with debris. They had departed in something of a hurry. He knew that Berthaud was safely settled in the palace, but he wondered how she had managed to detach herself from her people.

His mind should have been on the Hvassara army and the impending siege, but he couldn't help thinking of Noor. When they had returned from the mission to the Hvassara, the girl had refused to leave his side. He had offered to leave her at one of the oases on the way, with her own people, but she had explained to him that, because she had been taken as a slave and ill-used by the nomads, she would be unable to live amongst her people again. She would rather serve him, give him the gratitude that he deserved for saving her life, rather than be an outcast amongst the Harradim. So he had taken her with him, thinking things would change when they got to Melanthera, that she would go off on her own. There would always be work for a pretty girl like her, even if most Harradim women would never become pleasure girls.

The last words Asha had said to him, when he left the caravan at the East Gate were:

"That girl has suffered much amongst the nomads. You should either care for her or make sure she is cared for."

She said this with a serious expression, which then faded to the ghost of a smile:

"I think you may have found yourself a wife, Berendal."

But what Asha had said first was true. The girl had suffered much; the Hvassara were hard on their slaves, the women worse than the men. Noor was fragile, almost broken. And like it or not, and as ironic as it was, Berendal, who'd always been free as the wind, now had someone he felt bound to take care of. He'd never realised before the responsibility of saving someone's life and thought that he should probably avoid it in future.

He was also surprised by the chaste way he treated her, especially since she was such a beauty, but he somehow developed a strange sort of gentleness. All in all, it seemed that the Berendal of old had been somehow changed by past events and now was in thrall to this slim, graceful Harradim girl. He wondered what he'd ever seen in Piroushi girls; he'd now transferred his allegiance to Harradim women.

He turned back towards the Hvassaran army and took up position beside Gamelon and Asha. He knew that the priest and the warrior woman were the Empress's eyes here on Melanthera's walls. They would report back to her and she would make her dispositions in consultation with her generals. But he'd have to stay here with his garrison.

He'd sent Noor off that morning, up to the citadel, leaving the garret rooms that were theirs and

236

had become over these last few weeks a place of unexpected content for him. He knew he would miss her; he had hardly been able to watch as she joined the stream of refugees heading up to the old fortress. Melanthera was full of people from the east of the Empire; whole villages and towns had fled before the scourge of the Hvassara. Many of them had kept on going past Melanthera, no longer willing to trust in the strength of the old city's walls or the will of the Empress. The Hvassara had burst through the frontier like water flooding through a cracked damn and the deluge hadn't only washed over their defences, but it had also carried away many of the old certainties they had clung to.

Berendal heard the sound of horns and Asha pointed to a group of riders who had just rode into the Hvassara siege lines:

"So it is true," the woman said, "look at the standard and the man who rides beneath it."

Refugees had first brought the rumour, then soldiers falling back, fighting a rearguard action just in front of the nomadic horde. There were Melantherans riding with the Hvassara.

"Is that Quintal?" Gamelon asked, though he knew the answer.

"That's him," Asha said, "and let's hopes that the traitor doesn't keep to his tent. My blade is hungry for his flesh."

Chapter 21
Robyn In Melanthera

Just two weeks after her meeting with Sister Alethea, Robyn stood under the great arch of the Hwrathka Gate with Khamis beside her. She felt like a tourist, but of course tourists didn't come to Melanthera only miners and D.F. soldiers and the scores of military contractors that had flocked to the place, like 'kobo-flies to hwrathka dung' as Khamis had put it. It wasn't the place of safety that she had envisaged, more like putting you head in the lion's mouth. But Sister Alethea had put it another way; she had said it was like hiding in plain sight. The security apparatus wouldn't expect Robyn to run towards Melanthera, they'd expect her to flee the other way. That was the theory anyway.

Arranging the travel documents hadn't been difficult; Melantherans were always going to and fro between the planets, to or from work assignments, on leave or in transit. They, along with the other migrant workers from the outer planets, were a sort of human currency that had to be circulated around the inhabited planets to keep the towns and cities functioning. They were encouraged to come, when needed, and encouraged to go when their contracts were up. Nobody wanted them to stay anywhere overlong, so they were always in motion.

The difficulty had been the identity chip and the iris recognition scanners at the transport hub and the transit points beyond. All migrant workers were chipped and Robyn needed to be injected with one.

238

The problem was that the chips were coded to their points of origin, so the Melantherans had to copy this code while at the same time uploading the details of the person she was supposed to be. Robyn was told that the results wouldn't stand up to close scrutiny, but should be good enough to get her through the portals at the security checkpoints. The iris recognition issue was a different sort of problem as Robyn's I.R. patterns were on file. She was given contact lenses that copied the patterns of the person that she was supposed to be; a Piroushi woman from Melanthera, called Rahani. She didn't ask what had happened to Rahani, Robyn didn't want to know.

Robyn was a relatively small woman with dark hair, though not as slight as Khamis. She was given a compound to take to darken her skin and, when dressed in Melantheran clothes - the wide trousers, tunic-like top and head scarf - Sister Alethea thought that she should pass muster.

Khamis said, on seeing her: "You looked a bit like a Barossi before, but now you could be Piroushi. You look beautiful now."

Robyn felt herself blushing, feeling very flattered. Though she did also wonder what she'd looked like to Khamis before she had become beautiful.

There was the problem of language, but they came up with a surprisingly simple cover story. Rahani had been borne deaf and dumb, and though the technology existed to give her a hearing implant, no-one had yet designed an implant to help her talk, or at least not one a Piroushi could afford.

"You are Rahani, now," Khamis had said, a serious look on her face. "So from now on that's what I'll call you."

Robyn knew that there was wisdom in this, but she still felt a sense of loss. Losing her name felt too much like losing part of her identity

It had been decided that it was simpler not to give Khamis a new identity, just in case the forgery was picked up at some stage. She had only a tenuous link to Robyn anyway, so there was nothing to suggest she was at particular risk.

Leaving Hanis had been nerve-racking; she was sure that everyone would be able to see through her disguise. But the bored guards on the scanners had given her only a perfunctory check and the cruiser, full of migrant workers, had been running late, so everything had been hurried up.

"See! It's as I told you," Khamis whispered to her as they took off. "They look at us, but they don't really see us."

Waiting at the transport hub on Hanis, after passing through security, she was relieved at last to get away from the Library, but still felt vulnerable, almost as if she were naked, amongst the crowds of miners, librarians and migrant workers. She noticed men were looking at her and Khamis, probably more at Khamis she thought, but it was not with suspicion. Their thoughts were all, it seemed, lascivious. One or two even made lewd comments. Despite all that happened to her over the last few weeks, Robyn was still shocked by this. These men wouldn't dare make such comments to women of their own people, but Melantherans, it seemed, were fair game.

"We get this all the time," Khamis whispered to her, "especially if they think you are Piroushi."

Robyn had gleaned from some of the other migrant workers, what the other thing, apart from dancing, was that Piroushi girls were good at. Though she didn't want to put too much store in these rumours, it did make her look on Khamis in a new light, wondering what was behind it all.

She thought her heart was going to stop at one point when, after visiting the toilet, she walked across the concourse and, right in the middle of the place and under the great glass dome streaked with that red Hanis dust, she came face to face with Dr. Simeon.

She expected him to shout out:

"Ms. Harper what are you doing here?" And then call for security. But he looked straight through her, seeing just a Melantheran woman. No-one he needed to bother himself with.

She had always enjoyed space travel, getting an especial thrill out of worm-hole jumps that most people hated. There was always plenty to watch on the in-flight entertainment consoles - films, news and other programmes she liked, like documentaries - but she wasn't used to travelling the way the migrants did. The liners they were herded into were mostly old adapted cargo ships, with little more than seats and a few odd screens above the aisles, showing obscure, sub-titled soap-operas from places like Shabaz and Hephaestos. Food was served, as you weren't allowed to bring anything with you because of quarantine regulations, but it was poor fare compared to what she had eaten on the regular passenger liners she had always travelled on in that former life, when she was Robyn and not the deaf-mute Rahani,

On the long haul to Melanthera, Khamis slept, her head resting on Robyn's - or Rahani's -shoulder. Robyn could smell the perfumed oil that she dressed her hair with, a musky odour that was uncomfortably sensual. She couldn't sleep; there was too much snoring, muttering and gasping coming from the closely packed rows about her. The Melantherans were a social, open people, not really respecters of privacy. They were actually quite nosy, but she had rehearsed her mime, pointing to her ears and mouth and shaking her hand. They seemed to understand and accept this, though many of them would go on talking anyway, or feeding her, or even, and she was talking of the older women here, patting her face and stroking her hair in pity. Melantherans were also very tactile and had no concept of personal space. They'd sit so close to you that they were almost in your lap and wouldn't flinch.

She couldn't help laughing to herself as she thought about it all. She had started trying to find out about Melanthera, just to glean a bit more knowledge about the place, but had ended up becoming a Melantheran. She wondered if she wouldn't have just skipped it all - Asha's Lament, Berthaud, Berendal - if she had known it would lead to this. But, no, she thought, feeling Khamis's sweet, warmth breath on her cheek, I don't think I would have missed this for the world.

Somehow, and this was a strange thing to admit even to herself, she had felt more alive over these last few weeks than she had ever before. Living on

242

this knife's edge seemed to have made her life more distinct, to take away the blurred edges. Her time on Thera with Esmee seemed to belong to another person, a creature like her, but different in so many ways.

The spaceport on Elanthia was still a rudimentary affair, all prefabricated buildings and cargo yards, but construction crews were everywhere, laying down the foundations of the buildings, pouring concrete and clearing more land. Security checks here were even more cursory, the indigenous people being herded through one set of security gates, while miners and soldiers were quickly transferred to crawlers for the short trip to the city.

When they had been nodded thought the scanners, which Robyn doubted were actually working properly considering the number of false alarms and malfunctions that seemed to be occurring, there were no crawlers for the Melantherans. If you had luggage, which many of them did bringing all sorts of hard –to-get goods back to their families, you could hire a carriage drawn by haras. These strange looking creatures – well, strange if you were Robyn - looked a bit like llamas, but had short, cropped horns. Robyn thought their coats were denser and coarser than a llama's coat, but then she realised she'd never actually seen a llama, except in photographs, only an alpaca and wondered if they were the same.

In the end they did hire a carriage for the short trip. Khamis whispered to her that she had been told that it wasn't safe for two women to walk the road. From high up on the carriage, which they shared with five other people so they were packed in, Robyn could see the glint of what she at first thought was a great body of water out towards the horizon , but then she realised it was actually a vast array of solar panels, angled to catch the sun's rays.

Later when she asked Khamis about it, the woman told her that the electricity generated went to the refineries, the miner's compounds and the other Sung Yang establishments outside Melanthera.

"President Quintal has promised everyone electricity, but nothing happens."

Khamis had then gone on to voice her suspicions about electricity, saying that as it came from the Star People, the Melantherans couldn't trust it to leap around their homes, setting fires when it would. Robyn had laughed at this, till the tears came to her eyes.

"What is it, friend Rahani?" A slightly irritated Khamis had asked." Has a kobo-fly bitten you on the arse again?"

She explained that this, apparently, was the stock Melantheran retort if someone was laughing at something you didn't find funny. And this made Robyn laugh even more, to think that these people thought they had their funny bones in, of all places, their arses.

Travelling on, just on the outskirts of Melanthera, she could see encampments of conical, yurt-like tents on either side of the road. The Melantherans on the carriage all made a flicking motion with their left hands, which Robyn copied, a warding off gesture.

"That's why we can't walk down this road," Khamis whispered to her. "The Hvassara camp outside the walls now; many of them have given up their old ways and live on hand-outs from the Star-People, payment for their services. But they still take our women if they can."

Robyn almost let out a cry of excitement when she saw her first hvass, but stifled it quickly. She had read so much about the creatures, but on a second look she wondered why the Melantherans made such a fuss of the scrawny, goatish creatures. They looked comical with their perked up ears and staring eyes, like ill-favoured Bambis.

Just ahead of them, the high arch of a great gateway loomed up in front. It was as high and wide as a two-storey house on Earth, when they had houses and not just apartments, and was topped by towers and battlements; looking all the world like a medieval castle, but less angular, the crenulations rounded, the tops of the window arches curved.

"The Hwrathka Gate," whispered Khamis, "there is a famous poem about it, how they held it for the Empress during Kal Quintal's rebellion, but it's banned now. We are supposed to forget it. I can't even remember who wrote it."

At the Hwrathka Gate they had dismounted from the carriage; there was a sort of terminal, she thought you could call it, where wagons and carts milled around the carriage drivers touting for fares.

"We can walk from here on," Khamis had said and then they were there, standing under the great arch.

Where once the gate guards would have stood, scrutinising the travellers, a few traders had set up stalls, full of worthless trinkets to sell to off-duty soldiers and miners. Robyn and Khamis still took care, communicating in whispers, but they managed to have more of a conversation out of earshot of other people. It was the early afternoon, and the infamous Melantheran sun was high in the sky, fiercely pouring out its heat and light on the land.

"Will we see hwrathka?" Robyn asked, as excited as a child by the prospect.

"No friend Rahani," Khamis answered back, sadly, "the keeping of hwrathka was banned after the peace. They were too closely associated with the Empire. Only Emperors or Empresses were allowed to keep Hwrathka in the old days, so now they are banned."

They walked through what once had been the market square, past what Khamis said was a pleasure house, but now looked to Robyn like a brothel.

"This was all different when I was young, Rahani," Khamis said, "if a man wanted a pleasure woman he had to woo her, bring her gifts, sing to her. Now the miners just fling money at the women and they lie on their backs."

All around the market were bars, cheap eating houses and clubs of one sort or another.

"It's all for the miners and the soldiers," Khamis said. "They don't venture much further into town, they think it's still too dangerous for them, so they do their drinking here and take their pleasure with the women."

Robyn noticed that most of the eating places were serving off-planet food, synthetic chicken or soya burgers. There were a few Theran spice houses and a couple of pizzerias, but no Melantheran food.

"What do you expect," said Khamis, "they despise us. They only use our women so that they can feel their power over us."

For a moment, the woman's bitterness shocked her; Khamis was such a gentle creature. But Robyn knew she was right. What had been done here was a tragedy and a crime. She was still piecing the story together, but she well understood why it had been hidden.

After the market square it got better; there were only a few of the sleazy clubs and eating places on the road which climbed up to the citadel, sprinkled here and there with a number of up-market coffee houses.

"It's the one thing you people gave us that the Melantherans took to," Khamis told her, "coffee!"

Robyn stopped and put her hand on Khamis's arm, saying:

"Friend Khamis, I'll always prefer your durgan root tea."

She could see that the girl was touched by this, saw the tears that welled up in her eyes and found that she was also crying and they both smiled.

As they walked along the streets and then turned into the narrow lanes and alleys where most of the people lived, Robyn noticed that, although many people still wore traditional Melantheran clothes – the same sort of hooded tunic and trousers that Robyn was wearing - or the long robes of the Harradim and Barossi, there were a number of people wearing the orthodox, universal uniform gear of the inner planets; caps, jackets and fatigue

247

trousers. Khamis had explained to her that, after the war, there had been a lot of surplus military apparel which had found its way to the market stalls. She also saw a number of uniformed men, on patrol with side-arms or machine guns, and Khamis told her these were the Republican Guard, the new Melantheran police force.

One thing she didn't see were any women priests; there were a number of men wearing the red robes of the Elanta temple, but no women.

"The Sisterhood was banned, friend Rahani," Khamis said. "They were too close to the Empress for President Quintal."

A room had been arranged for them in small, neighbourhood tavern. It was in a section of the city that was mostly Piroushi and no questions were asked. Khamis was known to many of the people around and there seemed to be some safety and security in this. Many of the migrant workers that they had travelled with had been heading back to the refugee camps. Robyn had learnt that the camps, which were situated mostly to the east of the city on the plains outside Melanthera, were full of people displaced by the Hvassara, when they overran the eastern part of the Empire, but also with Melantherans who had been banished from the city.

Khamis had told her that they were better off in the Piroushi quarter. She said that the camps were not really safe, they were riddled with agents and informers, and the police, all Quintal's men, kept a close watch on any newcomers or strangers. "There are whole neighbourhoods empty," Khamis said. "President Quintal expelled anyone who supported the Empress. He left most of the Piroushi, Harradim and Barossi alone, thinking he could persuade them to change sides and back his cause."

They spent their first evening in the room. Khamis brought up some soup and bread from the kitchen. She was worried about the effect that Melantheran food might have on Robyn's stomach, which was not a comment on Melantheran food, but more to do with the exotic bugs and microbes that Robyn had not built up any resistance to. But the woman had dosed herself up beforehand with the various drugs that travellers used to combat this problem.

Their cover was that they were two travellers on their way home from work on Hanis, heading back to Piroush and its islands. While Melanthera was still a stew of intrigue and conspiracy, Piroush was a much quieter backwater of the old Empire and thus deemed safer for Robyn and Khamis. Since Quintal had been ushered in as a care-taker President by the Defence Force peacekeepers, Melanthera had officially become a Republic, so Piroush was technically no longer under Melantheran control, but an independent ally. In practise, this involved little practical change as the Empress's rule had always been benign and somewhat distant.

After they had eaten, Robyn felt utterly exhausted. It was not just the long journey they had undertaken in an unending series of ramshackle craft, but also that, for the first time in weeks, she felt the tension, the fear, lift off her. Khamis had taken their dishes down to the kitchen and returned with an earthenware flask and two earthenware mugs.

"Borriba wine!" She said and poured Robyn a glass. They sat on cushion by the fire, where the remnants of their hvass dung fuel smouldered, just taking the chill off the room. The Melantheran plains had a desert-like climate, with nights where the temperature dropped like a stone.

"This is really good, friend Khamis," Robyn said.

The Piroushi girl smiled, pleased at the compliment.

It wasn't long before Robyn crawled into the bed, which was incredibly comfortable and clean, if a little soft. Melantherans didn't have night clothes, they just slept in their clothes or naked, so Robyn was a little unnerved to see Khamis loosen and drop her trousers then take off her tunic and a short shift, before approaching the bed. The firelight's dying flames paled on the girl's skin, chasing the curves and plains of her flesh with a coppery blush. Robyn still had on her vest and pants.

The girl got in beside her and then turned, propping herself up on her elbow.

"We truly are like sisters now, Rahani, we have shared so much. Goodnight, sleep well on your first night in Melanthera. May Elanta protect you!"

She blew out the small, earthenware oil lamp and then pulled the cover over her.

"Tomorrow I will go and see if I can arrange our passage to Piroush. Then you will really start to see my country."

The girl's breathing became soft and steady. Robyn wondered at the way Khamis could just drop off to sleep like that. It was all too extraordinary for Robyn to be able to do the same thing, she listened

250

to the strange, sometimes familiar, sometimes totally alien, noises of the Melantheran night, thinking:

"I must remember that I'm on the run and not a tourist."

But she felt safer and more secure than she had been for weeks, if not ever before.

Chapter 22
The Star Woman In The Palace

Though the Empress's chamberlain had brought her dresses and robes made of rich silk and soft hvass wool, Berthaud had decided that, to keep focussed on what she thought of as the task in hand, she should continue wearing the Sung Yang contact team fatigues she had brought with her. This caused some amusement amongst the palace courtiers and servants, but she wanted to keep a separation, a certain distance, between herself and the Melantherans. She didn't want to be seen as joining their side, but rather as an observer, a witness to what was being done to them.

She did, however, allow herself, when alone in the evenings in the comfortable, airy pavilion room they had found for her, to try on the various pieces of finery and even to lounge about in them. She didn't take any pictures or film of these nocturnal fashion parades, knowing how easy it would be for them to be used against her. The ethnologist who had gone native. They would also find a lover, some Barossi or Piroushi perhaps, who had captured her heart, so that the story would conform to the pattern imposed on it; the bookish, academic spinster seduced by the barbaric splendour and sexual freedom of Mila's court. For she did not doubt that, ultimately, Sung Yang would win and she would find herself in a prison, or an asylum, if they didn't think it more convenient for her to die in the fighting. And they would construct a history to explain the way she had acted.

It had, it transpired, been hardest to explain it to Kev. She'd initially felt she had little in common with him when they'd first worked together years ago, finding that he could be boorish and insensitive, too scathing about indigenous societies and their customs and habits, too prone to make a joke of serious things. But over the years she'd grown fond of him, seen that under the bluff Tech's exterior, he had a nature that was caring of his comrades and friends. At heart, he was basically the soldier he once was and always would be; he might be bloody-minded about nearly everything else, but he'd sacrifice himself in an instant to keep his people safe.

He had been the only person that she had told about her decision. When she had come back to the base with Berendal and his silent Harradim shadow, everything had been confused and in turmoil. The order from the command team on the Sir John Franklin had arrived without any prior hint or warning the night before. It had been a 'Code Blue' for immediate evacuation, usually only issued when a base was under threat.

It was common knowledge among the base personnel that the Hvassara were on the march and heading for Melanthera; survey flights and surveillance drones had brought the news and it had spread rapidly, there was no keeping the lid on that box. They'd expected some sort of action to be taken, but an immediate and complete evacuation seemed very drastic. The next morning she and Kev had looked out over the market square and seen the usual, peaceful mix of stall holders setting up and people languidly resting in the shade of the trees and outside the pleasure house.

"Where's the imminent threat?" Kev had asked, to himself more than anyone else. But Johnson had insisted on a lock down and the highest level of security. When she'd seen Berendal, she'd managed to make some excuse about unfinished business in the town. Johnson wasn't too happy about it, but didn't yet have the authority to bar her from leaving; though by the look of him, she thought, he wouldn't be long in getting it.

On the walk up to the palace, she was still turning over and over in her head the course of action she was planning to take. She tried to dissuade herself, telling herself that she was losing her objectivity, her ethics, but she had a feeling in her gut, a visceral intuition rather than the result of a logical process of thought, that she must act in some way, must on this occasion take sides. Because, she thought, on this occasion there is no side-line to stand on.

Even an immediate evacuation of a compound, like the one under the Hwrathka Gate, took time. There were stores and supplies, the actual infrastructure of the place like the cabins and quarters, all had to be air-lifted or destroyed. There were rules about these sorts of things, procedures. There was a lot of high flown rhetoric about not polluting or unduly affecting the progress of cultures by exposing them to the products of a more advanced technology; it was all rather hypocritical when you thought about what Sung Yang were up to out there on the steppe with the Hvassara.

The disordered and frenzied activity that was the camp over the next few days, gave Berthaud time to prepare herself for the move to the palace. No-one questioned her when she took medical supplies or communications equipment from the stores; the supply Techs were happy to release anything as long as it was digitally signed for, as it meant there was less for them to catalogue and transport.

Moving the stuff was more difficult, but the compound was not totally self-sufficient; though they burnt or recycled much of their rubbish, organic matter, like surplus food, was dumped outside the walls of the city by Melantheran carriers using wagons drawn by haras, the job being too dirty and malodorous for the Star People themselves. Berthaud called on Berendal again for help; it was not difficult to smuggle out most of her supplies, which consisted of a number of small cases, on one of the wagons.

As the base was dismantled, the city around them grew busier and more agitated than normal. Berthaud could see refugees and soldiers flooding in through the Hwrathka Gate, while other soldiers and civilians left the same way. She could also see a rather glum and reluctant Berendal at the gate itself, supervising the supplies of food, water and arms that were being hauled up into the chambers above.

She knew, from what he had previously told her, that the Hwrathka Gate was the key to the city. To the north, east and south the great river of the Melantheran plains, the Khalamis, swept around the city, protecting the north and south walls, which had been built on its precipitous banks. To the east the

255

bridge over the Khalamis could be held against an enemy, its gate portal was a mini-fortress just like the Hwrathka Gate, or destroyed if the situation demanded.

Before the Hwrathka Gate the plains stretched out westwards, giving an enemy ample space to deploy an army and make the best use of siege artillery and other siege engines. Though it was terrible to think of the human toll the war would inevitably take and the death and destruction it would wreak, part of Berthaud was almost eager at the prospect of seeing what was, in essence, a medieval battle. But then she remembered the cannons and muskets and reminded herself that, whatever awaited them, it would be carnage and not a spectator sport.

In three days, the compound had been all but emptied of supplies and equipment; many of the Techs had gone and apart from the living quarters, there was very little left to air-lift out. That evening, Berthaud visited Kev in his quarters, where he was packing the last of his things, and told him what she intended to do:

Are you mad, Marie?" He asked. "This isn't your war, you know enough about how these things work not to get caught up in it."

She told him then about what she knew, or had surmised, about Sung Yang's dealings with the Hvassara and their interference in Melantheran affairs.

"I don't think any of this is a secret, Marie. I agree, it's really shitty and awful. But I don't know what you think you can achieve here. It's better to just get out of here, leave Sung Yang, and do something else. Get a teaching job or something."

In the end they had, as people say, agreed to differ.

"For god's sake, take care of yourself!" He finally said.

By this time, Johnson had taken over command of the compound, as Sung Yang regarded it as a security matter now. His detail would stay there while the living quarters were lifted out. In the end even the security fence would be taken for use somewhere else in Sung Yang's commercial empire. The security detail would be the last men out.

There was no way Berthaud could have got out of the base without Johnson's permission. There were sensors around the perimeter, along with infra-red cameras, and the guards in the towers were alert and itching to open fire on something. She had arranged with Berendal that there would be a request from the palace for her to visit the Empress urgently, delivered by a detachment of Barossi.

As it was, Berthaud had to argue with Johnson, who was not willing to open the gates, wanting to delay any further contact until it was too late and they were on cruisers in the air. In the end she'd confused him, by telling him he had no authority over her in this matter:

"You're security Johnson, not diplomacy. Sinclair has given me the authority to carry on this contact right to the end. He doesn't want there to be any incidents, or misunderstandings, leading to acts of violence or an attack on the compound."

Johnson had laughed at this, said they were ready for any attack.

"Sung Yang doesn't want to be responsible for a massacre, Johnson," she had continued, doubting there was any truth in what she said.

"Bad publicity is bad for business."

He'd let her go in the end, as if, though he was reluctant, he was glad to be shot of her. She'd left a log entry, which she'd entrusted to Kev, stating that she hadn't been taken hostage, but was staying at the palace of her own volition, because of her disagreement with the policies Sun Yang were following on Elanthia; that they were in breach of their contract due to gross interference in Melantheran affairs. She knew it would be suppressed, but guessed that, even so, some rumour of what she'd done would get out.

When she'd safely got to the palace, after being received by Mila and the Grand Council at a long, interminable, reception, when she'd finally closed the screen that served as a door to her quarters, she'd suddenly felt anxious and panicky.

"What the hell have I done?" She asked herself. "Why have I thrown my life away?"

Comfort came from an unlikely source. The priest, Gamelon, who seemed to think of himself as some sort of colleague, had turned up, calling at her door and asking for admittance. They'd talked, over a flask of that good wine they made here, and, after he'd given her a long-winded welcome, his usual conversation, a mixture of curious questions and random discourses on things Elanthian, had helped her regain her equilibrium.

It was obvious, thankfully, that he had no romantic interest in her. She wondered how Melantherans went about their dating rituals, how did they make passes and how, not coming from there, would you know when they were making one. She was sure that Berendal had said a few things in the past, which she had not understood or which were too obscure to comprehend, that were, effectively, sexual propositions. They'd gone over her head then, but now she was living amongst these people she thought that she would have to be more alert. At least Berendal, with his newly-found uxorious nature, wouldn't be trying to woo her. She did worry that Gamelon would be another sort of pest, especially if he made a habit of keeping her up half the night to discuss matters historical and ethnological.

Though that night had been only a few short weeks ago, her time here had felt like an age, so new had everything been to her. While she was in the compound, for all that time, she felt as if she had just scratched the surface of Melanthera. Now, every day brought new and strange things, often trivial. She'd be faced with a new food, or drink or a new custom she hadn't come across before. How was she to know, for instance, that it upset the serving girls to be constantly thanking them. For some strange Melantheran reason, it implied criticism of the service they were giving you. She'd learnt that one the hard way, sending a couple of girls off in sobs back to the kitchen, afterwards having to remember to be more economical and strategic with her thanks.

One of her biggest faux pas, amongst so many others, had been making an innocuous remark about the smell from the Hwrathka House, the creature's stables on the citadel plateau. Gamelon had explained to her afterwards, slowly and painfully, how, because the hwrathka was held in such affection, that it was regarded as impolite, positively rude in fact, to make any reference to the veritable stench that sometimes emanated from their quarters.

Customs and habits were bad enough, but the humour was even harder to understand. She had just about understood the general hilarity that Berendal was causing amongst the court, finally understanding that Harradim women were renowned as being moral and chaste; while Berendal, of course, wasn't, so his present domestic circumstances were regarded as highly ironic. But many of the jokes were totally impenetrable to her. One day she turned a corner in the palace garden and came upon two servant girls who were talking about a third:

"Kick her up the arse," one said, "that'll make her laugh."

She just couldn't understand it, thinking her Pad hadn't caught some nuance or subtlety. It also took her ages to figure out the comments that some of the younger men made about Piroushi girls and dancing, that used to make the Piroushi princesses at court so angry. In the end she got it. All of this was complicated even more by the fact that she was trying to use and practise as much Melantheran as she could, relying less and less on the instantaneous translator on the Pad.

She had though, by this time, fallen into a sort of routine. She would write her blog about the siege daily and then try and upload it. She had managed to send a few encrypted signals out through the Sung Yang communications net, dispatching them in short, compressed bursts, but she doubted they were all getting through. She'd piggy-backed some of them on the Sung Yang signals that were flying about the atmosphere, from surveillance pilots and drones, but she did not know if the security people were blocking them.

She wrote about the siege, how it was dragging on in a desultory way. She wrote about the cannon, which had first seemed ineffective, but were now starting to make a difference, battering at the walls on either side of the Hwrathka gate. She wrote about the military advisers, the Star People who, though they adopted Hvassara grab, stood out because of their height and skin colour amongst the nomads outside the walls. She wrote about the casualties from the barrages of cannon fire, the women and children hurt by the canister shot that, in a new, sinister development, was being deliberately fired into the residential areas. She wrote about the makeshift hospitals and the Sisters who staffed them, working with only the herbs and other natural remedies that they had at their disposal.

She talked about the men and women who manned the walls and towers, who sang as they faced the probing nights assaults that the Hvassara would send against the walls at regular intervals. She talked of the laughter that they sent, almost a weapon in itself, towards the besieging forces. She talked about the rationing and the hunger, how wives and husbands were giving up their rations to feed their spouses on the walls and keep them strong. And she wrote about the dignity of the Empress, the way that she rode around the city, showing herself to her troops, ignoring the musket balls and cannon shot as if they were, as she said, "an unseasonable plague of kobo-flies." She carried on writing, not knowing if anyone, anywhere, was reading her words.

She wrote about the One God One Church people, who had decamped from the city at the same time as the Star People and could be seen trying to gain converts amongst the ranks of the Hvassara for their prefabricated churches that had been flown in by cruiser one night. She wrote about Kal Quintal, how he had once, only once, ridden out from the Hvassara ranks with his entourage. A keen-eyed archer, on one of the ballista-like artillery pieces that the Melantherans had deployed on the walls, had hit his haras and thrown him from it. He'd taken to his tent and not shown his face again. The young Piroushi archer, when praised, had been grim-faced:

"I was aiming for the man," he said, "I feel bad about the haras."

She wrote and she wrote. Then in the afternoons she would go to the hospital that the Sisterhood had set up in the palace, doing what she could to repair some of the damage her own people had caused.

Chapter 23
Falling Heroes

It was all Asha's fault, Berendal decided as he lay in his bed in the high-vaulted chamber of the palace that the Sisters were using as a hospital. Noor sat beside him, holding his hand, her face stricken by fear and worry. He moved his neck, the little bit he could without feeling too much pain, and looked down at his body. There was a splint on his right leg and a bandage up his left arm to his shoulder. He also knew that there was another bandage on his head which looped over his right eye, he could feel it and it was partially obstructing his vision.

"It's alright, Noor," he tried to comfort her, feeling the hand that held his shaking." I will be fine, I won't leave you. I promise."

Yes, it was all Asha's fault, he thought; if she hadn't led that night sortie out of the eastern gate and across the Khalamis bridge, taking the Hvassara unawares, this tragedy wouldn't have happened. Because, the Hvassara had lost a lot of men and a lot of equipment. Asha surprised them, burst into their camp and spiked most of their cannon on that side of the city. Berthaud had told her how to do this; apparently Berthaud's head was full of obscure and obviously useful things.

"Hammering a barbed metal spike into the touch-hole," she had, of course, to tell them what a touch-hole was, "will put the cannon out of use."

Asha's force had spiked some of the guns, pushed a few in the river and actually managed to capture three, not that they knew what to do with them. Asha had led a swift, lightly armed force, a unit she had trained herself, supported by a cavalry force which protected her flanks and her retreat. They'd pressed the Hvassara hard, using the same hit-and-run tactics that they had previously made their own.

This raid seemed to have angered them even more than usual and the response had been the biggest cannon volley that they had yet experienced, aimed at the Hwrathka Gate and the walls adjoining it. They'd shored up the gates and strengthened them, so they weren't afraid of them being blown apart, but the towers and the battlements, already scarred by cannon-balls, took a fierce battering. Berendal had been on the battlements, giving orders to his men, when a cannon ball had sailed over the walls and taken the floor out from under him, shattering a big hole in the floor-boards. A canister shot had burst at the same time, sending a flurry of musket balls flying around the fighting platform, causing a chaos of metal fragments, wood splinters and stone chips, which cut into flesh, shattered bone and severed sinew.

Berendal had broken his leg in the fall, taken a musket ball through the arm and been hit on the head by flying masonry. But the tragedy wasn't that he had been wounded and had to relinquish his command of the gate. Having done his duty and not been killed in the process, he was quite content to be relieved of his post. No, the tragedy was that his left arm was his writing arm and he didn't want it removed.

He noticed that Berthaud was standing over him. He thought that he must have blacked out for a moment, as he couldn't remember her being there before.

"How do you feel?" She asked him, in reasonable Melantheran. She had to use her machine to understand his answer though.

"My arm," he asked, "will I lose it?"

"The Sisters think that they've saved it. I brought some antiseptics and antibiotics with me which seem to work here as well as back on my planet, so it seems that prospects are good."

"It's my writing arm," he said, then passed out. And when he awoke, Berthaud was gone, but Noor still sat faithfully by his bed.

It took him a good while to recover, the knock on his head seemed to have affected him in some way and he was prone to bouts of giddiness, when the floor seemed to shift under his feet and he could hardly keep his balance. Noor, partly to be able to stay with him, partly to do what she could to assist rather than standing idly by, had started helping the sisters with their nursing duties.

For some unfathomable reason, the Hvassara had started prosecuting the siege even more fiercely. One day when he had hobbled from his bed out of the great archway of the door and onto the terrace that looked out over the palace gardens, he had found one of the Empress's generals sitting there on a bench, his leg propped up on the balustrade before him in a cast. Berendal thought his name was Kern and he recognised him from his time spent in the palace, when he was, himself, briefly part of the Imperial court.

Since Quintal had turned traitor, the Empress was running the war herself. Kal Quintal had been a sort of commander in chief, but the generals in command of the various military arms were notorious for their disagreements and rivalry, so, in many ways, his authority had been notional rather than actual. The result of Quintal's defection had been a vacancy that it was impossible to fill without alienating and insulting three of the generals by raising up the fourth.

There were four branches of Melantheran arms; the hwrathka corps, the cavalry, the infantry and the archers, and each branch had a commander. This complicated matters no end as, in practice, the four arms had to work together closely on the battlefield. Squabbling between the commanders could have dire consequences, as had been proved in the Barossi wars of the last century, when the cavalry and infantry commanders were so hostile to each other that they had basically fought two different, separate wars with disastrous results.

Mila had thus decided that the easiest and most efficient option was to take over command herself. Not being a soldier, she was more than willing to listen to all the advice her generals could give her, but being the Empress she could give her orders when she had reached a decision without being questioned further. It had worked out well enough so far. It also allowed her to let Asha get on with her raids and sorties, without having to justify them to each general in turn.

The real problem with the war, or at least the way the Melantherans were waging it, as Berendal knew, was the fact that they hadn't actually been at war for the long years of the Empress's reign. It was true that there was a constant pressure on the eastern frontiers from the Hvassara, but apart from the garrisons of the outposts on that border, the Melantheran army had little to do and had become somewhat complacent. The hwrathka corps was mainly ceremonial; nobody had seen a battle charge by hwrathka for at least twenty years. Soldiers had a tendency to slope off home to their farms or to run stalls or taverns. This practise had become accepted, as the standing army's pay was effectively a pittance. They've had their baptism of fire now, though, Berendal thought, as he sat on the terrace a little distance away from the general.

The man greeted him and said: "I fell off my haras. Would you believe it? Twenty-five year in the saddle, riding out against the Hvassara innumerable times and I fall off my haras just outside the citadel gates. One of those cannon balls spooked the creature. They seem to have increased their range somehow."

They sat in the sun and talked in a desultory way. Kern had told Berendal his theory about the siege. That the Hvassara were being pressed by the Star People to finish it, once and for all. But he was more inclined to believe Asha and what she'd told him the night before when she visited him:

"The Hvassara aren't used to keeping such a vast army in the field, they are obviously getting some help with supplies of food and ammunition from the Star People, but it's still an enormous task for them, feeding their army and all its followers. They're just not that organised. Besides, they've got all those haras with them and hvass. They must be running out of pasture for them by now."

Whatever the reason, there seemed to be a feeling, intangible and fleeting like the scent of night flowers on the air though it was, that the siege was coming to its point of crisis.

Berendal had almost dozed off in the sun, the conversation with the old man drying up, when they heard a commotion from inside the ward. Some catastrophe, he thought, a wall collapsing or a house burning and then a flood of casualties, the Sisters doing what they could to preserve their lives. But then he heard Asha's voice, barking orders as usual and shuffled inside on his sticks.

He had been right. There had been an influx of casualties, but these were different. A noisy crowd of people, mainly civilians but with some soldiers amongst them, were bringing in three casualties on litters, but these were Star People. The litter-bearers deposited them on a raised platform in one corner of the room and the onlookers milled about, shouting and bickering in excited voices until Asha ordered them out.

"All of you, who are not Sisters or patients, leave now!" She commanded.

They did as they were asked. Very few people disobeyed Asha, and then usually only the once.

Trying to be as inconspicuous as possible, Berendal drew near the platform. There were a number of Sisters there, amongst them Sister Alethea looking drawn and haggard, from over-work and lack of sleep. Berthaud had been summoned and arrived soon after. Berendal could see Noor in the crowd around the bed and, catching

268

her eye, he made his way towards her. By the time he got to her side, Asha was telling Berthaud and Alethea what had happened.

"Apparently, the Hvassara sent a party over the south wall last night, on a stretch where it's been quiet up to now. They killed the guards and headed off to the cisterns that are on the slope of the plateau there. The Hvassara may have had the Star People along so that they could use their weapons to destroy the water tanks, to blow them up."

It made sense to Berendal that they would go for the defenders' water, but, still, it was a bold plan, as it would have involved moving through a number of the narrow, winding streets that sprawled down the hills there. The Hvassara's usual practise was to leave a decomposing corpse in a water-hole or well to poison it, but on this occasion they must have decided to do a more thorough job, with the help of the Star People, which had probably been their undoing.

"They killed the Barossi guards on the cistern, but were then surprised by a bigger force of Barossi. The Hvassara died fighting, these three tried to surrender, but the Barossi weren't having it."

Everyone knew that Barossi and Hvassara were mortal enemies and would give no quarter to each other and, within plain sight of the bodies of their comrades, the Barossi's blood would have been up.

"They'd have all been dead and gutted, if some of the city militia hadn't turned up and saved them." Asha said.

"One is dead," Sister Alethea interrupted, "and the other past help. As for the third one, I don't know." She sighed and turned to Berthaud.

Berendal leaned over and managed to get a good look at the Star People. They were dressed in Hvassara tunics and hats, but this was only a sort of camouflage which they wore over their black uniforms, helmets and body armour. The body armour, it turned out, had been no protection against Barossi spears; there were multiple wounds on their bodies. Before he grew dizzy again, he saw one of the Sisters taking off the helmet of the third soldier, the one that was still neither dead nor unconscious. Though the soldier had short, close cropped hair, he saw that it was a woman.

Berthaud had moved forward and was leaning over the woman, who was thrashing about on the litter as if trying to get up, and looking around in panic.

"You are safe now," Berthaud said. "You don't have to worry. These women won't hurt you and will try to help you."

The woman kept on rolling about.

"Do you understand?" Berthaud said. "You must keep still. Be calm. You are wounded. Lay still."

The woman nodded and quietened and Berthaud took her hand. The soldier looked up at Berthaud, a look of recognition on her face and said:

"You are her, aren't you? The one that went over to the other side." Then she grimaced with pain and closed her eyes.

"My name is Marie Berthaud. Can you tell me yours?" The woman's eyes snapped open and she answered.

270

"My name is Lieutenant Soledad Cruz, Inter-Planetary Defence Force."

"Soledad," Berthaud asked. "Do you know where you are?"

"I guess I do," the woman answered, looking around.

"We'd like to get you better, so you can go home." Berthaud said. "Where's your home Soledad?"

The woman's eyes misted up, but all she said was:

"My name is Lieutenant Soledad Cruz, Inter-Planetary Defence Force."

Berthaud and the Sisters worked on the lieutenant, treating the wounds the Barossi spears had made, doing what they could. The other soldier died in the afternoon, beyond help as Alethea had said. Just when the oil lamps were being lit on the ward, the Empress came in without ceremony or announcement. The Defence Force Lieutenant was awake.

Berthaud had thought that she should make a formal introduction:

"Your Highness, this is Lieutenant Soledad Lopez of the Interplanetary Defence Force. Lieutenant Lopez, this is her Imperial Highness Mila the Third."

For the first time, the Lieutenant looked perplexed, as if she couldn't quite believe what was happening.

"Lieutenant, in different times you would have been welcome as a guest. Now war had brought us to this and you lie wounded on that litter. I had no wish to be at war with you or your people. You must tell your generals, your leaders this. That all we Melantherans want is to be left alone."

The Lieutenant seemed confused, but then nodded and said:

"I just want to go home."

"Elanta willing, you will," the Empress said and then walked from the room.

But the Lieutenant didn't go home, she died in the night. Berthaud was still holding her hand and Berendal had remained close to the bed-side, his bedding spread on the floor, his hand holding Noor's who slept besides him. The Lieutenant had seemed to get lost in a sort of delirium for a while, but then, suddenly, she woke up and looked at Berthaud:

"I want to see my parents again. I want to go home just one more time."

"You will," Berthaud said, "just try and hang on, Soledad."

"Promise me..." the Lieutenant was having difficulty speaking me, "..don't let them bury me here... I want to go home..."

Then Soledad Cruz gave up the ghost and passed from the dry, harsh earth of Elanthia, heading for some other place.

Berendal could see that Berthaud was crying. She glanced angrily at him.

"I didn't sign up for this you know. I'm an ethnologist. I should be shut up somewhere with a computer screen and a report to write, not holding the hands of dying kids in this stupid, senseless war."

Berendal didn't understand what she was saying, but he moved to comfort her.

272

"No. Just leave me alone," she said as he tried to stand up.

Berthaud came back with Asha the next morning to make arrangements for the bodies. Asha told him that the Empress had got Berthaud to contact the Star People to arrange for the bodies to be sent back to them. They were to be carried out through the eastern gate and left just outside the Hvassaran siege lines, where the One God One Church people would attend to them.

Later Berthaud told them that she had picked up a broadcast from the Star People, which said that three civilian technicians had been murdered by the Melantherans.

"But I thought they were soldiers!" Asha said.

"Of course they were," Berthaud replied. "But my people will twist the truth when it suits them."

"But that's dishonourable," Asha answered. "Their people need to know the truth, what really happened."

Berthaud nodded sadly.

As soon as his head cleared and he felt he could walk without falling over, Berendal took Noor to Sister Alethea and asked her to marry them. Marriage in Melanthera was extremely simple, just a question of getting a Sister or a Priest to witness the vows and give Elanta's blessing. They would have to go through a more involved Harradim ceremony later, but that could wait. The important thing was that now Noor had someone, a husband, and a family. And they could face the future and whatever it would bring together.

Chapter 24
Kusha And Asha

When Asha was troubled, as she was now, she sought out Kusha. She found the woman sitting in the late afternoon sun, drinking durgan root tea. Kusha was one of the few people who could read the planes and angles of Asha's face, see the down-flickering of the eyes, the slight pursing of the lips that told what was going on behind the emotionless mask. She pulled Asha, reluctant at first, down beside her on the bench and made her drink some of the durgan root brew and eat one of the little cakes that the Piroushi always took with their tea. The cakes weren't as sweet as they should have been and were too dry, but they gave a little bit of comfort, a crumb of it.

Kusha and Annesh were no longer the vapid, languorous princesses that they had once been. The war had changed them, as it had changed everybody. Kusha had never really been the same since she had killed the would-be assassin on Khetmis. She had had to take on a mantle that she didn't really want. The Melantherans loved their stories, their heroes and their heroines and she had become one of them. But there had seemed to her to be nothing particularly heroic in what had happened. She had in fact been terrified, almost hysterical, and it had been the Empress who had calmed her. In truth, she felt that she had probably been more afraid of her own death, or rape, than the prospect of the Empress being killed, but she thought that was probably always the case; we are all selfish animals after all.

In retrospect she was most grateful to her mother, she who had taught her how to shoot the bow and given her the training that enabled her to calm herself, steady the shaft and kill the man who burst through the door panel. In the end, when she loosed the shaft, it was just like target shooting and the fear evaporated. She realised she could fight these men, defend herself; her arrow would pierce their hearts, however savage and fierce. She'd nocked another arrow to the bow string, kept her breathing calm and slow as she'd been taught. But no more of them had come; instead it was Asha who had burst through the door, bloody and enraged, looking for more of them to kill.

Up until then, she'd always thought that the strange woman, part priestess, part warrior, was unsophisticated and rather coarse, lacking in the refinement and manners she was used to. But Asha was a force of nature, not like other people, and if you won her friendship, which wasn't easy, she would be fierce and uncompromising in her devotion to you. She would die for you without a prior thought. Kusha knew that she had won Asha's friendship that day on Khetmis and that she wouldn't ever lose it.

Kusha had spent the day with the Empress's chamberlain going over the inventory of food, water and other supplies in the great storerooms under the palace. To everybody's surprise, and particularly hers, the girl who had never had to think about money at all in her life, had found that she had an aptitude for figures. To the chamberlain's evident

275

discomfort, she had given a detailed perusal to the ledgers of supplies, finding that they were short on a number of things.

"It's not my fault," the chamberlain had said, "people keep taking things without writing it down. Barrels of wine, grain, weapons. If it's not the army, it's the Sisterhood or the Elanta priests."

She had quietly, but firmly, told him that there was something he could do about it in future; he could do his job properly.

Now, as they sat together in the last warmth of the sun, she waited patiently. She had learned with Asha that it was no use asking her about her worries and concerns. You had to wait for the woman to tell you, however long that took.

"I'm much troubled today, friend Kusha," Asha said at last.

"And why is that, my dear friend?" Kusha asked.

"Because I no longer think we can win this battle. Whatever we do will not be enough."

Then Asha told her about the death of the Star People's soldiers, how the story had been twisted and turned about until it had been presented as an example of Melantheran treachery and savagery.

The Empress had even got Berthaud to broadcast a message from her regretting the deaths of the three Star People, 'in the fighting' as she put it. This was an unprecedented action; normally she would leave such a task to the grand council. But it had little effect. Mila couldn't punish the Barossi involved, she couldn't, after all, afford to alienate these people who had for years been her staunchest troops and formed her personal palace guards, but

276

she put out a proclamation to all her forces, that in future any Star People taken prisoner were to be delivered unharmed to the palace or severe consequences would follow.

"The truth to these people changes all the time, like wind on water."

She told Kusha she feared that, if they defeated the Hvassara, the Star People would find some new excuse to attack them. And there was no way that they could stand up to their flying machines and their weapons.

"You are weary, friend Asha," Kusha said, "you've led so many sorties, you'd done so much of the fighting. People tell me they've seen you on the walls and towers. They say you are everywhere."

She put her arm around her friend's shoulders, feeling the muscles tense and knotted under her fingers.

"You must spend tonight with Annesh and me. We will make sure that you sleep. We will guard the door against any interruptions. Then tomorrow you will feel strong again and refreshed. Then the Lady Asha will put these Hvassara to flight!"

Later Asha let Kusha lead her to her chamber. She let Annesh and Kusha feed her and undress her like a child. Kusha hugged her and kissed her, as she pulled the covers over her. Annesh was, in truth, still a little scared of Asha, so she just bade her good night. The two princesses were true to their word and they stood guard over her that night, allowing no interruptions.

"Even if the Hvassara are at the citadel gates, I won't wake you," Kusha laughed as she told Asha this, as the princesses undressed the woman. "We might wake you if they come through our door!"

And both princesses laughed even more when Asha said: "You'll smell them long before that."

That wasn't even a joke, she thought, as she immediately fell to sleep.

Apart from the dreams that came, the dead faces of the warriors she had killed looming up before her to be killed again, she slept reasonably well. She woke early, though, as she always had. When she was a herd-girl back in the Mountains of the Moon she had always slept at night with one eye open and would wake with the first inkling of light on the land. She had usually been cold and uncomfortable at night and too hot in the day. But that had been all her life had been then, she knew nothing else. Her uncle had been ready with his fists and his wife had treated her with contempt, so she had preferred the company of the hvass and the rugged, open pastures of the mountain slopes, to that dung-heap of a village.

She'd grown from girl to maiden on those mountains; a harsh mistress to serve, with only the strength of her arms, her staff and her throwing spears, to keep the herd safe from the lions and from the other tribes, for whom hvass rustling was a pleasant diversion from the mundane routine of their lives.

At a certain age, she could not remember when, men had started to pay her court, bringing her gifts and food to share, trying to get her drunk on kassa. She'd wondered at all the attention, but had looked down at herself one day while bathing in a mountain stream and seen the swell of her breasts and the way her hips had started to round out. She'd wondered then what her life might have in store for her; she could see herself at some corn crib, milking her hvass, making cheese with a baby on her back. But she had banished that future; she would follow the way of the warrior as Moon Maidens had in the past. Her uncle had given her a glimpse of how these men might turn out and she couldn't be in thrall to one of them. So when she saw the star fall, she decided to follow it and see where it landed, to wash the stink of hvass off herself for once and for all.

Lying awake there, she looked at the two Piroushi girls, sprawled on cushions on the floor, where they had slept so not to disturb her. She well remembered how, when she first met them, she had looked on them as delicate, excitable creatures, too ornamental to be of any practical use. But now, as she looked at Kusha, she felt such affection for her, such intense feeling, that she almost wished that she had not taken those vows of chastity.

She banished the thought from her head; she had chosen what she had chosen and that was not a path that she was any longer free to take. She thought that there would, one day, be some Piroushi noble who would make Kusha his wife. She would, no doubt, if any of them survived this siege, grow into her role as wife and mother. But Asha was just grateful for the moments of friendship that she was showing her now.

She dressed quickly and quietly and picked up her weapons, taking them from the cushions on which they lay by the bed. At the door, she turned just once, to look at the sleeping girls, and then went out back to the war.

Chapter 25
Over The Sea To Piroush

Khamis held on tightly to Robyn's hand as the wind took the ship's sails.

"We are truly on the way, friend Rahani. Soon we will see the islands, so lush and green, with the clear blue seas between them and the white sand of their beaches."

Robyn could see that the girl was almost ecstatically excited.

"My mother told me about Piroush, but I've never been there before."

Robyn tried to calm her, afraid they were drawing attention, but most of the travellers on the deck of the ship were too taken up in their own reveries, many of them, in a similar way to Khamis, long-time exiles coming home.

It had been a long hard journey, all of two weeks on the road. They had left Melanthera from its eastern gate as part of a caravan travelling to the coast. Khamis had told her that they would cross the desert, which would take them north of the lands of the Hvassara and through the oases of the Harradim. Harradim warriors rode with them as an escort, hiding their weapons until they were clear of the city and had passed over the great arch of the stone bridge which spanned the river Khalamis. President Quintal had proclaimed that there was a state of peace throughout the land, and whether it was a lie or not, he had forbidden weapons to be wore within his jurisdiction by anyone but the police and military. But as he effectively only controlled

Melanthera, the Harradim had got used to this pantomime of hiding their arms on the way into the city and uncovering them on the way out.

As they passed under the great gate house on the bridge, Robyn could see that it was deserted and in disrepair. They had no need for such defences now; the rockets and guns of the cruisers had made them obsolete. Looking back at the city, Robyn could see the red scars cutting into the hillside that marked the building work that was going on up the slopes that led to the citadel. Khamis told her that the houses the Empress's supporters had fled, or been deported from, were being cleared to make way for mansions and parks for President Quintal's new quarter, planned by and designed for Sun Yang personnel and executives from other corporations.

"He would sell every one of us to the Star People, if he could," she said.

From what Robyn had gathered from Khamis, who had in turn gathered it from the bazaars and markets of Melanthera, an admittedly convoluted route, Quintal had a number of advisers from Sung Yang. There was also a commercial embassy, headed by an Ambassador Carstairs, which also had his ear. So Robyn wondered whether the tail was in fact wagging the dog, an analogy she tried to use on Khamis, who took ages to get it.

"You see," she finally said, "though I now know what a dog is, we don't have them in Melanthera and I know little about them."

That explained why Khamis had been so terrified of the sniffer dogs they had seen at some of the transport hubs.

The caravan journey had started out as an almost magical experience for Robyn. Leaving the city, getting through the eastern gate past the Republican Guard, had been an anxious experience, but once through the gates she had felt liberated from the fear and paranoia that characterised life in Melanthera for people like her and Khamis. For now, like it or not, they were part of a demimonde of shadowy figures, dark streets and shuttered houses, that was the Melantheran underground.

Out here in the countryside, she felt free. The sheer, garish spectacle of the caravan, with its scores of haras, either being ridden or carrying cargo, seemed exhilarating. There were Piroushis dressed in colourful silks, Harradim women in robes with their golden nose rings, Barossi men with their face veils, and, riding on the flanks and in front of and behind them the romantic, dashing figures of the Harradim warriors with their headscarves, flowing cloaks and long lances.

A day in the saddle was enough to disabuse Robyn of her romantic ideas. Riding haras was not a particularly pleasant experience, the creatures could be quite vicious, trying to nip you when you weren't looking, and when they stopped, Robyn found herself almost unable to walk upright. Khamis was having similar trouble, not having ridden before either, so they managed to persuade one of the wagon drivers to take them up as passengers. He was a jolly, happy Melantheran, who, Khamis told her, talked unceasingly about his two wives; one in Melanthera and one at Hava Port where they were to take ship. He also, apparently, had hordes of children, and he talked about them at length too.

As Robyn could not understand a word he was saying, the journey was more pleasant for her than for Khamis, but only just. These desert tracks were dusty and rutted; they were bounced up and down unmercifully, the grit and sand penetrating the cloaks and headscarves they wore, making them cough and their skin itchy. There was no water to wash in either; they didn't carry enough to waste. Khamis said that they could bathe at the next oasis. You got used to most things in the end, Robyn thought, and after a few days of alternating between riding the haras and travelling in the wagon, she had inured herself to the trip.

After three nights camping in the desert, where Robyn huddled beside Khamis under their blankets trying to stave off the cold, they got to the first oasis. The desert plains suddenly gave way to a line of bluffs that formed a brittle, abraded crust of land. The track cut through a gorge and down into the valley beyond. Above the blank walls of the defile, Robyn could see, high above them, a sort of tower or emplacement built into the rock, where a couple of figures stood watching them pass.

Seeing her looking up, the wagon driver said:

"Those are Harradim sentries. That eyrie of theirs looks out over the plains behind us and watches for Hvassara raiders. They can look out a long way from there. They've probably seen our dust since this morning."

The oasis itself was a patchy, rocky shelf of green besides the trickle of a river and a collection of rock pools, where hot springs bubbled up from out of the earth. A squat, walled fort of mud-brick sat just beside the track, its gates open and their caravan stopped just outside the entrance; the wagons drawn up in their customary circle and the stock taken to water and pasture.

"Friend Rahani, take your things." Khamis said. "We sleep under a roof tonight."

Robyn gathered up the bundle of her bedding, and the hvass hide satchel in which she kept her money and her papers, and followed Khamis through the open gates of the caravanserai. The walls, low in height but with tooth –like crenulations for defence and watchtowers at each corner, enclosed a wide oblong of open space with all the buildings of the place built against the sides of the enclosure. The outer walls were old and thick, keeping the buildings that leaned on them, cool and comfortable in the day's heat and insulated from the night cold.

Indicating the open space of the courtyard Khamis said:

"This is so that all the animals and wagons can be brought in if there's a raid. It used to be enough to deter the Hvassara, closed gates and manned walls."

Khamis had told her that when the great Hvassara army had marched on Melanthera, some of the oases had fallen to them, the people being slaughtered or enslaved, even though the caravanserai had always been regarded as a sort of neutral ground, where the enmities and hostilities of the outside world were temporarily laid aside. There were two routes across the desert and the plains and they were taking the northern one, which hadn't suffered from the same Hvassara depredations as the southern route.

"They say the Star People have built their own track in the south," Khamis told her, "where their crawlers run and ordinary people are kept away."

Robyn thought that she must be referring to a road serving the miners or the Defence Force, though they were so closely aligned that you could hardly see a difference between the two groups.

The caravanserai was quiet, they had arrived in the heat of the early afternoon, but as they found their lodgings, a sort of women's dormitory in the shadows under the fort's walls, Robyn could see that people were beginning to stir. Harradim women were starting the cooking fires and carrying water and food back and forth between the buildings. Harradim women, like Harradim men, wore long robes and a head scarf, which covered their hair. They formed a contrast to the group of Piroushis, in their colourful silks, who had been part of her own caravan, but were now stalking about the grounds of the place like so many colourful birds.

Robyn had studiously avoided them, conscious of the fact that she was supposed to be one of their country women, but Khamis had spent some time in conversation with them, obviously excited by meeting her fellow Piroushis and the opportunity to talk about the country she had never seen. Khamis had found out that they were a troupe of dancers, returning to Piroush after a tour of Melanthera and the mining camps.

"Kal Quintal wants to show off our culture to his Star People friends," Khamis said, laughing.

They left their things in the dormitory, though Robyn was reluctant to leave the satchel.

"It's alright, Rahani," Khamis said. "No one steals in a caravanserai. If they did, the Harradim would kill them."

Khamis gave money to an old Harradim woman at a stall just inside the gate and she in turn gave her two rough, linen-like sheets. Then the Piroushi girl pulled Robyn by the hand towards the river and the pools beyond. They passed a little way from one pool, where they could see a number of men in the water, and, going between two rocks, came to another where Robyn could see a group of women bathing. Though they were naked, they were obviously Harradim, as they all wore a small gold ring in their left nostril. They smiled at the two foreign women and beckoned them in.

Robyn and Khamis took their clothes off and left them on a nearby rock. Robyn heard a stifled giggle from two young Harradim girls as she got down to her vest and pants. Her underwear wasn't an oddity in Melanthera, as many people, particularly the migrant workers, had adopted Star People clothing, but here amongst the Harradim it was obviously regarded as exotic.

In a few short years, the influence of the Star People had been pervasive, so the combination of awkwardness and misunderstood physical cues that would have marked Robyn out as a foreigner before their arrival weren't now so marked. Many of the migrant workers had adopted more than the clothes of the Star People, they'd also taken up the gestures and mannerisms of the people who had conquered them by stealth, as much as by military might. It was also not uncommon for words and sentences from the Star People's languages to pepper conversations. Even Melantherans said 'O.K.' now.

Though Khamis and Robyn had had to maintain the cover story that Kahani was a deaf-mute, Robyn was picking up more and more Melantheran. It was a blessedly straightforward language, much like the people who spoke it, so she was able to understand more and Khamis spent less time whispering explanations to her.

The water on her skin felt soothing and cool after the desert. Though it was hot, from the thermal springs, it didn't feel unpleasantly so and there was an effervescent quality to it, like soda. In halting Melantheran, a young Harradim woman told them that it was good for their skin, which didn't surprise Robyn as it seemed salty and mineral laden.

The Harradim women shared their soap and even washed their hair for them with it. It was a comforting and somehow touching experience for Robyn to have a young Harradim woman, who could only communicate by touch or gesture having no Melantheran, do this favour for her in such a gentle and considerate way. But it seemed the norm here; this was a woman's space, where no men would intrude, and there were no strangers or foreigners here, just other women.

Afterwards sitting on a flat rock with Khamis beside her, wrapped in her sheet, Robyn experienced a moment of peace and well-being unlike any other she could remember. That other world - of Hanis, of Thera before Hanis - seemed so far away. Out here she was nothing - or so she thought Abi, or Esmee, would think - a refugee or a runaway. Both women, though different in the way they looked at the world, would think, if they knew, that she had fallen a long way and was now on the margins of their society to be pitied or feared. But, looking at Khamis beside her and the sleek, dark bodies of the Harradim women with their long raven hair, given a sheen by the low, afternoon sun, she felt that she was something, or in fact more than something, part of this world, this Elanthia. She was Robyn, the enemy of the state, on Hanis, but here, in the desert, she was Rahani, friend of Khamis and sister to all these women.

Later, as they ate under the stars on the great tables that the Harradim women had set out in front of the dormitories, the Piroushi dancers, well-watered with borriba wine, gave a spontaneous performance of Piroushi dancing. As the men and women whirled about in their bright colours, dipping and rising, moving their bodies in strange, formal bird-like movements, which waved and flowed through the dancers as if they were possessed by some other, unearthly force, Robyn could feel their energy coursing out and being carried to the spectators. She could almost taste them, she thought, all her senses were so attuned to them. The rhythms of the music, repetitive but complicated, were almost hypnotic; the oils they used on their skins had a musky, sexual tang, which filled her nostrils; her eyes reflected that kaleidoscope of colours that the movement of their silks made, as they whirled around and around.

She now understood why Piroushi dancers were so renowned. She had seen ballets on Thera and other forms of dance from the old Earth cultures, but nothing had touched her like this. It was an experience that filled up all your senses, glutted them. A drunken Hvassara - there were a few amongst the travellers in the caravanserai - made a grab for one of the Piroushi girls as she passed. She just laughed and nimbly dodged his grip, but two grim-faced Harradim warriors seized him and hustled him out of the gates.

"He'll have to sleep outside tonight!" Khamis laughed.

Too soon, it was over. The Piroushi dancers sat down again at their table and drank more wine.

"Are our people not the best dancers, friend Kahani?" Khamis asked.

Robyn, who had also consumed a quantity of borriba wine, could only nod and agree. She felt strangely hollow; she didn't want the dancing to stop, it was as if she was addicted to it.

Khamis must have guessed what she was feeling for she said:

"They say that the Emperor Milo the First was so obsessed with a Piroushi dancer that he forfeited his throne to follow her."

She said more, told the whole story, but Robyn wasn't listening. As she watched the girl's face and the way the firelight played on the perfect curve of her nose, the fine arch of her eyebrows, that warm, sensual mouth, as they sat under the light of those cold, distant stars, Robyn wondered if she'd ever loved anybody so much before.

The memory of that night – or at least the early part of it - would later become for Robyn a precious, dream-like thing. When they eventually went to bed, she lay next to Khamis in the darkness listening to her soft breathing. But there were other women who slept less softly and there was a particular flea-like creature that seemed to relish her skin, so the night was much less perfect than it should have been and she woke up feeling somehow forlorn.

Oasis followed oasis and, in a number of days, they had come to Hava port, where ships had been waiting and it took only a little haggling from Khamis to secure them a passage. The two nights they had spent in Hava port had been uncomfortably hot, the thin strip of coastal plain that the town straggled, overshadowed by a chain of low mountains, gave it a humid climate so different from the dry heat of the desert they had passed through. They'd slept on the flat roof of an inn like the other guests.

Hava port was reminiscent of Melanthera, its narrow streets of tall overhanging buildings all feeding down to the port that was its reason for being. It had always been a Melantheran enclave, controlling the traffic between the capital and Piroush, walled and fortified and garrisoned by Imperial soldiers. During the days they'd spent in the desert, Robyn had been in a dream-like state lost in the landscape and in her love for Khamis, but in Hava port, seeing the black uniforms of Quintal's Republican Guard on the street, she was brought quickly and uncomfortably out of her reverie. The fear that had been somehow subdued, if not banished, while they journeyed, had come back.

She experienced one moment of real terror at the port, when, as the Republican Guard were checking the embarking passengers' documents, she noticed, as one of the guards lifted a curtain and disappeared into the back room of the customs building, two figures in the drab military fatigues of the Defence Force sitting at a table. Just a glimpse was enough to send her into a panic which, until she mastered it, made her want to run away from the line, to leave Khamis and take off. As it was the guards just gave their papers a perfunctory check - she wondered if they could actually read and comprehend the passports that the migrants carried - and gestured them on.

Now standing on the deck of the ship, she let herself relax a little, carried away and infected by Khamis's excitement. As the ship left the shelter of the bay that Hava port had been built on, Khamis's excitement lessened, Robyn could see from the look on her face that she was finding the motion of the ship strange and alien to her.

"I didn't know it would be like this, friend Rahani," the girl said. "My stomach feels like it is turning over."

"You'll be alright," Robyn tried to re-assure her, though she didn't feel much confidence in what she was saying. "You'll get used to the motion of the ship."

By this time Khamis had lain down on the deck on their bedding, like most of the other passengers. There were no cabins as such; they would sleep on the deck like the rest of their companions. Though she spent her days with Khamis and invariably slept besides her, what Robyn really wanted was to be alone with the woman. It seemed to her that in Melanthera, and its Imperial hinterland, a person was seldom alone. You lived your life out on the street, on the plain or in the desert, in the most intimate of circumstances. There was little concept of private space, especially amongst ordinary people, and everyone seemed to be markedly sociable, craving company as if it was as natural as craving food.

The Star People, as Robyn had taken to calling her own kind, spent most their lives away from each other, in cubicles or private rooms. Even when she lived with Esmee on Thera, she'd never been as physically close to her as she was with Khamis. There'd always been private spaces, even in their apartment, a closed bathroom door, time apart in the day when they were both working. She was hardly ever apart from Khamis now and this physical closeness had come to feel a natural part of things. She had noticed that Melantherans seldom did anything on their own, including going to the toilet. Occasionally she felt overwhelmed and irritated by this constant company, but, on the other hand, she seldom felt lonely or isolated.

She wondered at herself, whether she had changed so much over the past few months. When she was living with Esmee, there were times when she had to get away from the stifling atmosphere of their life together, to be alone, to be just Robyn. But with Khamis, things were so different, they might argue or snap at each other, that was normal, but it would soon pass. The bond between them was too deep; the girl had basically saved Robyn from imprisonment and worse.

"Have you never been on a ship before, friend Khamis?" Robyn asked, going to sit beside her, leaning her back against the bulkhead.

"Once, when I was too young to remember. When my family first travelled to Melanthera, but not since." Robyn thought that her friend was looking decidedly pale.

"Khamis, you've travelled light years in space liners. You've been to lots of different planets; a few waves and a fresh wind is nothing to you," she said, trying to reassure Khamis.

"Rahani, sister, the sky doesn't move about beneath your feet so. The sea of space doesn't turn your stomach over."

Khamis put her head on Robyn's lap and the older woman put her arm around her and felt her brow.

"You feel hot, dear." She said. "Perhaps you are unwell."

She knew nothing of Melantheran illness and, for a moment, she panicked, wondering what she would do if the girl fell seriously ill.

"Don't worry, Kahani," Khamis said. "It is just the sea."

Then, lifting her head a little:

"But why doesn't it affect you?"

"I've travelled on oceans before, Khamis, and where I lived until recently there was a large lake where we used to go sailing on weekends. So I'm used to it."

Khamis, looking around her at the other Melantherans, who all, apart from the sailors, seemed to be suffering equally, seemed astonished at this new-found attribute of Robyn's.

"So you are a sailor, Rahani," Khamis said, "so I should feel safe in your hands."

Robyn nodded:

"You will get used to it, Khamis, and my people used to say that a sea voyage is good for the soul, or the heart or something, so it may even do you good."

Robyn could see that, as much as she tried to make her do so, Khamis didn't quite believe her.

Chapter 26
Message In A Bottle

There it was again, the short encrypted message that had somehow got through the security net:

"You have friends outside. We are listening. Keep sending."

Berthaud had first started sending her reports, her diary of the siege as it were, out in short, encrypted data bursts. There was no way that the Star People – as she now thought of her erstwhile comrades - could turn the Sung Yang communication grid off, all they could do was erect a firewall, to stop her accessing their network from the citadel. But there was such a volume of military traffic being bounced up from the ground to the satellites which Sung Yang had put into orbit around Elanthia, that its wasn't difficult to piggy-back on these communications. The only problem with this was that these digital messages got no further than the Sir John Franklin and sat somewhere, hidden, in the main frame of its computer.

It had been, ultimately, a frustrating process. She could run her pad and her communications equipment off solar batteries and could keep sending, but no-one could receive her messages. Then she found an unexpected solution. The One God One Church people were still carrying on their proselytising mission amongst the Hvassara, convinced that the nomads would swap one sky god for another one. The One God One Church people were not as careful about security as the Sung Yang people. Berthaud had, after a few fruitless attempts, been able to hack into their ship's server and facilitate a sub-light channel to broadcast directly onto the Hub.

Travel between the stars had been impossible because of the time and distances involved, until the inner planets had learned how to use worm-hole technology to do so. In essence, when a ship needed to travel at sub-light speeds, it was effectively creating an artificial worm-hole to facilitate this. In the same way, the same phenomenon could be used to send communications.

Berthaud was publishing a blog called "reports from Melanthera", not a very original title, but a practical one. It was a 'pop-up' blog; she had effectively created a virus that would make use of different servers to publish her reports on the Hub. When it was shut down on one server, it would start up on another. Anyone searching for news or information about events on Elanthia would find it. That was the theory, anyway, though on days when she felt particularly low she wondered if anybody out there was listening to her, reading what was going on.

It was becoming increasingly obvious that Sung Yang were running the siege by proxy. The very fact that the Hvassara army were staying in the field so long was due mainly to the food and fodder that Sung Yang was providing, shipping it in using company cruisers. She also suspected that there were more and more undercover Defence Force soldiers and mercenaries amongst the besieging force. Some of the Hvassara units were acting more and more professionally. They were increasingly engaging in night sorties and showing much more discipline than was usually expected of Hvassara, who basically had two military tactics; the surprise attack and the quick withdrawal.

One of Asha's sorties had been ambushed on their way back to the safety of the city walls and had only been able to extricate itself with difficulty. Even Asha had been surprised:

"Usually, you can smell the Hvassara before you see them and they can't keep still, so they're not good at ambushes."

Asha was good at ambushes and counter-ambushes, though. While her party had been pinned down, she had almost single-handedly outflanked the ambush party and caused such confusion that it had had to withdraw.

This had caused much rejoicing amongst the Melantherans, but some consternation in the Palace. Berthaud had overheard the Piroushi princess, Kusha, telling Gamelon:

"She will be killed one day, taking those sorts of risks. She's mortal after all."

"But she's the people's hero," Gamelon had replied," and they need their heroes at this dark time."

The princess had replied:

"This is no longer a war for heroes; it is just a slaughter ground. There's no glory in it, just pain, suffering and death."

Berthaud knew that this was a new kind of war for the Melantherans, not the sort of skirmishing they were used to, but a full-on war of attrition against civilian as well as soldier. She wrote it all down in her next blog, leaving out names. For she didn't doubt that someone, somewhere was compiling a list.

Another sign that Sung Yang was getting more directly involved in the siege, was that the cannon fire was getting increasingly accurate, but, even so, the barrages aimed at the walls and the citadel weren't having much of an effect. The Melantherans had been frightened at first by the guns, but had, eventually, grown used to them. The Hvassara tended to fire twice a day - mid-morning and late-afternoon - and the city's inhabitants had got into a routine that involved being active between the salvoes and taking cover at firing times. Occasionally, the enemy would vary their time-table and a disaster might ensue, but it had amazed Berthaud how the Melantherans had learned to cope.

The cannon the Hvassara utilised didn't generally have the range or power enough to do much actual damage to the walls and the Melantherans would use the nights to carry out repairs and shore up damaged sections. The citadel had been hit a few times, but one of Asha's sorties had put paid to the brace of longer guns that had done the damage. That wasn't to say that people weren't dying every day, a steady drip of casualties, but the city was holding out.

There was one major concern. The Hvassara had started to concentrate their fire on the Hwrathka Gate and the walls on either side of it. It looked as if they were determined to affect a breach there and Berthaud knew that this would be the climax of the siege; once the nomads were inside the walls the final battle would have begun.

Gamelon had told her this a few days ago, when they had been out in the gardens by one of the fountains, drinking some of that odd-tasting durgan root tea that the Melantherans loved so much.

"Asha gives it a few days," he said, "the Generals are more optimistic. But, whoever's right, as fast as we repair it, they knock it down. And once they are through the walls..."

He left the sentence suspended in the air. Around the open ground of the palace gardens, domed tents had been pitched and refugees and soldiers were settling down for the night. Somewhere, Berthaud told herself, somebody is blackening their face and sharpening their weapons, with murder on their mind. And whether it's our people going over the walls, or their people trying to get in, some poor souls will die or get maimed tonight. She realised she had said 'our people', and then thought that there was nothing like a war to get you to take sides.

She'd made her way back to her quarters, more weary than usual, all the spirit gone from her. Just when she was thinking about going to bed, she noticed the light blinking on her pad. The message – the first one - read:

"Berthaud, we are listening. Keep the reports coming. Your friends on the outside."

On the outside of what, she thought. But even though she was suspicious, Sung Yang or even the Defence Force intelligence people could be using this as some sort of ploy, she felt her spirits lifting and she redoubled her efforts, sending out blogs daily. And messages kept coming in, all anonymous, unsigned, as if they were plucked from the ether.

They told her that people on the Inner Planets knew about the war on Elanthia and suspicions had been raised that Sun Yang was involved. Questions had been asked by delegates in the Assembly of Confederated Planets about what was going on in Melanthera. People were openly saying that Sung Yang had broken the rules of its commercial agreement with the Outer Planets territorial government. But the territorial government kept saying that it was an internal matter and the deaths of the Sung Yang personnel at the hands of the Empress's Barossi had leeched away some of the sympathy for the Melantherans, which, up till then, had been growing.

"Everyone likes an underdog," one of the messages had said, "and the Melantherans are the über-underdogs."

She had told the Empress about these outside messages, but the older woman had been unconvinced.

"Friend Berthaud," Mila had said, "will these friends you say we have on other worlds come with their airships to aid us?"

She tried to answer this, trying to explain to Mila how public opinion could influence things on her world, but the Empress just smiled.

"In the end we will get no help. People may ask questions when we are no more and mourn our passing, but we'll still be gone."

Though she couldn't convince the Empress, Berthaud was buoyed up by her contact with the outside. As she helped in the hospital, or watched the weary groups of soldiers changing guard at the gates and on the walls, she thought that it was possible help would come. Not the airships that Mila hoped for, but an intervention by the Defence Force to broker a cease-fire and help keep the peace. There must be people out there, she thought, amongst the powerful, who recognised the injustice that was being done, who would want to right this wrong.

But then the final message came. It blinked onto her screen like a beacon that would light the way home.

"Tell us where you are. Send the planetary positioning system co-ordinates and we will come and get you. You can do so much more on the outside."

She had turned her PPS off, fearing that she would be targeted by a drone or a bombing raid, and reading the message she was so tempted to switch it on again, to be done with this and get back to her own people. But her fingers paused on the keys of her Pad. They knew she was in the palace from her blog. They would also know that her quarters were part of the Imperial household. If the message was false, she would be providing precise targeting information.

Besides, how would her supposed band of supporters on the Inner Planets have the resources or ability to send a rescue force to get her out? No, she thought, the only people with the power to do so would be Sung Yang or, more precisely, one of its special security teams. She switched the Pad off, reluctantly powered down all her communications equipment, taking care to close up the satellite dish.

She became conscious that the light was going, but she did not get up to light a lamp. Sitting there in the dark, she realised that she was now cut off from that outside world, her world, and was left stranded in this one. Whatever happed to Melanthera would happen to her. Strangely, she did not feel any fear, though she told herself she should, she just felt a great sense of calm steal over her.

"When you can see the end of your life coming, see it close at hand," Berthaud thought or spoke aloud, she wasn't sure which, "you don't have to worry about the future anymore."

Her reverie was broken by a sharp rap on the door screen. That was Gamelon's knock. She invited him in.

"It's tomorrow!" He said and at first she wondered what he meant.

"The wall is breached," he said, "by the Hwrathka gate. The final attack will come tomorrow, probably at dawn. We are making preparations."

She asked what she could do.

"Nothing," he said, "you must be our watcher, our witness. Then you can tell the other worlds what happened here."

Chapter 27
In The Hwrathka House

Berendal found the stairs difficult; he had been furnished with crutches but it was still slow going. The Hwrathka House was ancient and had been built on a monumental scale, half sunken into the earth of the plateau to keep the great creatures cool in the Melantheran summer. It was as if the steps had been designed for bigger men, small giants or very tall people, he thought. He had difficulty keeping up with Gamelon and his head was aching and his shoulder smarted each time he landed heavily on the next tread.

The stairway they were descending dropped steeply from the surface level of the plateau near the Empress's apartments and would take then down to the stalls where the hwrathka slept. Before the siege, it was common to see the vast animals, with their shaggy heads and long curving horns, exercising on the parade ground or just grazing on the fodder that had been spread around. But since the siege, and the cannonading of the palace, the creatures had been kept in their stables. And it was obvious that they didn't like it. They were making that almost hypnotic, lowing sound, the bass note held at length until it ended in a sigh.

"Poor things," Gamelon said, turning towards him and waiting for him at a landing, "they miss the sunlight and the air."

A voice further off, down lower on the stairs said:

"They'll soon have plenty of that. Too much, I would say."

It was Asha speaking. Berendal could see by Gamelon's face that the remark had made him uncomfortable. Asha, being from the western mountains, did not have the same affection for these creatures that the city-dwellers had. To the Melantherans there was an almost sacred aspect to them, as they were inextricably linked to the goddess Elanta; you could see in the illustrations of her sojourn on the earth, in the ancient tomes of the Melantheran faith, that she was carried by one, as were her many consorts and companions. They were also, by association, living symbols of the Empire.

The two men caught up with Asha on the wooden walkway that spanned the hwrathka stalls below. The hwrathka drivers were with their beasts, grooming them and preparing their harness for the day ahead. Asha seemed pensive. She turned to the two men as they approached.

"It's a long time since the hwrathka have been to war. Can they still do it? Can they charge the enemy without flinching?"

"It's what they have been trained for," Gamelon said, "every day of their lives since they came here as calves."

"But training is different from fighting," Asha sighed, "and I think they are our last hope."

Berendal looked down at the drivers, who were now fitting the saddles to the creatures' backs. The hwrathka were as tall as the first floor of a building; some older ones even taller. They were wide enough to carry the driver and one or two archers on

305

their backs. The creatures would use their horns in the charge, lowering their heads, so the driver and the archers had to be well-trained and highly-skilled, just to keep themselves from falling, let alone fighting. The problem was that none of them had ever been in battle before. Most of their work was ceremonial, parading on feast days and religious festivals. The hwrathka force had not been tried in battle for over fifty years.

Berendal looked down at the great creatures. With the flickering of the lights, making their great shadows loom up and then diminish like the waves on the sea, with that deep, lowing sound that filled your ears, and, most of all, with that over-powering smell of dung, sweet animal breath and the acid tang of urine, it seemed that he was revisiting a dream he had once had. A dream he had dreamt when he was another person in another, different place.

"Berendal," Asha said, the irritation marked in her voice, "no time for dreams now, or composing poems in your head. It's time."

Later, before dawn, he watched the hwrathka units being assembled on the parade ground. Asha had gone down to the Hwrathka Gate, to the breach, getting ready to delay the Hvassara as long as posslble. Gamelon stood beside Berendal with Berthaud close by. Suddenly there was a commotion behind them and the Empress and her entourage erupted from one of the doors.

Her chamberlain was talking to her, dogging her footsteps, while simultaneously trying to fall at her feet, which made a ludicrous, impossible picture. He kept kneeling down, then getting up and scuttling a few paces, then kneeling down again.

"Your majesty," he said, "you have no need to do this. And it is not fitting. Please, refrain from this act."

The Empress was ignoring him and only stopped when she had drawn level with the commander of the first unit of hwrathkas.

"Is my beast ready?" she asked.

"Yes, your highness," the man replied. "It awaits you."

A large hwrathka was led up and Berendal noticed that it had a sort of roofed platform mounted on its back.

"I shall need assistance, men," the Empress addressed the hwrathka soldiers, "you'll probably have to haul me up."

The deed was done with some difficulty. No ordinary soldier could feel at ease manhandling an Empress.

"Your majesty, please!" The chamberlain went on plaintively. "Not in the front rank, please!"

"Nonsense," the Empress replied. "This is the most fun that I've had in years."

The hwrathka captain asked if she wanted an archer to accompany her.

"No, Captain," she replied, "friend Gamelon will ride with me. If we are bothered by the enemy, he will recite a few passages from his new history. That will put paid to the fiercest warrior."

They all laughed at this, even Gamelon. All except Berthaud, who was furiously fiddling with that machine of hers, trying to translate the joke.

307

"Friend, Berthaud," the Empress said. "Go to the top of the tower on the citadel gatehouse. From there you will either see us lose the Empire or win the day."

Then she looked down at Berendal.

"Are you not joining us, poet?" She asked.

"Of course, your highness," he answered and then added a rhyming couplet:

"Too wounded to mount a hwrathka and with a sore arse,

I'll have to make the most of a ride on a haras."

There was laughter again at this – nervous thought it was - and insulting comments about the quality of his poetry, as the units began to move out. And then Noor was beside him, moving almost silently out of the deeper darkness of the terrace. She hugged him, held onto him, as if she wasn't going to let him go, but then she suddenly stepped back.

"I know you have to go, husband," she said, "but come back to me. You are all that I have."

He had difficulty mounting, but felt better when he was on the haras, the sword in his good arm. He rode through the citadel gates, outpacing the slower hwrathka, who would save their speed for the charge. He joined a troop of haras cavalry descending the road to the Hwrathka Gate. The sun was rising up on the horizon and a wave of clear light was spreading towards them over the plain, highlighting the Hvassara camp and emphasising its vastness. Riding on with the cavalry, he wondered what use he would be. If his haras was killed or he lost his seat in the saddle, he would be helpless. But he knew that he could not miss this day of all days.

As they rode down the road they could see that the gates at the end of the side streets had been shut again, as they were that time before, when Quintal tried to wrest the throne from the Empress. Grim face men and women manned these gates. They all knew not to expect any quarter from the Hvassara. They'd been waiting too long to take this city, their vengeance would be terrible.

He thought of his life, the years he'd spent in a cup of borriba wine, the poems he'd written, the women he'd courted. All to end up with a shy, religious Harradim girl. But he was happy and regretted nothing. He was frightened, of course, but there was something about riding in a group of comrades that stirred the heart and kept the fear at bay.

On the final bend of road their commander called a halt and they regrouped. They could see that the attack had already started. Men were still at the walls and at the breach, but the Hvassara were in the process of overrunning them. As he watched he saw a unit of Hvassara musket-men forcing their way through the breach, firing in volleys, rank by rank, to clear a path. Then he saw Asha, but she was giving the signal for withdrawal, the trumpeter with her sounding the call.

The Hvassara understood the Melantheran trumpet commands and gave a cheer. Asha, and the remnants of the force that had manned the walls, retreated across the market square to a line of barricades, as the Hvassara poured in and formed ranks. Asha and her men crouched behind the barricades waiting for the Hvassara to fire, then they would try to rush them before they reloaded, Berendal surmised. Looking at the barricade, he was sure he spotted the tables from the Hwrathka Gate pleasure house, where he'd spent so many pleasant, but empty, hours of his life, longing after one pretty girl or another.

"Steady, my lads!" The cavalry commander said.

Then Berendal saw a strange thing. Asha's trumpeter gave a signal that he didn't recognise and suddenly, with a loud creaking of ropes and timbers the Hwrathka gate slowly opened.

"They have taken the gatehouse," Berendal thought, "or we are betrayed."

Then he heard a sound like he had never heard before. It was like the pounding of a thousand war drums and, at the same time, he heard a low, moaning noise that filled his ears as a cloud of dust enveloped him.

"Clear the road, men. Now!" The cavalry commander shouted and they scrambled to do so, their haras spooked as, out of the dust, came the column of hwrathkas, driving towards the gate.

"Oh, now I see," Berendal said out loud. "Now I see what Asha is doing."

The hwrathka were like a tidal wave or a landslide, an unstoppable force that rolled down into Hwrathka Square. Berendal now saw that Asha had left gaps in the barricade that the hwrathka drivers aimed for. Even so, some of the hwrathka just went straight through this flimsy defence.

The Hvassara on the square had formed ranks and were bringing some small cannons up. They had become complacent, victory had been in their grasp, only Asha's raggle-taggle force to break through. Their blood-lust was up and they had sharpened their knives the night before in anticipation of the pleasure that they would take in the day's slaughter.

Berendal had to give credit to the Hvassara, they tried to keep ranks, discharging volley after volley into the hwrathka, but the musket balls just seemed to anger the creatures. The cannons were more formidable, Berendal saw one hwrathka almost blown apart. But in minutes, the whole enemy force was swept aside by the horns of the hwrathka and trampled under their hoofs. As the dust settled, he saw Asha's soldiers emerging from their barricades to mop up the remnants of the enemy and the cavalry commander gave them the order to move out.

As for the hwrathka, they just kept going, out of the Hwrathka Gate and straight into the Hvassara camp. The rest of the morning was really just a mad race to catch up with the hwrathka.

Berendal passed Asha, outside the gates, making short work of a couple of Hvassara horsemen with the great two-handed sword.

"Can I give you a lift, friend Asha?" Berendal asked..

"There's no need for that, friend Berendal. I have two good legs." Berendal noticed that Asha was smiling, but, it struck him, that it was more of a grimace; Asha's killing face. She takes pleasure in this, he thought, which I could never do.

"Tell me poet," Asha asked. "Was that the Empress Mila I saw earlier sweeping by on a runaway hwrathka?"

"It was," answered Berendal, "and she's probably halfway to the Mountains of the Moon by now."

In the end, he couldn't keep up. His leg hurt, his shoulder was aching and the headache had got worse. He found himself almost alone on the battlefield, except for all the dead and wounded of course. He realised he was in some danger, as there were still stray Hvassara riding to and fro trying to escape the fray.

Suddenly, he saw a group of men looming up out of the smoke of one of the many fires that the Melantherans had started as they burnt the Hvassara's tents. He raised his sword and rode towards them, but then he recognised them as Star People; they were the One God One Church missionaries that Gamelon had told him about. One of them had a machine like Berthaud's that he used to communicate.

"Friend," the machine said, "we are not soldiers, we are men of God. We surrender to you."

He told them that there was no need to surrender, to head back towards the city, where they would be safe.

There were some bad sights he saw, amongst them the bodies of women and children. The hwrathka didn't discriminate, they mowed everyone down. He also saw some dead Star People, in military uniforms, their guns in their hands. But that was different, they had chosen to fight and consequently died; the women and children hadn't

He was thinking of turning back to the city, when a column of hwrathka lumbered out of the smoke, which had now got so thick that he suspected the grass had caught fire. On the first hwrathka was the Empress.

"Is that you, friend Berendal?" Mila asked. "Could you not keep up with us?"

"The hwrathka were too fast for me, your Highness," he answered." I didn't know they were capable of such a turn of speed."

"Neither did the Hvassara," the Empress answered. "We've routed their whole army. It seems that the siege is over at a stroke. They've thrown down their weapons and taken to their haras. Where they were one unified army, they are now so many tribes riding as fast as they can back to the plains."

Could it be true? Berendal thought. Could they have won victory with one swift stroke?

"It was the hwrathka, Berendal," the Empress said, as if reading his mind, "there's never been a charge like this in my lifetime. It put the fear of Elanta into them."

She turned around looking at the hwrathka units, which were emerging out of the smoke. It was as if she was counting them, calculating their losses.

"I can't tarry any more, friend Berendal. Your comrade Gamelon is looking decidedly green about the cheeks. I think he would rather be on a stormy sea in Piroush than on a hwrathka back."

As the hwrathka moved off, Berendal noticed a very forlorn Gamelon was slumped behind the Empress. He followed the hwrathka back into the city, over the debris of the Hvassara camp. Later on, he overtook the One God One Church people, who were marching beneath a white banner for some strange reason he couldn't fathom.

Once he was through the Hwrathka Gate, he saw that the pleasure house had already opened its doors, even though the debris of the battle still littered the square and the Sisters were yet tending to the wounded and saying words over the dead. There were no tables - they were still forming part of the barricade - but the girls were passing out cups of borriba wine to the returning soldiers. Alvara, one of the women who ran the place, kept saying loudly that she had three barrels of borriba wine breached and that she wouldn't take money off any soldier. Berendal stopped for one cup, but then feeling guilty about leaving Noor without news of him, he mounted again and rode back to the citadel. She was waiting at the gate amongst a crowd of people, all expectantly looking towards the plains.

She pulled him aside, away from the crowd, as he dismounted, clutching onto him, her eyes full of the tears that she had fought so hard not to shed all morning. She hung onto him like he was her last anchor in the world. Then Berthaud was beside them, unwilling to intrude at first, but then too curious not too.

"Is it true?" She asked. "Has the siege been lifted?"

"It seems so." Berendal replied, suddenly weary. "Asha is still out chasing what's left of the Hvassara army and hunting for Kal Quintal. So it looks like it is over."

Berthaud looked as exhausted as he was.

"I truly hope so," she said. "I truly hope it is over."

Chapter 28
The Dreams That Lovers Have

Piroush was both a surprise to Robyn and a relief.

A relief because the last few days of the voyage had not gone well. They had run into a storm, a tropical squall, and the boat had been tossed about like a cork. Each time the ship crested a wave and crashed down into the trough behind, Khamis thought that they would be swamped and that the sea would claim them. She clung to Robyn, as if the woman was the only secure thing in her world, while the other passengers on the deck prayed aloud to Elanta or wept from fear.

Robyn had told herself that if the sailors didn't look afraid, then she wouldn't worry. But, even so, there were moments when even she started to think that Khamis's gloomy predictions might become true.

Khamis wouldn't let her leave her side.

"Rahani, please stay with me, because I have a mortal fear of this sea," she squeezed Robyn's hand and looked plaintively up at her.

"Don't worry," Khamis, "Robyn said. "I won't leave you."

"You will stay with me if we go in the water," the Pirioushi girl said, "because I am frightened of being alone in the dark in that cold sea."

"I said that I won't leave you," Robyn replied.

After most of one day and them a night on that stormy sea, they awoke to a calm, milky ocean and the hot, spicy scent of the tropical islands that loomed up on each side of the ship.

"We are here, friend Rahani," Khamis said, seeming immediately to recover, standing up on unsteady legs to look out over the rail.

"These are the outlying islands of the Piroushi chain, I heard the sailors talking about it while you were sleeping and I lay awake. They said we should be safe now, these waters are calm and sheltered."

They rested throughout most of that day. All the passengers looked like refugees or survivors from some disaster, washed out and exhausted. The sailors seemed to find this highly amusing. There was one occurrence, though, that stopped their grins and laughter. In the afternoon as they passed between two small islands, two long, low craft glided out across the water towards them. The captain shouted some order that Robyn did not catch and suddenly all the sailors were on deck, bristling with swords and short pikes; other sailors up in the rigging with bows. The passengers were quickly herded down the ladders into the hold and the hatches were closed, so they were locked in the stifling half-light, the air full of the stench of the barely-cured hvass hides that were a large part of their cargo.

Soon, however, the crisis was over and they were freed from their place of refuge and allowed to emerge on the deck again. One of the sailors told Khamis that the two craft had been pirates, but they'd thought better of boarding, when they'd seen the crew standing to arms.

"I don't know what Princess Kusha will have to say about this," the man had gone on, "pirates this close to home waters."

Later Robyn had asked Khamis who this Princess Kusha was.

"Why, she is the ruler of Piroush, of course. When her father died she took the throne, though she is yet unmarried."

Robyn had thought that Piroush was part of the Empire and under Melantheran rule, but Khamis told her otherwise.

"Piroush was part of the Empire, but the Princes were always more allies than subjects, owing allegiance to the Empress who was their nominal overlord. When Kal Quintal took over, Piroush had to acknowledge his rule, because of the support he had from your people, but it has tried to stay as independent as possible."

Khamis laughed: "But every Melantheran child knows this, friend Rahani, why don't you?"

Robyn knew the girl was teasing her, but, even so, felt slightly irritated.

"Khamis," she replied.

"Yes, friend Rahani?"

"I should have thrown you to the fishes when I had the chance."

Khamis's face whitened in shock, but then realising it was a joke, she laughed.

"You people have a strange sense of humour," she said.

Piroush was a surprise because it didn't look remotely like Melanthera or Hava port, but had an exotic sense of otherness. The tropical climate had shaped the city and its architecture. There were no

318

roads as such, because the climate didn't suit haras, so everything was borne by hand or in litters, up and down the narrow stepped streets that ran from the port up into the wooded hills above the city. House were built on terraces, each in its own garden plot and, as a result, the city seemed that much less crowded than Melanthera. The buildings themselves, rather than being made of stone or mud-brick, were light wooden structures, with courtyards and sheltered verandas, so house and garden often merged into one.

There was one aspect in which Piroush resembled Melanthera, the market, which sprawled over the land between the harbour and the first of the town's streets, was as busy; the traders as insistent as their inland counterparts. Another resemblance was the customs post at the dock, which checked the papers of the disembarking passengers, but here the guards were Piroushi; soldiers who, with their head scarves and curved swords at their belts, looked to Robyn more like operatic pirates than members of the military.

As they'd waited in line on the dock, having climbed down the gang plank of the ship, many of the passengers seemed visibly excited, some even kissing the dry, flattened earth of the quay.

"Can you not smell it, friend Rahani?" Khamis asked. "It is like the perfume of paradise."

She was so excited and glad to have arrived that she hugged Robyn.

She was right about the smell Robyn thought, there was an amazingly alluring odour coming down from the mountains, of ripening fruit and dew-touched grass. There was also a rather rancid dock stink coming off the water, somehow countering this pleasanter fragrance, but Robyn didn't want to spoil these moments for Khamis by mentioning it.

She suddenly remembered that Rahani was supposed to be coming home as well, so she tried her best to look as pleased and excited as the other passengers. They went quickly through the perfunctory check of their papers that the Piroushi guards carried out. The soldier who stopped them, in fact, seemed more interested in flirting with Khamis than actually establishing her identity and he even gave Robyn an appraising glance. Khamis just shrugged, as if to say: "What do you expect? This is Piroush after all."

Beyond the customs post, in the open ground before the market stalls, crowds of people had gathered; relatives and families of the travellers, who had been alerted when the ship had passed the heads of the bay. The travellers quickly peeled off into their family groups and Robyn was surprised to see a young woman walking towards them as if she had been waiting for them.

"We are expected! Try not to look surprised, friend Rahani," Khamis whispered to her as the girl shyly approached. She embraced Khamis and touched her cheeks to hers and then Robyn's, in what Khamis would soon explain was the Piroushi way of greeting people.

"You remember friend Rehalla," Khamis said, rather loudly to Robyn and she had to pretend that she did, gesticulating enthusiastically in what she hoped was the Piroushi way. Melantherans and Piroushi had some many different hand gestures –

some only subtly different – that it was easy to make mistakes.

They followed the young woman through the market crowds and then up a stepped street, past gardens and latticed fences, climbing always upwards until Robyn, the humid heat taken its toll, whispered to Khamis:

"How much farther? This is hard work."

"Rehalla says we are almost there," Khamis replied. "Then she will explain all to us."

Soon they turned off the stepped way, onto a narrow path between houses until they came to a gateway farmed in a wood that resembled bamboo, but was more regular and symmetrical.

"We are here, friend Rahani," Khamis said "Rehalla says that she welcomes you to the Nishan woman's house."

The shy Piroushi girl took them across an area of shaded garden to a veranda and led them through a door into a cool, shaded room. She embraced them again and spent some time in conversation with Khamis before eventually leaving.

"Don't worry, friend Rahani," Khamis said as soon as the woman was gone, "this has all been pre-arranged. Rehalla was sent to meet us to convey us to this place, which she says should be safe."

"But how did she know which ship we were on?" Robyn asked, the old fear rearing up again in her.

"Rehalla and the other women have been meeting ships all week, trying to spot us," Khamis replied. "She told me that though Piroush is safer than Melanthera, there are still agents of Quintal and the Star People here, so they thought it would be better to lead us here, rather than have us wandering around."

Robyn realised that their roles had been reversed. On the ship, Khamis had been as dependent as a child on her, but now she, Robyn, was equally helpless, relying on these quiet, gentle Piroushi women to keep her safe.

"We have nothing to do now," Khamis smiled, "we can just rest and get our strength back."

Robyn slept through the mid part of the day. Though the houses were designed to catch every breath of air or passing breeze, the island was hot and humid and sapped her energy, leaving her feeling lethargic. Waking in the late afternoon she found Khamis sitting outside on the veranda of the house. Across the garden she could see a group of women preparing food in an open-air kitchen over a raised bed of charcoal.

"What is this place?" Robyn asked as she went to sit by Khamis.

"It is a women's house, Kahani," Khamis answered, "on Piroush young, unmarried women who have left their families for some reason live in such places. They are run by the Sisterhood."

Most of the women there were young. Khamis would explain to her that most of them had jobs of some sort, in the market or as traders. Some of them were girls who had worked in the pleasure houses, but had chosen to leave and take a different path in life. There were some older women, widows or elderly women without families. There were children too, mostly toddlers and babies. Khamis told her that, thought the house was intended as a place for single women, young women who had received an unexpected 'gift from Elanta', as the Piroushi put it, were also accepted.

They did not see any of the Sisters. Khamis told her that, while the Sisterhood had been banned in Melanthera because of its support for the Empress, and the wearing of the red robes by women also banned, the order had survived on Piroush by becoming less visible.

"Some say that Princess Kusha is one of the Sisters or, at least, that she is one of their patrons. But when the Republic outlawed the order, she could not be seen to openly champion it. So her government upholds the ban, but leaves the Sisters alone as long as they are cautious."

Over the next few days, as she became more familiar with the place, it seemed to Robyn that the Piroushi were playing the same game in all their dealings with Kal Quintal and the Star People; on the face of it they were allies, co-operating with the Defence Force and the Melantherans, but covertly they were doing what they could to keep the old order alive.

According to Khamis, their stay at the Nishan house was only a staging post on their journey. The intention was that they would be conveyed to one of the outlying islands where they could "disappear from view", as she put it. Robyn had been so caught up in the fact of flight that she had never really stopped to consider where she was fleeing to. Now the thought of being stranded on some isolated tropical island was bitter-sweet; while she could look forward with pleasure to the prospect of spending the time with such a gentle companion, the idea that her life would be circumscribed by the limits of beach, jungle and sea, made her uncomfortable. It was just another sort of prison really.

"It will only be until they stop looking for you," Khamis had replied, when she had told her some of this, "then other arrangements will be made."

Robyn noticed that the girl looked hurt and wondered if she'd been ungrateful in the partially grudging way she had reacted to the news.

Though no-one had confirmed it to her, Robyn had become certain that the Sisterhood had been mostly responsible for her escape and ongoing flight. She did not doubt that Khamis had acted out of a sense of friendship, or even love, but she doubted that the girl would have had the resources to act alone. Why the Sisterhood were prepared to put themselves, their networks, at risk for her was a question she sometimes asked herself, when she was awake in those dark hour before dawn, when Khamis slept the sleep of a child, waking clear eyed and full of the life that the new day promised. In the end, it did not matter, she thought. The fact was that their interests had coincided.

Piroushis were terrible at hiding their feelings, not at all like Robyn's people, and, later, in the early afternoon when they should have been sleeping, Robyn woke to find that Khamis wasn't there. She found her sitting on her own in the little courtyard that backed onto the house, where their bathroom was.

She went to her and hugged her, asking what the matter was.

"It is nothing. Please don't be concerned." The girl replied.

"Did I upset you?" Robyn asked." When I was talking earlier?"

"It was not you who upset me, Kahani, but the thought that there will come a time when I will no longer see my friend's face before me each day."

Robyn took Kusha back to their bedroom and held her until she fell asleep, but Robyn stayed awake. Khamis had come into her life suddenly and had then become this constant presence. She could not function here without Khamis, but it was so much more than that. She realised that she, too, could not think of a time when she wouldn't see her friend's face before her each day without sadness.

The Nishan house was not the sort of place where people asked too many questions. Though Piroushi, like Melantherans, were usually curious, or even downright nosy, the women's house was an exception. Many of its inhabitants had ended up there through a variety of life's misfortunes, so there was a sensitivity amongst the occupants about prying too much into other people's stories.

But saying nothing about themselves would have attracted more attention than saying something, so Khamis had let it be generally known that they were two friends, Piroushi from Melanthera, who had travelled back to visit their families in Piroush. They were resting awhile in Piroush before travelling on to one of the outer islands. Kahani was ill, prostrated by the heat and generally in ill health, so she kept mostly to her room. This story seemed to satisfy everyone, except Robyn, who was embarrassed and felt unworthy of the gifts of cold drinks and fruit which were sent in to her by the other women most days.

Every few days Rehalla would call on them, bringing any news, of which there seemed to be little, and sitting with them. Robyn suspected that Rehalla was one of the Sisters, but didn't think it was something she should ask her. A week or so after they arrived, Rehalla had decided that it was safe for them to take a walk outside the bounds of the Nishan house. Robyn had had many greetings as she crossed the garden, many Piroushi hugs.

"You need to look weak and frail, Kahani," Khamis had said to her before they set out. "You should take my arm as we walk."

She'd felt a fraud doing it, but all of the women they met as they made for the gate seemed to take her tottering steps as a sign she was getting better.

They walked up the stepped way and past the last streets of Piroush, soon coming to the forest, where the path became a narrow dirt track leading over the mountain. Rehalla talked and Khamis translated. Though Robyn understood more and more Melantheran, the Piroushi accent was still virtually incomprehensible to her.

"Rehalla says that this is not the real forest. To reach it you must first cross the hill and then descend into the valley, that's where the deep forest is."

Robyn nodded: "Where I come from we used to have similar forests, we called them rain-forests or jungles."

Khamis translated and then, after Rehalla posed a question, asked:

"Rehalla wants to know what happened to them Kahani?"

Robyn shrugged: "We cut most of them down. The rest died out from plant diseases or pollution."

Khamis and Rehalla talked for a while then, as if taking in the information, until finally Khamis said, with a serious face:

"Rehalla says that that was careless of you."

Then a smile broke across Khamis's face and both women laughed. And it was Robyn's turn to wonder whether she would ever understand the Piroushi sense of humour.

Rehalla had told them that it was dangerous for them to go down into the town, but that she would come and walk with them whenever she thought it was safe. From what the Sisterhood had gathered, having sympathisers in the Piroushi army and even in the Republican Guards, the Star People had put out an alert for two women, thought to be dressed as Piroushi in Melanthera, but it didn't seem that they had traced them to Piroush as of yet.

"Rehala says that the Sisters will try and move us in a few days, just in case they are on our trail."

They all knew who "they" were, the Defence Force security branch or one of their Melantheran allies.

"Rehala thinks we are safe enough for a while. She says where better to hide Piroushi women, than amongst other Piroushi women."

"I didn't think my people would give up," Robyn said, when they were back in the house. "They never do. They'll find me eventually, it's just a matter of time."

Then it was Khamis's turn to comfort Robyn. And then the kisses and caresses turned to something other than just comfort and Khamis's gentle hands were all over here, soothing and teasing at the same time, until they were on her breasts and then between her legs.

Later, much later, she lay back in a sort of peace, a moment in time taken from their lives, Khamis, besides her in their bed, smiled at her, head propped up on one elbow.

She said: "That was comfort, Kahani, the sort that women can give each other. And a need fulfilled."

It had been a long time coming, Robyn thought, all those night lying together, building to this.

"You were sad, Kahani, and I wanted to make you happy."

"You have, my dear," Robyn said, "and I did need that."

They lay like that for a long time, Robyn feeling somewhat self-conscious, almost shy.

"Tell me, Khamis," she said eventually, "what is the Piroushi word for love. How do you say it?"

Khamis laughed again: "In Piroushi to 'love' and to 'want' are the same word, we don't see any difference."

Robyn tried, haltingly, to explain what she meant.

"You know what my people mean by love, Khamis, and you know how I feel about you."

Khamis smiled: "Why talk of love, Kahani...Robyn...we are so close that we are part of each other. Is that not enough for you?"

"But people can love each other, Khamis and spend time together, even their lives," Robyn said.

"Women can comfort each other and spend their lives together, Kahani," Khamis said, "but we also need men or how would we make babies?" She was laughing again.

"But Khamis, where I am from women can choose a man or a woman; so can men. They can still have families."

Khamis shook her head: "You really are a strange people."

After that, Robyn decided to keep her own counsel about sexual politics and accept what Khamis had given her. For the Piroushi woman there seemed to be no real differentiation between love and sex, they just reflected the care and affection she felt for Robyn. And Robyn had to admit that it was all so less complicated than the relationships she had had with women in her own world.

Their days together now had an added dimension, an extra depth. They had always taken pleasure in each other's company, but now there was the physical pleasure too. Bathed in sweat one night, twisted and tangled in the covers, Robyn had said to Khamis:

"Did I make too much noise? Do you think anyone heard?"

"Don't worry," the girl answered, "it's normal. Nobody minds. Many of them are doing the same as us."

She had to admit that she looked at the Piroushi women in the compound in a different way after that.

On Rehalla's next visit, she seemed more relaxed. She told Khamis that they were planning to move them in three days' time. They were to be packed and ready on the third morning, when Rehalla would come to take them down to the quay.

They made the most of the two days they had left, not knowing when they would have the same opportunity to be together without other people around them. Robyn thought that Piroushi islanders probably lived their lives in close proximity to each other and she imagined them having to sleep in some communal hut, having to creep out into the jungle to be together. Often they just held each other or Khamis would run her fingers gently over Robyn's back tracing the curves there, sometimes teasing her.

"You have good child-bearing hips, Rahani. You'll make some man happy."

Robyn would frown and act annoyed, until Khamis would try and make things up and they would end up laughing together.

"I don't want a man," Robyn wanted to say, "or another woman. I just want you." She never said it though.

The next day Rehalla came and then they left the Nishan house for good. Robyn was touched by the farewell the other women gave them, the hugs and the tears shed, though she figured that they were more for Khamis than for her. She felt quite excited as they descended the road towards the port. This was another new stage of her life starting.

When they got to the market they turned left. They were heading for the smaller, fishermen's port. Rehalla told them that a small boat would be waiting to take them onwards across the water. From the corner of the market square they took a narrow street that climbed steeply down to the

330

harbour. As they turned a corner of the steps, Robyn saw a couple of men in front of them and as they passed she felt their eyes boring into her neck. She glanced back at them briefly and saw that they had started to follow. Then from a side alley another man emerged.

"Run!" Rehalla shouted turning towards the two men. "Go! Now!"

Robyn dropped her bag and grabbed Khamis's hand pulling her down the steps.

"Rehalla," the girl shouted, looking back, but Robyn pulled her on. Out of the corner of her eye, she could see that Rehalla was down, one of the men standing over her. They ran on towards the bottom of the steps only to see two men there waiting for them. Robyn pulled Khamis into another side alley, running through sheets of washing into an enclosed courtyard. Faced by blank walls, she looked around for a way to escape, but it was too late, the men were on them.

She felt herself knocked off her feet and some sort of sack pulled over her head, as tight restraints were fixed on her wrists and ankles. She struggled and was punched and kicked. She could hear Khamis screaming her name over and over again. Then she felt a needle pushed into her neck and the darkness came.

Chapter 29
Asha's Peace

For once in her life, Asha felt helpless. She could do nothing to stop the terrible moans of pain, alternating with sobbing, that seemed to engulf Kusha. She'd held her in her arms, stayed with her as long as she could, but the girl had been like this since she'd had news of Annesh's death.

"She was so gentle, so sweet," Kusha had said in one of her more lucid moments. "We were children together and I promised her mother I would look after her."

After saying this, the girl collapsed into a flood of tears again.

Though Asha felt for Kusha, and had also had affection for Annesh, she could not understand how the Piroushi girl could let her feelings overwhelm her in this way. What Asha wanted was revenge. She would not mourn Annesh, but she would make sure that the Star People paid for it.

She had to leave Kusha for a while to attend to her duties on the walls, but Noor, that gentle soul who had seen so much of her own hardship, had taken her place. When she'd looked in again, in the early hours of the morning, Kusha was asleep.

Annesh and the chamberlain had been killed in the first and only bombing raid that the Star People had launched against the citadel. She'd been outside in one of the palace yards with the chamberlain, trying to organise a distribution of food to the refugee families camped in the palace gardens. The bomb, or whatever it was, had fallen on them, killing her and the chamberlain instantly and killing or maiming a whole line of refugees who were queuing for the food.

The raid had abruptly stopped when the One God One Church people had rolled out a makeshift panel of white sheeting and their leader, Archdeacon Andrews, had called the Star People up on his communication device to alert them of their presence in the fortress. The God People, as the Melantherans had taken to calling them, had seemed as shocked as the Elanthians by the bombing raid.

"Tell them that you're not hostages. Make that clear." Berthaud had told Andrews. "You are under the Empress's protection and free to go if you want to."

Berthaud had told Asha that Andrews, who was after all an elderly man, seemed confused and baffled by everything that was happening around him. He didn't quite trust the fact that he and his people could walk out of the citadel, so they stayed put.

"It worked in our favour in many ways, as they probably won't try to bomb us again." Berthaud had said later. From what Berthaud had told them, it appeared that the force they were facing now, with its airships and its crawling iron wagons, was not the Sung Yang people, but an army called the Defence Force. Asha had thought the name ironic, as what they mostly seemed to do was attack.

The routing of the Hvassara army had saved them for a while, given them a short reprieve, but had ultimately undone them. A number of Sung Yang personnel had been killed on the field of battle or taken prisoner. Though they were fighting the

Melantherans at the time, the fact that the Melantherans were holding these Sung Yang personnel, plus some other Star People who were probably Defence Force soldiers - according to Berthaud - had been used as a pretext for an appeal from Sung Yang to the territorial authority for outside intervention. The fact that there were also missionaries supposedly being held hostage, only gave credence to their case.

They'd had a brief respite before the arrival of the Defence Force, which had swooped out of the sky one day and started bombing the citadel. At the same time soldiers from the Defence Force had occupied the site of the old Star People base and all of Hwrathka square. Within days, Kal Quintal had arrived back from a brief sojourn hiding in the hills, closely accompanied, or so it was rumoured, by Sung Yang personnel.

Berthaud had explained to Asha that the soldiers from the Defence Force were supposedly a peace keeping force, there to stop the fighting and help the civilian authorities to establish order.

"You know," Berthaud had said. "I'd once hoped for this. How could I have been so mistaken?"

The problem was that the peace that the Star People wanted to keep was Kal Quintal's. To them the Empress was a cruel, remote figure holding dozens of their people hostage. Sung Yang or Defence Force personnel, who'd gone through the Hwrathka charge and survived, were already putting around stories about the savagery of the Melantherans and were telling anyone who would

334

listen of how the Empress had personally led those monsters on that bloody rampage.

The Hvassara, like the skulking carrion they were, thought Asha, had started drifting back, camping outside the walls and selling themselves as mercenaries to Quintal. The city itself was an oddly divided place. Around Hwrathka Square the Defence Force held sway, but they were unwilling to spread out into the narrow streets and winding alleys of the residential neighbourhoods, where their superior weapons were of little use. Quintal held a sort of court in the Star People's compound and he would occasionally send his own forces out to penetrate into parts of the city. These patrols were often met by resistance, so there was a pattern of ambush and skirmishing going on daily.

This situation of stalemate would have been worrying enough, but what was going on outside the city was even more ominous. The Star People were using the Hvassara to cut off the citadel from the outside world, denying the Empress the food supplies and equipment the Imperial forces needed to withstand this second siege. They had been almost fatally weakened by the Hvassara's earlier blockade of the city and the brief respite that they had gained, after routing the nomad army, had not been long enough to rebuild their stocks and replenish their storerooms.

Though Asha did not doubt the martial spirit of her forces, newly confident after their victory over the Hvassara, there was little that she and the other generals could do to combat the twin enemies of hunger and exhaustion that threatened to overwhelm the garrison. They were also not only outnumbered, but literally outgunned. The Defence Force was an army that was centuries ahead of the Melantherans in terms of military technology. Whereas the Sung Yang personnel had adhered to the fiction that the weapons they supplied, the muskets and cannon, were developed by the Hvassara, the Defence Force had no need to adopt this pretext. Quintal's newly formed Republican Guard, a mixed bunch of mercenaries, political exiles and outlaws, had been supplied with the same automatic weapons that the Star People used.

In the street skirmishes that took place in the lanes and the alleyways of the city, the new weapons didn't give Quintal's forces that much of an advantage. This was close quarter fighting and the Republican Guards, widely regarded as traitors, were loath to close with such a fierce, vengeful enemy. They were also ill-trained and their fire was inaccurate, as they would often empty their magazines in the general direction of the enemy, rather than picking targets.

The Melantherans had also picked up a number of the Star People's weapons, supplies had been found in the overrun Hvassara camp and more had been captured from dead or wounded Republican Guards. Though Asha would have nothing to do with these on principal - she still though it more honourable to close with your enemy and deal with him at close quarters - the Melantherans had started to make use of them. The only person in the citadel who had any even a vague knowledge of these weapons was Berthaud. All Sung Yang staff, ethnologists included, had survival training and this training included a basic weaponry course, focussing on small arms. So Berthaud had some sort of familiarity, rather rusty though it was, with the captured weapons and, as a result, she was reluctantly pressed into the business of training the Melantheran soldiers.

Ammunition was a problem, as it was in very short supply. So all the soldiers were drilled, right from the start of their training, in the need to select their targets, lay down accurate fire and to use arrows or close combat weapons where possible. The result was that the Melantherans quickly proved themselves superior to the Republican Guards in the use of these new weapons. Berthaud also made sure they cleaned their weapons at regular intervals, it became a point of personal honour; this was something the Republican Guards seemed to be particularly lax about.

"I'm an ethnologist, I shouldn't be doing this," Berthaud had said to Asha as she brought her another group of recruits, "I've been patching people up all these weeks and now I'm training these young people to go out and kill."

Asha did not reply. Berthaud, like the rest of them, knew how dire the situation was, how each day survived was a minor victory. Unspoken, too, was the fact that Berthaud had further travelled the perilous path from being a dissenter to actively becoming a traitor, in taking up arms against her own people, if only by proxy. The irony was, Asha thought, that Berthaud was actually very good at it; she was a natural teacher, inspiring her pupils to go out and do something that she essentially could not condone.

But war was always like that, Asha reasoned, as she made her way to Kusha's chamber for that evening visit that had become part of her daily routine; just a half hour or so to take her away from the war, to sit in peace with the woman and think of other things, other possible lives. War always made you do things you didn't want to; war modelled your life as if you were clay in the Goddess's hands. In another life she would have stayed in her mountains and her world would have been girded around by the harsh, craggy landscape. Her days measured out in small achievements, keeping her herd of hvass safe, killing the lions that threatened them. A simpler life. But then there would have been no Kusha. And there would have been no honour or renown.

Kusha was much changed, like a ghost of her former self. Grief, hunger and exhaustion had honed down the sensual fleshiness of her body, thinned her face and taken the clarity from her eyes. But she still expressed her pleasure at seeing Asha, drew the woman down into a chair and made her, very weak durgan root tea. As Kusha leant over her with the bowl of tea, Asha was suddenly conscious of the smell of her own body. Water was rationed, so they all smelled, even the Empress, though nobody mentioned it.

It never bothered Asha, she never cared about it, only at this hour in the evening when she visited Kusha. Somehow, the Piroushi girl kept herself clean, used oils and perfumes to stave off the smell of sweat and sour clothes. It was the only time Asha felt even the slightest sense of self-consciousness. The Piroushi woman made her shy, that was it, the only person in the world able to do so. Perhaps it's worse tonight Asha thought, because I know what lies ahead for me tomorrow.

The council had met that day. Depleted as it was, there was still a representative from the merchants, who were sticking to a policy of studied neutrality, and the priesthood was represented by a junior cleric, the high priest also hedging his bets by staying away; only the Sisterhood, and of course the generals, were still unwavering partisans of the Empress. But even the council members who were still loyal, could foresee only one outcome.

Quintal, with the Star People's help, had gradually been taking control of the city walls and the main gateways. The Hwrathka Gate had fallen after a particularly bloody battle, brought to an end by the fire power of the Defence Force in the first days of their intervention. The few isolated garrisons in the wall towers had either disbanded or been overrun by Quintal's forces. The only lifeline remaining was the Eastern Gate and, everyone knew, it was only a question of time before that fell. One bombing raid from a Defence Force cruiser would wipe out the garrison of the gate-house.

"It is unclear why they haven't moved against it already," the old general, Kern, said. "But we have received news from a number of deserters, who have come over the walls, that Quintal is planning to complete our encirclement in the next few days."

It was sister Alethea who had spoken next:

"Your Highness," she had said, "we have all stood together throughout the first siege and now through this one. We've all strived and hoped that Elanta would deliver us from our enemies. But now

I think it's time to stop fighting. We need to talk to our enemies, negotiate a peace."

"But, Sister, it won't be a fair peace," Gamelon had answered her. Though he wasn't one of the council, he had been by the Empress's side throughout the fighting.

Then everyone had had their say, often at the same time, until the Empress's voice cut through the tumult like a shaft of light in a darkened room.

"I thank you for your advice, as I thank you for all the service that you have given me over all these years and through these long dark days that we have lately had to live through," the Empress sighed and was quiet for a while as if thinking. Asha noticed, as if for the first time, how tired she looked. These days have taken a toll on her too, Asha thought, even though she may be Elanta's representative here on earth.

"I have made my decision," the Empress said, "we will start negotiations with Quintal. I'm sure the Temple of Elanta would agree to broker them. But I find myself unable to trust all to Quintal's good nature. While the Eastern Gate is open, we will need someone to lead our forces out of this trap and away, to where they can keep up the fight. It will be our only insurance against total defeat."

Asha had stepped forward immediately and it had been agreed that she would lead this, their last, forlorn hope.

So Asha sat there with Kusha, knowing that it was, in all probability, the last time she would see her. Kusha didn't know this; the plan had been kept as secret as possible. Only the commanders of the selected units had been informed; others, like the

Barossi and the hwrathka corps, would stay behind. The Barossi would not part with the Empress anyway, their oath of loyalty was to her, and the hwrathka were too heavy and lumbering to be moved with the stealth and swiftness that would be needed to make the breakthrough.

There were many things Asha wanted to say to Kusha, but she knew that she wouldn't, ultimately, say them. Because, after all, what was there actually to say? After what they had been through these last few weeks, any profession of love seemed trite and irrelevant. They had an unspoken knowledge of each other that made the saying of words an unnecessary and banal extravagance. So she sipped her tea and watched her friend, drinking her face and form in with her eyes, remembering, fixing the memory like a fly in amber, for what little time she had left.

Then, too soon, it was the appointed hour and there were others she had wanted to say goodbye to, but she either couldn't do so, because of the secret, or had not had time. She would have liked to look on Berendal for one more time, to see his laughing face, though he had become newly serious with his Harradim girl and his war wounds. She would have liked to talk to Berthaud, have one last conversation about the war and what the Star People would do. And there was Gamelon, irritating old Gamelon, who now also seemed someone she would like to have just a few more minutes with. She would not think of Kusha, it was too painful, but would just hold that last memory of her in her mind's eye like a pennant, or a charm, which would guide her through the battle.

They assembled in the darkness of the early hours before dawn on the parade ground. There seemed so few of them now. Everyone who could be was mounted, speed would be of the essence, that and surprise. Even Asha was on haras back. There was a corridor of sorts leading from the citadel's back gates down through the streets and out onto the marshalling grounds before the Eastern Gate. The corridor wasn't totally secure; they would be liable to attack from Quintal's forces, which had garrisons and outposts at street corners and crossroads. Asha's instructions to her soldiers had been to keep going; to stop for nothing, to get as many out and away as possible.

The Empress had come to see them off.

"May Elanta make you swift and keep you safe. Know that you are our hope for the future, the hope of all Melantherans." Her voice trailed off as they rode out through the gates and down through the darkened streets. As she rode, Asha stole one last look at the shadowy figure of the Empress Mila the Third, still unbowed, still serene, standing there alone in the courtyard.

Elanta was with them, as they rode through the deserted streets. They took fire from one or two isolated posts, but it was desultory and ineffective. One startled Republican Guard detachment tried to block their path, thinking they were engaging with a sortie, but Asha's forces just rolled over them, cutting the men down or letting them be trampled by the hooves of their haras.

A force of light troops had been sent to secure the marshalling grounds, many of them trained by Berthaud and carrying captured weapons. As Asha's force rode past, she could see that these soldiers were engaged in a number of skirmishes with Quintal's forces, exchanging fire from the buildings around the square, but no serious attempt was made to block their path. The Republican Guards had not been expecting them to sally out in such force and were taken by surprise.

Their luck lasted until they had cleared the gates and were almost at the river bridge over the Khalamis. This had always been the flaw in the escape plan. Though they still held the river bridge – a small garrison still somehow holding out in the towers - it was a choke point and it would have taken only a small force of the enemy to block off the eastern end of the bridge. Ultimately, though, there had been little option. The eastern route was the only way open to them and they had to risk the passage of the bridge. Asha had sent a force of scouts ahead of the main body to secure the approaches to the bridge, but as she rode up with the vanguard, she could see, in the breaking light of dawn, that a large force of Hvassara were riding from the south to cut their route at the eastern end of the bridge and threatening to overwhelm the small force of scouts. The Hvassara had split into two forces; the smaller unit was riding to block the road, a larger force descending on the scouts to take the bridge and stop the Melantherans in their tracks.

It was a matter of moments to give the orders, put her heels to the flanks of the haras and lead the cavalry vanguard across the wooden planking of the bridge, clattering like all the demons of hell, raising such a clamour in the pre-dawn silence. She gave the cavalry commander his orders, telling him to stop for nothing and sent him up the road. She detailed an officer to keep the column moving as it passed over the bridge funnelling it up the road, and then she led two units of pike men and two of archers to reinforce the scouts.

The scouts had been hard pressed; the first wave of Hvassara had already clashed with them. The scouts had, however, taken shelter in the ruins of a small village that had once stood beside the road on the furthest side of the bridge, until it had been destroyed in the first siege. The Hvassara, faced with archers firing bows from cover, had reverted to their usual tactics, hitting the enemy hard then retreating to fire their arrows from horseback.

As more Hvassara came up, Asha deployed her archers in formation, supported by the pike men, who formed a protective cordon on the flanks and in front of the bows. Asha knew that there was no point fighting the Hvassara with cavalry; they were skilled riders and would always retreat from a direct assault, waiting to ambush or cut off their attackers, drawing them in. The Hvassara were in their element when on haras back, but didn't like facing a well-deployed infantry force or a fixed position.

Asha knew that they could hold the Hvassara here, at least for a time. The enemy had taken the bait and were throwing their forces at this rear-guard, rather than intercepting the main column, which was now well down the road. I'd have down exactly the opposite, Asha thought to herself. She made sure she was visible, walking out in front of the ranks, her red robes blowing behind her, the two-handed sword over her shoulder. She knew she was feared and hated by the Hvassara and that was another reason why they were pressing their attack at this point.

"All you have to do, men, is stand fast in your ranks and keep firing," Asha told the soldiers as the Hvassara attacked, "if we break formation we're lost, so keep your nerve and hold fast."

The first real massed attack came soon after, the nomads riding right up to the front rank of pike men and turning their horses at the last moment. Some miscalculated or were struck down before they could turn and man and beast fell into the Melantheran ranks to be speared and hacked to death. The second and third attacks were more of the same, each onslaught followed by a flight of arrows, which the Hvassara dispatched from horseback as they retreated.

By the fourth attack, Asha could see that they had taken a fair number of casualties, but they were still holding formation. The Hvassara then tried trading arrows with them from a distance, but the heavier Melantheran bows outmatched the Hvassaran ones. The smaller composite bow, that was so useful on horseback, did not pack the killing power of the longer Melantheran infantry weapon.

There was a lull in the fighting then as, it seemed, the Hvassara got bored. Asha could understand their feelings. It was not the way she was used to fighting, sticking hard to that perimeter under the hail of Hvassaran arrows. In the distance Asha could see the dust of wagons approaching and she feared that the enemy were bringing up cannons to finish them off. The Hvassara, while they'd become adept in the use of artillery, had not yet really mastered the skills of using mobile cannon on the battlefield, they still relied on slow moving wagons to tow their guns. Though the Hvassara fighting them seemed to lack muskets, a party of other Hvassara had worked their way around and were sniping at them from the cover of a ditch on the other side of the road behind them. And they were taking casualties from this.

Asha decided that they couldn't stay there any longer, so gave orders for the column to move off down the road and headed a sortie to clear the ditch of the snipers. She led a small, hand-picked party of men through the ruins towards the bridge, crossing the road and then working up the ditch where, unaware of the danger they were in, the musketeers still lay in position.

Feeling the soft, cracked mud of the ditch beneath her boots as she inched forward, hearing the buzz of kobo-flies in the air around her, smelling the scent of wild herbs growing by the way-side, she felt alive again; the blood pumping through her heart and pulsing in her head; all her senses heightened, even that tremor of fear she had learned to master.

Then they came on the first two Hvassara and in, a flurry of arms and legs, she stabbed one with her knife, the ditch too narrow for spear or sword. The other tried to scramble over the side of the ditch, but she pulled him down, by the back of the short pants he wore, pulled his head back by his greasy hair, and cut his throat. The moment of the kill, the pleasure she took, was like a wave engulfing her. She knew she was like an animal in this, like a mountain lion, having no pity or conscience for those she killed. She knew that Kusha was so different from her and she was glad, at least, for that. Glad also that Kusha had only once seen the beast that was inside her, that day on Khetmis.

By now her companions had passed her and put the rest of the Hvassara to flight. Then it was their turn to make a dash from the ditch, racing over the open ground to the welcoming ranks of the column, before a group of Hvassara horsemen that had appeared could close on them. As Asha shepherded her men in, a lone Hvassara, ahead of the group that had failed to catch them, tried to ride her down. She turned and drew her sword all in the one practised motion; she looked at him as he rode at her. He was young, a boy really, and had overreached himself in this, probably his first real battle. He was riding towards her, the uneven ground slowing him, riding into the death stroke that was awaiting him. For some reason - just before he closed, the fear evident in his eyes - she reversed her grip on the sword, grabbing the blade in her gloved hand and sweeping him out of the saddle with the hilt. Having dropped his sword in the fall, he lay on the ground awaiting the death blow that never came. Then he turned and half-ran, half-crawled away. Two pike men with shields came out of the ranks to usher Asha in.

"Now why did I do that?" Asha asked herself. "Perhaps Kusha has had a good influence on me after all?"

Keeping in formation, in the square of infantry protecting the archers, was difficult at the best of times and this was hardly the best. The Hvassara kept up sporadic attacks throughout the morning, as the soldiers slowly moved down the road, for all the world like a mobile, armoured beast. They were losing men; after each attack, their ranks were thinned, and it was getting harder and harder to keep their cohesion. Asha knew that if their ranks once faltered, if the line broke, the Hvassara horsemen would be amongst them in a minute, bent on slaughter and massacre.

She also knew that they had a chance; by the early afternoon they were approaching the fords of the Riparhin, a tributary of the Khalamis. Just below the fords, where the river spread in shallow channels over the plain, the Riparhin joined the main river and, in the angle the two watercourses formed, the landscape changed from the open, treeless plains to a land of broken scrub and stunted trees, swampy and wet in places. Asha knew that the Hvassara would be at a disadvantage in such a terrain, it was an infantryman's domain. As they neared the small settlement that marked the fording places - peopled by Harradim who in times of peace housed and fed travellers - she had expected the Hvassara to make one last, concerted effort. Instead it was all strangely quiet.

The reason for this soon became apparent, as the silence of the plain, as it drowsed in the heat of the afternoon sun, was broken by a drone like the voice of a thousand kobo-flies. Two of the Star Men's cruisers were fast approaching across the plain.

"Break formation. Get across the river as fast as you can and head for the trees," Asha gave the order as the first rockets hit the flanks of the column. Then it was chaos, as the first wave of men to cross the ford, running as fast as their armour and weapons would let them, were cut down by gun-fire from upriver. From where she was, flattened to the ground behind a boundary hedge of thorn bushes, Asha could see that the gunners were on this side of the Riparhin, in one of the houses of the Harradim. That was a mistake, she thought, as the river is not between them and me.

She managed to get together a small group of soldiers. Some of them were so startled and shocked by the assault that she literally had to grab them by their neck scarves and pull them down beside her. She gave her orders and they waited for a lull in the bombing. The cruisers had made three runs at them and, just when they were expecting a fourth, they turned for home. But coming across the plain, she could see the low looming shapes of the Star People's crawlers. Giving her orders to the few shocked survivors who would accompany her, she crossed the Harradim fields and made for the house, working through the narrow lanes of the village. The Star People were firing from the roof of one of the houses, which they had partially fortified. The men on the roof, in their dark, blank-faced helmets were, however, concentrating on the river, not seeing the danger that stalked them through the narrow, shaded Harradim streets.

There were two sentries positioned on the ground floor, one by the window, one behind the door. They had no time to wait, so they just charged in. One of the soldiers, the one at the window, threw some sort of bomb, which blew two of her men backwards in a bloody cloud, but in the act of throwing he exposed himself enough for one of the archers to get a clear shot at him, hitting him in the throat between body armour and helmet. The door was flimsy and fell under their combined weight. The second soldier fired a wild burst from his gun and ran up the stairs, Asha following closely. He turned to fire again, but it was too late, as she had closed on him.

As she pushed him away from her, she realised that he was the first Star Man she had killed. But, in truth, these people were no different than any of them. They bled and died the same way. She followed her men up the stairs. On the third floor a Harradim woman and two girls were huddled in a corner, with bedding over their heads. A Harradim man's corpse lay nearby. She could her firing, shouting and screaming above her. She drew her sword as she ran up the final stairs, emerging into a small hallway, which gave out onto the roof. One of her men had died here, the other two were kneeling in surrender on the roof top, a Star People soldier standing over them with a weapon; another soldier was treating a wounded comrade and a third one was still manning the large, blunt black thing that was killing her soldiers.

She lifted her voice and prayed to Elanta as she burst through the doorway. She cut the first soldier down before he could level his weapon. The second soldier turned where he was kneeling over his comrade and seemed more surprised than afraid. She cut him down as well. The soldier on the machine gun had by this time turned and brought up a hand-gun. Asha's two soldiers had retrieved their weapons and were fast approaching. The soldier coolly chose targets, firing a round into each of the men and then turning the gun on Asha. The two Melantherans went down, but the round missed Asha and, dropping her sword, she leapt on the soldier knocking the helmet off, revealing the face of a woman, hair cropped short, intense dark eyes looking up at her.

Asha's hand had gone to her knife; she was struggling to draw it, when she felt a strange sort of pressure in her side and she realised that she had been stabbed. Her hand found the woman's hand with the combat knife in it and with a superhuman effort wrenched it from her grasp, brought it up and stabbed down with it, into the exposed angle between neck and shoulder. The life seemed to go out of the woman's eyes like a candle flickering out.

Asha dropped the knife and stood up. She looked down at her hands and realised that much of the blood on them was hers. Our blood has mingled in death, she thought, two sisters of a kind. She had never killed another woman before; the Hvassara never put their women in the field, her foes up until now had all been men. She felt somehow hollow, as if she had betrayed some deep trust. But this war was like no other that had come before; men, women and children, young and old, none were spared the death it brought.

One of Asha's men still lived, though he was wounded.

"You must go as fast as you can," she said, "tell our soldiers that they can cross the river now. They must make all possible haste, as the Star People's wagons are coming."

The soldier ignored her words, and came towards her seeking to help her.

"Listen to me," she said, "leave me and go! I command it."

Reluctantly, he obeyed.

She felt tired, light-headed. She staggered down the stairs and tried to find a sheet or towel she could use to bind her wound. The Harradim woman, who was quietly sobbing, helped her, strapping up the injury.

"You must go! "She told the woman. "When the Star People see this, Elanta knows what they will do."

The woman and her daughters helped Asha down the stairs and out of the front door, but then she dismissed them.

"Go!" She said." Take your daughters and hide! Quickly, before they come."

Looking out towards the fords, she could see the last of the stragglers disappearing into the undergrowth on the far bank, just as the drone of engines got louder and bullets started to stitch the sand of the riverbanks and the placid face of the water.

"And so to die." She told herself. "I'll walk a while and find a quiet shady spot by the river."

She staggered off along the bank, keeping walking by telling herself that she didn't want them to find her body. Didn't want her corpse to be displayed on the walls of Melanthera. She found a good spot, a good enough place to die, she told herself and lay there in the shade. She realised how thirsty she was, but wondered if she should drink. But she didn't want river water; she wanted the clear, cold crystal of a mountain stream.

Later she had a dream or so she thought. She woke to find a Harradim child standing over her with a flask of cool water. She felt, after drinking it, that she had never ever really quenched her thirst before. But the child was also carrying something else. She bore a rose, a jungle rose from Piroush. How could that be? Asha thought Then she slept again.

She woke the next morning to a new day and the sun creating a lattice pattern on the floor of her shelter. Finding herself not dead yet, she decided to live some more.

Chapter 30
The Island Of Ghosts

When Robyn woke, drifting up from the fog of unconsciousness like as swimmer trying to regain the surface, finding it further and further away, she felt sore in her body and groggy in her head. Khamis was beside her. The girl had a bruise on her jaw and her lip had been bleeding, but she was alive. Her eyes flickered up at Robyn, the terror evident in them. Robyn tried to speak, but her tongue felt too thick for her mouth. Her hands were still tied, but she managed to move towards Khamis, lowering her brow to touch the girl's, the only way she could touch her. They were in the hold of a ship; it was a low foetid-smelling place with an inch or so of dirty water slopping about beneath them.

"Keep your head up, darling," she thought, "or you'll drown."

The boat lurched, as if hit by a big wave, and she suddenly found herself slipping down to the black depths again, all the time trying to form, to speak, the girl's name:

"Khamis..."

The next time she awoke, she was in a darkened room, a basement of some sort. Someone had injected her again; it must have been adrenaline or some sort of stimulant to wake her up. She was sitting on a chair and was tied to it by leather straps that were an integral part of it. She was glad the plastic restraints had been removed; they had left sore red marks where they had cut into her ankles and wrists.

"Robyn Harper," a voice said, in her own language, Terran, "thirty-four years old. Born on Mafusa. Moved to Thera to go to University. Trained as a Librarian as part of the Hub scholarship programme. Worked on Thera after qualifying, then suddenly she ups sticks and moves to Hanis, on assignment."

A man was sitting in front of her, but she could only see a silhouette, as a bright light was shining in her face. She uttered one word:

"Khamis."

The man nodded and said:

"Your little Piroushi girlfriend is safe for now. She's on ice, as they used to say."

"Who are you?" The voice didn't sound like Robyn's, her tongue was still thick in her mouth.

"The drug will wear off," the man said, not answering her question, "it was necessary to sedate you to get you here. And I owe you an apology."

Robyn lifted her head when he said this, not sure she'd heard him properly.

"Those Republican Guards can be a little rough, there was no need to beat you up, or that Sister who was with you."

"Rehalla?" Robyn asked.

"Safe as far as I know, we had no use for her. You see there's no arrest warrant out for her. We do things by the book, as they say."

"What do you want?" She asked.

The man sighed. "Robyn, I'm here to help you. Or to be more precise, I'm here to help you help yourself. Think about it!"

Then he left and two guards came and took her through a doorway and out into a corridor. The place looked like a palace or a temple, it was a complex of buildings, mostly unused. They crossed a courtyard and she was dragged down steps to a basement and to a passage-way with doors off it. One of them was her cell. There was a sliver of daylight from a barred window high up in the wall, opposite the door, and a pallet on the floor. In one corner there was a drain, which she supposed was the toilet, with a bowl of water to wash the waste away.

Time passed in a meaningless way here, only governed by the waxing and waning light from the narrow slit of window in the wall. All was quiet, except sometimes in the night she heard a woman screaming. She did not think it sounded like Khamis; she hoped that it wasn't Khamis. She slumped against the wall listening, willing on that other woman the torment she was going through, however bad it was, just as long as it wasn't happening to Khamis. She even appealed to Elanta, asking her to spare the girl. She's innocent, she told the goddess, and I'm the one at fault.

She didn't know if it was the next day, or the day after, that they came for her again; she lost track of time. There was no pattern to the time they fed her, it seemed at random. She thought that it was probably deliberate, done to disorientate her.

They took her to the same room, the same man was there, but this time they didn't tie her to the chair or shine the light on her. Instead he asked her to sit in a different chair across a table from him. He was a middle-aged man in his fifties, with short, white hair. His face wore a concerned look and his manners were impeccable.

"Please sit, Ms Harper," he said. "Can I call you Robyn?"

She didn't answer, but he did anyway.

"I told you that I'm here to help you. I meant it. To help you get out of this fix that you've got yourself into. But first would you like a coffee? I bet you haven't had any for a time."

She took a cup, but immediately wondered whether she had compromised herself by doing so.

"I don't know about you, but I can't be doing with that durgan root tea. I need the tannin and the caffeine."

She could see what he was doing; he was trying to be sympathetic, avuncular even.

"You've got yourself in the shit," he said, "if you'll pardon the expression, but I might be able to help you get out of it."

He had a Pad open before him on the table.

"Who are you?" She asked. "Who do you work for?"

He ignored the question.

"By the way," he said, grinning at her. She noticed that despite the smile, his light blue eyes were cold and seemed to look through her.

"By the way," he said again, "she's very nice, your little friend. Khamis is it? She's delightful."

He sighed, leaned back in the chair and sipped his coffee.

"She's Piroushi of course. When I was in the Defence Force, the lads were always going on what they called the 'Piroushi Pussy Patrol'. They're such delightful girls, so accommodating."

Robyn felt an ice-cold hand of fear gripping her, a physical pain in her gut. His voice seemed to bear an implicit threat.

"Oh, don't get the wrong idea. I'm just saying that I thought she was nice. After all, I'm a family man. You should know that."

He leant towards her: "I'm here to help you Robyn, remember that."

And that was the end of the second session. After an indeterminate time in her cell she was brought back on what she thought was the next morning. This time there was a bowl of fruit on the table, as well as coffee.

"Sorry the accommodation isn't better," he said to her, by way of introduction, "but you are, after all, in a detention facility."

He poured her coffee without asking whether she wanted it or not.

"I'd advise you to drink it black," he said. "Hvass milk just doesn't go with it."

He laughed: "The Melantherans have always cracked me up. They make such a fuss of what is, basically, a sort of scruffy goat. They definitely don't have an interesting fauna here, except for the hwrathka, of course, but they are nearly extinct. A page from history."

Abruptly he turned to his Pad, reading the screen.

"What about Robyn Harper's personal life then?"

She started to protest, but he cut her off:

"Here to help, remember?" He said. "It would be best for you to listen and only speak when required. Okay?"

He went on: "Robyn Harper. A few short-lived relationships in college. A few longer ones afterwards. You even went out with a man for a few months. Testing the water as it were. But I think we can safely say that you are of the lesbian persuasion. No judgement implied, nothing wrong with that. Girls will be girls and get it on with girls, as they say."

He looked up at her; those blue eyes piercing.

"Esmee Fallon. Very attractive, very chic. Part of the bohemian.... do people still say bohemian... let's say part of the art establishment of Thera. All those parties, operas, ballets. I bet you enjoyed them."

He looked down at his Pad again.

"Do you want to see her picture?"

Robyn shook her head. The tears, though unbidden, were coming. Her eyes felt brimful with them.

"Sorry Robyn, I didn't mean to upset you. Love of your life would you say, this Esmee? Your life so far? You don't have to answer."

He looked at her and paused, but she didn't speak. He pulled a packet of tissues from the pocket of his fatigues, but she left them on the table where he threw them.

"Then the rebound. Abigail Farim. Just the opposite of Esmee. Intelligence Corps. A sort of soldier spook. Didn't seem to end well. Then the rebound from the rebound. Our little friend Khamis."

The tears were now rolling down Robyn's face, she didn't know why. She almost wished the man would shout at her, hit her, rather than this.

"Sorry to upset you, you can go back now."

The guards came at his bidding, but just as they were taking him away, he stopped them and asked:

"What were you looking for Robyn? Was it love? Or was it something else?"

She thought it was the fourth session that he brought up about her father, but it may have been the fifth. By that time she was losing count; the days were endless, monotonous. Occasionally she would her screams or shouting, once or twice she heard shots and bouts of sheer terror would punctuate the apathy that she had slipped into.

"Your father died when you were quite young. Some sort of industrial accident. He was an agronomist, wasn't he? I'm not quite sure what this is, but apparently he specialised in hydroponics. You mother was away a lot, she was an anthropologist, so you were brought up by your aunt. A very female household."

He shifted in his seat, taking a long hard look at her. Each time she came, the table had more on it. There was chocolate as well as fruit, fruit juice as well as coffee.

"I hope you won't be offended, Robyn, if I tell you that you remind me of my daughter. That's why I want to help you. My interest in you is like that of a father. I see that you've taken a wrong turn and I don't think it should ruin your life."

For some reason the mention of her father had angered her, a red-hot pulse of fury coursed through the mush that her brain had become.

"How dare you even talk of my father, you bastard," she said." You don't want to fucking help me, you just want screw with my head and get what you can from me."

The guards had moved towards her. She hadn't noticed, but she was standing up. The man motioned the guards away.

"Let me prove something to you, Robyn. Let me tell you something."

He sighed.

"Do you know what the Republican Guard officer, who is in charge of this establishment, wanted to do with your little friend, Khamis? Until I managed to dissuade him, that is."

Cold fear replaced the anger in a moment and she sat down.

"They have their own way of dealing with dissidents like her, pretty female ones. They ship them to the Hvassara, sell them to the nomads. That way they get rid of them and they get paid. A lovely little thing like Khamis - what is she twenty three or twenty four - she'd last ten years at the most with the Hvassara. Five if she was lucky. I'm sure I don't have to describe to you what they would do with her."

She knew then that he had broken her. It was now only a question of how much she could tell him without doing too much harm.

The next session was strangely low-key. He brought her in, gave her coffee and dismissed the guards.

"Frankly, Robyn," he said. "I can call you Robyn, can't I?" He went on doing so, not giving her time to answer.

You can call me anything, she thought, just don't do anything to Khamis.

"Frankly, Robyn, I don't know why they are so bothered about getting you back. It seems to me you turned over a stone and found something nasty underneath. I think most people on the inner planets know that corporations like Sung Yang are up to no good out on the frontier. Nobody really cares as long as they can keep living in their lovely little lakeside apartments above Lake Thera. Like your old lover."

He sighed, stretched and walked around the room.

"I actually admire you, Robyn. You really did your job too well. They should be recruiting you, not trying to lock you up."

He paused as if thinking hard. Then turned to her.

"What if I made a recommendation for clemency. Suggested that you get a short sentence on some farm-prison of a planet. I could pull some strings, get them to employ you afterwards; no-one else will. Otherwise you'll be cleaning rooms like your friend Khamis was. Think about it. You're a bit of an expert on Melanthera, you could do some good, be a friend of theirs on the inside."

Robyn dare not speak, daren't utter a word, she felt as if she was manning the last barricade, as if her defences were about to crumble. Part of her wanted to say:

"Yes. Do it! Just let this end."

"You see, what I think happened is this, Robyn. You were very unhappy, heart-broken and lonely, and then you opened a book, a fairy tale book. It was about a place called Melanthera, which never really existed in the way you imagined it. And you

362

became obsessed with it. You got ill, remember! And that illness just pulled you down into that fantasy world, deeper and deeper."

He sat down again and pulled his chair close to her.

"And the fantasy world became real, because a beautiful young girl from that world came into your apartment one day and you fell for her, head over heels in love. Then you did something silly at work. You hacked into secret records, copied them. They couldn't ignore that. You were conspiring with enemies of the state, terrorists. Then you went on the run with the girl and you lived your fantasy, culminating in a honeymoon on Piroush."

He had leaned over now and put his hand on her arm, she tried to recoil but his gaze was almost hypnotic.

"But you know now, deep down, that this place is gritty, shitty and wild. These people are their worst enemy. They are savages really, going through all the stages of civilisation at once, like a run-away elevator."

His grip tightened.

"The old Empress was a dinosaur, an antique. Quintal is trying to deal with the problems that she never bothered with; like hunger, poverty, lack of hygiene and health care. Which side would you rather be on Robyn? With The Empress and the Sisterhood, or for the poor and indigent. You have to grow up, take the rose-tinted spectacles from your eyes and see the real world of Melanthera. This is not your private erotic fantasy, Robyn, these people need the same things as our people; development, industry, wealth. So they have to crawl into bed with Sung Yang or North Star or someone else. So what? Would you rather they were kept like animals in a zoo, stuck in their ignorance and their own filth. Would you Robyn?"

The last defence fell; the tears came and would not stop. He put his arm around here.

"I'm sorry Robyn," he said. "I don't mean to hurt you. I just want to make you see things clearly, so I can help you."

By the next session, which came too soon, she was telling him everything that he wanted. At first, though he tried to hide it, she could see that he was pleased with her eagerness. It was the smug smile that stole over his face on occasion, until he resumed that blank mask that he usually wore.

He was very keen to establish who else had conspired in her escape, especially if any library staff had been involved. She told the truth, said that she didn't know, but he fished for names. Suddenly he seemed to get bored with his own questions and sat back in his chair, silent for a while. It was late afternoon, they had come for her around midday she thought, and the day was being worn down, eroded away by the stultifying heat.

"Do you know, Robyn," he said eventually, "what they call this island, the local Piroushi?"

Suddenly alert again, he looked at her with those piercing blue eyes.

"The island of ghosts. They won't come here, they think it's haunted and I suppose it is. It used to be called - still is officially - Khetmis. It was the Empress's summer residence. That's where you are, in the old palace."

364

He rose from his chair abruptly, walked over to a sort of cabinet and took out a flask of the kind that the Melantherans kept their wine in. He brought the flask over and two cups. Poured her some without asking if she wanted any.

"This is one of the only things I really like about this place, the borriba wine. They should forget the mining industry and export this stuff."

She didn't touch her wine at first, but he urged her to and she took a sip, realising how biddable she had become, what power he had over her.

"Robyn, listen carefully. I need you to be absolutely truthful with me. The only way I can stop the Republican Guards from questioning Khamis is if you tell me everything. If my bosses think you are holding anything back, they'll get it out of her and their methods are much less subtle."

She nodded, told him she would tell him everything. That she wanted to co-operate. The mouthful of wine had gone straight to her head, making the scene even more surreal. She felt like a schoolgirl in front of the head-teacher for some misdemeanour.

"I will tell you everything, but tell me who you work for." She said the words without being aware of actually speaking them.

"Why does that matter, Robyn?" He replied.

"It just does." She answered.

He shrugged and said: "I'm a private contractor, Robyn. This isn't anything personal, it's my job."

Days later they came into her cell at night and injected her again. When she awoke next, she was

365

in what she took to be the hold of some small boat, from the way the boards of the floor were moving under her feet. The hold had been partitioned into cubicles separated from each other by flimsy walls. She heard someone coughing in the cubicle next to hers. She shouted:

"Khamis?"

But only heard a muffled noise as a reply.

The movement of the craft seemed to settle down and two guards came and pulled her from the cell and up a gangway to the deck. She could hardly walk, it was as if her limbs had seized up. They manacled her hands and as she looked around her, she saw the one person she wanted to see. Khamis was on the other side of the mast. The girl was dressed in some sort of jump suit, but was standing and, at first glance, seemed uninjured.

"Khamis," she shouted.

One of the guards motioned her to be silent with a graphic demonstration of how she would otherwise be gagged. Another one said, in Terran:

"Talking is forbidden! It will go hard on the girl, if you disobey."

She thought he had been chosen as her guard because he spoke her language; assigned by her interrogator because of this skill.

As they led the two women to the rowing boat that waited, all they could do was look at each other and try to communicate with their eyes. The Piroushi girl looked exhausted, with a sallow, grey pallor from the weeks in the cell. But Khamis gazed at her with tear-filled eyes that told how glad she was to see her after all this time. Robyn tried to meet her gaze, but she bore such a burden of guilt that it wasn't easy. All I did, I did for you, my love, she thought to herself. But would you understand if I could tell you? Would you be angry with me, despise me for it?

They were put into the stern, chained on a thwart, a guard behind them; Khamis leaned against her, the closest to a touch that she could come without being detected. She moved a manacled hand onto Robyn's thigh, touching Robyn's hand. The guard must have seen, but he chose to ignore it. Robyn was thankful for this small mercy, just the fleeting touch of Khamis's hand on hers.

Then they had no more time to look at each other as they were roughly hauled up steps to the harbour - the same fisherman's harbour where they had been taken- and marched up a street of steps.

"We're heading for the main port," Robyn thought.

It was what White Hair had promised her. A swift passage to Hava Port and from there to Melanthera. She would be extradited back to a Defence Force base on Hanis or elsewhere. Khamis would be tried and sent to a prison colony.

"Best I can do," he'd said. "You get to have a trail of sorts. It won't be public, of course, but they'll take your co-operation into account. Your girl will get a slap on the wrist, some sort of short prison sentence."

She had paid a high price for this and Khamis would probably never know how much. Whenever she could, without raising the ire of the guards, she stole a look at Khamis. The girl looked back at her; she looked tired and frightened, but there was something else there that she was trying to convey.

A fierce, little flame seemed to flicker there. Was it love, Robyn asked herself, or hope? Or am I just imagining it?

The guards were having a hard time of it. The streets were crowded and it was evident that the people did not appreciate being pushed around by what they regarded as foreigners. Though they had taken the two women's clothes away and dressed them in prison wear, Khamis still looked like a Piroushi and the crowd didn't like seeing one of their own being taken away in chains.

The crowd thinned as they descended the steps into the main market square. Ships lay at anchor in the Piroush Roads or were tied up to the quay. She wondered which one would bear them away, hoped fervently that they would allow them to be together, at least for some of the time on board.

Around the custom house, as they approached, Robyn saw that there were more soldiers than usual and, scanning the crowd looking for a friendly face, she was surprised to see one. Rehalla was standing some way off watching their party. As Robyn looked, she saw the women give a signal and suddenly a rank of Piroushi soldiers formed in front of them, others lapping around the flanks of their small party. All in all, there were seven Republican Guards with them, in uniform, and two other sailors in civilian garb. There were around thirty Piroushi soldiers, so the Republican Guards were outnumbered and, though many of them carried automatic pistols, the Piroushi were armed with bows and spears.

A Piroushi Captain had words with the Republican Guard squad leader. She couldn't really follow what they were saying, but the exchange seemed heated. Both had papers, hvass skin scrolls or Star People documents and were poring over them. Eventually, the Republican Guard officer said something, which sounded to Robyn very like a Melantheran swear word, and stalked off.

Then something truly surprising happened. The officer walked up to Khamis, grabbed her roughly by the arm and hauled her to the Piroushi Captain. Two Piroushi came out of the rank of soldiers and ushered Khamis away. The girl looked stunned, shocked and then suddenly she turned and shouted:

"Kahani! The Princess Kusha won't let them take me."

She shouted something at her guards; they paused until the Piroushi Captain came up and said something to Khamis.

"Kahani. I'm sorry. I asked them to take you too."

She turned and struggled with her guards and she shouted something else, but her voice was drowned out by the collective voice of the crowd, who had started that ululation that passed for a cheer on Melanthera.

The last Robyn saw of Khamis was the sight of her being dragged away, her eyes never leaving Robyn's, as she, in turn, was dragged to the ship.

Chapter 31
The Passing Of The Empress

Under the eaves of the pleasure house at the Hwrathka Gate, a man dressed in Harradim robes sat on a shaded balcony. Though the awning above him kept off the afternoon sun, he still wore the head-scarf of a Harradim man, over his head and around his face. He sat on a cushion on a low ledge against the wall, just by the doorway that led onto the balcony; a crutch lay next to him. Built into the wall was a small niche, in which sat a flask of borriba wine and two cups. A woman stood nearby in the doorway of the room, occasionally glancing down at him and then looking out, past the rail into the square, where the crowds were assembling. Though she was dressed like a Piroushi, her light hair, pale skin and height marked her down as a Barossi.

"You'll have a good view of proceedings from here, Berendal," she said, "and no-one will disturb us. They think I'm with a customer."

Berendal looked up at her and smiled. The Barossi woman was known as Sky in the pleasure house, though her name was actually 'sky that comes before the dawn of a spring day' following the Barossi style of giving long, rambling appellations. She remembered Berendal in those years before the war when he'd been a regular at the house, staying up all hours to get roaringly drunk and declaiming his poems to the crowd, sometimes ending up in her bed, though she would quickly usher him out in the mornings.

370

She could see something of the old Berendal in his smile, not as wide or wicked as before, but the embers of the flame that had once burnt there were still smouldering. He was though, much changed; he walked with a limp now and still felt the ghost pains of his wounds. The war had changed them, changed everybody. Even she, Sky, who'd once lived life for the day and to the full, couldn't free herself from all that happened these last few years; things she had seen, done and things that had been done to her.

But, to Sky, the biggest change in Berendal was the way that he had been transformed from that consummate pursuer of women, moving from romantic tryst to romantic tryst, a poem always at the ready, to a sober and serious married man. They said, or at least the rumour-mongers in the market did, that his wife was a Harradim who he'd rescued from the Hvassara. That exploit, combined with his command of the garrison which held the Hwrathka Gate against Quintal's men, had made him into an unlikely sort of war hero, something which he'd once traded on until he was wounded in the siege of the city and then married.

On reflection, though, she thought that one thing he retained from the old Berendal was his luck. After the Empress had come to terms with Quintal and the Star People, basically surrendering all her power for peace, many of her supporters had suffered the consequences. Kal Quintal was a very vindictive man and had never gotten over the indignity of fleeing Melanthera in a dung cart after his revolt had failed. Many had now suffered to salve his injured pride.

As part of the peace agreement, there were supposed to be no reprisals. The idea had been that peace would bring reconciliation, an intention that had run through Quintals' inauguration speech when he had been sworn in as President of the Republic. But once Quintal was in power, it was relatively easy to dispose of his enemies with trumped up charges of sedition or subversion. Sky herself had spent a few nights in one of his dungeons, after an altercation over a drinks bill with some of the new Republican Guards. It was their way of warning her, telling her they could do what they wanted now.

Berendal's luck had run true because of the circumstances of his marriage. By all accounts his wife was a traditional Harradim woman and had insisted on a Harradim religious marriage as well as a civil one. She had wanted to live in the Harradim quarter of the city, those streets above the market square that were almost exclusively inhabited by her people. Because the Harradim had always been regarded as a people that kept themselves aloof from wars and political conflicts, Quintal's forces had left them alone. In fact, because of their role as guardians of caravans and providers of safe havens for travellers, Quintal had sought to make them allies. So Berendal's marriage and his adoption of Harradim ways, including the wearing of their clothes, had provided a measure of safety for him. He'd effectively disappeared into the Harradim streets where few knew, or were concerned about, his past deeds.

Sky looked down at him again; such a change, she thought.

"You should be safe here," she said, "but keep to the room as there's a few Republican Guards in and who is to say that they won't recognise the old Berendal lurking somewhere under those robes."

A Harradim in a pleasure house might also be something they would remark, she thought.

"So keep to the chamber and if you need to piss, I'll bring you a pot."

Berendal smiled at this. He looked at Sky as she, in turn, looked out over the square at the crowds assembling there. He'd always thought that she was a good-looking woman, with the fairness of the Barossi, the long elegant legs, the graceful curve of her back; memories came flooding in of nights spent in this room and mornings as the sun's beams fell through the slatted blinds and lit up the gold of her hair. Sky, so different from his Noor. He could feel a poem coming on, he thought, but then he told himself that he'd have to stop thinking this way and he'd have to let the poem go, to evaporate into the hot, afternoon air. He couldn't let himself think about other women, tempting though those thoughts were, and his poems these days had a more serious air and purpose.

It was Gamelon who had dismissed him from the palace. Berendal had hung around with the other maimed and enfeebled, the garrison of hungry ghosts that had manned the walls after Asha and the last of the army had gone. It had been a strange in-between sort of time; they were not defeated yet, or so it seemed, and it wasn't until the peace was sealed and the Empress had agreed to go into exile that he and his comrades had realised that the end had really come.

The High Priest of Elanta had been the mainstay in the negotiations, but he had been so eager to ingratiate himself with Quintal and his allies, that the treaty had been balanced to their opponent's advantage. In truth, it had been the Star People, behind the scenes, who had dictated the terms. It had been agreed that the Empress would retire to her summer place on the island of Khetmis, nominally still the Empress, but to be replaced by a representative government drawn from all parts of Melantheran society. Kal Quintal would be what the Star People described as a 'caretaker' President, who would serve for a number of years until elections could be arranged.

This idea had confused the Melantherans at first, because, as it had been described to them, it meant that each person would be free to choose who ruled them. But it was pretty obvious to everybody that the Star People wanted Kal Quintal to rule and wouldn't actually allow anybody else, or at least someone they disagreed with, to take the reins of power. It seemed a lot of bother for everyone, just to get a pre-ordained result. Most Melantherans, if left to their own devices and being, it had to be said, naturally lethargic, would probably have voted for the Empress, so things could go back to being what they had been before. But this, apparently, wouldn't been possible, as the Empress was technically still their 'head of state', so she wouldn't be able to stand for election.

Gamelon had told Berendal that there had been a lot of head-scratching and confusion at the Grand Council meetings where they had discussed these issues, the Empress always remaining aloof and distant from such trivial details.

The sticking point in all the negotiations had been the fact that the Empress's army, or what was left of it, was still at large and out there in the countryside fighting a guerrilla war against any force that tried to impose the new republic's will on the farthest parts of Melanthera. According to Gamelon, the Empress was told that she could stay in the city, remain in the citadel, if she would order the army to lay down their arms and come back to Melanthera. The Empress's answer had been:

"If I'm going to be a powerless figurehead, I may as well be one on Khetmis rather than stay here in Melanthera, if it means I have to surrender all the hope that remains to us."

In the days before the treaty had been finally sealed, Gamelon had come to him and asked him to walk with him in the gardens of the palace:

"Old friend," he'd said, "the game is nearly at an end and I'm afraid that we've lost. It's time for you to leave."

Berendal had protested, said that he couldn't leave his Empress at this the worst of times.

"This order comes from her Highness," Gamelon had continued. "You won't hear it directly from her mouth, as it would only do you harm to bring you into her presence. There are spies, even amongst us, and someone somewhere is making lists."

He paused, suddenly needing to sit down by one of the fountains. We're all exhausted, Berendal thought sitting beside him, we all need this to end.

"You should go now, today." Gamelon started speaking again. "Take Noor and go to the Harradim. Hopefully they won't look for you there."

So they had left that night, just before the curfew that the Star People's troops had imposed on the city. A Harradim couple walking through the Citadel gates, their bundles on their backs, heading down the hill to their own people.

Finding a place to live had not been difficult; there were plenty of empty houses as so many people had either been killed or fled. The Harradim looked after each other and though Noor was as much a stranger to these people as Berendal was, they were soon provided with food, shelter and the safety of neighbours who would look out for them. And for once in Berendal's life, money wasn't a problem. The Empress had expressed her gratitude to him handsomely in coin.

So Berendal lived to all appearances, in his little courtyard house on the Street of the Dyers, like a contented Harradim husband; Noor taking care of him in the home she had always wanted and now had finally got. But both of them were troubled. Some nights Noor would wake up from dreams where she was still on the plains, still amongst the Hvassara.

"Some mornings, even when I open my eyes, I feel that they are still there. In our house or on the street, waiting to take me back."

He tried to comfort her, did his best, but she could see the way the shadows fell over his face, the way his eyes held a sadness, that he wasn't happy.

He told her what the trouble was:

"I wake up each day. Get up, dress, break my fast. Do all the little things that make up this life of ours together, but all the time - outside, just up that hill- the Empire is going through its last death agonies."

They were lying in bed together; he was sitting up, hiding his head in his hands, ashamed that her love was not enough for him, that he should feel this way. She took his hands from his face, prying the fingers loose one by one, gently - she was always gentle - but firmly.

"Husband, you have it in your power to do something. You can write. Put it into words for all of us, what we are feeling. You can fight with your pen, as well as with your sword."

From that day on, after thanking Elanta for giving him such a wise wife, he set to his work. He would spend the mornings writing. In the afternoons he would go the shops in the Street of the Scribes to buy ink, obsidian nibs and the thin, fine hvass hide that was used for scrolls.

The first poem he wrote was the 'Hymn to the Star Men'. It was a satirical piece, on the surface a paean of praise to the first contact team that had landed on the planet, but, just under the surface of the elegant phrases, it poked fun at them and their clumsy attempts to understand Melantheran culture. He felt a little uncomfortable writing the poem, because Berthaud had been part of that team. He did, however, think that she would be able to see the funny side of things; he'd always thought she had an almost Melantheran sense of humour.

He'd tried his poem out on Noor, she was full of praise for it, but he didn't think she had any great

377

critical faculty when it came to poetry. His wife could hardly read; her life among the Hvassara had not only left her scarred, it had also robbed her of the chance for any sort of education.

In the past, he had always been used to reading his poems out in pleasure houses and taverns, spreading them through the words and mouths of others as well as his own. If a verse or a couplet was clever or funny, or both, Melantherans would memorise them and repeat them. That had always been the way poets had communicated their work to an audience under the Empress. But, because of the subject matter of the poem, and the fact that he was effectively in hiding, that was out of the question for him. He had idly mentioned this to one of his neighbours, a Piroushi artist - another exile amongst the Harradim, who lived a couple of doors down from him - over durgan root tea in the tea-house. The artist had commiserated with him.

"You have to be careful these days," he'd said, "the Empress hasn't departed yet, but, even so, the Republican Guards are throwing their weight around. Anything critical of Kal Quintal or his Star People friends could land you in jail. But there might be another way!"

The artist had told him that one of the things that the trade with the Star People had brought was a new way of producing poems and other written documents.

"They can do it on their machines," the artist said. He frowned. "They don't seem to value things created in the way we always done, hand-painted or hand-written; it is all too slow for them. So there is a way of making copies of a poem like yours, it's called the printing press."

In this way, he was directed to a small warehouse near the market square, where he met the ex-soldier who was putting out hand-bills and leaflets critical of Kal Quintal.

"I know you," the old soldier said. "You're Berendal. I was under your command when we held the Hwrathka Gate."

So the 'Hymn to the Star Men' was printed and distributed by the network of urchins, who scrabbled around in the early hours of dawn, leaving copies on tavern tables, stuck to walls or deposited on doorsteps.

The people were eager for a chance to strike back, even if only with the pen. The poem was read in corners in the taverns, women around the wells would giggle over it, even the Republican Guards were seen huddled over copies. More and more pamphlets and poems were being churned out by the printing presses that grew up in Melanthera. It was like a vast creature feeding the hunger of the people of the city. Quintal's men would close them down, but more and more would spring up. In the end, the Defence Force put a ban of the import of such machinery, primitive though it was to them.

Other poems were written. Berendal was flattered when he saw one entitled 'How Berendal held the Gate'. He was past any need for fame, or indeed notoriety, but he could see the way that having his name bandied around like this would be put to the service of his next work.

This would be his masterpiece, the poem he was born to write. He would call it the 'Asha's

Lament' and it would chronicle all the events of the last few years, from when the Star People first landed until this very day, when the Empire was in its death throes.

And who better to have as the hero? Asha, the Moon Maiden, who had come to the city following the Star. Asha, the warrior, who had saved the Empress and then become the hero of the siege, taking the fight to the enemy; never tiring, always on one part of the wall or the other, wherever she was needed, driving them on, giving them hope. Asha, his friend, who had ridden out with the army, in that last great breakout. Some said that she had died there, on the plains to the east of the city, others that she was in the mountains still leading the fight. But what everyone said was that she would come again, she would return to deliver them.

"Here they come!" A voice said. Berendal snapped out of his reverie. Sky was smiling at him.

"You were far away." She said. "Look it's the Empress!"

And then he saw them; that sad parade. The Empress was riding in an open carriage drawn by six stark, white haras, descending the road from the citadel. She still had her Barossi guard marching in front and behind her, though he knew they were just ceremonial and would be disbanded and sent back to their homes as soon as the Empress had arrived at Khetmis. There was a train of wagons and riders, the remnants of the Imperial Household, stretching out behind her.

The crowd in the square was silent. Republican Guard units were positioned around at regular intervals and the Star People's Defence Force

380

soldiers were also in evidence, stationed on roof-tops and behind the walls and on the towers of the compound, which they had re- populated.

It had been determined that this would be a low key event. There would be no religious ceremony; no members of the interim government would be present. No announcement had been made and no-one had any idea of the timing of the departure, but, somehow - as if through some sixth sense - the crowds had been gathering since early morning.

It had been made clear, by the Republican Guard patrols that had re-doubled their efforts on the streets over the last few days, that there would be no demonstration at this event. They had used their new, Star People derived, loudhailers to make the point. Any resistance or disturbance would be met by force of arms. Deportation would be the penalty.

Berendal could see the figure of the Empress in the carriage, coming ever closer. She had eschewed the company of any of her officials and, apart from her driver, she was alone. She wore the high-headdress and long robes of her office, the costume worn by all those Emperors and Empresses over the years, since time, or at least recorded time, began.

As the carriage turned into the square, it was so quiet that you could clearly hear the snorts of the team of haras as they laboured to pull the weight of the old, ornate vehicle. The Hwrathka Gate stood open and, for a moment, Berendal thought that the Empress would leave without any sort of farewell, that she would just pass under the gate and out into history. But then it started, the murmuring, like a swarm of kobo-flies.

The Republican Guards started raising their weapons; the Star People soldiers could be seen aiming their guns down into the crowd. But still the muttering went on and, suddenly, several Harradim women on the market stalls beside the square, started the ululating cheer that was the Melantheran way of showing appreciation and soon it spread through the crowd. And just before the gate, the Empress stopped the carriage and stood up.

The ululation was deafening now, the crowd surging forward. Shouts were going up as well:

"Mila! Mila! Mila!"

And then, from one corner of the crowd, then from another:

"Asha! Asha! Asha!"

The Republican Guards looked around them, unsure what to do. The crowd had pressed up against a number of the units and scuffling was breaking out between some of the younger onlookers and the soldiers. Suddenly, the Empress lifted her arms for silence and everyone complied immediately.

"Melantherans! Friends! Don't let my departure be marred by bloodshed!"

The crowd quietened down, the hot-heads were hustled backwards from the ranks of the Republican Guards.

"Today, my body has to leave you, but my heart remains here with you in Melanthera. May Elanta guard you and keep you safe! "

The Empress gave a signal to the carriage driver and the Barossi guards and she rode on, passing under the Hwrathka Gate. The crowd took up their cheer again and carried on until the

Empress was well out of ear-shot on the road to exile.

Sky came and sat next to Berendal and he put his arm around her. She was crying, but Berendal had no tears left.

"The world was turned upside down today, friend Berendal," she said.

Later, when the crowd had dispersed, he made his way up the steep streets behind the market to his home. He had to be discreet, to blend into the shadows of the narrow, high alleys and by-ways, a lame Harradim man on his way back to his people.

It was when he turned the corner into the Street of Dyers that he heard the noise, a low rumbling first, then a bellowing, followed by the staccato of heavy gun-fire. Looking up towards the citadel, he saw a pall of smoke pouring up into the air and as the wind changed direction, it brought with it a terrible stench of burnt flesh.

Stumbling up the road, nearly at his own door, feeling in his gut that something terrible was happening, though he did not know the reason why, he almost collided with a little Piroushi girl, the artist's daughter, who ran out of her doorway almost straight into him. She was weeping piteously, inconsolably.

"Whatever is it, Khamis?" Berendal asked her, holding her close to him.

"It's the hwrathka," she cried. "They are killing them!"

He got the child back to her house, into her mother's arms, where the woman tried to comfort her. Then he sought out his own house and Noor. He found her in the garden, ashen-faced.

"Husband," she asked, "you have heard?"

He said he had.

"They waited for the Empress to go and then they went in and slaughtered the hwrathka," she said. "The cries are terrible and the smell of their burning corpses."

He sat down by her on the stone bench and held her hands. The slaughter went on for hours, but they didn't move.

Chapter 32
Desert Of The Heart

It was two days out from Hava Port that Kahal admitted to her that they were not heading for Melanthera. She was sitting in a corner of the courtyard of the ruined caravanserai, around a fire, where she and the other prisoners had cooked their food. The Republican Guards had posted sentries on the walls, but they knew that it was unlikely that any of the prisoners would try to escape. All that was out there was the desert and the roving Hvassara, who would treat them even worse that the brutal Republican Guards.

Kahal had been assigned to her as her personal guard throughout the voyage to Hava Port. She had, in fact, spent most of the voyage locked in a cell in the hold of the ship, a bigger vessel than the one that she and Khamis had taken on the outward journey. Despite all the discomfort and danger of that first voyage, the memory of it seemed idyllic, especially compared to the time she spent on that other ship. It was called the Black Ghost, which she thought was an appropriate name, for the way it had spirited her away from all that had become precious to her. She thought she could have borne the voyage if Khamis had been near or with her, but, heartbroken and lonely though she was, she was glad Khamis was elsewhere. Somewhere that must be better than this place.

They obviously had some interest in keeping her alive, or so she told herself, because they brought her food twice a day and would allow her on deck, closely watched by Kahal, tied to him in fact, where she was allowed to walk and empty the pot they had given her to piss and shit in.

Strangely enough, Kahal had become something of a comfort to her. He was a bluff, crude, soldierly type, but not cruel. He had learnt her language after serving with a Defence Force unit in Melanthera as a guide and, eventually, an interpreter. He was Kal Quintal's man and was vocal in his disdain for the old Empire and the people who still supported it, but he seemed to have some general affection for the Star People and so, even though she was a renegade, he seemed to treat her in a way that was , if not sympathetic, at least not hostile.

It was Kahal who explained to her, once they were on board the ship, what had happened on Piroush.

"Apparently, there was a local arrest warrant issued for that Piroushi girl, which superseded the warrant we carried from Melanthera. They do it all the time. It's their way of dealing with their own people; they don't like us getting our hands on them."

He was quiet for a time, evidently thinking.

"I don't blame them really. Each to their own, I say."

He told her that Princess Kusha had personally intervened to stop Khamis being taken away. This gave some comfort to Robyn; even if Khamis was in a Piroushi prison cell, she was probably safer than in the hands of the Republican Guards, but it did nothing to stop the ache in her heart or fill the terrible void that seemed to be at the core of her being.

Kahal had sought to argue with her, to dispute the whole question of Empire and Republic; the benefits the Star People had brought, weighed up against the war and the death that had gone with it. But she had not proved to be a worthy opponent. She had sunk into a terrible apathy, a black, depressive state. She no longer cared what they did to her. Sometimes, looking at the deep, pitching ocean as she threw her piss over the rail - not making the same mistake she made the first time and getting it flung back in her face by the wind - she really felt like jumping, taking Kahal with her into the depths. But ultimately, she couldn't even raise the energy to take that one, last, decisive act.

The voyage had been a sort of limbo, a lost time. She had spent most of it lying on her cot, sleeping or staring into space. When Kahal took her up onto the deck, she was like an automaton, obeying his every command, hardly reacting, as if she was sedated. She often didn't eat her food and then Kahal would get angry with her.

"You worry me," he'd say, "you won't last a day where you are going unless you keep your strength up."

He also showed a clumsy sort of gentleness, trying to feed her as if she was a child, holding the ladle to her mouth. But all the time she was thinking of what he had said, "where you are going." She thought she was going home, she told herself, but then realised she didn't know where home was anymore. The closest she could get to picturing home in her head was the Nishan house in Piroush and Khamis lying there beside her.

At Hava Port they became part of a caravan, but not of merchants this time, instead solely made up of Republican Guards and their prisoners. While the guards rode on haras or in wagons, the prisoners spent most of the day walking. For some reason, she was regarded as having importance and was allowed to ride in one of the wagons if she showed signs of fatigue.

The ruts of earlier wagons were clearly discernible on the desert, so they needed no guides. The Republican Guards did have a number of Hvassara scouts, who rode out into the desert every day coming back with news for the commanding officer. In her insular state of mind, she was not paying much attention to her surroundings, but she did notice that many of the guards seemed alert and jumpy. She also thought that she didn't recognise this route as the same one that she and Khamis had traversed on their outward trip, but she thought little of it.

Though the guards could be brutal and ready with their fists and riding whips, if any prisoner gave them offence, she had to admit that they were disciplined and adhered to their own standard of behaviour. When a Hvassara had tried to force himself on one of the women prisoners on the first night, he'd been summarily dismissed and sent away.

That first night they had camped in the desert, but on the second afternoon they had come to the caravanserai. It was a burnt-out ruin, but the walls were still intact and the wells still in use. Kahan had sought her out by the fire that night. He seemed pre-occupied. He spent a long time telling her about the Harradim who had lived there.

"They'd run this place for travellers from time immemorial. These places were like refuges, havens of peace. Enemies would sit down next to each other and break bread together. No-one could draw a sword here or the Harradim would throw them out."

She asked him what had happened here, not really out of any interest, just to keep the conversation going.

"Over ten years ago, the great Hvassara army that besieged Melanthera rolled over this place on the way. They killed the men and sold the women and children into slavery. The Harradim wouldn't come back after that. The tribe than ran this place were wiped out and no other tribe would take it over. Too much death happened here."

He was silent then, just sitting by the fire. The other prisoners, made uncomfortable by his presence, had drifted away to one of the other fires.

"Robyn," he said, the first time he had used her name. "You should know that we are not going to Melanthera. I don't know what you were told, but we are going to one of the camps."

Momentarily, Robyn felt a sick feeling in her stomach, a physical pang of fear. But then she asked herself: "What did I expect? Did I think White Hair would tell me the truth?"

"They want to keep you alive for now," Kahan went on, "but they want to keep you somewhere out of the way until they decide what to do with you."

He sighed.

"I don't know why I'm telling you this. Well, I suppose it's because I don't want you to think I've lied to you."

Abruptly he stood up and disappeared into the darkness.

So this is it, thought Robyn. I'm not leaving this place after all. She had heard of the prison camps, more by rumour than through anyone's actual experience of them. Because very few people survived them, or escaped, to tell what went on there. It seemed to be something that the Republic had been tutored in by the Defence Force, a way of dealing with dissenters and political opponents. Putting them out on the steppe, in the desert or the mountains, where they could spend a life of toil in the mines, working the salt pans or cutting timber. Why kill your opponents when you could make them economically useful? If they succumbed to the heat or the cold or were crushed under a tree or in a cave-in, that was too bad.

Just behind the fire were the remains of an old stable that had been assigned to the prisoners by the guards. They had spent some time cleaning debris and rubbish from the floor of the place and now it was a reasonable shelter from the cold desert night. She was loathe to leave the fire, but eventually pulled herself away from it and found a place amongst the other sleepers. As usual, the Melantherans weren't great ones for privacy, so they were all huddled up together in two different parts of the building; one reserved for the men, the other for the women. The Republican Guards were quite strict about keeping the sexes apart, but she had seen couples trying to sneak off to get some

390

time together, a little bit of mutual comfort against the dark days ahead.

As she made her way amongst the women, many sleeping, but others still awake talking softly, a figure motioned to her. She made her way, somewhat reluctantly, over to the woman who beckoned her. The prisoners' attitudes to Robyn tended to be either one of general, benign friendliness or one of rank suspicion. She could deal with either; she didn't want to make any more friendships and risk the chance of them being brutally pulled asunder. But the woman who waited for her now was different, she had courted Robyn from the first day they met, making every effort to talk to her, to spend time with her. Her name was Mara. She had worked as a migrant worker and so spoke Robyn's own language. She informed Robyn that she had a Barossi father and a Melantheran mother, but it was clear, even to Robyn, that the other women held her in disdain and this was because they suspected her of having Hvassara blood.

Even Robyn, with her incomplete and scanty knowledge of things Melantheran, knew that this was something no-one would admit to in other peoples' company here. The Hvassara were known as raiders and slavers and no Melantheran she had come across, including the Piroushi, had one positive thing to say about them. She suspected that this was partly because they were nomads and, as was often the case, the settled peoples, who usually had something of value to be stolen, both feared and despised their footloose counterparts.

She also thought that it was because, although Melanthera was far from an equal society, amongst the Hvassara, women were treated - or so she had been told - as chattels, one rung up the ladder from slaves and one rung down from the warrior's favourite haras. It had been one of Khamis's favourite nightly pastimes on their journey out in the desert, telling her tales of Hvassara raiders and their evil intentions; rather like the way children tell each other ghost stories around a campfire.

Thinking involuntarily of Khamis, gave her a small pang of grief, so in the end she was almost pleased to lie down by Mara. Pleased for some sort of company. She thought the woman was older than her, in her forties or thereabouts, though it was difficult to tell age here. If she had Barossi blood, she favoured her mother, having the olive skin and dark, curly hair of the Melantherans.

"Come rest, friend Robyn," she said. "Look I will spread this blanket over both of us to keep the heat in. I suspect tonight will be very cold."

Mara was very knowledgeable about the desert and the route they were taking, which Robyn put down to her Barossi blood. She was always constantly seeking to engage Robyn in conversation, to pry as it were. It had made Robyn suspect that the woman was, at best, an informer and, at worst, a spy, planted deliberately to pump her of any information that the white-haired interrogator had missed.

Because, although she had basically told him everything, she had managed to leave out most of the names, or change them. She'd pleaded ignorance as her excuse for this, that she'd never known names, could not recall which street she stayed on in Melanthera, or remember the faces of those who'd helped her. This was perhaps why she'd ended up here, that she hadn't been a convincing enough informant, a good enough traitor. Or perhaps this was always the plan, perhaps there was never any deal; perhaps she'd never really saved Khamis from the Hvassara, Princess Kusha had done that.

She also wondered if Mara had been told to seduce her. The woman was always trying to get close to her, offering to brush her hair, help her wash, offering to comfort her. Even if Robyn had felt any physical attraction to her, which she didn't, she didn't want anyone after Khamis. She'd never really understood what was meant by the term 'heart-broken' before; she did now. This was different from Esmee, different from Abi; it was something deeper, more profound.

Considering how she felt, it was surprising to her how easily sleep came these days. She thought it was the long days of travelling, the heat of the sun in the day and the coldness of the desert nights; all conspiring to exhaust her. So she slipped off easily, Mara's voice, soft and insistent, lulling her to sleep.

The noise woke her abruptly and she couldn't quite figure out what it was or where she was. Suddenly, the stable and the desert came back to her. Other women were awake or waking, but Mara was gone. Then she saw the woman coming back from the big, open doorway of the building. The noise coalesced into something she could make sense of; gunshots, shouts and cries.

One young woman screamed in terror, then shouted: "It's the Hvassara. Elanta save us!"

"Don't be stupid, child," Mara shouted back, "the Hvassara wouldn't attack the Republican Guards, they are their allies."

The tone of Mara's voice struck Robyn; it no longer had that plaintive, wheedling quality. It was commanding, bearing authority.

"Come," she dragged Robyn up, "you're not safe here."

As she pulled Robyn up and took her hand, they brushed against each other for a moment and Robyn felt something poking into her. Mara was wearing a weapon underneath her tunic, a pistol of some sort. Robyn was shocked by this, but said nothing, as the woman led her from the stable and out beneath the curtain wall.

The fires were still burning, but they had died down; the light they gave was flickering and uneven, mixing shadows and light, distorting the shapes of the buildings and the people who could be seen on the walls or running across the yard. Robyn had difficulty making sense of it all, but amongst the dark uniforms of the guards, she could see other figures, like phantoms emerging then merging again with the shadows, their faces muffled in head-scarves, bodies shrouded in Harradim cloaks.

As she tried to make some sense of the chaos around her, it seemed to her that the guards were being driven back from the front gate and the wall that flanked it. They were taking positions in the ruined buildings around the courtyard, behind the well and in the open kitchen. Their habitual arrogance and easy brutality - that could be read on

394

their faces, in the way they carried themselves and in every act - had been replaced by something else; they were confused and terrified.

As they walked from the ruined stable, two guards ran past them towards the other prisoners, herding back the few who were tentatively emerging from the doorway, threatening them with their guns. They ran past Mara and Robyn, as if they were invisible. Mara led her along the curtain wall away from the fighting, gripping her hand tightly, pulling her towards another dark veranda that fronted another building. Robyn suddenly realised that Mara was taking her towards, not away from, the Republican Guards. She tried to get away, but the woman's grip was vice-like and then in one deft move, Mara twisted Robyn's hand and her whole arm behind her back.

"Don't be stupid, girl," Mara said. "You'll be safe with me, so don't fight."

But then it was too late, the Republican Guard Captain emerged from the shadows of the terrace in front of them, flanked by another figure.

"Bring her in here," the Captain said. Mara pushed her towards him and then the other Republican Guard had taken her other arm and she was shoved through a doorway into another one of the caravanserai's guest quarters. She realised that the guard who had taken her arm was Kahan. In the little light there was, she looked hard at him, locking her eyes with his, trying to appeal to him. But his face looked blank, she could read nothing there.

The room had been used by the Captain as his quarters. It was a small chamber, furnished with a sleeping platform. A hand-set of some sort lay on a shelf by the window. It was turned on; voices talking or shouting, then a scream. "Why doesn't someone answer?" She thought.

The Captain looked at her and then spoke to Kahan. Mara listened, expressionless. Kahan drew his side arm, the black, blunt-nosed pistol looking small in his big hands. He seemed to be arguing with the Captain, who shouted something at him, and then went to stand by the door, looking out.

"I'm sorry," Kahan said to Robyn, "they don't want you to be taken alive."

He raised the automatic pistol, two hands around the butt and aimed it at her head. She stepped back against the wall and shrank down, putting her hands up in a futile effort to shield her face. No thought came into her head, there was just the harsh, metallic taste of fear on her tongue and, though she was hardly aware of it, she had started crying.

"Oh, fuck it!" Kahan said – in Robyn's language - and lowered the weapon, his hands shaking. The Captain, turned, shouting angrily, drawing his own pistol taking two strides to cross the room.

"Now it comes," she thought, "the end of me."

Two shots rang out, deafening, stunning. Then two more and a groan. A small noise like a yawn or an expression of fatigue. There was blood on her face and the floor was pooling with it. Mara stood above her, pistol in her hand. The Captain lay dead in front of her, splayed out on the floor, dark matter oozing from the back of his head. Kahan lay in a corner, as if curled up in sleep. Mara took her hand again.

"Come!" She said. "Now! We have to go!"

"Why?" Robyn asked. It was the only word she could get out.

"Shut up and do what you're told!" Mara said.

It seemed like a dream, or rather a nightmare. Mara led her onwards through the fighting, always keeping to the shadows of the curtain wall. They passed guardsmen, crouched behind walls or wagons, but after a quick glance they ignored them. They passed bodies too, mostly of guards with arrows bristling from them or bearing gashes inflicted by edged weapons.

One of the Hvassara guides loomed out of the darkness towards them and Mara shouted at him in what Robyn presumed was his own language. But whatever she said had no effect on him. He laughed at her and raised his sword. She shot him, as easily as swatting a kobo-fly.

They passed the bodies of prisoners too. Many had tried to make a run for it, taking advantage of the chaos. Some of them had been shot down, killed or wounded. They passed one woman who Robyn recognised, crouched against a building with a leg wound, trying to staunch the blood. But when Robyn tried to go to her, pulling at Mara's hand, the woman just said curtly:

"Leave her!"

And when Robyn broke free and started towards her, she said without any trace of emotion in her voice:

"If you take one more step nearer, I'll shoot her in the head!"

There was a small gate or sally-port at the back of the caravanserai. It was more of a tunnel really; steps descended down a narrow shaft, giving out on a passageway which emerged some distance from the walls in an outcrop of rocks. The entrance to the sally port had been partially concealed; charred roof beams and scraps of roof matting had been laid over the entrance to the shaft, though it was obvious that Mara knew its exact location. A tinder box and a little oil lamp had been left just inside the tunnel's mouth and Mara knew exactly where to find it.

As they emerged into the outcrop of rocks, Mara said;

"Don't think of running, girl. There's nothing but desert between here and the frontier. You'll either die of thirst or the Hvassara will pick you up and you'll soon wish the heat had finished you off."

They huddled together amongst the rocks for some time, listening to the sounds of battle that came from the fort. Mara pulled her close.

"We need to keep warm," she said, but the woman took a firm grip on the sash of Robyn's tunic. "Just in case I try to escape," Robyn thought.

When the shape of the rocks around them began to emerge in the early light of dawn, Mara led her down towards a hollow, where the springs that the caravanserai had been built close to, emerged in a green swathe of shrubs and grass. She allowed Robyn to quench the burning thirst that had gradually come on her through the night and to wash the blood off her face and hands. Then she pulled her into a low stand of shrubs.

"What are we doing now?" Robyn asked.

"We wait, girl," Mara said. "To see what happens."

The woman laughed, but there was little humour in it.

"Those Republican Guards are amateurs. That's what you say, isn't it! They're not good soldiers. They didn't expect to get attacked at the caravanserai. They expected to be ambushed in the desert, not when they were behind walls."

She was still holding the gun in her hand, it was like an extension of her arm, Robyn thought. She seemed used to it, comfortable with the weapon.

"The guards were complacent. They got their throats cut. And that Captain was not up to the job. So, unless a relief column is on the way, I think we can predict the result."

"But who attacked us?" Robyn asked. She looked warily at Mara. The woman scared her; it was the way that she had killed Kahan, the Captain and the Hvassara scout. Without feeling, without any compunction.

"Why, the rebels, of course!" The woman answered. "I don't know if you've got anything to do with it. The guards obviously think you've got some value, or they wouldn't have tried to kill you."

She laughed again.

"Though I wonder what a scrawny thing like you can be worth. Anyway, you should try and get some sleep. We'll see how the land lies in an hour or two."

"With you here, not knowing what you've got in store for me, how do I sleep?" Robyn thought. But, suddenly she was waking up, sometime later, as the sun was higher and getting hotter, its heat and light penetrating the lattice of shrubs they lay under. She looked up, forgetting where she was, until her eyes fell on Mara. The woman was asleep; though the pistol was still firmly clutched in her hand, her eyes were tightly closed.

Robyn made her decision and started moving in a split second. She crept as quietly as she could, out from under the canopy of shrubs, and made her way back towards the spring. She was thirsty again and, looking around first, she bent down to drink, feeling the cold water on her face like some sort of simple blessing. But abruptly her head was pulled back by the hair and she was hauled from the water's edge.

"I'm sorry, Mara," she started to say, but it wasn't Mara. The face that looked down on her was expressionless, all except for the eyes which flickered from her face and then down over her body. It was a Hvassara, one of the scouts, she thought, and his curved blade was drawn, hovering just above her throat. The man seemed to consider her for a time, his tongue flicking between his lips. Then, he pulled her to her feet, by the hair again, and started dragging her towards his haras, which was hidden under a stand of trees. When he got her there, he pushed her down to the ground, landing a savage kick in her stomach, which winded her and temporarily disabled her, then reached for the rope on his saddle.

"He's saving me for later," she thought, struggling to get up. He hit her again with the riding whip that was looped around his wrist. But, as he turned back towards his haras, he suddenly grunted and, as he slumped down the side of the beast, she saw the tip of the spear point that had emerged from his back, just breaking the skin. Then a shadow loomed over her, blocking out the sun, a tall figure she could only see in silhouette. With a quick movement, the figure knelt down, grabbed the Hvassara scout's head by the hair and pulled it back exposing the throat, cutting it with a quick, adroit movement of the knife in its right hand.

Robyn rolled onto her side; she'd had enough of the sight of blood for one day, though she couldn't block the butcher's shop stench which filled her nostrils. She tried to crawl away, but it was futile. The figure took hold of her by her hair and turned her over on her back, kneeling on her arms, the bloody knife at her throat now. A few drops of blood fell on her face as the figure brought the knife up. That was the scout's blood, she thought, feeling no pity, knowing what he had intended for her.

She was looking up into an angular, thin, dark face; a hood thrown back to reveal a close-cropped head. There was no expression on the features, just a fierce light burning in the eyes, which fixed on her own. Beneath the Harradim cloak that the woman wore, Robyn could see the red robes that she knew were the badge of the Sisterhood. But she'd never seen anyone wear them, as they'd been banned throughout Melanthera and Piroush. And she'd never seen a Sister cut somebody's throat. The woman's gaze did not waver off Robyn's face; Robyn looked into those eyes that were for all the world like those of a predatory beast.

The woman was so close, she could smell her. The tang of her sweat, the spicy scent of her breath.

"It's strange," Robyn thought, "but she smells salty, like the sea."

Abruptly, the woman got off her and motioned for her to stand up. As she did so, Robyn saw all around her warriors dressed in the same Harradim robes, armed with swords, spears and bows, not a gun in sight. The woman was busy retrieving her spear from the dead Hvassara. Robyn looked away again, as this seemed to involve some rather grisly knife work. The woman cleaned off the head of the spear and stowed it with two others in a sort of sheath that hung over one shoulder, beside the great two- handed short that also hung there.

"Star Woman!" The woman said and beckoned to her to follow. She didn't speak Robyn's language, but she knew those two words, which were spoken somewhat dismissively or so it seemed to Robyn. They were walking back to the spring, the other warriors around watching the flanks of the party, quiet and alert. As they got nearer to the water's edge, there was an eruption from the clump of bushes and shrubs where Robyn had spent the night and she saw two warriors appear dragging Mara. The woman was chattering on in Melantheran and, when she saw Robyn, shouted to her:

"You must tell them what I did! How I saved you!"

They brought Mara close up to the red-robed woman and made her kneel. The woman had already drawn her knife, spitting out a word that Robyn could not understand.

"You must tell them!" Mara entreated her; the woman seemed somehow deflated, her legs scrabbling at the ground as the two warriors held her firmly in place.

"You must tell the Lady Asha that I'm your friend! That I saved you!"

Robyn felt the shock break over her, it was an almost physical feeling like being hit and pulled under by waves breaking on the shore. And in the same way, it took her breath away. That name had started all this and, in the woman standing next to her, it had coalesced into flesh. She stared at Asha, open-mouthed and awe-struck. The woman stared back. Then she heard Mara's voice again.

"Tell her!" She kept saying. "Tell her!"

"But how I tell her," Robyn shouted in frustration." She doesn't speak my language."

"But I do," another woman, younger than Asha, had stepped through the circle of warriors around them; she was also dressed in the red robes of a Sister. "Is what this woman says true?"

Robyn told her it was.

"You can explain later," the woman said, "now we must move quickly, in case a relief force comes."

Suddenly all was movement around them, other warriors rode up with haras and Robyn could see amongst them, a fair number of her fellow prisoners.

"The woman can live for now," the young sister said, "until we hear what you have to say."

The Sister's name was Mila, she told Robyn.

"There were many girl children given that name after the Empress was exiled," she said, laughing, as they rode along, "it used to get confusing when I was at Temple school."

Mila, considering their circumstances, seemed to be surprisingly jolly, chatting amiably to Robyn and cracking jokes.

"I've been among your people," the young Sister said. "I worked as a servant for one of your families and learnt the language, while also ministering to the Melantheran community. It's a path that Sisters often take." Robyn thought of Sister Alethea on Hanis, hoping that she hadn't been taken by Security.

"It's good to have a chance to practise Terran," she said. "I get little enough chance now."

A few hours later their caravan stopped in a territory of shallow valleys and rock outcrops.

"It's dangerous to travel too far by daylight, we throw up too much dust," Mila said. "We had to risk it to get away from the oasis, but we'll stay here for the rest of the daylight hours. It's easily defensible, if we're attacked by anything other than cruisers."

Sister Mila seemed to have been assigned as Robyn's companion, or guard. She saw that Robyn was fed, some sort of rough bread and hvass cheese, a strong taste she had almost got used to.

"We can't risk a fire, friend Robyn," she said, "though I'd dearly like a cup of durgan root tea."

Robyn had told the woman everything; there seemed no point in holding anything back. They could do with her what they would, she was beyond caring.

Later, she was taken into the space formed by two rock outcrops which leaned towards each other, a sort of partial cave. Asha was sitting there, still and silent. They both waited for her to speak, it took some time. Then she asked Mila something in

Melantheran and they chatted for a while. Then Mila said:

"The Lady Asha would like to ask you something."

"Ask away," Robyn replied and when Mila didn't understand. "Please ask me anything."

"Lady Asha asks," Mila went on, "since she has heard from me that you were in Piroush, she asks how fares the Princess Kusha."

Robyn nodded: "She is still on the throne and the people seem to love her. She saved my friend Khamis from the Republican Guard."

Mila translated and Robyn saw just the ghost of a smile push up the ends of Asha's mouth and creep into her eyes.

"Now this other one!" Mila said and clapped her hands.

Two guards dragged Mara in. The woman fell on the ground in front of Asha and started babbling away in Melantheran.

"Do you know who she is?" Mila asked and before Robyn had time to answer said: "She's Republican Guard, a spy, what your people call Intelligence or Security."

Mara glanced up at Mila, the terror now evident in her face. She said something to her.

"The question is whether she was trying to save you, as she says, or whether she was trying to stop you being saved."

Mila looked down at the other woman, the smile suddenly gone from her face, replaced with a look of contempt. She looked like she was about to spit on Mara.

Mara said something in Melantheran and repeated it in Terran: "I've come over to you! I want to join you!"

Asha stood up, as if to signify that her patience was at an end, she motioned to the guards who advanced.

Mara was almost screaming now: "I could be useful to you! Really useful! I have lots of information!"

Asha sat down once more and the guards stopped. Mara started talking again in Melantheran, the words tumbling out of her as if she daren't even pause for breath.

Chapter 33
End Of Empire

Mila the Third, last Empress of Melanthera, sat on the divan in her palace on Khetmis, trying to cool herself with an ornamental fan, reflecting on past glories. She had sent most of the servants away, hence the fact she had to fan herself. She did not want too many people around her, especially the younger ones, as she knew it was only a matter of time before they came for her.

The result was that the palace was much quieter, much less busy. The bright, idle chatter of the young maids, like bright plumaged birds drifting around the place, no longer echoed in the corridors. Their high-pitched delighted laughter no longer sounded in the gardens, spreading with it an infectious humour, an outbreak of smiles. The young lads, the footmen and grooms, who spent much of their time chasing after the maids, no longer had to suffer the complaints of the stewards, being constantly told to keep their voices down, to stop running in the corridors. They were no longer there.

Now the palace was filled with old people. Her chief steward - who had taken over the Chamberlain's duties after his death in the siege, even though he was advanced in years and seemed to have lost some of his faculties - ruled over a household of elderly cooks they'd brought with them and old Piroushi maids who were too slow and too short-sighted to keep up with the domestic chores. There were no more Barossi. Her faithful household guards had been sent back to their homeland before she embarked on the ship at Hava Port.

At their final parade, before the gates of Hava port, many of those stoic, impassive warriors had ripped off their face veils and cried openly, such was their grief. Mila, alone in her carriage, had been equally moved; she'd had to grasp the handrail beside her so tight that her fingers started to ache, to keep the tears from falling from her own eyes. Because, of course, an Empress couldn't be seen to cry, that would never do. As they marched away, an orphan army heading out into the desert where their Hvassara enemies awaited them, she wondered what she had ever done to deserve such unswerving, unquestioning loyalty.

It had been part of the peace agreement that she would give up her household guard. The Barossi had always provided her with what was, in essence, her own private army. The republican authorities, effectively Kal Quintal and his Star People cronies, would not stand for her having a military force under her command. The agreement had also stated that the republic "would provide adequate security" for her exile on Khetmis. This had turned out to be a detachment of Republican Guards under a drunken Lieutenant. The men had spent most of their few weeks on the island, lying on the sand and swimming in the sea, when they weren't causing trouble for any the younger women maids who had yet to depart. Eventually, after a series of complaints, the detachment had been withdrawn, but no other guards had come to replace them. Mila knew then that the end would not be long in coming..

It was a heavy, hot day; that enervating heat that seemed to seep from the ground of the island and sap all will. She thought of how, over the years, she had taken such pleasure from her summer place, how she had enjoyed getting away from the dust and noise of Melanthera. Though she dearly loved her city and its inhabitants, she had to admit that they were a particularly noisy and argumentative people. Even in her palace gardens, in the midst of the green lawns, shade trees and gently flowing fountains, the bustle and energy of the city penetrated. You could hear the carts and wagons passing by, the raised voices and laughter. The dust was blown in over the walls, too, the blades of the grass and the leaves of the trees were often touched with a fine film of red dust. And whatever scents the plants gave out, whatever flowers the gardeners grew, there was always the stench from the shambles and tanneries outside the east gate to be reckoned with. You'd sit quietly at peace in the garden and suddenly the vile stench would assail you, filling your nostrils.

So Khetmis had always been a haven to her, a place where she could rest her weary bones and escape the daily routines of court, the audiences and disputes, the petty squabbles she would have to settle. But Khetmis had always been a place of vibrant life, of long-drawn out dinners under the stars, midday picnics under the forest canopy and lazy afternoons spent in the gardens, surrounded by her ladies-in-waiting and her other attendants.

Thinking back, she smiled when she thought of Annesh and Kusha, the afternoons they had spent here with her; those two golden girls who'd laughed and played as if life was an endless joy and there was no end to it. But Annesh was dead, killed by the Star People's bombs, and Kusha was no longer so young and so care-free. The young woman had accompanied Mila as far as Piroush, but there she had left her, as Kusha's father had been ailing and she was the heir to the throne.

That had been another parting that Mila would have liked to forget; there had been too many partings over these last few months, people who had had to leave her or been sent away. Kusha had wept and knelt down in front of her, her head in Mila's lap. The Empress, singularly unused to human contact, had found her hands stroking the girl's hair, comforting her as you would a child.

"Don't cry, dear Kusha," she'd said, "or you will make this woman cry too."

But she knew that Kusha was not only crying for that moment of parting, but also because of all those things that had happened over these last years, for the way their world had been torn apart and turned upside down. Mila knew there would be a formal leave-taking, you couldn't avoid ceremony if you were an Empress and a Princess of Piroush, but she quietened the girl and got her to listen, while they were still just an old woman and a young one, alone together in this room.

"Before we part, I want you to listen to me. You will always have a special place in my heart, Kusha. You are like a daughter to me, the child I never had. We have to part now, but you will always be with me."

Mila sighed. So many partings, she thought, but there were some still with her. Gamelon, no longer the verbose, slightly pompous priest-historian, was still with her. The war had taken a toll on him, as it had on everyone else, but, she had to admit, he was better company now; still asking lots of questions, over-fond of his own voice, but somehow sadder and gentler too.

And she also had Berthaud. Mila had thought that the Star Woman would have left her by now. Though she had grown to like and respect the woman, knowing that that small, slight body held a will and a soul equal to any Barossi warrior, she had not looked for the same loyalty to her cause that Gamelon so readily gave. But Berthaud had been insistent that she would follow her into exile.

This in itself had been accomplished by a process involving what Berthaud had called "smoke and mirrors". As part of the negotiations, prisoner and hostage exchanges had been arranged, but Berthaud was a special case; she was neither of the latter categories, regarded as a traitor by her people and a soldier who had, legitimately, changed sides, by the Imperial forces.

When the Star People had grown insistent, pressing for her return, Berthaud had suggested that they report her missing presumed killed. Though they all knew that the Star People would be suspicious, the story was plausible, as the bombing of the citadel and the chaos of subsequent events did mean that numbers of people were unaccounted for. As the Republican Guards has insisted on checking the identity of the people who were accompanying Mila into exile, smuggling Berthaud out with the caravan could have presented a problem. But, because Melantherans didn't carry identity papers - or at least hadn't then - it was easy enough to add another name to a group of Harradim women in the entourage. With Harradim robes and a head-scarf, Berthaud looked the part, being small of stature, dark-haired and olive-skinned.

It turned out that the Republican Guards, who were assigned to inspecting the members of her party, did just a perfunctory job; they were too few to scrutinise every individual and, instead, maintained a surly, hostile vigil as the party passed. Even if they had been more industrious, it was very unlikely that a male Melantheran would have spent any length of time examining a Harradim woman, especially when there were armed Harradim men nearby.

Berthaud's escape had only been a partial one; she was still unable to shake off the things that she had seen and done during the war. It was the same for all of them, Mila thought, they had all seen death and destruction, cruelty and pain, but in some ways it was worse for Berthaud, because she bore that added burden of guilt; it was, after all, her own people who had inflicted this on Melanthera and, ultimately, they had done it all for a few more bags of gold. So Berthaud spent much of her time alone in her apartments, dealing with her own personal demons. She no longer had any equipment she could use to transmit, though she still had the little machine she wrote on. And that was what she seemed to spend her time doing, recording everything. Mila had asked her about it, teasing her.

"You spend too much time with that little machine, friend Berthaud," Mila had said. "Surely we are not that interesting?"

But the woman would not be drawn into laughter, instead she replied with as serious look on her face:

"You Highness, I need to write all this down. To record what has been done to you and your people, by my people. Somebody, someday, must read this and know what happened."

Mila had smiled at the woman, seeing how care-worn and aged she seemed lately.

"Friend Berthaud, we still put our trust in Elanta. We have had a difficult time, a trial set by her, but she will take care of her people."

After Berthaud had left her, she had thought to herself: "After all this, do I still believe that? Do I still think Elanta's hand is guiding us?"

She couldn't give herself an answer.

As Mila sat there, the morning drifting away like smoke on a sea-breeze, she thought that what she missed most was the laughter. And thinking of laughter, she thought of Berendal. Thought of his love poem to Kusha that had caused so much trouble. But the war had changed him too, he had become a different man and there was little of the old laughter left in him.

Just before noon Gamelon knocked on the door screen and, when bidden, entered.

"Your Highness," he said, "a ship has been sighted approaching the bay. It carries no banner or

413

flag; when the watchman attempted to signal to it, it made no response."

It was as she had expected.

"So," she thought, "today is the day! They are coming at last!"

"Highness, I've sent word to the next island by fast boat, but we can't expect any help for hours yet."

She nodded an acknowledgement.

"Gamelon, inform Berthaud and the servants that they must leave now and take to the hills. They should make for the other side of the island."

He turned to leave, but she stopped him.

"And you must go too. You must leave with them."

"But, your Highness, aren't you coming too?" Gamelon asked.

Mila smiled:" I'm too old to go traipsing around the woods. I'll wait here to greet our guests."

Gamelon hesitated for a few moments, lost in thought or feeling, then spoke:

"Your Highness, grant me the favour of letting me wait with you."

Mila could see by his face that he understood the meaning of what he had asked.

Berthaud had also wanted to stay, but Mila had told her that she must go: "You have more to set down, friend Berthaud, the story is not yet at its end."

When the palace was quiet at last, the two remaining inhabitants sat calmly together, waiting.

"Have you any news to give me, Gamelon?" Mila asked. "Something to pass the time."

The man sighed wearily, but answered her question:

"It is rumoured that an epic poem called the 'Asha's Lament', by one Berendal, has been circulated in Melanthera. The authorities are burning every copy they can find of it and seeking out Berendal, but it has caught the people's imagination."

"Let us hope that it is better than some of his earlier work," Mila said and they both laughed.

"And Asha?" Mila asked. "Is there news of her?"

"She is still out there, Highness, and from what the authorities say, she's everywhere. They see her hand in every raid, every act that is taken against them."

"Ah," said Mila, "she was always fearless. She'll never stop fighting, until they kill her."

"Even if they kill her," Gamelon said, "no-one will believe she's dead. She's more like a force of nature than a mere human."

They were silent for a while, then Mila said:

"They killed my beautiful hwrathka. They say some of the drivers wouldn't leave the creatures, they'd been with them all their lives, brought them up from calves. They shot them down alongside their beasts."

Mila sighed.

"I do regret that. If I had still been in Melanthera, they would never have dared do it. I'd have never left them there, unable to defend themselves, if I'd known that was going to happen. That treaty was all empty words and lies."

The Empress smiled.

"We should have had one last magnificent charge. They'd have shot us all down, but at least my hwrathka would have died with some dignity, not slaughtered in their pens."

Later, they heard movement outside, soft footfalls, doors being kicked in, and shots being fired. Suddenly, abruptly, a voice was carried to them from some sort of loudhailer. The words were spoken in broken, badly accented Melantheran.

"Throw down your weapons and surrender. We have a warrant for the arrest of Mila, once known as the Empress, for treason. If you come out now, you will not be harmed."

Mila frowned: "The world has changed so much, Gamelon. These people now think they have the authority to arrest me! Who gives them that! The goddess chose me and it is for her to depose me."

She stood up, her legs stiff from sitting so long.

"All in all, what's done is done. But so many have died in my service, there's no need for one more. Go, friend Gamelon, write your histories! Live!"

But Gamelon smiled and made no move to leave.

"Well then!" Mila said. "Let's not keep our guests waiting any longer. Let's show them how an Empress dies."

Though it was against all protocol, she took his arm and they walked out together.

Berthaud, climbing a jungle trail towards the summit of the mountain and the pass that would take her and her companions over the ridge, turned as she heard the fusillade of shots. Some of the old people with her started weeping, a few threw themselves on the ground, inconsolable.

"So it is over," she thought, "they crept in like the cowards they are and killed Mila when she was defenceless."

Berthaud was wearing her side-arm. All of the Sung Yang survey teams were routinely issued with weapons, even an ethnologist was expected to carry an automatic pistol in her luggage in case of emergencies. She thought that the assassins would probably not bother to pursue a party like this, of the old and infirm. But, on the other hand, she almost wished that they would. For the first time in her life, she really wanted to shoot somebody. Anyone of those killers below would do.

Night found them on the other side of the ridge, covered them and gave them the peace they needed. Some of the older people were exhausted; this sultry tropical heat was taking a toll on a relatively young, fit woman like Berthaud, so it was having a disastrous effect on the others.

The next morning, leaving some of the party in hiding, Berthaud along with the Chief Steward, who insisted on accompanying her even though he found the going hard, set off down the trail towards the beach on this, other side of the island. As they descended they could see sails in the bay; she hesitated before going on, but the old man said one word:

"Piroushi!"

417

They staggered out of the jungle and onto the sands. Piroushi soldiers were being landed from small boats and amongst them she saw a familiar face.

"The Empress?" Kusha asked. Berthaud's silence was the only answer.

Later on Piroush, in Kusha's palace, Berthaud sat in the terraced gardens looking out at the sweep of the bay, waiting for the princess. The Piroushis had had prior warning of the plan to kill the Empress and Kusha had personally led out a force to try and prevent it. Ill luck and bad winds had been against them and they were too late, but the craft carrying the assassins had been intercepted.

The crew of the ship, facing execution, had been all but too eager to talk. The captain professed innocence, saying that he had just conveyed a party to Khetmis, not knowing their purpose. It was obvious from what he said, and even more obvious from what he didn't say, that the soldiers involved were Republican Guards. But they had disappeared. The island where he had landed them, after the raid on Khetmis, was uninhabited and there was no trace of them. It was equally obvious to Berthaud, that the Defence Force had been involved and that the assassination squad had been picked up by a cruiser.

The captain and all the ship's officers were executed and the crew members sent to the Piroushi galleys. Princess Kusha had been in no mood for clemency. A protest from the Melantheran authorities had been scornfully rejected. The Piroushis were furious, but unable to threaten their more powerful overlords.

Berthaud heard a noise and saw Kusha approaching, accompanied by her bodyguards. She took no chances now. As she approached, Berthaud, thought how much the woman had changed.

"She was just a young girl when I first met her," Berthaud thought, "but she grew up fast."

They had no need of a translator. Berthaud was almost fluent in Melantheran by now and could even cope with the Piroushi accent.

"Friend Berthaud," Kusha said, "you are welcome to stay in Piroush. Always welcome! But for your safety you will need to go into hiding. I can provide a safe place for you on one of the outer islands. After the Empress..." Kusha paused, almost losing her composure. She carried on.

"After the murder of the Empress, you, too, are at risk. We can't take the chance."

Berthaud thanked her and then said.

"I've decided to go back."

"Back?" Kusha asked. "Back where?"

"To my people," Berthaud said.

Chapter 34
The Turncoat

The old convent of the Sisterhood was a shadow of its former self. There were fewer Sisters; where once the halls and the corridors of the place had been thronged with the holy women and their lay assistants, now only a handful of them still lingered in the place, mostly elderly and with nowhere else to go. The buildings themselves were in a pitiful state; what had once been a pleasant complex of courtyards and cloisters, chambers and dormitories, was now in a state of disrepair, tiles were missing from the roof, window lattices stood broken and unrepaired, the lawns were overgrown and the supply of water to the fountains had been choked off. Where once a crowd of Melantherans would have fronted the gates, waiting to receive alms, be fed or treated in the infirmary, now the city people had been forbidden by law from seeking such aid.

To Robyn, the building seemed haunted by its past; she could almost hear the whispering voices of the Sisters who should have been there, the laughter of the young novices. But no more. The convent was like a ship abandoned at sea, it few denizens like stranded mariners.

The place had only survived by a set of random, fortuitous circumstances. The reason it hadn't been appropriated by the Republican Guards, was that the convent was part of the greater perimeter of the Elanta temple. Though the Sisterhood had been outlawed and suppressed, the wearing of the red robes made a crime punishable by imprisonment, Kal Quintal's coterie of mercenaries and carpet-baggers had courted the High Priest of Elanta and the other members of the religious establishment. The Temple and all its property had thus been left alone and the convent formed part of that property.

This had not been the case everywhere. In the smaller provincial towns, Republican Guards had expropriated convent buildings and expelled the Sisters, sometimes using violence, always brutal. In two of the towns, this abuse of the Sisters, including cases of rape, had provoked popular uprisings. The rising had been easily put down in the town of Verna, which was close enough to Melanthera for the 'peace keepers' of the Defence Force to intervene in support of the Republican Guards. But in Amaris, on the frontier of Melanthera, the Republican Guards had still not wrested control back. The town's citizens supported, it was rumoured, by the Lady Asha's rebels, had resisted all the Republican Guard assaults.

Though the republican authorities wouldn't openly admit it, they had been chastened by these shows of resistance and had carried on their persecution of the Sisters at a more subtle level, targeting individuals piecemeal rather than taking on the whole convent community. Because the Sisters, though banned, were still there. They were less visible, dressing as ordinary Melantherans, but their network still existed, though it had become an underground movement.

Robyn's presence in the building went unremarked. The Temple authorities tolerated the convent's continued existence, unwilling to close down a place that was, in truth, dedicated to the goddess Elanta. Even the High Priest had no stomach for doing anything that might offend her. She might already be looking down from the heavens shaking her head at some of the things her male priesthood were involved in.

As the Sisters could no longer function as a religious order, the convent had become, by accident rather than design, a sort of hostel or half-way house for women refugees, many of them ex-Sisters, who had been displaced by the war and the new regime. Mara fitted in less well; despite all her years as an intelligence agent, or perhaps because of them, the other women were wary of her and untrusting, which was also exactly the way Robyn thought of her. She was a strange companion, Robyn reflected, oddly acquired and not always welcome. She was hardly an ally or friend; it was just that their plans ran parallel.

It had not been an easy task for Mara to persuade the rebels of this latter fact. It had also taken her a long time. The woman been roughly handled and Robyn had got the distinct impression that Asha would have preferred to have killed her outright. The intelligence corps of the Republican Guards was particularly hated by the rebels on account of their brutality and this was not a conflict where prisoners were usually taken. But Mara had made a persuasive argument and Mila, who seemed to have more of a grasp of political issues than Asha, a fighter rather than a talker, seemed ready to be persuaded.

"I may be for the Republic," Mara had said, "but that doesn't mean I'm on the side of those who want to pillage the planet. To take everything from us and leave us with the dregs."

They had been sitting in the sheltered space between the two outcrops and it was early evening, the light fast going.

"I don't want the Empress back," she went on. "As far as I'm concerned I'd like to get rid of the rebels, the Sisterhood and everyone who's been keeping us back, stopping us progressing. But then we'll need to get rid of the Star People. We'll learn enough from them to take over the mines and the factories and then we'll drive them out."

Eventually, Mara had been taken away by the guards and Robyn had been unsure what fate the Melantherans intended for her, but next day she saw the woman again, her hands tied and under guard on the back of a haras, but alive.

The rebel forces kept constantly on the move and seemed to break up and come together again in a confusing pattern of planned and random co-incidence. If they had an over-all strategy, it was by no means clear to Robyn. She questioned Mila about it, but the woman laughed and would not answer her.

"It's best for you, friend Robyn, that you know as little as possible, then if you are recaptured you can't tell them anything."

From what Mila told her, it had become clear that she had been luckier than she thought, in being rescued in the way she had been. Though she had wondered if she had been the rebel's target when they attacked the Republican Guards' camp at the caravanserai, Mila told her that the raid had been planned to free all the prisoners. She had just been an added bonus.

"You were luckier than you knew, friend Robyn, that party was destined either for the desert work camps or for the Hvassara. The Guards have a side-line in slave trading. There would not have been much to choose between either fate."

Mila told her that they'd had some news of her from the Sisters in Piroush, but had presumed that she had been conveyed straight to Melanthera by crawler, on the southern desert road that was used almost exclusively by the Defence Force. That she hadn't been, was a surprise to them.

"It means that they were trying to lose you, friend Robyn. To make you disappear. If you had been transferred to the custody of the Defence Force, there would be a record or your detention, perhaps even a trial. Sometimes they prefer to let people vanish."

After all she had been through in the last few weeks, Robyn found Mila's company a comfort. Like all the Sisters, she seemed to have an innate kindness and gentility in all her dealings with people, all except Mara.

A few night after she had been rescued, as they sat alone around a fire on the high desert plain they were crossing, the night so cold she was wrapped in a blanket, she started, haltingly and painfully to tell Mila about White Hair and her interrogation. The woman just sat there, passively, an encouraging look on her face. After a few moments, Robyn found that she was crying and then the tears wouldn't stop. Strange, she told herself, I thought that I'd become numbed, deadened to the pain of it all.

Mila came over to her and held her, making soothing noises, as you would to a child who had woken from a bad dream.

"There are many of our people who have been in the Guards' cells, in Khetmis or elsewhere. Some have suffered terrible things, far worse than anything you did."

She used the sleeve of her red robe, dusty and faded though it was, to dry Robyn's face, smoothing her hair off her forehead as she did so.

"The clever ones, the interrogators, will always pick your weakest point, a flaw they can work on. For you it was your friend Khamis. Once they had her at their mercy, they had you in their power."

The desert wind suddenly gusted strongly and the flames shot up from the dry, scrub wood, lighting Mila's face. Though she lived a hard life and hardly got enough to eat, her face was still round and fleshy like the rest of her. So different from my Khamis, Robyn thought.

"You feel guilty, Robyn. That's why you are crying. But, you know, once those people have you, it's only a question of time, of how long you can hold out until you tell them what they want to know."

"But what about Sister Alethea and the others I told them about?" Robyn asked, through her tears.

"Sister Alethea and the others are used to this life. As soon as word got around that you'd been taken, they would have acted. Besides, you tell me you didn't give them names and were vague about details."

Robyn nodded.

"That's probably why they decided to get rid of you." Sister Mila said. "All in all, you had little further value to them. You never really had much to tell them, anyway. "

When she had stopped crying and Mila had gone to sleep, Robyn lay awake by the fire thinking of what the woman had said. In reality, hers was a just one little strand of the story, part of the greater narrative thread of these people's history, a miniscule part of what they had suffered over this last cycle of time.

She doubted if her own people had ever regarded her as much of a threat. She had broken the rules, transgressed, that was all. She'd always thought her work was about gleaning information, a quest for knowledge to inform the greater objective truth, but that was a lie she had lived. The Hub had one, orthodox stream of history that you signed up for when you joined. It was more like a religious text than a history, a justification of all the things her people had done. She'd just been a kobo-fly to be swatted, a minor irritation.

Over the next few days, they kept moving. Every so often, in the remote villages or larger towns that seemed to be almost exclusively in rebel hands, she was taken to gatherings of people, mostly Sisters, but also military commanders and civilian officials. There was much discussion, most of it totally inexplicable. It was after the last meeting, in a pretty mountain village which clung to the side of a high pass in the foothills to the north of the desert, that Mila took her aside. As they sat by the village well, under a stand of borriba trees, which seemed to flourish in the warm, dry climate of the place, Mila said to her:

"They want you to go back, friend Robyn. Here you are just a fugitive, moving from hiding place to hiding place, but if you go back to your own people, work with the Sisters and the other Melantherans amongst your own kind, you can tell our story. Tell your people what has been done to us in their name."

So it was arranged, and though she could have said no, she saw that she really didn't have any options. With Mara's help, they thought that she could be smuggled off the planet. Mara was part of the Republican Guard establishment, a high-ranking intelligence officer, so she would be able to facilitate Robyn's return to Melanthera and her trip onwards.

Mara's one condition had been that she would accompany Robyn off planet. The rebels had questioned this, they had hopes Mara would be their double agent in the Guard's headquarters in the Citadel, but she had simply asked:

"How long do you think I'd last if they found out what I'd done?"

Robyn was still not sure she could trust Mara and neither, she thought, was Mila. The Sister's last words to the woman were:

"Lady Asha has asked me to give you a message. She says that if you betray us, she will make it her personal task to hunt you down and kill you."

Mara said nothing, just nodded.

"She does not make idle threats," Mila continued, talking now to Robyn. "Farewell now, may Elanta keep you safe on the road. I'll see you in Melanthera."

As they'd ridden away on their haras, Mara had turned to Robyn and said:

"Are you as glad as I am to be away from all that goodness and grace? It's enough to turn your stomach."

So far, Mara had proved true to her word; she'd got them back to Melanthera, through the Guard checkpoint at the eastern gate and had installed them, as planned, in the old Sisters' convent. It seemed to Robyn that Mara could come and go as she pleased without question. She often disappeared for a day or two, but would, without fail, turn up again.

"It will take a while to sort out papers and arrange a flight out of here, so you may as well make the most of it," Mara had said to her. "Get as much rest as you can."

Mara was not an easy companion. She was prone to long, sullen silences and seemed to hate being cooped up in the chamber they had been assigned. As in most Melantheran inns or hostels, there was only one bed and Robyn did not find it easy to share it with the other woman. Mara suffered from vivid dreams or nightmares and would sometimes spring up in the bed - or once or twice actually spring out of the bed - and rattle questions and accusations off at her in Melantheran or some other language. When she'd finally come to and realised where she was, she'd say nothing, just climb back in the bed. It got so that Robyn was loath to close her eyes at night.

Thankfully, she didn't make any sexual advances. Robyn had suspected that any interest Mara had shown in her, when they were prisoners, had been purely professional, part of her arsenal of ways and means of suborning her subject to her will.

The only time Mara was even remotely companionable was when she was drunk. Every so often, she would come back to the room with a few flasks of borriba wine and, having consumed the lion's share of it, she would first become affable and then eventually maudlin.

"I've killed people," she said to Robyn, one night when she was well in her cups. "I've had to."

"I know," Robyn said. I know too well, she thought, I've seen you do it.

"What do you know?" Mara said, slurring her words. "I didn't want this life. I was happy once, when I was a girl."

Just before she slipped into unconsciousness, she said:

"It was your people... Your people made me a killer... Made me what I am..."

Soon she was snoring.

One day, when Mara was away, Sister Mila appeared at her door.

"It's cold out today," she said. "Do you have a cloak?"

The prospect of an outing was welcome. She collected the hooded, poncho-like cloak that she had been given, the standard and ubiquitous piece of Melantheran clothing, and they strode out together.

Since Robyn had been at the convent, she'd hardly ventured out of its grounds. When her chamber go too claustrophobic, she had taken the occasional turn around the gardens that flanked the square in front of the citadel, listening to the sermons of the One God One Church people, who seemed to be picking up more followers as the days went on, but had not gone any further.

"Is it safe?" She asked Mila.

"We are all in Elanta's hands," the woman replied. Robyn saw that she no longer wore the red robes of the Sisterhood. In civilian clothes, Robyn thought, she looks just like any Melantheran housewife on her way to market.

They walked across the square and made their way down the road, which descended from the citadel to the town. For the first time ever in Melanthera, Robyn felt cold, huddling into her cloak with her hood up.

Mila smiled. "You've yet to experience our seasons," she said. "In truth we seem to just have two. A short, cold, wet winter and the long, endless hot summer."

"How are you faring with friend Mara?" Mila asked after they had walked in silence for a while.

"She is not an easy companion," Robyn said. "A difficult person at the best of times."

"But useful," Mila replied, "though she seems to be taking her time in arranging your passage. I hope it is not difficult for you. All this waiting."

"No," Robyn replied, and then laughed. "What I'd really like to do, is go for a run."

Mila looked bemused.

"You know. Get some exercise and get fit at the same time. But that would look really odd here."

"But, friend Robyn, why would you run if you weren't going anywhere?" Mila asked, not understanding at all. "You could just as easily walk and not tire yourself."

They made their way down the hill, until Mila abruptly turned into a narrower street where the houses seemed to lean in over them, making Robyn feel as if she was in a tunnel. As they made their way down the winding street, Robyn saw that more and more of the people were dressed as Harradim, men and women wearing the long robes and head scarves. She remembered the day that she and Khamis had spent at the Harradim caravanserai and the afternoon they had spent bathing with the Harradim women. The women they passed now seemed less open, less friendly. Their eyes followed them and they cast surreptitious glances after them.

"Don't be too concerned," Mila told her. "There are spies everywhere in Melanthera, so everyone is cautious."

They seemed to walk aimlessly for half an hour or so and just when Robyn was on the verge of asking Mila what she was doing, the woman took her arm and steered her into a tea-house. They passed through a gateway and up a few steps into a garden, shaded by a number of wide-leafed trees she couldn't identify. Tables and chairs had been set out on the earth beneath the trees and people, mostly Harradim men, spent their time talking or playing a complicated game with different shaped pieces of wood on a small, oblong board. Many were calling out words, numbers she thought, and either looking down-cast or elated after their round in the game.

"The one vice that Harradim have, or so I'm told, is gambling," Mila said. "Whole fortunes have been squandered on the flip of a tile."

The game was called Kings and Emperors. Mila started trying to explain it to Robyn, but then gave up. It seemed to be some sort of stylised wargame, like chess. By now, the sun was high in the sky and the day was warming up, the chill going from the air.

An old Harradim man was passing amongst the tables selling the little triangular pendants of Elanta that many Melantheran women wore, even Mila had one around her neck. The little figure was simply worked out of some sort of sheet metal; its crowned head made the apex, above a sort of bodice and a long skirt which flared out to form the base of the triangle.

The old man made his way to their table and held out one of the figures to her, saying something in Melantheran that she couldn't understand.

"He says you must have one of these. He says that it's a memento, a souvenir from Elanthia."

There was something about the man's face, about his eyes as he smiled at her, holding out the pendant. But then Mila passed him some coins and he was gone, that feeling of recognition departing with him.

They had durgan root tea, which Robyn had acquired a taste for, and a plate of small, sweet cakes.

"Piroushi style!" Robyn said and Mila nodded.

"Yes. It's a habit that the Melantherans picked up from the Piroushi. It cuts the bitterness of the tea."

They drank and ate.

"Friend Robyn, you know a lot about us now," Mila said, smiling at her. "You are almost one of us."

But Robyn wasn't listening. A thought had suddenly struck her. That old Harradim man had wanted to give her a souvenir of Elanthia, which implied that he knew she wasn't from Melanthera or even the planet itself. Perhaps it was a mistranslation she thought, perhaps he had meant something else, but she couldn't help feeling a little uneasy after that, sitting there in the tea house. She was glad when Mila stood to go and paid the waiter.

On the way back to the convent, they passed two women in Defence Force military fatigues coming from the direction of the citadel gates.

"Star People," Mila said. But the women didn't even glance at them. Robyn had a mischievous urge to go up and engage them in conversation, but she soon suppressed it.

Mila took her to the convent gate and then made to leave.

"I must say goodbye to you now, friend Robyn," the woman said, giving her the Melantheran hug. Robyn had got used to this by now and she knew how to keep her balance.

"I'm glad Elanta willed out paths to cross in this world and I'll pray she keeps you safe, even amongst those cold, far stars."

Robyn gave her a Terran hug, which made the Sister a little uncomfortable.

"One last thing," Mila said, "that pendant. You must keep it on you at all times and never give it to anyone else. There's a message inside it, for you to open when you have left our world."

Mila turned her back and was gone, leaving Robyn with so many unanswered questions.

Sitting in the room later, she fingered the pendant tempted to open it, but then Mara came in and eyed the thing in disgust.

"I hope you haven't suddenly got religion, Robyn. Anyway, if you have become an acolyte of Elanta, it's a bit too late in the day. We're leaving tomorrow afternoon."

Chapter 35
The Hwrathka House Hotel

If Berthaud stood on the sleeping platform that had been built into the wall of her cell and stretched her arms to the narrow window sill, she could just pull herself up enough to get a fleeting sense of the gardens, a brief impression of the space they enclosed beneath that blank, blue sky which haunted her. She could, it was true, only catch a glimpse of the tops of the trees and, at the extreme angle of the window, the end wall of one of the towers that flanked the rear side of the palace, but it was enough to assure her that the outside world was still there, that there was some reality beyond this.

When she had first seen the Hwrathka House, on that initial visit to the palace all those years ago, she had been in some awe of it. Though the Melantherans had always seemed a people without much sense of grandeur, without the need that her people seemed to have to display and impress, the grand building that quartered the Empress's great war beasts had had a magnificence all of its own.

It was an enormous excavation, built into the top of the plateau on which the citadel and the palace within it, was spread out. You would thus enter the Hwrathka House from a series of nondescript gates and doorways on the upper, ground level, and suddenly come out onto a succession of terraces and staircases, which looked out on the great cathedral-like space. Far below were the pens of the animals, making their strange, lowing sounds, with that hypnotic, soothing quality. From the lower gates, through which the animals entered and exited, a series of ramps and platforms led up to the pens, which were layered in storeys beneath the upper balconies and walkways. Corridors led from the upper levels to covered stairways which, in turn, led directly down to the animal pens, but the series of terraces were built in this way so that the Empress and her court could walk slowly and descend gradually to the lower levels, giving them ample time to marvel at and appreciate the great creatures below.

At the lowest level, vast tanks of water fed from springs had been laid out, where the drivers took the creatures to bathe them and remove the ticks and insects that made their lives a misery. On the level above were the ceremonial gates that were used when the hwrathka, fully-caparisoned and accoutered, progressed out of the House to the parade ground beyond to be drilled and inspected by the monarch, or to give a demonstration to guests.

Berthaud remembered the first time she had seen the creatures on that parade ground, the thrill, the exhilaration of that charge. The fear too, that the creatures wouldn't, couldn't stop. That she would be trampled under their hooves. But most of all she remembered the sadness she had felt; knowing even then that their day was over, that the creatures' time had inevitably elapsed when that first Star Ship had taken its orbit around the planet and dispatched the first contact team.

She'd never seen the Hwrathka House full, of course. By Empress Mila's time the herd was much reduced, not like the great hwrathka force that the first Emperors would put into the field; the military tool that actually won them the Empire. When Berthaud had first seen the Hwrathka House, only the pens at the lower levels were occupied; the upper pens were vacant or used for storage. She could only imagine what the place must have looked like when it was full of the creatures. And the stench, of course. Even when it was more than two thirds empty, it carried an overpowering reek of dung, urine and fermenting fodder. It never seemed to concern the Melantherans, they loved their hwrathka and seemed to have some particular affinity for the creatures, but it took some getting used to for a Star Woman.

It was strange, but ultimately understandable, how her people had always looked for Terran equivalents to describe Melantheran things. And that, in the very act of comparing, they often devalued the thing itself. Her people always described the hwrathka as "like elephants", or "like mammoths", but that only partially described their size. They were in fact bigger than elephants, broader and their great horns were more impressive than elephants' tusks. Facing a charging, bellowing hwrathka, was like having a train bearing down on you at speed, as Berthaud well knew.

Nobody knew who had given the order to kill the hwrathka, or at least nobody would admit to it. Kal Quintal's people had blamed the act on the Defence Force, which had, in turn, denied any responsibility. It was rumoured that some of the Star People, who had been amongst the Hvassara when the last, great hwrathka charge rolled over them, had carried the slaughter out as an act of revenge. It had taken a couple of days, she had been told, to kill the creatures and drag their bodies out onto the great pyres they had constructed to burn them.

The atrocity had cut deep into the souls of the Melantherans. Even those who had little love for the Empress had been shocked by it and it had galvanised resistance to the new Republic; a resistance that would grow underground, and in the shadows, to manifest itself in occasional acts of sabotage or the distribution of a new political pamphlet.

The Defence Force had sought to partially expunge the memory of the hwrathka massacre by turning the Hwrathka House into a prison. Using the shell of the old building, they had either imported pre-fabricated cells or converted the storerooms and warehouses that were part of the place into jails. Prison guards and soldiers had shared the building; it was also a convenient barracks for the various military arms of the Star People and those troops had given the place its ironic new name, the 'Hwrathka House Hotel'.

After the initial bout of fighting, when a peace had been imposed, most of the Defence Force troops had departed and the prison was put under the command of the Republican Guards, but it was common knowledge on the Melantheran streets that the Star People still lingered on. There were various units of intelligence corps agents and special services soldiers, who used the place as an interrogation centre and for special categories of prisoners. And Berthaud knew that she was one of these.

She was, in fact, no longer Marie Berthaud, but was now addressed as "Prisoner DF- 81560" or usually as the "the prisoner"; as in the phrase "the prisoner will" or "the prisoner must not". She thought that the DF in her prisoner number stood for 'Defence Force', but didn't know what the numbers signified, only guessing that they in some way referenced the electronic files that the Defence Force had compiled on her. These must comprise quite a substantial library of information by now, she thought.

The jailers that she saw most days were Republican Guards, Melantherans, but occasionally Hvassara or even the odd Barossi. They spoke to her in Terran, with varying degrees of fluency, but didn't seek to communicate any more than the basic, mundane routines associated with her day. In fact, in the first days, she had never once been told why she was been held or by whom; it all had a surreal and Kafkaesque quality.

The guards always behaved correctly to her; she thought they had been well trained by their Defence Force mentors. Since arriving at the prison she had not been subjected to any violence, or any other treatment which might have demonstrated that her guards had any less robotic qualities. It was true they never slapped her or swore at her, but it was also true that they never smiled at her, shared a joke with her or looked on her with anything more than professional, clinical concern. She knew it was all part of the process, all part of the dehumanisation, the deconstruction of her personality.

On her bad, black days, she thought back to that last conversation with Princess Kusha and wondered why she had been so adamant that she would return to her own people. Looking back now, analysing it, she thought that she had had some vainglorious idea of being able to restore her professional status as an ethnologist, even if only to her own person. She had wanted to re-assert her old self; to go back to her people and give an objective, academic account of all that had happened here. She supposed that in some ways she wanted to justify herself, to prove to herself that she hadn't transgressed, crossed some invisible frontier and become the subject of her own study.

The attempt had been doomed from the start. She knew that she would be arrested, but had thought that, as a citizen of the Inner Planets, she would have been subjected to some sort of due process, would have her day in court. But now she realised she had been colossally naive. She had seen what had been done to these people by her own people, so it had been foolish to think that she was somehow immune, would be treated differently. She was surprised in some ways that they hadn't just killed her and this told her that they, whoever they were, must fear something, even if it was just a fall in the price of Sung Yang shares.

She had travelled back to Melanthera from Piroush in one of the caravans that crossed the desert. Kusha had assigned her a couple of Piroushi minders to watch over her until she got to Melanthera; they were quiet, cautious types and not exactly good company. In fact the whole trip had been a melancholy affair; the travellers were mostly Piroushi women travelling back to the space port at Melanthera and from there to their various domestic jobs on the Inner Planets. The Piroushi women were already mourning their imminent departure from

Elanthia and their sombre mood spread to the rest of the party, even it seemed to the Harradim guides.

The desert journey had given her time to think about what actions she would take; by the time she got to Melanthera and through the checkpoint at the eastern gate of the city, she was ready to shake off her Piroushi protectors and go about the things she had set herself to do before her final day on the planet. She'd planned that final day in some detail, rehearsing it over and over in her mind. She would change out of her Piroushi clothes into her old Survey Team fatigues, leave the old Convent by the citadel where she was staying, and present herself at the Defence Force headquarters within the citadel gates. Ultimately a small distance to cross geographically, yet it seemed like a yawning gulf of uncertainty set to swallow her up.

As it was, it didn't work out that way. Perhaps she had been too confident, cocky even, that she could function on the streets of Melanthera as a Piroushi, fade into the crowds and not be remarked. She had set herself two days to accomplish the tasks in hand and say goodbye to the place, but on the second night, on the eve of her surrender to the authorities, she had been taken just outside the convent gates. Four men in civilian clothes had jumped out at her from the shadows, pinned her to the ground, bound and gagged her and covered her head with some sort of sack. She didn't even have time to resist.

Ironically, they hadn't taken her far. It was a short enough walk across the square, past the citadel gates and into the Hwrathka House. They must have passed close to the Defence Force headquarters,

441

which was to be her destination the next morning. She had known she had been taken to the Hwrathka House as soon as they pulled her hood off. It had changed enough inside to be unfamiliar, but, whatever they did, the ghost of a smell still lingered. The animals had made their imprint here and the people who had come after them, would never totally extinguish it. She learnt later that some prisoners swore that they still heard the creatures lowing in the night.

She'd been led down a stairway to a small, brightly lit room and stripped by a female guard in front of her erstwhile captors, who looked on blank-faced. Then she was pushed towards a shower room, where she was shoved through a series of water jets. On the other side she was given a towel and then a physical examination by the female guard, which included an examination of her rectum and vagina, in case, she thought, she was smuggling something in. She'd protested once and pulled away and had then received the one and only blow she had got here, a slap across the face followed by a tug on her hair, grown quite long now, which was more painful than the slap.

She got the message and stopped resisting. There was no more casual violence, it had only been applied so that she would become biddable. They gave her a jumpsuit to dress in and fixed a plastic band around her wrist. She thought it probably had a chip in it. She was then walked up a few flights of steps, past pre-fabricated buildings, which had been dropped into the vast space, to her cell. When the door closed, she took a deep breath and tried to gather her wits. She must not let the sense of separation overwhelm her, she told herself.

Day and night were marked by the switching on and off of the lights in her cell. She was given meals at regular intervals. These were all Defence Force rations, which took some getting used to after Melantheran food and didn't sit that well on her stomach.

"I've got Melantheran bacteria in my gut now," she thought, "and they can't deal with Terran food."

There was a flush toilet in the cell, which she was glad of, though this seemed strange after the more primitive Melantheran toilets. Where there were any of these, they were often communal, so pissing and shitting turned into a social occasion, whether you liked it or not. She was not allowed any reading material or any communication of any sort. Exercise was a walk back and forth along a blank corridor, under the watchful gaze of a silent guard, once a day.

Eventually, after countless days - perhaps weeks - of this, she was taken out of her cell one morning to a small, brightly lit room where a young woman in Defence Force uniform sat waiting for her.

"Dr. Berthaud," she said, greeting her. Her own surname sounded strange after all this time. The woman did not introduce herself, but, by the flashes on her fatigues, Berthaud thought that she was Intelligence Corps.

"I hope they are treating you well here," the woman said. Berthaud noticed that she was wearing captain's bars.

"Why am I being held here?" Berthaud asked, her own voice sounding as strange as her name to her.

"Doctor, you have committed a number of crimes in Melanthera. You have been arrested for those." The captain replied.

Berthaud asked what the crimes were and the captain rattled off a list. The list included espionage, rebellion and political assassination.

"You face a number of serious charges, Doctor. The Republican authorities consider you to be an enemy of the state. They regard you as having been an influential member of the circle of conspirators around the Empress. These are capital offences."

So, Berthaud thought, they are going to kill me, but they'll get the Melantherans to do it for them.

The captain stared at her, her face framing a look of concern.

"You are in a difficult position, Doctor. Marie. Can I call you Marie?"

Berthaud didn't answer, but the captain did anyway.

"Marie. I'm here to help you. There is something we can do."

That was how it started. From then on the captain came to see her once or twice a week. She soon introduced herself as Captain Susan Walker.

"Please call me Susan," she said.

And, increasingly, the meetings took place in the palace gardens, which hadn't changed much, apart from the cruiser landing pads which had been installed there. As the weeks progressed, she was also granted small, but sweet, concessions. She was given a Pad, with no external access, but pre-loaded with books, articles and news archives. She started getting hot meals sent to her, from the Defence Force mess. She knew what they were doing, but had not been prepared for how seductive it was. They were, after all, her own people and they were offering her a way out.

Susan told her what they were offering, one day as they sat by the fountains, where Berthaud remembered the old Empress once sitting in better times.

"Marie," Susan said, "there's only one way out for you and you are not going to like it."

It was simple really and in some ways ingenious. A Defence Force doctor would be given access to Berthaud, who would them be diagnosed as mentally ill. The exact diagnosis wouldn't matter. The Inner Planets government would then petition the Melantheran Republic to leave the charges against her pending, but to allow a transfer to a Defence Force medical facility on Hephaeston on compassionate grounds. Susan was right, Berthaud didn't like it. She asked to be taken straight back to her cell. But then a week later, they played their next card. She had a visitor. It was Kev.

When she was told she had a visitor, she was so astonished that she felt in shock. She was taken to a small room, where for a few awkward minutes she looked across at her old comrade opposite her. He looked equally uncomfortable, as if he wanted to be somewhere else.

"Well, how are you, Marie?" He asked.

She didn't answer, just shrugged and spread her arms as if to say: "I am as you see me."

"You know, Marie," he went on, "when I was in the Defence Force, we always had a saying, a code of honour really, that we never left a man behind and that's why I'm here."

"You didn't leave me behind, Kev," she said. "I left myself behind."

"Whatever, Marie." He went on speaking. "You're in this place now. They'll either leave you here or they'll try you and probably execute you. Or just throw away the key."

He sighed and looked down at his big, meaty hands.

"I know you did what you thought was right. I know that. I know what was done here wasn't all right. We made mistakes." He paused and looked at her again.

"But Marie, we lost a lot of our boys and girls here. It was messy, fucked up, but it's over now. You've got to come home."

"It won't be home, Kev," she said, feeling herself choke up, angry with herself because of it. "It will be a psychiatric ward. All I did, they'll put down to an illness; some flaw in me."

"I know, Marie," he replied, "but that way there is a chance."

A week or so later, Berthaud sat at the back of a cruiser, ready to lift off from the citadel. The craft was nearly empty, the other passengers sitting in the front rows of seats, leaving the back to her. She'd caused something of a stir among the Defence Force personnel that had boarded before her. They knew who she was and kept giving her surreptitious glances, which her companion, Captain Susan, returned angrily. Berthaud knew that the Captain wasn't concerned for her or her feelings.

"She just doesn't want me to change my mind," she thought.

As they lifted off, and when the dust cleared, she looked out over the city, trying to catch a glimpse of the streets below and a certain street particularly. It was impossible, of course; it was a maze down there, a random pattern of alleys and streets that few could really fathom.

That first day it had taken her ages to find Berendal and when she had eventually found the street and seen the man in Harradim robes, sitting on his step at what seemed to be the right address, she had, at first, hardly recognised him. It had taken him what seemed like an age to recognise her, too, but then he'd laughed and smiled. That smile, that unique grin of Berendal's, that she would know anywhere.

He took her arm and conducted her off the street.

"Berthaud," he said to her, "you make a good Piroushi. If I wasn't a married man, I could fall for you myself!"

Her Melantheran wasn't perfect, but she understood that. And then, in his cool, shaded parlour, open to the inner courtyard of the house and its garden and fountain, she met Noor; a delightful, gentle person, who served them the ubiquitous durgan root tea.

"Berendal," she said. "I've got something I want you to keep safe for me."

She took the memory card out of the pocket of her tunic, held it out to him.

"You've seen one of these before," she said and he nodded.

"This one has got everything on it. The whole history of this place over the last few years. My logs and dispatches. Your poems. Gamelon's histories. All the things they want to suppress, all the events they want to pretend didn't happen. Keep it for me."

He bowed his assent and then they drank tea and spent a pleasant afternoon, remembering.

When she left – after hugging them both in the Melantheran way and then in the Terran way - Berendal walked her to the end of the street, the tears in his eyes.

"We may not see each other again, Berthaud," he said.

"Elanta willing, we will!" She said and he smiled at her use of the customary farewell. Melantherans never like goodbyes that were final.

But those were not his last words. As she walked off down the road, he ran after her and asked:

"But who shall I give the card to?"

"You'll know who. The right time will come and you'll know who to give it to."

Then she was gone.

Chapter 36
The Leaving Of Elanthia

It wasn't until she was sitting in her room, in one of the space port hotels in Thera, that she allowed herself to think of Khamis.

In truth, she'd been too scared to think of anything else but the prospect of arrest and interrogation during her final day on Elanthia. Mara had manufactured for her a new identity. Robyn was now Sarah Peters, an ethnologist on contract to the Defence Force. Mara had acquired papers and contact lenses that would fool the Iris Recognition scanners. Citizens of the Inner Planets weren't chipped, that was reserved for migrant workers like the Melantherans, so that did not present a problem. However, Robyn still had Rahani's chip in her neck and feared that Mara would be quite prepared to dig the little thing out with a knife if she had to. Fortunately for Robyn, Mara had got hold of a chip coder and decoder from one of her intelligence contacts and it was a matter of moments to wipe the data. That's the end of Rahani, thought Robyn, with a sharp pang of regret.

When Robyn asked Mara how she had got Sarah Peters' papers, Mara simply said:

"Don't ask!"

Which made Robyn suspect that she was filling a dead woman's shoes, but eventually Mara admitted that the character was one of a store of false identities kept by the Guards' intelligence department, so their operatives could come and go as they pleased.

"You see, Robyn, we've been keeping an eye on the Sisterhood and their activities amongst the migrant workers."

She laughed, a strange, cheerless sound.

"I don't think your Defence Force realises what good students we've been over the years. They have no idea about our activities off planet."

Mara was travelling as Sarah Peters' personal assistant, a Melantheran by the name of Khira Khamza, which amused Robyn as she thought it sounded like a superhero's name from some old comic. The woman had provided Robyn with Defence Force fatigues and a combat jacket; she, herself, wore Melantheran clothes. Robyn had packed her own Melantheran clothes in her luggage, wrapping the pendant amongst them.

They set off from the convent in the early afternoon, making their way down the hill towards the Hwrathka Gate. The journey was endless to Robyn, at every turn of the road she expected to see a squad of Republican Guards waiting for her. She was still sure that Mara would betray her.

"Perhaps they'll take me when I get on the crawler," Robyn thought, but the journey in the stuffy, crowded vehicle - from the gate to the space port - was uneventful. Then she went through an agony of waiting at the port, Mara trying to make conversation with her, so that all would appear normal. Then finally, they went through the scanners and boarded the space liner, assigned seats next to each other.

"Say goodbye to Elanthia," Mara whispered as they took off.

At the space port on Thera, she and Mara parted ways.

"Be honest, Robyn," Mara said, "you never thought you'd get this far. You thought nasty, old Mara would turn you in. But as I told you long ago, we basically want the same thing."

Robyn doubted it, but she didn't answer.

"Well, I doubt you'll see me again. I've got some money stashed away in one of your banks, so I'm thinking of taking a holiday. I hear the lake is lovely."

With those parting words she was gone.

Now, in the hotel room, Robyn thought of all she had lost. Her job, her identity, her old life. But none of that really mattered, she told herself, because she had lost something else, someone more precious than all that. She'd had a glimpse of the life she wanted to live, the person she wanted to live it with and that had been taken away from her. It was like being shown a vision of heaven and then denied it.

She sat in the dark and she couldn't stop thinking of Khamis. She could see her face in her mind's eye, but then, suddenly, she worried that that too would fade with time. She tried to remember every detail of it, the shape of her nose and the curve of her cheek bones. It was impossible, she thought, memory was so treacherous.

She looked for a distraction and found the mini bar. There was a half-bottle of Theran wine there, along with various spirits. As she poured herself a glass, she noticed her hand was trembling, quite violently. She was obviously not cut out for this sort of life. The Theran wine tasted different, alien; she thought that she had probably got too inured to borriba wine.

She opened her suitcase and remembered the pendant. It took a few moments to prise the back off it with her Defence Force issue pen knife. Inside, she saw a small, black memory card and reached for the Pad that had been part of Sarah Peters' equipment. She loaded the memory card and brought up the files on it. One document was entitled 'message'. She opened it.

"This is a message from Marie Berthaud, in the hope that this card will be conveyed to someone who is sympathetic to the Melantheran cause. It was left in the safe keeping of the poet Berendal."

"The old Harradim man," Robyn thought, "so that was why he was so familiar." She'd seen the same smile, the same eyes looking out from a photograph she'd seen so long ago, in that other life.

The message went on:

"This card holds all of my blogs, diaries and records from my time on Melanthera. It also holds a comprehensive selection of work by poets, including Berendal. Amongst these is 'Asha's Lament'. I have done my best to translate this work from the original, though I fear that I may have not done it the justice it deserves. Also on the card is the last, unfinished work of the priest-historian Gamelon, which covers the reign of the Empress Mila the Third. It is unfinished because Gamelon was assassinated by the same squad that killed the Empress, after he refused to leave her side. The Empress was assassinated as a result of a criminal conspiracy planned by senior Defence Force officers and officials of the Sung Yang Corporation.

452

This card holds the untold, unofficial history of Elanthia and the last Melantheran Empire. It is a story that needs to be told."

"And it will be," thought Robyn, "because I'll tell the story. So that even though I can't be with Khamis, I can at least help her and her people with their fight."

Robyn packed a small bag with her Melantheran clothes, the Pad and the memory card. It was time for Sarah Peters to disappear. She took the lift down to the lobby and walked out of the hotel, smiling at the receptionist on the way.

It was a glorious day and Lake Thera was shining in the sun. She crossed the square before the lake, where the theatre and the opera house were, but her eyes were fixed ahead of her. She would find somewhere to change and then she would become Kahani again, the Melantheran migrant worker, she would disappear into that underground world of servants and cleaners and all the time she would be hacking into the Hub, challenging its version of events, changing history.

Two women, dressed in the latest Theran fashions, were crossing the square on their way to lunch in the Opera House restaurant. One of them looked hard at the woman, who walked by in front of them.

"Robyn," she said, softly to herself. But she knew that it couldn't be Robyn, dressed in Defence Force fatigues, here on Thera. Robyn had had some sort of schizophrenic episode and had disappeared on one of the Outer Planets. It couldn't be her and yet...

"What's the matter Esmee?" Her companion asked, looking forward to lunch and irritable that she might miss it.

"Wait here!" Esmee said. "I won't be a minute."

She ran after the woman, the one she thought was Robyn Harper, but when she turned a corner by the mono-rail station she was gone. All Esmee could see was a migrant woman, a cleaner or the like she thought, waiting for the train to take her to work.

THE END